Bello

hidden talent rediscovered

Bello is a digital-only imprint of Pan Macmillan,
established to breathe new life into previously published,
classic books.

At Bello we believe in the timeless power of the imagination,
of a good story, narrative and entertainment, and we want to
use digital technology to ensure that many more readers
can enjoy these books into the future.

We publish in ebook and print-on-demand formats
to bring these wonderful books to new audiences.

www.panmacmillan.com/imprint-publishers/bello

Richard Mason

Richard Mason was born near Manchester in 1919. He served in the RAF during the Second World War before taking a crash course in Japanese and becoming an interrogator of prisoners of war. His first novel, *The Wind Cannot Read*, which drew on these experiences, won the 1948 John Llewellyn Rhys Prize and was made into a film starring Dirk Bogarde. Several of his following novels were also cinematised, most famously *The World of Suzie Wong*, about an artist's romance with a Hong Kong prostitute. His last novel, *The Fever Tree*, was published in 1962. Mason moved to Rome in the early 1970s and lived there until his death in 1997.

Richard Mason

THE FEVER TREE

BELL◎

First published in 1962 by Collins

This edition published 2017 by Bello
an imprint of Pan Macmillan
20 New Wharf Road, London N1 9RR
Associated companies throughout the world

www.panmacmillan.com/imprint-publishers/bello

ISBN 978-1-5098-5246-8 EPUB
ISBN 978-1-5098-5245-1 PB

Visit **www.panmacmillan.com** to read more about all our books
and to buy them. You will also find features, author interviews and
news of any author events, and you can sign up for e-newsletters
so that you're always first to hear about our new releases.

FOR SARETT

Part One

Chapter One

Birkett had forty-five minutes before his appointment at the tomb. Allow twenty-five minutes to get there, and that left twenty to go.

He pushed his glass across the bar. "Same again. Scotch."

"Double, sahib?"

"Single." Birkett could hold his own against drink.

The fans twirled like aeroplane propellers under the high vaulted ceiling, fluttering the blue silk sari of the girl along the bar. She had huge dark sad eyes like the eyes in Persian paintings, and a red spot on her forehead to match the red paint on her nails. She looked bored with her middle-aged companions and kept glancing at Birkett as if yearning to talk to him.

Birkett avoided her eyes and looked away through the arch to the big sombre dining-room, where waiters in white turbans and red cummerbunds moved barefooted amongst the tables under the marble pillars. A few couples twirled to a fox-trot on the dance-floor, the men in European dinner-jackets or Indian jackets buttoned to the neck; the women in bright silk saris. Even the solitary English woman wore a sari to camouflage her nationality and big blonde English frame, whilst back at the table her husband, a hydraulic engineer from the Midlands, chatted over-heartily to his Indian hosts to camouflage his lack of ease.

Birkett sipped the small whisky. His gaze fell on the mahogany honour-board behind the bar, listing the Club presidents in letters of gold. They went back over thirty years. Fotheringay, Whittington-Smith, Sir R. Boland, Bell-Carter . . . You could see the hands holding the whisky-sodas, the moustaches bristling under sun-helmets as they set off for polo or sticking pigs. You knew from the names they had all been pig-stickers: you only wondered that there had been enough pigs to go round. Smedley-Cox, Athelston . . . And so on until, with Sir Joshua Hindcliffe, 1947, the pig-sticking names came to a resounding end. And then: Sen, Desani, Muckerjee, Singh . . .

Yes, a decade ago, Birkett thought, the only Indians you'd have seen in this place were the waiters in compulsory white gloves to conceal the grey hands. And now the few British who came here fell over themselves to behave like Indians while the Indians behaved more like the British than the British themselves.

"Major Birkett! My dear fellow!"

It was the Sikh doctor whom Birkett had met at the Club the night before. He wore a European lounge suit and pink spotted turban, and his face was covered by an explosion of grey beard.

"My dear Major! You like our Club, isn't it? I am utterly delighted! Now, I wish you to meet my son." He turned and waved a pudgy hand towards the tall shy youth who soundlessly followed him. "Young fellow, I wish you to meet my dear friend Major Ronnie Birkett, the famous explorer and writer."

The young Sikh wore a pale blue turban and a black immature beard, neatly trained round his chin. He placed his long sensitive fingers together in the attitude of prayer, saying very politely and diffidently, "It is a great honour, sir."

"Thanks." Birkett's speech was dipped like his moustache. He brought his hands together smartly, performing the Indian gesture of greeting with practised ease but with a foreign briskness reminiscent of a military salute. "Not that I'm famous or an explorer—your father's got his wires a bit crossed."

"But you have explored everywhere, isn't it?" the Sikh doctor said.

"Travelled around a bit. But seldom off the beaten track, so hardly call it exploring."

"But your books of travel are utterly famous. You are a famous writer."

"Oh, rubbish." Birkett had no use for the gush.

The youth said gently, "I have heard your book on India is most interesting, sir."

"Bit dated now."

"May I ask how you write your books, sir? You write with a pen or a typewriter?"

"Bash 'em out on the old machine, much easier."

"Who is your favourite author, sir?"

"Conrad." He had not read Conrad for years but a decisive answer saved trouble.

"I understand you have just come from China, sir. What was your opinion of Chinese Communism?"

"No corruption in China now—I'll hand that to those Reds, they've wiped out 'squeeze'. And some very impressive material achievements. But not my cup of tea. Not all that brain-twisting."

"You don't think Communism is the answer for India, sir?"

"God forbid."

He glanced at his watch. Thirty-five minutes to go: ten before he must be off. He looked up and caught the glance of the girl in the blue sari, whose eyes had kept slipping back to him. He abruptly switched away his gaze and found himself confronted by a lean sunburnt face with trim moustache, and the stare of two steely ice-blue eyes: his own reflection in the mirror behind the bar. He noted the spare erect shoulders, the disciplined bearing. Spare and trim, he thought. Forty-eight, but not an ounce of unwanted flesh, not a single capitulation to age.

Spare and trim like the cheetah, he thought.

"My dear fellow, your glass is empty!" the Sikh exclaimed. "An empty glass is utterly forbidden! Another drink for my old friend Ronnie!"

Birkett hated to be called Ronnie. He did not care for Ronald: he preferred to be called Birkett. He avoided a wince, and said, "Thanks, I'm through."

"But you are with Sikhs now isn't it? You cannot be with Sikhs and not drink!" The doctor caught sight of the girl along the bar. "Hello, there is my girl-friend! There is my utterly ravishing girl-friend Mrs. Kapoor!" He propelled Birkett along the bar with an exuberant hand on his shoulder. "Lakshmi, my dear, I wish to introduce my old friend Major Ronnie Birkett, the famous explorer and writer."

The girl's face lit up eagerly. "Oh, how exciting!" she exclaimed, bringing her red-tipped fingers gently together under her chin as Birkett's hands briskly met and dispensed their greeting. "I felt sure you were somebody famous!"

"Ronnie is famous all over the world," the Sikh said. "He is world famous."

"Nonsense," Birkett said. "Just the doctor's bedside blarney—didn't know me from Adam when I walked in yesterday."

"Of course I knew your name at once! You are just being utterly British and modest!"

"I knew it," the girl said. "I read in the newspaper that you were in Delhi and I longed to meet you. I am your fan!" Her features had a classic Indian delicacy, and her face was an inverted triangle spreading outwards from the neat little pointed chin to the huge wide dark Persian eyes that reached to the outer corners. The black hair was drawn smoothly back from the forehead, with its decorative red spot, into a chignon. It was a face of remarkable beauty, that made the girl's rather bright, brittle, pseudo-sophisticated manner seem as incongruous and ill-fitting as some tawdry sequin dress imported from the West. And she went on, with the kind of hungry eagerness with which bored and unhappy people clutch at straws of distraction, hoping each time to have found a permanent raft, "I have only read your Indian book, but I simply adored it."

"Thanks, bit dated now."

"I think it must be wonderful to be able to write! Do you write with a pen or a typewriter?"

"Old machine as a rule."

"But you do write so beautifully!"

"Nice of you to say so." His eyes fell momentarily to the smooth bare sliver of waist, visible between the loose diaphanous folds of her sari, which floated like blue mist in the breeze from the fan. It was the colour of warm dark honey, and so slender that he could have encircled it with his hands . . . He abruptly averted his eyes and looked away through the arch towards the gyrating couples, the soft-footed waiters carrying their trays amongst the marble pillars. Women were like drinks for Birkett, he could take them or leave them. "Only not true, I'm afraid. Bash out the stuff for a living, that's all."

"That adorable modesty!" the girl laughed. "I simply adore it!"

"Ronnie, what a hit you have made with my girl-friend," the Sikh exclaimed. "I am utterly jealous. But I shall help you for the sake of friendship. I shall take you both to dinner and you may hold hands and carry on a flirtation."

"Thanks, but can't manage this evening," Birkett said.

"You are afraid of my girl-friend's husband turning up with a horsewhip while you are flirting, isn't it? Don't worry, my dear fellow, he is in Lucknow. She is on the spree. You are perfectly safe to come for dinner."

"Sorry, previous engagement."

"Then we shall meet after dinner at the Volga where you and my girl-friend may dance and flirt. You know the Volga in Connaught Place?"

"No, and don't think I'd fancy it—sounds too Russian for me."

"It is not Russian. It is quite British and civilized. It is also air-conditioned."

"I wish you would come," the girl urged, with hungry eagerness.

"And only wish I could—but tied up the whole evening." The Sikh winked a little roguish eye. "He must be dining with a girl. Ronnie, you old rascal, you have a secret girl!"

"I'm sure he has lots of girls," the girl said, with a new tension perceptible under the bright, brittle tone.

"He is utterly wicked—he is worse than a Sikh!"

Birkett looked at his watch again. Twenty-five minutes exactly before the rendezvous. "Well, I must skip."

"You are not leaving Delhi just yet?" the girl said. "We shall see you again?"

"Certainly hope so—plans a bit uncertain. Anyhow, nice meeting you. Most enjoyable."

He brought his hands smartly together before his face, and before

7

the girl's red-tipped fingers had touched in response, had already turned and was walking away across the brisk and soldierly and trim; and the girl watched after him, her fingers poised under the little pointed chin, whilst the Sikh watched beside her, his two little eyes twinkling roguishly on either side of the big pock-marked nose. The spare erect figure disappeared through the arch. They were silent for a moment. And then the Sikh, who did not really know the girl very well, and whose joke about her being his girl-friend required the presence of a third party to make it harmless, grew uncomfortable and looked around for his son; but the tall shy youth was lost in a day-dream farther along the bar. He turned back to the girl, and said awkwardly, for something to say:

"Well, what do you think of my old friend Ronnie Birkett? Don't you think he is a great fellow?"

The girl nodded dreamily, all her sadness welling up in the huge brown pools of her eyes. "He seems very nice."

"So utterly British."

"Yes, he is very typical."

"That's it, he is utterly typical and British. He is a great fellow, Ronnie. He is a great asset to our Club."

Chapter Two

Birkett crossed the fan-cooled entrance hall of the Club with his brisk British step. He came out between the tall classical pillars into the wall of heat, and descended the steps to the drive.

A hot yellow moon had just risen over the trees. Insects swarmed round the electric lamps along the drive, bombarding the glass with suicidal frenzy. A bunch of drivers squatted on the grass, smoking cigarettes through their fists.

Birkett made his way past them to his hired car. He drove out of the Club driveway and round the curving colonnade of Connaught Place, with displays of cheap magazines and murder books on the pavement, the jut-boned horses waiting between the shafts of the idle tongas, and turned off along a radial road. It brought him into the wide triumphal avenue leading to the Secretariat. The great twin pink sandstone buildings, the crowning achievement of Imperial rule, glowed under their floodlights; the ornamental fountains sent up their shimmering jets and collected the falling spray in their pink sandstone bowls. He swung off the avenue to the left of the Secretariat, and in a few minutes was clear of the town. Now there was nothing in his headlights but the narrow strip of tarred road, stretching away emptily into the distance, flanked by dusty bullock tracks and a few dusty straggling trees.

He felt the first touch of exhilaration. He was on the job again. The cheetah was off on a new prowl.

He drove swiftly. On either side of the road the parched stony plain lay deserted under the moon. And he remembered the African plain, and the cheetah sitting alone under the tree in the hot African afternoon. And then the sun going down, and the cheetah lazily rising, and yawning—and a sudden uneasiness running like a shiver through the great herds of wild creatures that filled the plain: the fat zebra interrupting their grazing with anxious backward looks, the bearded wildebeest restlessly tossing their heads, the wagging metronome tails of the Thomson's gazelle suddenly missing the beat. And then the first stir of panic, and the dust rising from the hoofs as the herds moved away from the danger they had felt but not yet seen—from the lone cheetah whose yawn had spread fear through them like a contagion. And the cheetah sensuously stretching and yawning again, and strolling out from under the tree: trim-waisted, self-sufficient, and serenely alone, the strongest and swiftest animal on the plain. The perfect animal-machine . . .

He saw movement ahead. It was an old ramshackle horse-drawn tonga lurching along in the same direction as himself at break-neck speed. The solitary passenger gripped the hood struts for support with one hand and a huge khaki solar topee to his head with the other.

The tonga swerved off the tarmac to let Birkett pass. The dust spurted from under the wheels, billowed in a cloud across the road. It threw back the beam of Birkett's headlights like fog so that he was obliged to slow down. It filled the car with a fine soft powder that tasted dry in his mouth and tickled the back of his nose. He emerged from the dust cloud and regained speed. Shortly he saw two little green lights ahead on the road—the eyes of some animal, probably a wild cat. They stared stupidly into the headlights.

Well, I'm not slowing down again, Birkett thought. So you'd better look sharp.

He pressed his horn but the green lights did not move. He caught a brief glimpse of the animal itself in his headlights as he was almost upon it: it was not a cat, but a jackal. It turned indifferently away. But too late—there was a soft thud on the front of the car, a bump under the left wheel. He waited for a bump from the back wheel but it never came.

Well, you must have got flattened good and proper, Birkett thought. But you can't say I didn't warn you.

He thought of the mess of crushed ribs and burst flesh left behind on the tarmac. The disagreeable image disturbed him—too mildly to have ordinarily mattered: but on occasions of this sort, when there was enough already to disturb equanimity, such an untoward incident was to be deplored. And he wished now that he had slowed down to avoid the creature.

He glanced at the dashboard. Four and a half miles from the Secretariat—almost there. He reduced speed, keeping an eye on the left side of the road, and presently caught sight of a dim mass looming against the sky. Its shape became clearer as he approached.

That's the chappie, he thought. And by Jove, it's a tidy size. It's as big as a cathedral.

He saw a track leading off the road to the left and turned along it. The moon had already cleared and cast a brilliant light over the plain. He could see the tomb in almost as much detail as if it had been daylight. It was built according to the familiar Mogul pattern with a massive central mausoleum surrounded by a broad high terrace, and slender minarets rising from the corners of the terrace like guardian lighthouses. It had fallen into neglect and the sandstone was badly weathered, and several of the lofty ornamental pavilions on the main structure were missing. The row of white half-eggshell domes above the main facade grinned down from crumbling gums of pink sandstone like the broken remnants of an old man's teeth.

He ran the car out of sight into some scrub. He sat for a moment listening. There was not a sound. He got out and approached the tomb. He walked round until he came to some steps leading up through a dark slanting tunnel. He groped his way up them and emerged in the middle of the terrace. The moonlight, after the darkness of the steps, had an almost blinding brilliance. His shadow on the white marble terrace floor was like a shadow from the sun. He felt as conspicuous as if he had stood in a spotlight on a stage. He went to the arched entrance of the mausoleum: the door was heavily padlocked. He turned away and followed the long finger of shadow thrown by one of the minarets to the corner of the terrace. He stopped in the shadow at the foot of the minaret, and stood leaning against the curved wall, looking out over the low balustrade.

The air was hot and still. The dry dusty plain lay silent under the moon.

He lit a cigarette. He shielded the flame of the lighter with his hands and smoked with the burning end of the cigarette cupped in his palm.

He thought about the jackal he had killed on the road. He remembered the soft thud on the front of the car. The bump under the wheel, the crunch of ribs ... Had he really heard the ribs crunch? No, it was impossible. He had imagined it. All at once a howl shattered the silence like a stone through glass. It seemed to come from right beside his ear, and he jumped. He glanced round him but the terrace was empty. He peered over the balustrade: nothing moved on the plain. The howl had stopped and silence returned.

Another jackal, he thought. Must have been somewhere down in that scrub. And my God, I jumped.

There's no getting out of it, he thought. I jumped. That little beggar made me jump.

It had not been much of a jump, and most people under the circumstances would have jumped out of their skins—but most people were not in this game. And in this game you had no right to jump at all. You trained yourself against jumping—against all outward manifestations of surprise. And normally nothing could make him jump. Even if Beelzebub had appeared at his elbow in a sulphurous flash, he wouldn't have batted an eyelid.

No, it hadn't been like him. But he understood how it had happened: at the moment that the howl had broken out in his ear he had been thinking about the jackal he had run over, and for a split second he had absurdly imagined that it was the dead jackal howling—that it had come to avenge itself for its death on the road.

Well, that just went to show how much the incident had disturbed him. My God, squeamish as a ruddy kid—over a jackal. He ought to be ashamed. They were filthy creatures, jackals. Vermin. He had done a good job flattening out that jackal on the road. His good deed for the day.

Yes, it's a bad weakness that squeamishness, he thought. I must get on to it. I must lick it.

He knew that he could lick it once he put his mind to it—there was no weakness you couldn't lick, no mastery over yourself you couldn't achieve, by the power of the mind—and the confidence that he could do so reassured him. No, nothing really wrong with his nerves. There couldn't be, or he wouldn't have been here at all: you needed nerves of steel even for routine occasions of this sort. Because you never knew. No matter how careful you were, no matter how scrupulous with your precautions, you could never feel absolutely, one hundred per cent secure—for you were not the only person and there was always the risk of the other man letting you down . . .

He wondered if the other man today would be Indian or European. Probably Indian. But you never knew. Once in Valparaiso, when he had been expecting a Chilean, the other man had turned out to be a Finn.

At least he had thought he was a Finn. But you never knew.

He heard the jangling harness and grinding wheels of the tonga he had passed in the car. It was just going by on the road. He wondered what it could be doing so far out of Delhi . . . The sound of its wheels was suddenly deadened: he realised with astonishment that it had turned down the track to the tomb.

The tonga lurched into view. It pulled up before the tomb with a final flourish of harness and horse-bells. The driver stuck his whip beside his seat; he hoiked and spat, and then pinched his nostrils between his fingers and leant over and blew the dust from his nose. The passenger stepped down gingerly from the back, like a sea-sick voyager from a gangplank finding his feet strangers to dry land. He carefully felt his bruises, dusted down his creased white suit with anxious flapping hands, adjusted the solar topee.

Well, I've had all sorts of headgear in my time, Birkett thought, I've run the whole gamut from a fez to a knotted handkerchief on Southend beach, from a burnous to an Italian workman's cap improvised from *Il Messaggero*—but if this is my chap, it'll be my first good old-fashioned woolsey helmet.

The man approached the tomb uncertainly. He went out of sight below the terrace, and presently Birkett heard his clumsy Indian sandals on the steps, and saw the topee emerge as though from a trap-door on the stage of white marble.

Birkett strolled out from the shadow of the minaret. He said amiably in Urdu, "Good evening, doing a bit of sightseeing?"

The Indian ignored him. He gazed up with studied absorption at the decorated façade of the mausoleum, at the row of broken eggshell domes grinning down from their crumbling pink gums.

Birkett tried again. He said, "Yes, those Mogul emperors certainly used to get put away in style."

The man continued to ignore him. Well, not even the Taj Mahal ever held a genuine sightseer quite as spellbound as that, Birkett thought. It's the worst overacting I ever saw in my life, unless he's trying to impersonate a deaf-mute.

He strolled nearer. He said, "Not a fisherman, are you? I'm wondering where I can get a bit of sport round here. Of course, no use hoping for salmon or trout. I'll have to take what's going." He waited for the man to reply. The answer to salmon was dogfish.

The man turned his head slowly towards Birkett. His face was a shiny ebony, like an African's. His features merged in the blackness, making it impossible to see more than that he was a youth in his middle twenties. At last he spoke. He said, "Uh?"

Birkett concealed the irritation that he always felt when they sent along half-baked youngsters hardly out of their nappies—they were a menace when it only needed one little slip-up to land you all down the drain. He said patiently, still speaking in Urdu, "I was talking about fishing."

The Indian said diffidently, "Excuse me, I do not understand Urdu. I am from Madras." He spoke English with loving precision, bringing out each word separately and delicately as if unpacking pieces of glass. "I speak only English and Madrasi."

The Southern Indian origin, of course, explained the ebony complexion; and the educated English showed that at least they hadn't just raked in some half-witted sweeper. Birkett grinned, reassured. "Sorry, old chap. I was just saying how I hankered for a bit of fishing. If you want to see a happy man, laddie, just lead me to a river full of salmon!"

"Salmon?"

"All right, I know, they're about as common around here as Mogul tombs in Scotland."

"We also have no salmon in Madras. We have no rivers, we are on the sea."

"What do you catch in the sea?"

"Dogfish."

Birkett nodded indifferently. "Dogfish, eh?" So much for the first party game. And so on with the next. "Of course, it isn't really fishing for me unless it's rod-and-fly. But I've been told of one place up in the hills—hang on, I've got it scribbled down—where the fishing's tip-top, streams fairly boiling with . . . Hello, what's this?" He stared in puzzlement at something that he had pulled out of the breast pocket of his bush-shirt. It was a triangular piece of playing card torn diagonally across from corner to corner. "By Jove, that poker game must have been a rough house! I wonder who got the other half?"

The Indian took off the topee and held it inverted to the moon. He peered inside. A piece of playing-card similar to Birkett's was stuck into the lining like a bus ticket.

He took it out and handed it to Birkett. Birkett held it in his left hand, and the other piece in his right, and placed them together. The torn edges fitted snugly. The two pieces made a perfect ten of spades. Birkett briskly pocketed the pieces of card, his manner becoming business-like and impersonal. "Right, I'm with you."

The Indian beamed happily, exclaiming as if they had only just met, "Good evening, sir! That was very exciting, wasn't it? But I am so glad we can now talk properly."

Birkett glanced at him sharply. But the Indian was too happy to notice, and went on blithely:

"This is my first responsible duty, you see, sir. I was very nervous at first, but it turned out much easier—"

Birkett interrupted brusquely, "What about that tonga-wallah?" He nodded over the balustrade towards the old driver who was putting out the lights of his carriage to save oil. "What d'you mean by bringing him up here?"

"It was an error, sir?" The Indian's happiness had been extinguished by the rebuff to his friendly overtures: he looked like a wounded animal. "But I was instructed to take a tonga, sir. I was given my fare."

"You should have left it at a distance. Where's your common sense? All right, we'll go round the back—we don't want the tonga-wallah snooping."

He marched off round the terrace. The young Indian struggled to keep up with him, the big clumsy sandals slopping noisily on the marble. He was not used to Birkett's brisk British pace and began to drip with sweat.

Birkett said, "Right, let's squat over there." He sat down cross-legged with his back against the mausoleum. He saw the Indian squatting several yards away. "What's the idea, laddie? Are we supposed to shout? Or communicate with walkie-talkies?"

The youth rose and came nearer, sweating through every pore, and knowing that all the bad drains in Madras would smell sweet as jasmine compared to himself. He said miserably:

"I have an order for you, sir."

"Let's have it." Birkett concealed the excitement that he always felt at this moment: the moment when a new job began, and he might hear "Djakarta" or "Pago Pago" or "Goa"—the moment when his whole being, trained to slip swiftly and smoothly into whatever gear was required of it, became dedicated to a new end.

The young Indian said, "Tomorrow afternoon at four-thirty you will call on Mr. Prem Kumar Gupta at 42, Mehta Road, New Delhi."

"Go on," Birkett said.

"That is all, sir."

"Eh? What about identification?"

"There was nothing about identification, sir."

"And no other order?"

"No, sir."

"Right, I'll repeat it. Tomorrow afternoon at four-thirty . . ."

It sounded like a ruddy invitation to tea. After being keyed up for days, anticipating a new assignment, he found it hard to hide his disappointment at the let-down. He only hoped that tomorrow this Prem Kumar Gupta would have something better to pull out of the hat. Prem Kumar Gupta? . . . The name struck a chord.

"Wait a minute," he said. "P. K. Gupta—isn't he in the government here?"

"Yes, a minister, sir."

"Minister, eh?" But how was he to approach him? And to what end? And anyhow, how could a minister be in this game? He felt sure now that the order could not be complete. He said, "Now, think again. Isn't there some detail you've forgotten?"

"No, sir."

"Nothing about how I'm to introduce myself?"

"Nothing, sir."

"What I'm to say?"

"No, sir."

"You're positive?"

"Yes, sir."

"Well, my life's in your hands, laddie." He remembered the small detail once omitted from an order given to a colleague—it had thrown a whole plan out of gear and his colleague had gone to the wall. And that's just where he'd go if this youngster . . . He checked himself. None of that, he thought. Your job's to carry out orders. And if an order is wrongly given, *tant pis*—you're not in this game for your health.

"Right, nothing else? Then no hanging about." He rose smartly. "You clear off first with that tonga-wallah."

He listened to the Indian's big clumsy sandals slopping away round the terrace and down the steps. A jackal whooped, and the whooping spread from jackal to jackal, from pack to pack, until the whole sky was ripped to shreds by their cries. Yes, I did a good job killing that jackal on the road, Birkett thought. After all, they're vermin. It's absurd to feel squeamish about destroying vermin. I'm going to lick that squeamishness. It's the only weakness in the whole streamlined, efficient machine.

Chapter Three

"Yesterday we spelt Kathmandu with an 'h', so today we'd better leave it out," the news-editor said into the telephone. He was a Parsee with a dry sense of humour and an Oxford education, and he smoked a cigarette in an ivory holder. "If we spelt it the same twice running our readers would think they'd got hold of the wrong rag."

He glanced at Birkett's card on his blotter. He put his hand over the receiver and said:

"Ah, Major Birkett, you're really in Delhi? Forgive my surprise, but our gossip column reported you were here—and it usually manages to hit even fewer nails on the head than the Swami's horoscopes. Make yourself comfortable—won't keep you a moment."

Birkett propped his walking-stick against the desk and sat down. The news-editor continued his conversation on the telephone. He was discussing the dismissal of the Prime Minister of Nepal, which had been reported in the morning papers.

"Not content with being the only newspaper in India that can't tell its readers why the King booted the P.M. out, we have to run a special leader to emphasize our perplexity . . . Who cares if the others were only guessing? If they could guess in Ootacomund, why couldn't we guess in Delhi?"

The desk-fan moved to and fro, fluttering the papers on one side of the desk and then the other. The news-editor rang off, saying, "What a fate, to be scooped by the *Ooty Courier*!" He tapped the ivory cigarette-holder fastidiously over a big glass ashtray. "Well, what can I do for you, Major Birkett?"

"I want to pick your brains," Birkett said. "I've been asked to write an article for America about the leading personalities in the Indian government. I know about most of them, but there's one or two I'd like to get a line on . . ."

He mentioned various names, to take the emphasis off the real object of his curiosity, and then said, "And P. K. Gupta—minister, isn't he?"

"Building and Communications."

"Good chap?"

"Doesn't like journalists, so that's a good start. He and Nehru attended the same British institutions."

"Harrow . . .?"

"No, I meant Ahmadnagar and Dehra Dun," the news-editor said dryly.

Birkett smiled, recognizing the names of two jails in which political prisoners had been accommodated during British rule. "So he was one of the 'Quit India' boys, was he? Funny, I can't place him at all."

"He's the sort that avoids the limelight and gets on with the job. But we must have the odd photograph." He picked up the telephone and asked for a picture of Gupta, and then resumed, "Of course, Gupta was also a devoted disciple of Gandhi, and a staunch advocate of Gandhi's doctrine of passive resistance and Satyagraha. I once heard him speak about non-violence—he was so violent about it that it seemed a contradiction of terms."

Shortly a girl came in with the photograph. The news editor handed it to Birkett. "That was taken on the day of Gandhi's funeral . . . He does *usually* wear clothes."

The picture showed a barefooted, dark-legged figure in middle-age walking in a procession of mourners. His loins and shoulders were swathed in white homespun cloth. He had a big smooth round face, and a big head slightly out of proportion to his body like a baby's. Birkett carefully studied the features and then handed the photograph back.

"Well, that gives me plenty to be going on with. Thanks for the help."

He took his walking-stick and left the office. He glanced at his watch as he descended the stairs. Not yet eleven o'clock—still a good few more hours of suspense before his meeting with Gupta this afternoon. The visit to the newspaper office had only served to increase his perplexity, for if Gupta had been one of the Gandhi boys—a Gentle-Jesus-Meek-and-Mild believing in non-violence, passive resistance, turning the other cheek—well, he could hardly be in this game. Good God, certainly not! And if he wasn't in this game, what the devil could be the purpose of the meeting . . .? Still, he had achieved the main object of the visit: he had seen the photograph. A superfluous precaution perhaps, but whilst the object of this afternoon's meeting remained so obscure, it was necessary to be prepared for any eventuality. Even for the eventuality of its turning out to be some trickery of the other side's, and of not being confronted by Gupta himself but by some impostor. . . . Well, he'd be on to that one quick enough now.

He came out of the building on to the scorching no-man's land of the pavement. The sun blazed down from an incandescent sky. The town had already been crushed into its daily submission, and the defeated inhabitants had abandoned the open spaces and crawled off into the shadows, patiently enduring the sun's oppressive imperial rule and awaiting its eventual withdrawal, the recovery of independence, at sun down. It was no wonder that submission and humility were part of the Indian character—they were practised here as a daily exercise.

Birkett set out in the direction of his hotel with his brisk foreign step. His walking-stick beat a sharp, decisive tattoo on the hot flags. The perspiration began to prick on his shoulder blades. He noted the feeling with satisfaction. Nothing like a bit of sweating for cleaning the system, keeping spare and trim . . . He avoided the arcaded pavement round Connaught Place and set out straight across the great open circle of grass, feeling the sun like a weight across his shoulders. He turned up the avenue towards the hotel.

Well, six hours from now I'll know the answer, he thought. Devil of a long time, but nothing to do but possess my soul. And I'm bound to say . . . Hello, that one's nice!

He gave his critical attention to a girl in a pink sari some distance ahead on the pavement.

Yes, very nice, he thought. Nice neat figure. And nice and small—right up my street.

The girl wore a pair of big black sun glasses. She stood near the gates of the hotel looking at the pavement display of Kashmir boxes, numdah rugs, silver anklets, and other well-tried tourist lines presided over by an old pan-chewing woman with red-stained teeth dressed as a Tibetan. Her interest in the familiar wares struck Birkett as a trifle odd.

First Indian I've ever seen stop and look at that junk, he thought. Most of them are surfeited with the stuff before they're knee-high to their amahs, and can never look a Kashmir box in the eye again.

Just then the girl looked up rather surreptitiously towards the hotel, and Birkett recognized her. It was that Mrs. What's-her-name from the Club. That girl who'd kept giving him the glad-eye at the bar.

The hotel drive was empty except for the majestic turbaned figure of the Sikh commissionaire on the steps, and the girl returned her gaze to the display at her feet. The old squatting woman turned her head and ejected a stream of red spittle. She paid the girl no attention: she had evidently long since abandoned hope of her custom.

No, I reckon it's not those Kashmir boxes that have tickled her fancy, Birkett thought. I reckon it's somebody in that hotel. And if it's me, I'm afraid she's out of luck. Because I'm entering into no commitments until I find out the score this afternoon.

He decided to slip past her and get safely through the gates before she had time to recognize and detain him . . . Then he began to waver. After all, no harm in a chat, he thought. It would help to take my mind off the suspense. And that's a nice neat little waist, there's no denying it. And never know, might come in handy, a little something like that, if I'm going to be stuck in Delhi. No sense in looking a gift horse . . . Now what was her name?

Kapoor, that was it. Lakshmi Kapoor. Well, into the fray.

He approached briskly from the flank.

"Morning!" he said cheerfully.

The girl gave a start and looked round. She was momentarily overcome with guilty confusion, but she quickly recovered herself and affected a show of astonishment.

"Oh, it's Major Birkett! What a surprise!" She remembered the big ugly dark glasses and hastily removed them, uncovering the huge dark Persian eyes that made the brittle manner seem so incongruous.

Yes, if she could get rid of whatever's eating her, she'd be a real bonny girl, Birkett thought. Still, there's nothing brittle about that neat little waist.

"Not buying anything from these sharks, are you?" he said.

"No, I just saw them as I was passing, and simply couldn't resist stopping to look . . . But how extraordinary meeting you here!"

"This is where I'm staying."

"Oh, I thought you were at the Imperial!"

Now, that's very untidy of you, Birkett thought. If you'd been in my game you'd have known the maxim about never telling a lie unless you could be sure it was tidy, with no loose ends. And you'd have remembered telling me that you'd read the bit about me in the newspaper, which mentioned where I was staying, and you'd have considered the possibility that I might have read it too—and decided that the lie was too untidy to tell.

"I've never been into this hotel," the girl was saying. "It looks so beautifully modern—I'm sure I'd adore it!"

"You should see the swimming-pool. It's so modern that it's shaped like a kidney bean, and there's many an old-fashioned guest been drowned trying to find the shallow end, before they'd caught on that the modern idea was to put the shallow end in the middle. Like a squint? We can get some coffee by the pool."

"Oh, I've so much to do, I'm afraid I can't . . ."

But she quickly decided, of course, that she could after all come just for a moment—just for a glimpse of the pool that he had made sound so irresistible. And putting on the dark glasses again, she cast anxious glances up and down the road to make sure she was not seen going into the hotel; and as they walked up the drive she kept up a stream of compulsive nervous chatter, scraping words together like pebbles to fill up a hole.

"I can't get over—I mean, running into you like that . . . Oh, your walking-stick! I simply adore it! It's so typical!"

God, I was out of my mind to stop and talk to her, Birkett thought. I should have left her to her Kashmir boxes and gone past like a scalded cat. Well, the harm's done now. But only one quick cup of coffee, young lady—and then out you go on the end of my boot.

2

"That girl is beautiful. It is a pity she has spoilt herself by lying in the sun. She must have such a beautiful fair skin, but look how it is all dark and spoilt!"

Lakshmi watched the bronzed Nordic girl with the cornflower blue eyes and long flaxen hair dive from the springboard into the electric-blue water and swim side-stroke across the pool, the hair streaming behind her.

"I can't understand European girls," she chattered on. "If I had a beautiful skin I would never go out in the sun . . . You know what I'd simply adore? A cigarette!"

Birkett silently offered his case and then his lighter. She held the cigarette an inch or two from her mouth as she applied it to the flame, then glanced anxiously at the tip that was blackened but not alight. Birkett continued to hold the flame in silence. She tried again with the cigarette tentatively between her lips. She gave the tip another anxious glance and saw with relief that it was aglow. She drew in a little smoke, hastily blew it out again. She returned her attention to the flaxen-haired Nordic goddess in the pool.

"I'm sure she has heaps of lovers—she's probably even naughtier than me. Oh dear, now I've given myself away! But I don't care. I think it's so boring to be proper, don't you? I'm not ashamed to admit I've had lovers . . ."

At last Lakshmi dried up. There was an awkward silence as she cast round for a new topic.

"All right, now come off it," Birkett said suddenly. "What's the game?"

He had seemed scarcely aware of her existence until this moment; now all at once she found herself fixed by the steady ice-blue eyes. They impaled her like skewers.

"Game?"

"The big sophistication act—what's the idea?"

She shook her head in confusion. "I don't know what you mean."

"You've never stopped acting since the minute I met you in the bar," Birkett continued bluntly. The bluntness was partly natural and partly cultivated, for he had long ago perceived the advantages—especially in regard to the peculiar requirements of his life—of this north-country characteristic in himself, and deliberately developed it. Sometimes people found him boorish, but none questioned the absolute integrity that it conveyed: it was unthinkable that this plain-speaking soldier could be practising deception, hiding any cards up his sleeve. "And you're the worst actress I've ever seen in my life."

She protested feebly that she had not been acting.

"No? All right, tell me straight. How many lovers have you had since you were married?"

"Really, what a tactless question!" She tried to laugh it off archly. "I refuse to answer!"

"I'll answer for you if you like."

"How many do you think?"

"None."

Her last defences crumbled. She was speechless.

"And none before you were married. In fact, I'll bet you've never been to bed with anyone except your husband, and I don't suppose you enjoyed it much even with him. So what's it all in aid of?"

She could only shake her head miserably, and he went on:

"Well, I'll give you my idea, and you can tell me if I'm right. I'd say for a start you've been married seven or eight years. Arranged marriage, of course. Husband picked for you by your parents. Well, that was all right. You weren't exactly a pair of love-birds, but you hadn't expected much anyhow. Then you started reading

European novels, seeing European films—nothing but a lot of tripe, but you took it all in deadly earnest and began to think you'd missed out on something. You started fretting and hankering: bursting into tears for no reason at all. You wanted to be swept off your feet by a great love affair like the emancipated girls in the books. No chance of getting into trouble at home, but this trip to Delhi was just what you'd been waiting for. You came with your head full of dreams of romantic adventure. Indian men are inclined to stick to the conventions where married women are concerned, so of course your best bet was a European, and you were so scared of finding yourself back in Lucknow without anything to show for yourself that you were prepared to settle for a chap like me. And just in case I didn't take the hint and mistook you for a conventional Indian wife, you put on the sophistication act to show me you were up to all the tricks; though thank God you stopped short at inhaling that cigarette, or I'd have seen you carried off on a stretcher. You were trying to act just like those emancipated heroines in the novels—and succeeded in looking about as much like them as my Aunt Fanny."

Well, that's one way of getting rid of her, he thought. She'll have to walk out now to save her pride—because if she doesn't she'll be lost.

He watched with amused detachment to see what she would do. She sat staring at the pool with big brown wounded eyes.

"Well, it's your move," he said. "Aren't you even going to slap my face?"

She said flatly, "Why should I? I deserved it."

"That never stopped a girl."

"I feel so ashamed. I just want to shrivel up and disappear."

He felt a mixture of contempt and pity for her because she had not even tried to save her face. It was that Indian submissiveness again. You only had to look as if you were going to hit them and they grovelled at your feet.

He said, "Well, cheer up and have another cup of coffee. I was going to boot you out ten minutes ago. But I don't mind you like this."

She suddenly noticed the forgotten cigarette in her fingers, and looked round helplessly for somewhere to put it. She stubbed it out gingerly in the ashtray on the table, and then reached for her handbag and took out a little engraved silver box. She opened it and began to prepare some pan. She had been longing for pan ever since they had arrived at the pool but had been afraid that Birkett would think it too "native." But now she had been so utterly stripped of self-respect that she had nothing more to lose.

"You make me feel like glass," she said tonelessly. Her fingers moved deftly, smearing the pan leaf with a thin coating of lime paste, adding some arica nut, a pinch of saffron. "How could you know so much about me? You were right about almost everything—except that I've been married longer than seven years. I was married at sixteen. I'm now twenty-seven."

"Well, you're certainly very bonny for such an old married woman."

"This is the first time I've ever been away alone. My husband only allowed it because the doctor said I needed a change. I couldn't go to a hotel alone—I had to come here to stay with his relatives. Afterwards I'm going to other relatives in Indore."

She folded the pan leaf to make a little packet and put it in her mouth. She began to chew.

"And it isn't true that I—well, that I ran after you to have a love affair. I wouldn't have dared even imagine it. It seemed terribly daring just to meet you like this for a cup of coffee. This is the first time in my life that I've been alone with a man outside the family. You've no idea how fast and wicked I feel! And how scared I was of coming into the hotel! Indian society is so provincial— there would be a dreadful scandal if I was recognized."

"Yes, I saw that you weren't just using those dark glasses for the sun."

The flaxen-haired goddess with the cornflower blue eyes paused beside the pool, shaking her head to dislodge some water from her ear.

"I wonder if she's married?" Lakshmi said.

"She's not wearing a wedding-ring," Birkett said.

"But you can't see . . . You mean you'd already noticed? You are extraordinary, you notice everything!" Her jaws moved mechanically as she watched the girl walk off along the pool. She said presently, "I never saw my husband at all before our marriage ceremony. Even then I didn't see him properly because of my veil. But afterwards, when I took off the veil, I thought him so fine and good-looking and was so terribly happy! I was full of romantic ideas about marriage—oh, you can even feel romantic about a marriage that's arranged!—and I knew I should love him and make him a good wife. I longed for him to speak, say something tender. But when he spoke, his first words were to tell me that he loved another girl, that he was only marrying me at the will of his parents. That night he went with a prostitute. It wasn't the fact itself that hurt so much—I'd been frightened of that side of marriage and in some ways felt almost relieved—but the shame of knowing that everybody knew. His family, his friends, our own servants—they all knew that he'd left his new bride on the wedding night and gone to a woman of the town. I know it's stupid, but in India we care so much about what other people think. I wanted to die . . ."

Well, I've let myself in for it now, Birkett thought. The story of her life, complete and unabridged. Including details of ailments since birth, and Appendix A. relating the true facts about how Auntie Madge met Uncle Joe.

Her voice went on. It was a low voice with a rather attractive velvety purr, but a sing-song Indian intonation that irritated him.

He noted his irritation with paradoxical satisfaction. An item for the catalogue . . . He always made a catalogue of faults of a woman who physically attracted him. It provided a safe guard against the danger of becoming too deeply involved.

He noticed Lakshmi's jaw working mechanically as she chewed the pan—like a ruddy American woman chewing gum. Yes, another item for the catalogue, that pan.

The girl went on: "He plays polo in the morning and gets drunk in the afternoon. And in the evening—well, you can guess! It's not even as though he can afford it, but his parents encourage him because debauchery is the privilege of their class. Only sons of good families can spend their lives riding horses and drinking with dancing girls. Only the sons of zamindars."

"Oh, they belong to that lot, eh?" The zamindars were the petty raja landowners who for generations had lived in idle luxury on the rents extorted from their tenants, until the recent Zamindary Bill had deprived them of much of their wealth and power.

"Yes, I remember you wrote about the zamindars in your book," Lakshmi said. "It was one of the bones I wanted to pick with you. You sounded almost as if you were on their side and didn't approve of the new reforms."

Birkett said, "That was because it looked too much like the thin end of the Russian wedge for my liking. It reminded me of that old cut-throat Stalin's efforts at land reform—regular blood bath, remember? Enough kulaks massacred to fertilise a real bumper crop in the Ukraine—but there was no crop at all, only famine and starvation and general muck-up And I could see the same thing happening in India. But it didn't. I was wrong—it was nothing like Communism. In fact I'm not sure now that it went far enough. They've still got too much money, those zamindars, many of them."

"Not enough to go on living in the same way as before," Lakshmi said. "That is what happened to my husband's family. It was only my dowry that saved them."

"So you were given away with a nice bit of brass, eh?"

"Brass?"

"Money. Brass we call it in Lancashire. Your father had plenty, did he?"

She explained that her father was a building contractor and his firm had branches all over India. Her grandfather, who had founded the firm, had started as a labourer in an English warehouse on the Hooghly River. He had been born in the Calcutta slums. "So you see we are not 'good family,' and my husband's parents would never have chosen me for their son except to save themselves from ruin. It was a great triumph for my father. He had never been accepted by zamindar society: that was one thing that all his money had never bought him. But now it had bought acceptance for his daughter. Or so he thought, for really his fortune was thrown away.

Because I've never been accepted . . . But in India you marry for life. And you learn to bear your sufferings in silence."

Birkett was listening with only half an ear. He seemed to have heard it all before, for India—despite all the sex in the Hindu religion, all those religious friezes showing you how to do what, and how, and to whom—was full of frustrated wives. The trouble was not so much the system of arranged marriages as the high walls of convention with which the Indian woman was surrounded. Confined to her domestic prison, she had too few distractions for her mind, too much time to brood on her own frustrated soul.

The girl was saying, "I was disappointed at first—I'd always wanted a boy. But soon I was just doting on Kusum, living for her; Wait, I've got a picture, though it's not very good—you can't see her lovely fair skin." She rummaged in her handbag, "I was so proud once, somebody told me, 'Why, Kusum's so fair, she could be a little Italian girl!'"

"What's wrong with being Indian?"

"Oh, nothing. But a fair complexion is so beautiful! So aristocratic! Look, there she is . . . Oh, isn't she pretty! You know Kusum means a flower? I know I shouldn't say it myself but don't you think she is like a lovely flower?"

Birkett looked at the snapshot of the girl posing stiffly on some verandah steps. She struck him as remarkably plain. "Yes, very bonny." He handed it back. "How old is she now?"

"Kusum? Now?" Her face clouded. "You mean how old *would* she have been?"

Evidently the child was dead—that must have been one of the bits he had missed. "I mean how old was she when—er—?"

"When we lost her? Just five. It was soon after her fifth birthday that the epidemic broke out . . . Nothing has really mattered since I lost my little Kusum."

She fell silent. Her huge dark yearning eyes absently followed the flaxen-haired girl as she scaled the ladder to the high-diving board. She said, "I wonder if she really has lovers?"

"She could count me out."

The girl dived, moved like a quivering shadow through the water, and emerged with the grace and ease of a naiad.

"Don't you find her attractive?" Lakshmi said.

"No, too emancipated—she's lost half her feminity. You can't behave like a man and be a real woman at the same time. It's one or the other." The girl in the pool swept the long wet strands of flaxen hair from her face, arranged it to trail decoratively, and swam across the pool—effortless, exhibitionistic, completely self-sure. He said, "No, not my type. Not that Valkyrie type."

"What is your 'type'?"

"You—you're my type."

"Me?" She stared at him in disbelief. There had been no design in her question. All her dreams and pretensions had been so effectively shattered that she hardly thought of herself any longer as a woman at all—never mind as capable of attracting a man.

"You're teasing me, aren't you?"

"No, you're a very bonny girl. Nice and feminine and small, how a girl should be. Only I don't like to see you chewing pan."

"Oh, I'm sorry, how awful!" She turned her face away guiltily, hiding her mouth with her hand, and swallowed the pan that remained.

"You'll spoil your teeth if you're not careful. You don't want to look like that old harridan selling the Kashmir boxes, do you?"

"I don't use tobacco—that is what stains."

"Never mind, I'd forbid you to touch the stuff if I had anything to do with you—not that that's likely." His eyes impaled her again. "Though I wouldn't mind having something to do with you at all."

She said uneasily, "I hope we can meet again. I've enjoyed talking so much."

"Don't fool yourself. If we met again it wouldn't be to talk."

She was silent under his ice-blue gaze.

"And in case you're still thinking you'd fancy a little flutter," he went on bluntly, "I'll tell you straight—it would suit me very nicely, but I wouldn't give you what you're after. It's the romantic trappings you want—the secret looks, the touching of knees under the table, the lovers' talk. But I've grown out of all that lovey-dovey stuff. I don't give a hoot for girls now, except for going to bed—and that means no more to me than a good meal or a glass of beer. So now you know the score. You'd get no fancy words from me, only a roll in the hay—though so far as that goes you might go farther and fare worse. So what about it? Like to come upstairs?"

Despite the irony in his tone she knew that his words were not wholly in jest, and she felt their bluntness and crudity almost like a physical assault. And yet whilst part of herself was repulsed, the other half was simultaneously drawn by something about him she could still not define.

She said wonderingly, "You are extraordinary . . . So extraordinary. I thought I knew what you were like—so typical English army. But you are not at all. What are you really like?"

He smiled quickly. "A cheetah."

"A cheetah—why?"

"Never mind, skip it."

"Please tell me what you meant."

"Once came across a cheetah in Africa—sitting by itself under a fever tree on the Serengeti. Struck me it was a lone sort of chappie like me, that's all."

She shook her head in bewilderment. "I still don't understand."

You're doing your best though, he thought. And I'm not sure that you're not brighter than I've been giving you credit for—and that it's not time to pack up.

He glanced at his watch. "By Jove, if I'm to get a spot of work done before lunch . . ."

She said reluctantly, "Yes, I must go."

"Don't want to rush you. Like a taxi?"

He accompanied her across the lawn. He felt her dragging reluctance to reach the hotel, arrive at the moment of parting. She was longing for him to propose another meeting. But now his thoughts had returned to his meeting this afternoon with Gupta; he was making no commitments before he found out the form.

They reached the front entrance. The magnificent Sikh commissionaire, autocratic as a maharajah and as splendidly outfitted, gave a commanding blast on his whistle. An old eight horse-power taxi hurried anxiously up the drive.

"I've enjoyed it so much. If only we'd had longer," the girl said, fishing.

Birkett did not bite. "Well, chin up," he said in cheerful dismissal.

The Sikh held open the taxi door. Suddenly she gave way to the impulse she had been resisting. "I know you're awfully busy, but I suppose there's no chance . . . ?"

"Plans still uncertain—but bound to run into you at the Club if I'm around."

Her face collapsed in misery. She gathered up her sari and got into the car, and he caught a last glimpse through the window of her pale little face, finger-tips touching under the delicate pointed chin, as she was carried away; and she looked so forlorn that he wondered momentarily if he might not have indulged her. Besides, if the meeting with Gupta turned out to be another let-down, he might have been glad of some distraction this evening.

Still, you could bet your life he hadn't seen the last of her. If he knew anything about women, she'd soon find some excuse to turn up on his doorstep again, call him on the phone. He'd give her a couple of days at the outside.

Then he remembered how she had sat tight at the swimming-pool when she ought to have walked out.

No, she wouldn't need a couple of days—not a girl as handy as that at sinking her pride. She'd be much quicker off the mark. He'd be surprised if that phone didn't ring within twenty-four hours.

3

It rang within four hours—at exactly five minutes past four as he was about to leave the room for the meeting with Gupta. He laid down his walking-stick again and picked up the receiver. "Birkett here."

"This is Lakshmi . . . Lakshmi Kapoor." Her quavering voice betrayed how great an ordeal it had been for her to make this call. "I just wanted to say how grateful . . ."

"Sorry, just going out. Can't natter now. Come for dinner, if you like."

Joy overwhelmed her. "Oh, I'd adore . . . !"

"Right, eight o'clock down in the hall. Now excuse me. Must skip. 'Bye."

He hung up. He took the walking-stick and left the room. He went down the corridor to the lift. He felt the beginnings of exhilaration. He was on the job again. The cheetah was strolling out from under the tree: he was off on a new prowl.

Chapter Four

He found his way in a few minutes to Mehta Road. It was lined with bungalows set back in watered gardens. The air was filled with the sweet, sickly scent of frangipani. A wailing female voice came from some unseen radio—that ubiquitous female whose mechanical caterwaul began somewhere about Naples and was passed on like a torch, from open window to bar doorway to open window again, through the Middle East and across India, until finally extinguished somewhere on the borders of China. The voice faded behind him. It had almost died out of hearing when the torch was taken up by another open window ahead. Just then he spotted No. 42 on a gatepost above the name Jehangir House.

He found the flat on the top floor. The door was opened by a plump middle-aged Indian in white muslin shirt and dhoti. He had sullen resentful eyes on the look-out for slights. He said, "Yes?"

"Prem Gupta?"

"Out."

"My name's Birkett."

The Indian hesitated, and then ungraciously jerked his head for Birkett to enter.

"The Minister is busy. I don't know if—" He broke off, as if suspecting that his use of English might appear to Birkett as an acknowledgement of inferiority, and resumed in Urdu, "—I don't know if he will see you." He started to lead the way across the hall but then, as an added measure to restore face by keeping Birkett waiting, turned aside and picked up a telephone directory, and became absorbed in an improbably laborious search through its pages.

After a while Birkett said mildly, "Come on, George, get a move on."

The Indian's brow knitted, his absorption became more emphatic.

Birkett brought his walking-stick down with a sharp rap on the parquet. "Wake up, George!"

The Indian put down the directory and gazed elaborately round the hall. He said in Urdu, "I must go to an oculist. My eyesight is evidently failing. I cannot see the person to whom you are speaking."

"You."

"Me?" He showed exaggerated surprise. "But I am the Minister's private secretary. I am not accustomed to being addressed like a sweeper."

"You're a bit behind the times, George," Birkett said. "The British Viceroy packed his bags over ten years ago. So why keep on fighting?"

The Indian lifted his nose contemptuously in the air and led the way along a corridor. Reaching a door at the end he knocked, stepped inside, and shut the door behind him, leaving Birkett to cool his heels. A moment later he reappeared. He said to Birkett with fussy anxiety, "The Minister is a busy man, you know. You must not stay long."

"That's up to him."

"It is my duty to see his time is not wasted. I have looked after him for twenty years. I am privileged, he is a great man . . . Now, you understand? You will conclude your business as quickly as possible?"

Birkett smiled to himself. The old hen's jealous, he thought. He wants the cockerel all to himself. "Do my best," he said.

"The Minister will introduce himself. You will call him 'sir'."

He opened the door and Birkett felt a gust of cold air on his face, and stepped through into an air-conditioned room that after the heat of the corridor had an Arctic chill. The Indian closed the door behind him. A big plain desk squarely faced the door and behind the desk sat Gupta.

There was no doubt that it was Gupta, although he had lost the remainder of the hair that he had possessed in the photograph.

The shiny bald dome made the big head, with the smooth round heavy-lidded face, seem more than ever like a baby's. He sat stiffly, occupied with some papers. His Indian jacket, buttoned tightly round the neck, gave the impression of austere military uniform. He glanced up and began to rise rather wearily, unhooking steel-rimmed glasses from his ears. He extended a hand across the desk. He said remotely:

"My name's Gupta."

"Birkett."

Gupta repeated, "Birkett, Birkett?" as if he was hearing his visitor's name for the first time. "You're not the writer, are you?"

"That's right, sir."

"Ah, the writer. Well, won't you be seated?"

Birkett sat down, laying his stick beside the chair, and the Minister seated himself again behind the desk.

"Well, what can I do for you, Birkett?"

"I was going to ask you the same question, sir."

"Really? But what brought you here?"

"I just had a hunch you might want to see me."

"How curious! Why should I?"

"No idea," Birkett said flatly, and waited for Gupta to make the next move. Gupta was silent. It was another minute before he said absently, as if making conversation only for the sake of politeness.

"You know anything about yoga?"

"Yoga?"

"No firsthand experience, I suppose?"

A shot in the dark? Birkett wondered. Or has he been boning up on me? He said, "Yes, I've had a bit. Long time ago when I was soldiering out here in the war—I spent two months leave in an ashram near Madras."

"Surely an unusual interest for a soldier?"

"Probably but I wanted to find out what was in it."

"You were impressed?"

"I'll say so! Should have seen me after that leave when l got back to Burma—sitting cross-legged in my forty-pounder tent, while the shells roared overhead like express trains, concentrating on the end of my nose and uniting myself with the Infinite. And maybe not such a bad idea at that—nothing like yoga for taking your mind off unpleasant reality."

"So that explains it," Gupta said.

"Explains what?"

"How you got your material for this." He opened a drawer and took out a book. It was Birkett's book on India. "I got this in case you ever had a 'hunch' about coming to see me. I have not read it. I have no time for reading. I have to rely on Desai—you met Desai, my secretary, didn't you? He kindly made this report." He took a piece of paper from inside the cover. He scanned the paragraphs of neat typing. "I gather you were finally disillusioned about yoga. How was that?"

"I just came to my senses."

Gupta, his eyes resting on the typewritten paper in his hand, let the remark go unchallenged. After a bit he said, "Desai, at any rate, seems to approve of your conclusions."

"Debagging the fakirs—yes, I'm not surprised. That chap's got so many chips on his shoulder, if you'll forgive my saying so, that he'd enjoy seeing anybody debagged."

Gupta again let the remark pass. He said, "The rest of the book, however, was evidently less to his taste. You'd like to see?"

He handed the paper across the desk. Birkett ran his eyes over the neat typed paragraphs.

Major Ronald Birkett. (Biographical notes from jacket and text.) Born Longhulme, Manchester, England. Son of ecclesiastical minister. Educated Rowan House Preparatory School, Staffordshire, and Longhulme Grammar School. Early journalistic career in Manchester and London, followed by wartime military service in Europe and Far East, and in forces of occupation in Germany. Has since travelled widely. Since visiting Australia, 1956, has remained in Far East.

Author shows authentic knowledge of yoga cult, and appreciates the obstacle to Indian progress imposed by religious superstition. His facetious humour on this subject, however,

*ill becomes an author from the country that deliberately
fostered Indian superstition and ignorance to assist its task of
imperial oppression.*

*The book is otherwise a worthless parade of reactionary
platitudes under the guise of sympathetic liberalism, which
will no doubt find appreciation in certain quarters.*

Birkett slid the paper back across the desk with an indifferent
shrug. "Can't satisfy everybody."

"But you satisfy yourself?"

"I try to make a balanced judgment. There's not much in that
book that I'd go back on now. It's mostly pretty well in line with
your present government policy, so presumably you'd agree with
it yourself."

"I think not, since I don't agree with the government."

"Eh? How's that? How can you be a minister if you don't believe
in the policies you're carrying out?"

Gupta said, "How can you be a writer if you don't believe in
what you're writing?"

Birkett frowned. "Sorry, I don't follow. Of course I believe in
what I write."

Gupta rose stiffly and walked across the room. He stopped before
a geographical globe which he spun with his finger. "You can see
this is old. India is coloured red."

"Good old British Empire," Birkett said. "Yes, plenty of red in
those days."

"I remember looking at India in my atlas as a boy, and dedicating
my life to changing its colour."

"Must give you a bit of satisfaction to see it looking that nice
green now," Birkett said, nodding to a map on the wall.

"Not as much as I once thought. I used to believe that the British
were the root of all evil—that when the red was changed to green
all our problems would be solved. It wasn't until Independence
was already in sight that I was shaken out of my complacency.
You were here during the war, so perhaps you remember the Bengal
famine?"

"Yes, never forgot it," Birkett said. "Those starving kids with swollen bellies in the streets of Calcutta. Not to mention the odd corpse or two."

"There were two or three million corpses altogether. I toured Bengal during the famine and the villages were littered with the dead and dying. I once saw a woman, who had lost three children, try to kill herself with a knife. The knife was snatched from her hand. She ran off and beat her head against a wall to batter out her brains."

He crossed to the window and stood looking out, his hands behind his back. He went on, "Of course, the ultimate blame lay with the British overlords. But it was impossible to ignore the guilty negligence of the local Indian government, and the criminal activities of profiteers who cornered the rice to make fortunes out of suffering. How could such a catastrophe be prevented from happening again? Clearly the answer was not only in changing the colour of the map. That was only the beginning. Once Independence was achieved, how could we awaken four hundred starving millions from their sloth and poverty? Make use of our great natural resources, turn India into a rich productive land? What manner of government was needed? It took me a long time to find the answer—three years."

The telephone rang. He picked up the receiver and said, "Gupta, yes?"

Birkett waited. Nearly there, he thought. In a minute or two he's going to show his hand.

"*Tiek*, tell him to see me tomorrow at Parliament House," Gupta said and rang off. He remained standing stiffly behind the desk. He said, "Yes, it took me three years to find the answer—the only possible answer for India, And that, of course, was Communism."

"Communism?" Birkett stared with the ill-concealed beginnings of distaste, "You weren't a Communist?"

"I am still a Communist."

"You're not serious? No, you must be pulling my leg. I know old Nehru's fond of buttering up the Reds, but you can't tell me he'd stand for a Red in his cabinet."

"Probably not. Fortunately the question does not arise, since I was persuaded at the outset that I could best serve our cause by concealing my beliefs. We are birds of a feather."

"Eh? I don't get the point."

"You are also a Communist, aren't you, Birkett?"

"Me? A Red? A Bolshie? No ruddy fear!"

Gupta said patiently, "You are quite safe, Birkett. You may trust me."

"Look here, Gupta, I'm still not quite sure if this is a leg-pull or not," Birkett said. "But I'll tell you straight. I don't like Commies. I spit on 'em. They twist people's ruddy minds until they'd sell their own mothers down the river. Treachery's their stock in trade. There's only one thing you can be sure about a Communist. If he's got a dove of peace in one hand, he'll have a knife ready to stick you in the back in the other. And if you're one of 'em, I'm off."

"That was good, Birkett. That was very good. For a minute I was almost deceived myself."

"Listen, Gupta, I just want a straight answer. Are you really a Communist or not?"

"Of course."

"Then excuse me." He reached for his walking-stick beside the chair and stood up.

"I congratulate you, Birkett," Gupta smiled. "You have passed my test. I wanted to see if you would take me on trust. Of course you are perfectly right not to do so. Now, please sit down again, and I shall present my credentials."

Birkett gave him a look of contempt and turned away to the door.

"Before you go," Gupta said, "you don't happen to have heard of a place . . ."

Birkett opened the door and started to leave the room.

"A place called Omputon," Gupta said.

Birkett stopped halfway out of the door. He said, "Eh?"

"Omputon."

Birkett stood without moving for a moment, and then came back into the room and carefully closed the door. He returned to the desk without hurrying and without looking at Gupta. He propped his walking-stick against the desk. Omputon, he thought. Well, I'm blowed, Omputon. After all this time.

He remembered the first and only other time that he had heard the word spoken. It had been three years ago in Australia, and he remembered waiting on the street corner in the King's Cross district of Sydney on a wet blustery evening, beside a vacant lot occupied by a mountain of old rusting buckets and bedsteads, and an unattended display of second-hand cars with prices marked in white paint on their windscreens, and a huge hoarding on which a loose poster had been flapping about in the wind like a wet bedsheet. And he remembered the tall enormous tart, like a giantess from another planet, sheltering near the hoarding under an absurdly tiny umbrella, who had kept calling to him every few minutes, "Waiting for your cobber? Where's your cobber? Hasn't your cobber come yet?"—and wanting to take him into one of the cars for two pounds: "That's in the Rolls, dearie . . . All right, thirty shillings in the Holden . . . A pound in the Vauxhall." And then the giantess finding a client and taking him into a car that was so small that it was a wonder she could get in at all, never mind earn her fee; and at last the repair truck with the hulking moronic-looking driver stopping and picking him up and taking him to a dark cul-de-sac, and the driver turning off the engine and speaking in a voice of such hard cold precision that Birkett had sat up in astonishment, and in considerable awe, realizing that so far from being a moron the driver was a man of ruthless intelligence and authority. And he remembered the driver telling him, in the cold steel hammer of a voice that drove home each word like a six-inch nail, that he would remain seconded to the Pan Asian Communist Service Agency for further duties, receiving orders in the normal manner through the branch network, unless PACSAG should for any reason wish to short-circuit the network and contact him directly, in which case they would use a special code. "The code will indicate direct communication from the founthead. The alert word is Omputon."

Birkett remained silent a moment longer, savouring his excitement.

So it was top-level stuff this time-straight from the founthead. Well, that made up all right for yesterday's let-down.

He said smartly, "Right, I'm with you, sir."

"Good," Gupta said brusquely, "now we can get on. We've a lot to get through. Sit down, Birkett."

Splendid, Birkett thought. No time wasted, no natter—straight to the point.

"I've an important job to be done in this sphere," Gupta went on. "I've already turned down two men who weren't suitable. Now PACSAG has highly recommended you."

"I'm flattered, sir."

"What do you know about Nepal?"

"Nepal? Well, I heard the news this morning, about the King kicking out his Prime Minister. I gather the Prime Minister was a secret friend of ours."

Gupta waved an impatient hand. "Nonsense. You don't still believe that rubbish in the sensational Press? I only wish he had been our friend. We need friends in Nepal."

He abruptly pushed back his chair and got up, snatching a ruler from the desk. Birkett followed him over to the map of India on the wall. He reached up with a ruler towards the barrier of the Himalayas across the top.

"There you are—Nepal."

He struck sharply with the ruler on the little island of pale blue squeezed between the green of India and the yellow of Tibet. Kathmandu, the only town marked within the blue boundaries, stood in perfect isolation in the middle, innocent of connecting railways or roads.

"Independent kingdom," Gupta said. "Nearly all mountains. No economic importance whatever, and so inaccessible that even the British couldn't be bothered to annex it. But its position gives it an importance out of all proportion to its population and size."

"Yes, with Tibet in the Chinese sphere, I can see it must have importance as a buffer state," Birkett said.

"And a bridgehead!" Gupta reached up and struck the ruler into Tibet, and then drew it down in a straight line through the centre of the little island of blue into the green continent below. "A bridgehead for Communism into India! A Communist government in Nepal would advance our cause further at a single stroke than could be achieved by any other means. And if PACSAG had listened to me earlier, there would be a Communist government there now."

He explained that for several years an invisible battle had been waged between China and India for possession of Nepal's soul. But neither China nor PACSAG had fully understood the importance of the outcome to the future of Asian Communism, and ignoring Gupta's warnings and his advice on strategy, had allowed India to win all along the line. It had set back the cause of Communism twenty years. But now at last PACSAG had woken up, given Gupta a free hand to do what he could to redeem the situation.

Birkett said, "A tough nut to crack! Still, given time . . ."

"Time?" Gupta turned. "We are not given time. India's position is too strong. If we took 'time,' every move we made would be countered. For every inch we gained we should lose a yard."

"What's the position there now? Have we an organized Party?"

Gupta waved this away. "Forget it, Too slow! It must be done in one decisive stroke."

"Have you a plan, sir?"

"A very good plan. Six weeks from now the tables will be turned. I shall have a Communist government in Nepal."

By Jove, I don't know what the devil he's got in mind, Birkett thought. But if he says he'll do it, I believe he will. Nothing will stop him. Or me . . .

Gupta returned to the desk, motioning Birkett to be seated. He sat down also and said, "You will be under no obligation to carry out this job. I should feel no confidence in you if you were acting under compulsion."

"I've never turned down a job yet, sir," Birkett said.

"You have probably never had a job of this nature. Your main task in brief. . ." The telephone rang. He picked it up. "Gupta, yes?"

Birkett waited. The Minister said impatiently, "*Tiek, tiek* . . . I can't talk now." He rang off.

He left his hand on the receiver, and after a moment lifted it again and laid it on the desk. He said, "My colleagues can wait. They think they hold the fate of India in their hands—but now you hold it in yours. For just that reason I don't want you to make your decision without thinking it over."

Birkett said nothing,

"Our future hangs on the success of your mission," Gupta said. "It must not fail. It is the assassination of the King of Nepal."

Chapter Five

It was ten minutes to nine when Birkett turned through the gates of the hotel. He walked up the lamplit drive.

> *Oh, Mr. Middleton,*
> *I've got such a pain!*
> *Quick! Some Osbaldiston's Syrup*
> *To make me well again!*

That jingle again! It had come into his head as he was leaving Gupta's and now he couldn't get rid of it. He had walked back to get some fresh air into his lungs after the air-conditioning, and it had gone on jingling all the way.

> *Oh, Mr. Middleton,*
> *I've got such——*

A girl in a green sari rose from a chair in the entrance hall and came towards him. Good God, Lakshmi Kapoor—still here. He thought she'd have packed up long ago.

He greeted her cheerfully.

"Hello, bit late, am I?" Nearly an hour to be exact. But she was looking as pleased as Punch now that he had turned up—so no point in rubbing it in. "Never mind, I'm here now, that's the main thing. By Jove, you're looking bonny!"

"I was afraid you'd forgotten!"

"Not a bit, no. Just one thing and another. Now, you don't mind possessing your soul a bit longer, do you? There's a girl! Just while I slip up for a quick wash—down in a jiffy." He collected his key from the desk. The absurd little rhyme began jingling in his head again as he went to the lift. He remembered the Osbaldiston's poster on which it had appeared. It had been as familiar a sight on the north-country railway platforms of his childhood as the trolleys of milk cans and the red penny-in-the-slot machines with Nestlé's chocolate. He could still remember every detail of the picture of the schoolboy rushing into the chemist's shop with falling socks, twisted tie, hands clutched to his belly—and an expression of agony half turned to joy as he saw Mr. Middleton, the rubicund dispenser of cheer, flourishing the bottle of Osbaldiston's Syrup of Figs over the counter.

> *Oh, Mr. Middleton,*
> *I've got such a pain . . .*

He wondered if the roomboy had thrown away the morning newspaper. The lift gate sighed open at his floor and he went along to his room and looked round for it.

He thought for a moment that it had gone. Then he spotted it in the bedside cupboard.

Well, that's him, he thought. That's the chappie.

The photograph was no bigger than two postage stamps. It showed the face of a man of about thirty-five wearing Nepali cap and dark glasses. It was an agreeable face of no particular distinction. The dark glasses deprived it of any expression.

Gupta had mentioned the dark glasses. Apparently he was never seen without them in public. "He grew up overshadowed by his father, a man of extravagant charm. It no doubt gave him feelings of inferiority. His nature is shy and retiring—the dark glasses give him something to hide behind. He is a worthy, hard-working young fellow who has done a great deal for his country. We have nothing against him personally. It is just his misfortune to be King. And not only King but, according to popular Nepalese belief, a reincarnation of Vishnu and therefore a semi-divinity. . ."

That, of course, was all to the good. It meant that the passions aroused by the wanton murder would be all the greater, the wrath of his subjects all the quicker to seek expression . . .

He stood for another minute staring at the face of the young

King with the dark glasses looking out from amongst the columns of print. His eyes were reluctant to leave it. He dragged them away with an effort and went into the bathroom. He adjusted the shower and stepped into the hot spray.

I shouldn't hesitate, he thought. I've got two days to make my decision, but I should make it here and now . . .

Those had been a nasty few moments, he had to admit, before he had realised that he wasn't expected to pull the trigger himself. Assassination was a mug's game. But of course the whole point was that the trigger should be pulled by an Indian—from the Indian Embassy in Kathmandu. That was what made it such a pretty plan, because inevitably it would suggest to ignorant Nepalese minds, already suspicious of India, that the crime was officially inspired. That sly old Nehru up to his tricks again. My God, they'd go wild—tear the Embassy brick from brick. Those tough little Nepalese hillmen, whose national sport was lopping off the heads of goats with one swipe of a kukri, were going to exercise the same skill on any Indian they could lay their hands on. And within twenty-four hours of the young King's murder, you'd be more likely to see an Abominable Snowman than an Indian face in Nepal. Close your eyes and count ten, and . . . Hello, what's that? By Jove, the hammer and sickle flying over Kathmandu!

He adjusted the shower to "cold." The heat abruptly withdrew and his body tingled agreeably under the cold impact of the spray. He felt newly livened as he reached for his towel and briskly dried.

The big question mark, he thought, was the Indian. Everything hung on the Indian—and on Birkett's ability to handle him.

Gupta had known little about him. He had only the details from the records. Name: Krishna Mathai. Age: 27. Occupation: Third Secretary, Indian Foreign Office. Category: ST3a. (In other words, Communist affiliations kept secret and available for underground duty.)

"You may find the young man eager to grasp such an opportunity to serve our cause." Gupta had said. "On the other hand, assassination being a spectacular career but of somewhat limited future, he may feel certain—reservations. Your task will be to make him appreciate, and willingly accept, that after shooting the King he must pay the same compliment to himself . . ."

My God, some task, Birkett thought. Still, right up my street. I don't know why I should feel the least hesitation. After all, it's only two lives—you lose more than that from heat stroke in a May Day parade. And look what you're getting for your money—the price is sheer bargain-basement . . .

But somehow his mind still jibbed at making the decision. Right, skip it for now, he thought.

He gave two quick dabs at his moustache with the corner of his hairbrush, one to the left side, one to the right, and left the room. He stepped from the lift in the hall below and sailed up to Lakshmi breezily.

"Sorry, bit long, was I? By Jove, sorry to keep repeating it, but you really are looking bonny tonight! Now let's stoke up with a bit of grub."

The big gloomy dining-room was deserted except for a few old despondent waiters standing about with faraway eyes.

"Bit of a barracks," he apologized, as they sat down at his usual table. He had briefly considered taking her down to the Palmyra Room, but the hotel's all-in rate only covered meals in the main dining-room and it would have meant paying for his meal twice over. And although nobody could call him mean, he wasn't a man you'd catch throwing away a penny on some thing only worth ha'pence—least of all for the sake of a girl.

Lakshmi was scarcely aware of her surroundings: her face was radiant, and her huge long Persian eyes shone with inner illumination.

There's only one thing that can make a woman look like that, Birkett thought. God, what idiots women are! She's only met me twice and doesn't know the first thing about me—I'm only a dummy on which she's hung a romantic image of her own. Still, she can't say I didn't warn her.

He said, "Taking a bit of a risk coming along tonight, aren't you? What yarn did you spin to the people you're staying with?"

"I pretended I was having dinner with an old school friend that

I'd met this morning." She looked mischievously pleased with herself. "I invented a whole story about her—it sounded terribly convincing!"

"Same all the world over, you women—can't beat you for shameless intrigue. Only what happens if somebody walks in and recognizes you, and tells your friends that Phantom Fanny, or whatever your girl-friend's supposed to be called, is an Englishman with a moustache?"

"I don't care," she glowed. "I'm so happy tonight, I don't care what happens."

"Well, I'm having a nice time myself. Not every day I have such a bonny—sorry, skip it. But anyhow you're a very pretty girl, my dear." No denying it. And that red spot on the forehead—well, by Jove, he was beginning to find it quite disturbing. Like the crucifix of that girl in Manila that was the only thing she hadn't taken off at the drop of a hat.

The old waiter served their soup with quivering hand. Birkett tasted it. "Sorry, awful muck." He suddenly gave way to impulse. "Come on, let's go to the Palmyra Room."

"But really, I don't . . ."

"It'll be a bit costly, I'll be paying for my meal twice over—sheer highway robbery. But no harm in throwing your bonnet over the windmill once in a while so long as you know what you're doing."

There was a dance-band playing in the Palmyra Room. They sat side by side at an alcove table lit by the soft glow of its own lamp. Couples in close embrace appeared like phantoms from the dark shadows round the dance-floor, drifted across the circle of rosy twilight, melted again into the shadows. The music palpitated softly.

Lakshmi said presently, "You never told me if you were married."

"I told you I was a lone ranger."

"You mean you've never been married?"

"Yes, I went through the mill as a youngster. Only the price was too high—the girl I married wanted to possess my soul, keep me haltered and chained like a performing bear. Lord, the scenes! Every time I went to the odd stag party, met the odd friend for a drink. And every Tuesday night, regular as clockwork, after I got back from volunteer training down at Chelsea barracks—floods of tears, and 'Boo-hoo, you love the army more than me!'" He suddenly remembered the time he had come home to find Dorothy in one of her states, and it had finally turned out that this time the theme that had been occupying her during long hours of brooding, culminating in the inevitable tears, was his failure to be like other husbands who called their wives by pet names. Good God! And what "pet name" did she fancy? No, she couldn't say—it wouldn't be the same unless it came from him. All right, suggestions please. And at least, "Well, for instance, it would be nice if you called me Dot, or Dotty. . ." Dotty! Imagine it! Brooding like an old hen, weeping bloody buckets, because your husband didn't call you Dotty! The memory was so embarrassing that he decided not to tell Lakshmi. It would only make him look a fool for ever having become involved with a girl capable of such imbecility. He said, "You can't treat a man like that. You can't swallow him whole. You've got to leave him a bit for himself."

Lakshmi said, "It must be difficult for a woman if she loves a man so terribly."

"Love! You should have heard her talk! Oh, yes, the times she used to tell me she could only love one man all her life, couldn't understand women capable of infidelity!"

"I think that is beautiful."

"Beautiful words are cheap—I prefer beautiful deeds."

"You don't mean she was unfaithful?"

"How's your arithmetic? I went off to France at the beginning of the war. I returned to London after eleven months to find Dorothy in the family way. Five months gone—rough estimate, but near enough. Five from eleven leaves six—wide enough margin to cover all possible vagaries of nature as hitherto known to parish records."

"Oh, how awful!"

"Bound to say it hurt my pride. But a blessing in some ways. Quick release from that halter and chain—no need for paying some woman a fiver to trot off with you to Brighton. So that was the end of Dorothy and I never saw her again, though I heard she successfully hooked the chap who'd been keeping my slippers warm. And good luck to him. I hope he took to harness better than me."

"You've never wanted to marry again?"

"Don't make me laugh! Now, don't let's spoil the evening with muck-raking. Come on, let's take a spin."

She was flushed and exhilarated when they returned once more to the table. She kept exclaiming that it was the happiest evening of her life.

"I wish all women were as easy to please," Birkett said.

"I can't believe I'm not just dreaming."

"My word, it doesn't say much for your dreams, if you can't manage to dream up something better than an old stick like me!"

"I can't imagine anybody better."

"You can't be trying very hard—still, does me good to hear it. Hello, here's Broken-hearted Blondie back to give us another treat."

The crooner with the shoulder-length platinum hair caressed the microphone in the spotlight and moaned of the pain of rejected love.

"Don't you find her attractive?" Lakshmi said.

"Now if you'd asked me twenty years ago . . ."

"You wouldn't rather be having dinner with her than me?"

"Come off it."

The crooner continued to suffer into the microphone.

"Mr. Middleton would see her right in no time," Birkett said. Lakshmi looked puzzled, and he grinned. "Good dose of Osbaldiston's is all she needs for that pain—Osbaldiston's Syrup of Figs. Filthy muck. Bane of my childhood."

He told her about the poster rhyme that had started jingling in his head. He recited it to her. While he was doing so he thought of his mother. He saw her face, sickened with anguish, beside the Osbaldiston's poster on the platform of London Road Station, in the gloom of a Manchester fog, on the morning he went off to boarding-school. And then she was stooping nervously to kiss him, and he was pushing her away because he could see all the smug, polished, sniggering little faces under the Rowan House caps watching from the windows of the train, and was suddenly afraid that kissing one's mother might be thought babyish. And then his mother was saying, "Dear, it's almost time . . ." and he was tugging her away anxiously behind the poster to kiss her out of sight . . . He pushed the memory from his mind: it still held too much pain. He said, "Yes, filthy muck, Osbaldiston's. There wasn't a kid alive who wouldn't have settled for the stomach-ache sooner than take a dose. It was a barefaced lie, that poster."

He told her how it had worried him as a boy—he'd been brought up to believe that telling lies was the shortest cut to the Eternal Fire. He had finally put the problem to his father, enquiring diffidently if the persons responsible hadn't landed themselves in for a lengthy toasting.

"He was an old non-conformist windbag, my father, who spent so much time in prayer that he'd got chronic housemaid's knee. But he was also a north-countryman. And no matter how passionately he inveighed against the vanity of worldly goods in chapel, there was nothing he respected more than a bit of brass. That was how a man showed his worth, by making a bit of brass. And I can see his face now, flushed with anger as he scolded me for daring to question the integrity of a Lancashire family firm like Osbaldiston's. The Osbaldistons had 'shown their worth' by making a packet of brass. And he refused to discuss the poster, because, as he put it, 'it is impossible for you and me to know what is behind these things.' His advice to me was to hold my impudent tongue, and remember that 'The fear of the Lord is the beginning of wisdom'—nothing to do with the matter under discussion, but it was his favourite text and engraved on the chapel wall. That was my first lesson in differential morality. It was all right for Osbaldiston's to plaster its lies over every railway station in Lancs and Yorks, but if you said you'd washed your hands when you hadn't, and had the sort of father who'd leave the table to go and see if the wash-basin was dry, you were a safe bet for the everlasting barbecue . . . My God, as if Dorothy wasn't enough for one evening, without dragging my father up, too. Come on, let's take another spin."

She entered his arms on the dance floor. Her bare waist was smooth and slender under his hand. He tried to remember the last time he'd had a woman. Good Lord, it must have been the old Walkie-Talkie in Hong Kong on the way through to Pekin. Eight months ago! And that one-night stand with the Walkie-Talkie hadn't been exactly the ideal experience to carry him through an eight-month siege. He had met her in the hotel bar. Her real name had been Mrs. Walker and she had never stopped talking about her abortions. She had had first-hand knowledge of the facilities available in nearly every country in the world—she could have written an international guide on the subject for the help of peripatetic lovers who didn't take care.

Well, Mrs. Kapoor was certainly a step up from Mrs. Walker. On the other hand, she wasn't necessarily waiting to fall over backwards at the first puff like the Walkie-Talkie. He fancied that she was probably the type who kept it all in the head—who was ready to talk about love until the cows came home, but once it came to the brute physical facts—clang! Up went the drawbridge! No, he must step easy. He always took care never to give a woman a chance to make a fool of him, humiliate him—never to push an attack beyond the point at which he could be certain of holding it. Still, he certainly fancied her. So best foot forward . . .

But back at the table, separated from the embrace, his interest began to flag. He stifled a yawn. No, blowed if I can be bothered, he thought. Not worth all the ruddy preliminaries. And the harder a woman is to get into bed, the harder she is to get out . . . No, I want my bed to myself, I want a good sleep. So skip it.

Just then Lakshmi said, "I suppose we couldn't—no, it's not fair to suggest it."

"Come on, let's have it."

"I just remembered it's full moon, and thought how lovely to take a drive."

"Getting past my bedtime. Not a youngster any more, you know."

But he could not fail to see the disappointment in her face, for a moonlight drive was clearly part of the romantic idyll for which she had yearned through the long loveless years of her marriage, and he weakened. He decided to indulge her.

"Well, there must be plenty of young fellows in this room who'd be ready to oblige if I didn't. So I reckon I'll take up my option. Come on, off we go."

They took a taxi outside. It had a grey-bearded Sikh driver and no side-windows. The driver was very old. He sat hunched over the wheel, his head in an untidy turban, never turning to right or left. He found it an effort to change gear, and to save trouble changed straight from bottom into top at ten miles an hour. The car limped and shuddered as it struggled to gain speed.

"Your engine won't last long at that rate," Birkett told him.

The Sikh lifted a hand from the steering wheel, twisted it weakly back and forth in the characteristic gesture that meant, "It can't be helped, nothing to be done."

They drove out into the moonlit countryside. The hot wind blew on their faces through the open sides of the car. Lakshmi covered her head with a fold of her sari to protect her hair. She held it clasped under her chin with one hand, and with the other held Birkett's. Suddenly she exclaimed, "Oh, look, how beautiful! What is it?"

He followed her eyes, and in the moonlight that drenched the plain saw the tomb where he had met the Indian the night before.

"It's an old Mogul tomb," he said.

"Can't we go and look at it?"

"Why not?"

The car faltered along the track in top gear and expired before the tomb. They climbed the steps through the slanting tunnel, and strolled round to the back of the terrace where he had sat with the Indian. Lakshmi exclaimed at the stillness of the plain, the mystery of the Indian night, the beauty of the moonlit marble.

"Yes, quite a place this," Birkett said, amused to think how little she could have guessed that he had been here so recently, or for what purpose. And enjoying the irony of repeating the exact words that he had spoken to the Indian, he added, "Those old Mogul emperors certainly used to get put away in style."

They stood in silence. The parched plain was itself like a lunar landscape under the moon. I suppose she's waiting for me to kiss her, he thought. She obviously expects a bit of kissing. Well, here we go, though once we start that business I won't promise where——

A jackal howled. The howl was answered from across the plain as if by an echo, and then a whole chorus of cries broke out as though every jackal in India was raising its voice to the moon.

"Christ," he said, "what a din!"

"You can't see them."

"No."

Nothing moved, no life was to be seen in the dead landscape of scrub and stones. The cries were disembodied, like the cries of the dead. He remembered the jackal he had killed on the road: the soft thud against the car, the bump under the wheel. And jumping, when that other jackal had howled.

Yes, I promised myself to get on to that weakness, to lick it, he thought. I ought to have licked it long ago. He remembered when he had first become aware of it, back in Burma during the war, and the incident was as clear as if it was happening now . . .

He had volunteered to gratify the M.O.'s whim for a Japanese skull to study the prognathous jaw, waving aside his dubious reminder that they were advancing too fast to find skulls—the dead Japanese would still have heads—and blithely reassuring him, "Don't worry, I'll get a head and stick it on an ant heap, and it'll soon be picked clean." And he remembered approaching the Japanese bunker, braving the stench that had made a sergeant-major vomit at a hundred yards, and taking his orderly's kukri for the purpose of decapitation and lowering himself through the narrow hole into the darkness below; and just being able to discern in the light from the entrance a pair of feet, in Japanese cloven rubber boots, and the lower half of a pair of legs, and feeling his way along the body in the blackness intending to drag the head into the light so that he could get to work, and getting a grip on the shoulders and lifting the body from the ground—and just then his orderly wrenching off part of the roof and a shaft of daylight falling on the dead man he was holding, and revealing the face with the gaping jaw as if caught by death in the midst of an agonised cry, the rotting remnants of lips, the huge white maggots seething in the sockets of the eyes . . .

Oddly enough it had not been the maggots that had most affected him. It had been the tiny neat gold fillings in the teeth of the yawning jaw. Until that moment he had thought of the exploit quite impersonally, as a quest for a skull that would simply be the skull of "a Jap"; but now, all at once, the gold fillings had brought home to him that the body in his hands that he had been about to decapitate had been the body of an actual person to whom the idea of a ghastly death in a bunker in Burma, with maggots feasting on the eyes, had been so unthinkable that he had concerned himself with making appointments for the dentist, having his teeth probed for mere pinpoints of decay, acquiring these trivial little dental refinements . . . And he had been seized by some primitive, irrational, utterly unexpected fear, and he had let the body fall, the maggots spilling from the eye sockets, and turned and scrambled from the bunker—and thereafter, whenever he had encountered death, it had never been without a repetition in some degree of that same fear and revulsion. And although he had somehow managed to avoid betraying that weakness for the rest of the war, he had been bitterly ashamed of it, for it was a weakness that ill became a soldier.

And that becomes a cheetah no better, he thought. A cheetah can't afford to shrink from the kill. And yet that's what I'm doing now. It's that weakness that makes me hesitate over this job for Gupta . . .

The cries of the jackals had ceased. The sky was silent again. Lakshmi sighed and said :

"It's so beautiful! Oh, Ronnie, I wish tonight could last forever!"

He resisted the wince. He said, "Not Ronnie, if you don't mind—couldn't stand it even as a kid. Silly. No idea why."

"You like Ronald?"

"Much better." She could hardly call him Birkett.

He smiled, "Well, the night's still young. So now those ruddy animals have piped down, I suppose we might as well make the most of what's to come."

2

Her first stiffness in his embrace melted as quickly as fresh snow in the sun, and soon she was yielding with upturned face, closed eyes, and searching tongue. He had seldom encountered such frank sensuality, such eagerness to explore every possibility in the meeting of lips. And he had been afraid it was all talk, all in the head—that was a good one! No, no need to worry about the drawbridge going up with a clang of outraged virtue. This time it was "Welcome" on the city gates. . .

He took off his jacket. He folded it neatly and placed it on the floor, and then glanced back at Lakshmi. "Not the most comfortable place in the world, but at least the marble's clean." She stood with face averted.

"What's up? Feeling shy?"

She shook her head dumbly.

"Well, don't tell me you're getting cold feet?"

She said miserably, "I hate disappointing you, I'm terribly sorry . . ."

"Sorry? Ruddy hell, what a ruddy time to start feeling sorry! Look, I'll tell you straight, if there's one sort of girl I can't stick . . ." Rage choked him. Leading him on—making a bloody fool of him. It was the old pain that he'd always tried to protect himself against.

She went on unhappily, "You see, it's such a special occasion for me, and somehow here . . . It doesn't seem right. I'm frightened of something going wrong—someone coming . . . Couldn't I come to your hotel tomorrow?"

His rage subsided as quickly as it had flared up. Well, that's different, he thought. I thought it was a real slap in the face with a wet fish.

He made a grim face and shrugged. "All right, best make it after lunch tomorrow. Two-thirty suit you?"

"I'll come any time you want," she murmured. "I'll come earlier if you want."

"No, two-thirty. Then it won't cut across my nap."

She sighed and leaned against him. "Oh, what are you doing to me? What are you doing?"

His good humour returned.

"Now, don't blame me. I warned you from the start I was just a ruddy old ram."

Chapter Six

Birkett came briskly down the hotel steps into the early sun shine. He sang a catchy tune to himself. It was a minute before he realised the words that he was absently fitting to it.

> "*Oh, Mr.* MIDDLE-
> *Middle-Middle-*TON
> *I've got such a*
> GOT *such a*
> GOT *such a* PAIN!*"*

It's not a pain that's my trouble, he thought. It's a jingle.

> "*Oh, my trouble's not a* PAIN!
> *Not a* PAIN? *No, a* JINGLE!
> *A* JINGLE? *Yes, a* JINGLE!
> *A ruddy silly* JINGLE
> *That* JINGLES *in my* BRA-I-I-I-N!*"*

Anyhow, he'd got his walking-stick back. Who cared about a jingle when he'd got his stick back?

It had been a nasty few minutes. He had returned from an early breakfast to find the stick had vanished from his room. He had turned the room upside down, but it was nowhere to be found. There seemed no reason why anybody should have pinched it—it wouldn't have fetched a couple of annas in the bazaar. It wasn't even a proper walking-stick. It was just a sturdy, knobbled piece of wood that he had fished out of the Irrawaddy near Mandalay over fifteen years ago, to fill some temporary need, and that afterwards he had kept trying to discard; but every time he had done so his orderly had produced it again, saying: "You forgot your stick, sir." He had got the idea that the stick must like him and he had stopped trying to throw it away, and it had been his inseparable companion ever since in more countries than he could count. It was the only personal possession to which he allowed himself any feeling of attachment. He would sooner have lost a leg than that stick . . . Then he had discovered the roomboy out in the hall using it to prod open a skylight to release a panic-stricken bird, and he had sent the boy packing with a warning never to touch the stick again.

Now, feeling his sturdy old friend safely back in his hand once more, he was in the best of moods. He remembered that Lakshmi was coming to see him this afternoon. Splendid, nothing like a bit of recreation after lunch—roll on two-thirty!

He sang to the tune of *Away in a Manger*:

"Roll on Two-THIRTY!
'*Who's* THAT *at the* DOOR?'
'*Why,* LAK-*shmi, your* TRUE *love,*
Come to ROLL *in the* STRAW!'"

Quite a budding Wordsworth. Change from Mr. Middleton, anyhow . . . Blast, started it off again—should have kept quiet.

"Oh, Mr. Middleton—"

He suddenly thought of his mother again. The memory of saying goodbye to her on the Manchester platform had kept returning as persistently as the jingle. This morning when he had woken he had found it there waiting for him, instead of the decision about Nepal as he had hoped, and he had lain in bed recalling forgotten details of that scene on London Road Station—the great canopy of glass over the platforms smothered under the dirty yellow blanket of fog, so that although it was only eleven o'clock in the morning the station was as black as night; and the gas-lamps along the platforms burning with foggy halos, and the hungry yawning cavern of fog at the end of the platforms swallowing the trains as they pulled out. And he had remembered the black ache in his stomach, as if all his insides were being gnawed away, as the hand of the clock over the platform bit off the half-minutes, eating its way through the remaining slice of time, and his mother, her face greenish-grey like the time she had been seasick going to the Isle-of-Man, making nervous conversation that was even more inconsequential than usual . . . And the black clockhand continuing to snap off the half-minutes until only a sliver of time remained, and then leading his mother behind the poster and hugging her quickly and breaking away, feeling already alone as he crossed the platform to the train with all the sniggering polished little faces in the windows, and then catching a last glimpse of his mother's anguished face as the train jolted and pulled out and was swallowed up by the great hungry mouth of fog. And then the other boys inviting him into a compartment and asking him if he liked strawberries, and promising to give him all he wanted that night before they went to bed, and their kindness filling him with such relief and gratitude that he could almost have cried . . .

He saw a bookshop across the road and went over. He glanced in the window, wondering if they would have anything about Nepal—it had occurred to him that a bit of background reading might help him to make his decision. No, all stationery and paperbacks. He turned away and continued his walk, making for a bookshop he knew off Connaught Place.

Yes, they'd given him his strawberries that night all right. He'd never forget it—stripping off his pyjamas in the bathroom, in obedience to a message which they pretended had come from the Headmaster to prepare himself for his "newboy's flea inspection," and then being set upon, as he stood there stark naked, and carried to an empty bath in which he was held down by a dozen eager hands whilst the promised "strawberries," the ceremonial pinches to initiate the new boy, were delivered by each boy in turn on some carefully chosen tender part. And just when he had thought it was all over, "Now for the cream! Do you like it hot or cold?"

"Neither!"

"Well, you're going to get it hot!" And seizing a duckboard from the floor and placing it over the bath to imprison him, they turned on the hot tap, and peered through the slats with squeals of delight as he tried to avoid the scalding splashes and gushing steam . . .

Christ, the cruelty of little boys—those Nazi warders at Belsen weren't in it. He had never experienced as an adult anything like his stark terror that night in the bathroom. Not even in six years of war.

There had only been one other occasion during that term that stood out equally—when classes had been interrupted by an order for the whole school to assemble in the Big School room, and after a long hushed wait in an atmosphere of growing suspense, the Headmaster, dressed in mortarboard and gown and clutching a bundle of canes, had swept down the aisle and mounted the rostrum. He had proceeded to jaw them about a certain crime which some boys had committed, but he had never actually named the crime and Birkett had understood nothing except that it had taken place in the bushes behind the gym. He had been to those bushes once or twice himself to collect red click-beetles, and he had begun to suspect with growing alarm that this was what the Head meant. Then the Head had declared that the evildoers, engaged in their "self-indulgent pursuit," had taken advantage of those "smaller and weaker" than themselves, whose very innocence made them easy "victims." Obviously the "smaller and weaker" were the click-beetles, whose innocence was such that they would often jump right into your pill-box and become victims of their own accord. There could no longer be any doubt that he was guilty. He had broken out in a sweat, heard his own teeth chatter. The Head had finished his jaw and consulted a list of names. "Handforth! Come here, I want to thrash you." The red faced boy had stumbled past feet and knees to the rostrum and knelt on a wooden chair, and the Head had given him six strokes. He had returned blindly to his seat and the Head had called out another name. Birkett had thought of slipping out before his turn came and hanging himself in the lavatory. But his limbs had been petrified—he could not move. The Head had called out six boys and broken two canes, and Birkett had felt sure that his turn must be next—and just then he had heard the Head say, "Now back to your classrooms," and seen him sweep off down the aisle . . . He had scarcely been able to believe his eyes. His guilt had been overlooked. He should have owned up, but had spoken of the matter to nobody; and it was not until years later that it had dawned on him that the crime had had nothing to do with click-beetles, but must have concerned some sort of adolescent fun and games. The public thrashing had been to gently urge the feet of the guilty boys, at the outset of sexuality, into the right path . . . My God, the right path! If the six of them between them hadn't trampled down more flower beds since then than a herd of rogue elephants it wouldn't be the fault of the Headmaster.

After he had been two years at Rowan House, his father had found even the reduced fees for the sons of ministers too much of a burden, and he had been taken away. He had started at the Longhulme Grammar School as a day-boy—and he could remember coming home on dark winter evenings on the tram, which would come grinding and clanking to a standstill at the end of Mostyn Road, and then getting off with his second-hand satchel and threadbare scarf, and hearing the tram grinding away down the High Street as he walked up Mostyn Road, past the genteel semi-detached houses with the spindly hedges of privet, the little front paths lined with shells from Llandudno; and feeling a thrill as he saw the crack of light between the curtains of No. 17, where some Roman Catholics had just moved in, thinking that perhaps at that very moment they were engaged in their orgiastic rites, drinking intoxicating liquor, burning incense, indulging themselves in every possible sensual excess. And then he was pushing open the gate of No. 43, with the shabby peeling paint round the bay window and the coloured leaded-glass of the front door, and entering the little hall with the umbrella stand and dead musty smell; and hearing the muffled sing-song voice of his father, on his knees beside the roll-top desk in his study, as he beseeched Almighty God to hear a miserable sinner's unworthy voice; and then going into the living-room with the framed text over the mantelpiece, the sooty piece of newspaper in the grate, the single gas-mantle burning over the chair where his mother sat turning the collar of a shirt and crying . . .

He could not remember how many times he had come home from school to find his mother crying—and sometimes her face and neck would be covered with great red blotches, like an archipelago of red islands, from an affliction of the skin which for years had caused this intermittent eruption. The trouble had originally been diagnosed as food poisoning, and she had given up fish, and then fruit, and then every other sort of food in turn—and just when it had begun to look as if she had found the offender, her skin would suddenly erupt again. There was only one thing that his mother had never tried giving up, the one thing that he now knew would have worked—and that was his father.

He remembered how she had cried in a steady hopeless way, as if she had given up the struggle of trying to make herself stop. "I'm a sick woman," she would sob, when he had asked what was the matter. "I'm a sick woman." He had not dared to press her further. And when at last he had summoned up courage to do so, she had shaken her head as if she had not known herself—and then suddenly burst out, with a kind of passionate bitterness of which he would never have believed that nervous, crushed little woman capable, "Oh, your father's a hard man! I know I shouldn't say it, but he's hard and bigoted, that's what he is!" He had little enough affection for his father, but his mother's disloyalty had profoundly shocked him; and he had stood speechless, in an agony of embarrassment, until she had gone on; "He's been such a disappointment to me. When I married him I thought he had vision, but he's just hard and narrow. You're all I live for now, dear. I know you won't disappoint me. You won't be content with your father's narrow little world. You'll discover new worlds of your own—you'll have real vision!"

His discomfort had not prevented her words from affecting him more profoundly than any other words he had ever heard spoken. He had seemed all at once to grow up, changing from his mother's child into her champion and protector. And it had been with her words still in his mind that, soon after her death four years later, he had given his allegiance to the Blackshirts and become the leader of the small band of adherents at school whose secret activities had continued in defiance of the Headmaster's ban on "Fascist badges, slogans, and the juvenile theatricals of our would-be Hitlers." And he had only wished that she had lived to see how triumphantly he was fulfilling her ambition for him—breaking away from his father's narrow little world and dedicating himself to the bright new Fascist world of the future. For the Blackshirts were, above all, men of vision . . . And it was only years later that he had come to realize that it had been the wrong vision. Then he had started searching elsewhere—the army, yoga—until finally he had found the truth in Communism, to which he had remained dedicated ever since.

He had reached the bookshop that he wanted to visit. He paused a moment at the window and then went inside.

He found the section devoted to East Asia; and glancing over the shelves, his eye was caught by the familiar jacket of his own Indian book. He paused a moment and then passed on indifferently. The indifference was no affectation. He had no illusions about himself as a writer. He had never thought of himself as anything more than a journalist, with a handy knack of recording impressions vividly, in a staccato style that the kinder critics called "highly readable." It was odd how it had worked out. He had taken up writing when he had left Grammar School not for its own sake, for his ambitions had never been literary, but as an instrument to serve his political beliefs. Then it had been the sword he had carried into battle. Now, a quarter of a century later, it was a shield to hide behind—to distract and lull his opponents while he carried on his real work. It did not trouble him that he wrote falsely. To lie was necessary. He was prepared to do much more.

His eye fell on a book entitled *In Secret Nepal*. He took it down and glanced over the list of chapter heads: "An Abominable Snowman at Last?" "More Footprints," "Another False Alarm." He replaced the book on the shelf.

He tried another bookshop without success, and then started back for the hotel.

He couldn't go on putting off the decision. No more evasions—he must look the problem squarely in the eye . . .

But somehow his mind kept slipping away from the centre of the problem to the perimeter. He wondered how much it would harm him at PACSAG if he turned down the assignment. Bound to go against him. Still, his stock must be high enough—he could probably afford it. He had never put a foot wrong in ten years. Not a job skimped. Not an end left untied. Ten years without a single black . . .

He entered the hotel. It was just then that he saw Potter.

He was coming out of the lift in the hall. Birkett had not seen him before, and did not know at that moment that his name was Potter or that he would ever see him again. The occasion in fact had no significance for him then, but only acquired significance later in retrospect, when he remembered where and when he had seen Potter before.

It was probably only the moustache that made him notice him at all. It was a big, bushy moustache of the kind sported by fighter pilots during the war. It was rather absurd. He also wore horn-rimmed goggles, a striped English cricket blazer, and suede shoes.

Chap from one of the oil companies, Birkett speculated idly. Those Battle-of-Britain moustaches all seemed to have congregated in Sheil.

He got into the lift and promptly forgot the man's existence. He fetched his bathing-trunks and then came down again and went out to the pool for his swim.

The swim refreshed him splendidly. He climbed out of the electric-blue water, dried off in a few moments in the sun, and then found a comfortable chair in the shade. He ordered an iced drink.

The boy went off with his tray and just then the man with the big absurd airman's moustache came out of the dressing room. He wore blue bathing-trunks and the horn-rimmed goggles. There was something odd about the shape of his left thigh.

He came round the curved edge of the pool to the steps nearest to Birkett. He was a hefty well-built chap with a big chest. He began to descend the steps into the water rather cautiously and Birkett saw that the left thigh was covered for the extent of about a foot with callouses of healed flesh. It was thinner than the other thigh. It looked as if a slice had been taken off with a knife.

War wound most likely, Birkett thought. Crashed his machine. Lucky to be alive.

The man launched himself into the water. He swam across the pool with a rather laborious breast-stroke, holding up his head with difficulty to keep the goggles dry.

Birkett lost interest, and paid him no further heed. He looked at his watch. Eleven-thirty. Only three hours before the girl would be along. By Jove, looking forward.

> "*Roll on two*-THIRTY!
> "*Who's* THAT *at the—?*'"

Skip it. Work before play. Head as clear as a bell after the swim—now he'd have that problem licked as easy as pie.

Chapter Seven

Birkett's irritation grew with each minute that the girl was late. He was a stickler for punctuality. And already twenty to three . . .

There was a tapping of fingers on the door. His irritation instantly vanished. He went cheerfully to open it.

"Good, found the room all right? I say, Mata Hari!"

Lakshmi wore her big black sun glasses and a scarf round her head. She came in quickly. Her attempt at disguise, and her ascent by the stairs to avoid the eyes of the liftman, had done little to lessen the ordeal of entering the hotel and coming up to his room, and she was in a state of nervous agitation.

"I can't stay," she said at once. She removed the sun glasses but avoided his eyes. "I've only come for a moment." Her manner was remote, disclaiming all memory of their embraces at the tomb, the tacit understanding about their renewal.

Birkett was neither surprised nor dismayed. He took the situation in his stride.

"That's all right, my dear. Anyhow, sit down a moment to get your breath."

"No, I really mustn't." But she sat.

Birkett smiled to himself. Women, he thought. They're like ruddy kids with their play-acting. And transparent as glass. She's no more intention than I have of changing the afternoon's programme. But makes her feel cheap coming along here by appointment for you-know-what as if it was an appointment at the hairdresser's, and so she has to go through this little pantomime to satisfy her pride. The eternal female problem: how to be a naughty girl without losing your virtue. Also, of course, it's a useful insurance policy in case I'd changed my mind and no longer wanted her.

Anyhow, she was here, that was the main thing. He'd certainly been glad to see her. He had still not made that decision for Gupta—his mind had been nagging at the problem ever since his swim but somehow he could not come properly to grips with it—and her arrival, apart from anything else, gave him a good excuse for a respite.

"I say, that's a pretty sari you've got on. That's really pretty." He added that he had been struck by her taste in dress from the start.

Lakshmi searched his face anxiously. "You don't mean it? You're not just being kind?"

"Of course I mean it. I know that when a girl manages to look like you it doesn't just happen, my dear. She must have a real flair. Now take that necklace you were wearing with that blue sari that first night in the Club . . ."

"You mean you remember it? But that cost absolutely nothing!"

"All the more power to your elbow."

She began to glow. She explained that at home she could not buy anything without her husband's family criticizing it. Her mother-in-law had told her so often that she had no taste whatsoever that she had begun to believe it.

"Don't you listen to that old zamindar witch," Birkett said. "The only thing she'd have good taste in would be broomsticks."

Soon they were back where they had left off the night before. Presently Birkett detached himself and stood up.

"Well, no point in beating about the bush, my dear. Get yourself into bed."

He pulled back the bedcover, slid home the catch on the door, and retired to the bathroom. He always left a woman to get stripped by herself. He wasn't the sort of chap who got a kick out of messing around half-dressed like a homeless couple on the Common, trying to master the sartorial mechanics, fumbling a slow tantalizing passage through the labyrinth of buttons, zippers, and bits of elastic, and press-studs that wouldn't unpress and turned out in the end to be hooks-and-eyes. No, leave 'em alone to get on with it—and then if they'd got some guilty secret like a corset or truss they'd at least have a chance to push it out of sight.

He pottered about for a bit and then returned to the room. Lakshmi's sari was lying over the back of a chair. She was sitting up in bed in her brief Indian blouse that ended below her breasts. She had let down her long hair, and it was spread in a black fan behind her shoulders off-setting the delicate little triangle of her face with the small pointed chin, the huge wide dark eyes, the red spot on her forehead. Her gaze was fixed on him. He felt its intensity—even was vaguely aware of the nervousness, the timid appeal she was making that this meant more than what it appeared to be.

"By Jove, that's a picture," he said. "That's a real picture."

He was a satisfactory lover. His detachment was to her advantage on this occasion, leaving him unhampered by excessive ardour, nervous impatience, or any of those other afflictions that may beset a lover in such an initial embrace. He found her as tremulously responsive to his touch as some delicate musical instrument—an instrument on which such notes had never been struck before, and which did not know its own range nor of what harmony it was capable. This inexperience gave her a charming innocence and he was much pleased with her. And afterwards, enjoying a peaceful cigarette as she lay with her head in the crook of his arm, he felt an agreeable sense of well-being. He reflected that it had been achieved with the minimum inconvenience, and was glad that he had been ready to put himself out for her.

She whispered that nothing so beautiful had ever happened to her in her life.

"You've led me into a new world," she murmured. "A new enchanted world!"

He disliked such poetic expressions. They made him feel uncomfortable. But at least they sounded better on Indian lips than on the lips of a European; and indeed she spoke with such genuine wonder that she made it seem almost natural.

"Well, it may be a new world, but you certainly took to it quick enough," he said. "Like a duck to water."

He glanced down at the small neat brown body pressed against his own. He told her that he liked her nice colour—just right for his taste. He felt her stiffen a little.

"Don't tease me," she said.

"Tease? Who's teasing?"

"I can't help being black." She pulled the sheet over her body to hide it.

"Black? You must be colour-blind. You're just a nice brown."

"I'm black. I hate the sight of myself."

"Never heard such rubbish in my life."

"I'm the family freak."

She told him that she was much darker than her older brother and her two older sisters, and her darkness had caused her parents much distress. It had been an unwelcome reminder of her father's family origins in the Calcutta slums—for in India the rich protected their complexions and colour roughly corresponded with class. They had tried to conceal their dismay from her, but inevitably she had become aware of it, Once, indulging her childhood passion for dressing-up, she had improvised a nurse's white uniform and headdress from an old sheet, and had gone to show herself off to her mother who was entertaining guests on the verandah. Her mother had stared at her in horror and quickly hustled her away. She had been quite bewildered. Afterwards her mother had come to her crying with shame, and exclaiming, "Oh, how awful! In front of those people! You must never, never do that again!"

"Do what again?"

"Wear white next to your skin. It shows up how—I mean it makes you look so much darker than you really are, You've got such an awkward complexion, you'll always have to be so careful what colours you wear. And you must never, never expose yourself to the sun. We're going to have a big enough problem to find you a husband without you making matters worse."

However, when the time for match-making had arrived her father's generous dowry had enabled her colour to be over-looked.

At least until after the marriage—for once the dowry was secure her husband's family had not hesitated to use her complexion as a means to humiliate her. Once her mother-in-law, looking through some photographic negatives in which black and white appeared in reverse, had exclaimed, "Oh, look at our little Zulu, she's got a white face! You'd never know she really looked like Chanda Mohan!" That was the charcoal merchant in the bazaar whose face matched his wares.

Birkett said, "Well, that accounts for the way you were looking at fair-skinned people at the swimming-pool, like a penniless kid at a sweetshop window."

"I once heard about a woman who went to London for an operation to change the shape of her nose," Lakshmi said. "I thought 'If only I could have an operation to change the colour of my skin!'"

"It would be over my dead body. I like you just as you are. Why d'you want to go and make yourself look like something turned up with a spade?"

Her belief that her colour must be offensive to others was so deeply ingrained that it was only with the greatest difficulty that she could persuade herself of his sincerity. And then she was moved by such gratitude that tears sprang to her eyes; and urgently pressing herself against him, as if to seal their bodies into one, she began to cover him with desperate little kisses and caresses.

"Here, watch out or you'll have the bed on fire," Birkett said. He had just lit another cigarette. He was not going to waste it.

Lakshmi continued her urgent persuasions. By Jove, she certainly had a way with her—he hadn't known he had such resilience . He remembered the old Walkie-Talkie coming back for a second . helping, with her whole international repertoire of tricks including something that Eskimos were supposed to do when they took liberties under each other's furs, and been dismayed to find the cupboard remained stubbornly bare. But the Walkie-Talkie was one thing and Lakshmi another. The contents of the cupboard depended on who opened the door.

He stubbed out the cigarette. Pity, still half left. But no matter. Bonnet over the windmill.

"My word, and you say it's a new world," he said. "Well, you're going to cause a packet of trouble when you're an old inhabitant."

And then a strange thing happened—something that had occasionally happened to him before in the arms of a woman, but rarely enough for it now to take him completely by surprise. It was as though he had been proceeding blithely along some woodland path and become suddenly and acutely aware of imminent danger, and glanced down to find himself on the very verge of a whirlpool— another step and he would have been swallowed up by the dark swirl and sucked down into its depths. Now the source of danger whose imminence possessed him was the moist soft-lipped sensuous mouth of this girl, whose depths, like the depths of the whirlpool, he felt all at once to contain unknown terrors into which he was on the verge of being sucked—and abruptly, as if he had been stung, he pulled away his own mouth, and then recovering himself, and trying to reassure her for the rough unexplained withdrawal, returned it to her eyes, her nose, her cheeks: anywhere but to her mouth where the danger lurked.

And then something else occurred that was equally unexpected— suddenly there came into his head, ready-made and with perfect clarity, the solution to the dilemma that had weighed on him all day. And he knew that tomorrow he would tell Gupta that he would go to Nepal.

The decision had arrived out of the blue, like some religious revelation, without argument to support it. But no argument was needed. He knew with absolute conviction that it was right and subject to no second thought.

He felt as if a load had been lifted from his mind with this resolution of the problem. And now the absurd sense of danger vanished as suddenly as it had come—no longer was he in fear of being sucked down into the unknown terrors of the whirlpool. And soon the lost ground was recovered, the jarring interruption forgotten—for now, the decision made and his future committed, he could abandon himself utterly and in perfect safety, as a sailor at the end of shore leave might abandon himself to a girl he had hitherto cautiously avoided, safe in the knowledge that his ship was already getting up steam and was shortly to sail.

2

Birkett called on Gupta at ten-thirty the next morning. The secretary in the white muslin dhoti opened the door. He said sullenly, "The Minister is out."

"Come off it, George."

He stayed with Gupta for two hours and afterwards walked back to the hotel. He was in the best of moods. It was Sunday, which meant the traditional curry for lunch at the hotel. And after lunch he was expecting another visit from Lakshmi.

He stopped at the desk in the hall of the hotel.

"I'll be keeping my room another week, then I'm off to Nepal," he told the porter. He had to hang on for certain items of equipment which would take Gupta a few days to obtain.

"You have a visa, sir?"

"No, where's the Nepalese Embassy?"

The porter wrote down the address. Just then he saw the man with the big moustache, whose name he still did not know was Potter, standing farther along the desk. He was glancing at a travel leaflet as he waited to speak to the porter. He wore a striped Guards' tie—evidently not an airman after all. Birkett took the piece of paper with the address and went off to the dining-room.

The curry was excellent. He ate his lunch with relish. He watched the flaxen-haired Nordic goddess from the swimming-pool come across the room, her taut dress brazenly proclaiming the big round swellings of her breasts like the prow of a Viking ship. Her bronzed complexion was darker than some of the Indian waiters'. It was emphasized by a fashionably pale lip-stick. She sat down at the next table.

Well, she'd help to pass the time between trains, Birkett thought cheerfully. But I've something better than that on the menu this afternoon.

The man with the big moustache came into the dining-room. He caught sight of Birkett and came over to his table.

"Excuse me, old man, but I couldn't help overhearing that you were off to Nepal." There was a big grin stretched out under the bushy moustache. "Damn' funny, so am I. Off in a couple of days when the wife gets out."

"You'll beat me to it."

"Still, I suppose us white chaps will be a bit thin on the ground in a place like that. Bound to run across each other. Mind if I join you, old man?"

"Help yourself."

"Jolly good show." He extended a big fist across the table. His hands were well-kept with manicured nails. "Pilot Potter."

"Birkett."

Potter sat down, His eyes goggled behind the horn-rimmed glasses as he caught sight of the girl at the next table. He pawed roguishly at one end of the moustache. "You'd know you'd got hold of something with that girl, old man." He suddenly let out a guffaw, leant back in his chair, and slapped his knee, "That reminds me of a real corker! The one about the actress and the man with the telescope in the stalls—you haven't heard it, old man? Well, one night this actress . . ."

Birkett did not bother to listen. He hated dirty stories. Finally Potter reached his pay-off. He guffawed and slapped his knee. "And that reminds me of the one about——"

"What line are you in?" Birkett quickly interrupted.

"F.O."

"Diplomat, eh?" God, even worse than the usual run of pansy-boys and stuffed-shirts who represented Britain abroad. They should post him to Moscow—the Russians would award him the Order of Lenin for his invaluable contribution to anti-British propaganda, and exhibit him behind glass in the Park of Rest and Culture with a loudspeaker relaying the dirty jokes.

"Always dreamed of the gay diplomatic life in the flesh pots of Paris and Rome. But trust old Pilot Potter. First Ecuador, then Liberia, and now Nepal."

"Why 'Pilot' if you were in the Guards?"

Potter stuck a big thumb under the striped tie. "Oh, you mean this? Just a line-shoot, old man. Not quite Guards' colours. Near-miss—intentional of course."

"So you were really a flyer?"

"No fear, nothing so dangerous as that for Potter, old man. Potter fought his war in the Ministry of Supply."

"Then what about the 'Pilot'?"

"Pilot's whiskers—nickname in the Ministry." He tugged at the bushy moustache. "Just a line-shoot, of course. But worked wonders with the girls. Wife still makes me keep it." He took a photograph out of his wallet. "That's the wife, old man."

The girl in the snapshot was blonde with a pretty babyish face. She was staring into the camera with a rather affected look of wide-eyed innocence.

"Bonny," Birkett said and handed the photograph back.

"You'll meet her in Nepal." The old waiter, with dithering hand, put a plate in front of him. He goggled at it through the horn-rimmed glasses in disbelief. "Doesn't mean me to eat this, does he, old man?"

"Vindaloo curry," Birkett said. "Delicious."

"Looks a disaster to me, old man. I thought I'd struck gastro-nomical rock bottom in Liberia. But trust old Potter."

Birkett finished his meal and went upstairs to his room. Still half an hour before the girl came. He removed his bush-shirt and slacks and stretched himself on the bed. He closed his eyes, emptied his mind, and in a few moments fell asleep. His facility for falling asleep at will, and waking at a given time, was a legacy of his yoga days—for his rejection of yoga metaphysics had not blinded him to the practical benefits of the yoga training. The posture and breathing exercises, which he had continued to practise regularly, were invaluable for the development of bodily and mental control, and for the maintenance of sound health. He put it down to this regime that he had not known a day's illness in ten years. He had not even had a common cold.

Presently he woke. He was fully awake at once with no

intermediary drowsiness, his body refreshed and his mind clear. He glanced at his watch. He had slept for nineteen and a half minutes. Good enough—the prescribed period for his afternoon nap was twenty minutes and he allowed himself a margin of error of one minute either way. For longer periods he allowed ten minutes, and seldom failed to wake within this margin even after a night's sleep of six or seven hours.

He took a shower and dressed in clean khaki. He was just buckling the belt of his bush-shirt when the girl arrived.

She removed her scarf and sun glasses. Her eyes shone.

"Well, I've good news," Birkett said cheerfully. "I'm not shoving off for another week."

The light went from her face. She stared in dismay.

"What's up?" he said. "Aren't you glad?"

"Only another week? And you're not coming back?"

"No, I'm skipping up to Nepal to nose around for a new book. Anyhow you'll be leaving Delhi yourself in a week or so."

"No, I'm not going to Indore. I put it off to stay in Delhi with you."

"You'll be fed to the teeth with me in a week. Anyhow, no use nattering about it. Let's make best use of what time we've got."

She came every day after that and sometimes twice a day, and once so early in the morning that she had to hide in the bathroom when the roomboy brought his breakfast, and afterwards they shared the breakfast in bed. He did not mind the frequency of her visits because their inevitable end was in sight; and besides, she did not expect too much of him.

"I know you're not in love with me," she said. "I know you only give me a tiny bit of yourself. But I'm grateful for even that tiny bit, because it's more than I ever had before. Though sometimes I wish I knew what went on in the other great big part of yourself that you keep shut away."

"All writers keep part of themselves shut away," he said. "It's where their next book is brewing."

"Perhaps . . ." she said doubtfully. And after a minute, "Anyhow, it doesn't seem to stop us getting on wonderfully together. We're so well suited—I mean physically. I used to hate being so small; I thought it almost as great a misfortune as being dark. But you say I'm just the right size for you. And you're exactly right for me. You're so straight and'—'thin' isn't the right word . . ." She groped for the word she wanted.

"Spare," he supplied. "Yes, I'm still quite spare and trim for forty-eight."

"You remind me of an English officer I used to see about in Lucknow. He had an Indian wife and I pretended to despise her for marrying an Englishman. But really I envied her; it was just that I knew no Englishman would ever want to marry me because I was so black. I hated the English. And loved them . . ."

She was always remarking about how well they were suited. She believed that they had been made for each other, that their love-making must be unique—that for no-one could it ever have been quite so wonderful before. "But perhaps that's just silly . . . Perhaps it doesn't seem at all special to you. Have you got on just as wonderfully with lots of girls?"

"Well, I won't say that," he said.

"No, please tell me," she pressed. "I want to know the truth."

"I couldn't say," he said evasively. "Anyhow, we certainly do get along very nicely. No denying it, very nicely indeed." He might have put it more strongly, since he could not remember any girl who had pleased him better. But no point in giving her ideas.

"I know it couldn't be the same for me with anybody else," she said. "Not with anybody else in the world."

She loved to touch things that belonged to him: ran her fingers tenderly along his walking-stick, toyed affectionately with his toothbrush and razor in the bathroom, and went right through his clothes hungrily seizing on loose buttons, frayed hems, any sign of wear or tear that offered the least excuse for setting to work with needle and thread: she would be able to remember those little darned patches afterwards as one mark, at least, that she had left on him. And she began to yearn for a baby. It would have needed only the smallest encouragement to make her throw all caution to the winds, and she even started tentatively to feel him out, saying,

"Supposing I had a child by mistake . . . my husband would throw me out and I'd have to go back to my parents. I wouldn't really mind if it happened . . . Would you?"

"Yes," Birkett said bluntly. "I would."

"But I wouldn't hold you responsible. You needn't ever know."

"Well, the question's not going to arise. So bluntly put all that nonsense out of your head." He wasn't falling into that old feminine trap—a baby was the death-blow to a man's independence. And he knew all about those assurances that you'd not be held responsible, need never know. You'd know all right. She'd see to it—and no matter that you'd taken refuge a thousand miles up the Amazon, you'd hear those pathetic little baby cries come floating on the breeze . . . No, no kids. No ruddy fear.

The next day was Birkett's last in Delhi. He called on Gupta in the afternoon to collect his equipment and spent the evening with Lakshmi. Her tears were never far away. She resisted them as they dined together in the Palmyra Room, managing to appear deceptively cheerful; but upstairs in his room again they suddenly overwhelmed her, and breaking her resolution to accept the parting as final, to make no demands on him, she begged him with streaming eyes to take her with him to Nepal—to prolong their precious happiness just a few more days. "Out of the question," Birkett said.

"I promise I won't be a nuisance—and I'll pay my own fare."

"And what about the people you're staying with? Are they supposed to give you their blessing?"

"I'd pretend I was going with my old school-friend."

"Good old Phantom Fanny! So now she's off to Nepal! My dear girl, I can assure you the cat would be out of the bag before we got to the airport."

"I don't care. I don't care what happens if only we can be together a few more days."

"I don't even know what I'll be doing after I get to Kathmandu. I may be pushing off into the wilds."

"I could come later when you know your plans. I'd have my

visa ready and you only need send a cable. I'd come straight away. You'll remember, won't you?"

"My dear girl . . ."

"Promise you'll remember."

"All right, I promise. Now take this handkerchief and mop yourself up."

His departure the next morning was at dawn, and although he had told her that on no account must she come to see him off, he arrived at Safdar Jang airport to find her already there; and they watched the first wan light spread up from the horizon, and Safdar Jang's tomb emerge in silhouette against the sky and the big black bulky shadows along the tarmac take the shape of aircraft.

"You won't forget your promise?" Lakshmi pleaded.

"Promise?"

"That you'll send a cable if you want me."

"No, I won't forget."

Her pale drained face, stricken with anguish, reminded him of his mother's face beside the poster on the Manchester platform on that other occasion of parting. Well, thank God that he wasn't suffering now as he had suffered then, that he hadn't that great black ache in his belly.

> *Oh, Mr. Middleton,*
> *I've got such a pain!*
> *Quick! Some Osbaldiston's Syrup*
> *To make me well again!*

Only there had been no cheery rubicund Mr. Middleton ready with an answer for the pain he'd had then, no medicine to relieve it—no anodyne, no escape, no alternative but to endure it and make sure that he never laid himself open to it again, but learned to avoid it, protect himself . . . And he felt pity for Lakshmi because she had never learned, had no protection, could still get hurt.

A loudspeaker called for passengers for Benares and Patna. "Well, now I must skip," Birkett said. "Very nice week it's been. Only sorry it wasn't longer."

He walked away across the tarmac, carrying with him into the aircraft the image of the girl's stricken face, half confused with the image of his mother's face on the platform; and the confused images still haunted him five minutes later as the aircraft lifted from the runway in the grey dawn light and began to climb steeply, and was caught by the first gold rays of sun slanting up from the horizon.

Oh, Mr. Middleton
I've got such a pain . . .

The airport was lost from sight. Below them was the stony deserted plain, riven with thirsty gullies. He watched the sunlight spilling over the plain in a shimmering glory of pink and gold; and then the glory was fading, the sun already shining with that flat white incandescent light that would lie like a burden on India all day long.

He looked at his watch. Only a couple of hours to Benares, and another hour to Patna where he would go through the Indian customs before the short hop over to Nepal. He wondered if the customs would be sticky. He felt the gun below his armpit under the shirt. Firm as a rock—nice bit of workmanship, that harness. The customs weren't going to frisk him, so no difficulty there. He opened his briefcase and took out a book. The memory of the girl's face had faded. He gave her no further thought. He began to read.

Part Two

Chapter Eight

"Good morning, Major Birkett."

The plump Indian customs officer beamed amiably across the trestle table on the verandah of the airport building. The traffic at Patna airport was largely domestic, and the customs post existed solely for handling the few passengers passing through on the daily flight to Nepal. The officer liked to treat them with friendliness. He always glanced at the labels on their baggage and addressed them by name.

"You have anything to declare, Major Birkett?"

"Few cigarettes."

"No prohibited articles, Major Birkett? No arms? Ammunition?"

"Good God, no!"

"Thank you, Major Birkett." He squiggled with a piece of chalk on Birkett's suitcase and canvas hold-all. He beamed, "I hope you will enjoy your stay in Nepal."

Twenty minutes later Birkett was again in the air. The aircraft crossed the wide brown meandering Ganges and made for the long line of the Himalayas ahead.

"Soon be going over the top," the man across the aisle said gloomily. He was a tall stooping Englishman in a creased tropical suit, with a long pale face and thinning hair.

"Pretty clear today," Birkett said. "Should get some splendid views."

"I'm always kept too busy on this flight to look at the view." He saw Birkett's puzzled glance, and added, "I mean, crossing my fingers and saying my prayers."

"Why, lot of accidents on this line?"

"No, I'd feel safer if there had been. Their luck can't hold much longer—especially with me on board. My luck's always been filthy. And I've already made this trip thirty-two times, so by the law of averages our chances of a safe landing must be practically nil."

"You sound like an old hand in these parts."

"No need to rub it in."

He told Birkett that his name was Wilson, and that he had run a hotel in India until the British had scuttled and left him "high and dry"—just his filthy luck. He had struggled on for a few years, and then taken advantage of the opening up of Nepal to foreigners and started a hotel in Kathmandu. "That is if it's not presumptuous to call my little place a hotel."

"I'd been wondering where to put up," Birkett said. "I'll give it a try."

"I'm afraid it's pretty filthy. I suppose it's cutting my own throat to say so, but if I was in your shoes I'd go to the Royal. That's where most tourists go."

"I prefer to keep clear of tourists."

"Well, if you're determined, I can't stop you," Wilson said." And at least there'll be some whisky going for once—I've brought a case back from Calcutta." He peered dismally out of the window. "Not that we'll necessarily survive to drink it."

The jungle-covered foothills below them looked like a rumpled cloth of green velvet. They became rapidly higher, exchanging the velvet of the jungle for a dark green mantle of deodar and fir, and then shedding the trees altogether as they rose to bare tawny ridges and soaring peaks. The aircraft's shadow skimmed effortlessly below them like a bird, shrinking as it plunged down a steep escarpment into a valley, expanding as it shot upward again—almost converging with them as they passed over a summit.

"Must have been a tidy walk over here in the old days," Birkett said.

"Still, at least you knew you'd get there—not that you'd have been allowed into the country in the first place."

"What made them open up Nepal?"

"It was after the Ranas were deposed." The Rana family, Wilson explained, had held autocratic power in Nepal for a hundred years, keeping the Kings virtual prisoners in their own palace. The entire wealth of the country had flowed into their pockets, enabling them to indulge the three traditional Rana passions for power, women, and hunting big-game. However, some years ago Nepalese exiles in India had provoked a revolution resulting in the restoration of the King's power, and the progressive-minded King had decided to open up his country's doors.

"What happened to the Ranas?" Birkett asked.

"They were kicked out." The aircraft bucked like a wild horse trying to throw its rider. "Hello, here it comes. The last five minutes are always the worst."

"You mean we'll be down in five minutes?" It seemed impossible that they could arrive so soon at any place flat enough to land, for below them the jagged peaks and ravines followed each other in unbroken succession; and ahead was the great white barrier towering to twice the height at which they were flying—the barrier whose peaks included Everest and Annapurna, and that was known as the roof of the world.

"It won't be more, if it's at all," Wilson said.

Birkett gazed out of the window. Suddenly the mountains came to an end, and he found himself looking down on a flat green cultivated valley—so improbably flat, after the wild disorder of ridge and ravine, that it suggested the work of man rather than nature, as if a giant bulldozer had been used to push the mountains aside. A big brown sprawling town came into view. It straddled a winding river. A cluster of pagodas with tiered roofs formed its nucleus. The golden roof of a temple glittered in the sun.

The aircraft tilted its wings and dropped down on to a runway amongst emerald paddy-fields, and soon they were stepping out into the fresh invigorating mountain air. It seemed impossible to believe that only an hour ago they had stood in the suffocating air of the Indian plains. They had been transported to another world.

A crowd of Nepalese were gathered outside the small new reception building. The men were dressed in white cotton jodhpurs and round brimless caps and the women in bright saris, and many of them wore clusters of scarlet-dyed rice on their foreheads. Their faces were round and light-skinned and there was laughter in their long Mongolian eyes.

"Now, all the usual fuss and bother—awfully sorry about it," Wilson apologised as if he were personally responsible. "Let's have your passport."

"I'll have to come along, won't I?"

"No, why? I don't want you troubled."

"Then you'd better take this key for my suitcase in case they want to open it."

"My dear fellow, you don't want these blighters putting their dirty paws into your shirts. No, hang on to it, I'll manage."

He went off and returned within five minutes.

"Sorry I was so long. Now, my boy should be here with the car, but he usually breaks down on the way. You'll understand when you see the roads. They'd reduce a tank to scrap metal in a couple of miles."

They found the boy waiting outside, but the sight of the vehicle brought Wilson no cheer.

"I'm afraid that'll mean a breakdown on the way home," he said.

The car was an ancient open model that dated back to the Rana days, when cars for a few privileged citizens had been carried in pieces over the mountains from India and assembled in Kathmandu. It had lost its hood, and springs sprouted from the seats. They climbed in and clattered off towards the town. "We'll go through the bazaar," Wilson said. "Filthy place. Still you'd better see it once and have done with it."

The car turned down a narrow unpaved street seething with pedestrians. It was lined with shops, their open fronts supported by carved wooden pillars and richly carved windows and balconies above. The driver blasted the horn continuously. The car crawled forward, tilting in and out of potholes. They avoided a dead dog lying in the road. It was covered with flies. They passed a squatting beggar, hung with such an abundance of small filthy rags that he looked like some monstrous, tattered bird. Deformed and fly-infested children thrust hands into the car for coins.

Suddenly they emerged into a spacious square, a fairy tale world of temples and pagodas like a scene from a Christmas pantomime. The decorations that encrusted the sacred buildings—painted woodwork, coloured tiles, brass bas-reliefs, carved figures in permutations of the sexual act—were variegated as the buildings themselves, the confusion of Indian and Chinese styles clearly demonstrating that here was the meeting-point of two cultures, two religions.

They continued through the labyrinth of narrow streets, and came out at last on a road running alongside an open area of grass bordered with eucalyptus trees. In the centre of the grass a big shady peepul tree, surrounded by a stone platform, stood in solitary magnificence.

"This is the maidan," Wilson said. "It's where you take your girl when it's not being used for military parades."

Birkett nodded towards a procession of a dozen figures in quilted jackets and embroidered felt boots crossing the grass in single file. The leader had long black hair and the flushed complexion of a Red Indian, and walked with long swashbuckling strides. The women were loaded with necklaces and bangles of jade. One tiny old woman was being carried piggyback by an old man. "Look like Tibetans," he said.

"Tibetans or Sherpas from up near the border," Wilson explained. "They come down to trade skins and enjoy a bit of high-life in the fleshpots."

"Tidy walk from the border, isn't it?"

"Three or four weeks. That's the Palace, by the way—not that you can see it." They had left the maidan behind and now a long high wall ran alongside the road.

"The Royal Palace?"

"Yes, filthy great place. Still, I suppose His Majesty's got to stretch his legs."

The wall was interrupted after several hundred yards by a big entrance gate with tall stone pillars. The pillars were painted yellow and topped with plaster icing-sugar dripping down the sides, like magnified versions of the gateposts of some modern seaside villa trying hard to be different. There were sentries at the gate, and several officers and soldiers standing about outside the guardhouse.

"His Majesty's taking no chances," Birkett said.

"All just for show," Wilson said. "Filthy waste of money. His Majesty could stroll out to buy his cigarettes if he wanted, and nobody'd lay a finger on him."

"Never know," Birkett said. "Always the odd crank about."

"Well, I can easily get you in if you want to go rubbernecking. I'll speak to His Majesty's secretary for you."

The Palace wall came to an end. A few minutes later they came to another wall along the road with a gateway as grandiose as that of the Palace, but with rusting gates and crumbling pillars from whose cracks sprouted weeds.

"Well, here's the Everest," Wilson said.

"The Everest?"

"Everest Hotel—my little place."

The car turned through the gate into the drive, pitted as though by shell-fire and littered with stones. Trees on either side, thrusting their arms above the matted vegetation, blossomed out in luxuriant purple—even a palm tree had burst into phenomenal purple flower. Birkett was momentarily perplexed, and then noticed the parasitic fingers of bougainvillaea entwining the trunks and branches of its half-smothered host. They jolted and rattled round a bend, where a building confronted them—a Gargantuan white wedding-cake of a palace with colonnades running the full length of both ground and upper floors, and huge pillars supporting the porticoed entrance.

"My God, this isn't your 'little place'?" Birkett exclaimed.

"It's much bigger than it looks, I'm afraid," Wilson said gloomily. "You can't see half of it. That's just one side of a square." He added, "Of course there's just the orange garden in the middle— that's what we still call it, though it's gone back to jungle now."

"It's the size of Buckingham Palace! How many rooms?"

"Don't ask me, I'd rather not know. Somebody did once work

it out mathematically, but luckily I've a filthy head for figures and I've forgotten. Of course it's all shut up except for this front part."

"Even that must take a bit of filling. How many guests do you average?"

"Well, we've five at the moment, unless we've lost somebody while I've been in Calcutta." The car crunched to a standstill before the entrance, the tyres spurting gravel tipped on the drive to counter the ravages of the rainy season.

"I'm surprised you can afford to keep the place going," Birkett said.

"It depends on what you mean by going. Of course the rent isn't much—roughly what I used to pay in London for a bedsitter in the Cromwell Road."

He explained that Kathmandu was full of such white elephants, built by the Ranas whose families, impartially incorporating both legitimate and illegitimate offspring, had commonly numbered thirty or forty. The Everest had been the palace of a former Rana commander-in-chief, now in exile in India. Wilson had taken it over "lock, stock, and barrel."

"Which just meant with the stuffed heads left on the walls . . . I've never been a fancier of stuffed heads myself, and I finally got the boys on to burning them. But before we'd cleared out one room the guests were complaining of the smell. Anyhow, if you like stuffed heads you're welcome to all you can take away."

They mounted the steps between the stucco pillars. A stuffed tiger with shabby skin snarled unconvincingly in the entrance hall. It had lost a fang, and the dusty pink mouth looked as artificial as a dental plate. Across the hall a crocodile stretched its jaws in a perpetual yawn, sawdust spilling from a hole in its side.

"Rats," Wilson said. "I was hoping they'd come back and finish it off, but they lost interest." He nodded to the clutter of antelope heads on the walls. "I'm afraid those chaps have suddenly started dropping their eyes. I don't know why, unless it's the weather. Some days you'll find them rolling all over the floor like marbles."

There were more antelope heads on the stairs and in the upper corridors, interspersed with buffalo and rhino, and photographs of Ranas with sun helmets and drooping Edwardian moustaches posing with guns before prostrate animals.

"I'm giving you our best room, but it's pretty dreary," Wilson said. He fumbled with the handle of a door but it refused to open.

"Must be locked," Birkett said.

"No, we haven't any keys. It seemed rather pointless to impose further obstacles when most of these doors were already so warped that . . . Ah, done it—wonder of wonders! Well, sorry, I'm afraid this is the best I can do for you—and if you want to change your mind and go to the Royal I'll be the last to blame you."

It was a huge bleak room with high ceiling and uncurtained windows. There were two leather chairs that looked as if they had proved a more enduring attraction to rats than the crocodile in the hall, and two crude Indian-style beds.

"It's a double room really, but of course I'll only charge you single," Wilson said.

"Thanks, suits me fine." Birkett preferred a plain room with no fancy trappings.

"The bathroom's through that door. Well, if you're quite decided, I'll send up the boys with your stuff. And I only hope your stay here won't be too miserable."

"It's going to be a great success, don't worry about that."

After the boys had brought his baggage he unpacked and then took off his bush-shirt and unfastened the webbing that secured the gun under his arm. He put the gun and harness into the empty suitcase. From an inner pocket of his trousers he took the throat-pastille tin containing the heaven-helpers. He opened the lid. The lethal pills lay huddled like elongated eggs in their nest of cotton wool. He closed the tin and put it in the suitcase with the gun, locked the suitcase and placed it at the bottom of the wardrobe. Then he put on the bush-shirt again, took his walking-stick, and set out for a walk.

He walked until sundown, exploring the town and its immediate outskirts, getting the general feel of it—making himself as familiar as possible with the background before proceeding to the next move, which would be to find and tackle the young Indian, Krishna Mathai.

He returned to the hotel for dinner. The dining-room was a large sombre hall, with portraits of Ranas on the walls and a high moulded ceiling etched with dust. It was lit mournfully at one end by the inadequate town electricity, whilst the other end faded into darkness. Birkett was indifferent to the gloom, but took exception to the stained tablecloths, bunged-up salt-shakers, and knives whose loose handles kept parting company from the blades, which offended his taste for cleanliness and efficiency.

His fellow-diners included a quiet neat Indian timber merchant, an English lady with severe haircut and sturdy shoes on a sight-seeing visit, and a middle-aged American employed in a United States training mission. Half-way through dinner they were joined by an Englishman with red hair, red face, and red knees exposed under sweat-stained shorts.

"Sorry if I make you all feel over-dressed," he said. "But I was just packing up tonight when one of our local mechanical wizards dropped a bolt into some cogs at five hundred revs to 'watch it bounce.' So that was three hundred quid down the drain." He sat down. "We'd have done better to save time and dump the machinery at Gibraltar. It'd have been in better hands with those apes."

"Excuse me," the English lady barked, as if firing an opening salvo to start hostilities, "anybody here done Bhautgaon? I'm not going to hike nine miles just for another street of mangy pie-dogs. Anything there worth seeing?"

"Plenty of dirty carvings." The red-faced Englishman winked at Birkett.

Sloe-eyed boys in jodhpurs and brimless caps moved barefooted amongst the tables, removing the plates of rejected greasy soup, bringing the wild-boar stew garnished with dark soggy cabbage. Wilson appeared from the kitchen and stood regarding them gloomily.

"How is it tonight? Pretty filthy?"

"Glad to see our old friend again," said the red-headed

Englishman with heavy humour. "We'll miss that boar when one day it stops turning up."

"I know you must be getting sick to death of it," Wilson said. "I'm awfully sorry, Mr. Hobson. But you know what it is with those boars. You can't just say, 'I'll take the left trotter.' It's all or nothing and then you get it into the kitchen and think, "Well, that'll mean a few grumbles before we're through."

After dinner they all adjourned to the bar. Wilson opened a bottle of the whisky he had brought from Calcutta.

"We'd better make the most of it tonight because it'll all be gone by tomorrow, and we'll be back to drinking the local poison."

"You're not expecting us to get through a dozen bottles between us?" Birkett said.

Wilson replied with gloomy foreboding, "I'm afraid this bar's going to look very different an hour from now, Major Birkett."

"Expecting some more customers?"

"A few may drop in."

"That's a joke," said the red-haired Hobson. "He means the whole town'll be here. They all know the day Wilson gets back from Calcutta with the booze."

Birkett talked to Misra, the Indian timber merchant, and brought the conversation round to the Indian Embassy and its personalities. Misra mentioned a number of names but not Krishna Mathai's. The bar began to fill up. A man and two girls from the British Embassy came in, and then several small shy Nepalese in jodhpurs and high-necked Nepali shirts. The shirt-tails hung loose below the European-style jackets. There was one tiny frail old man of almost midget proportions who must have been at least eighty.

"General Ranju Shamsher Jang Bahadur Rana," Wilson said, introducing him to Birkett. "Though I'm not sure it goes in exactly that order."

"Perfectly correct." The General had little humorous eyes like an elephant's, and spoke beautiful and precise English, acquired sixty years ago at Oxford when Ranas alone had been permitted the benefits of foreign travel.

"Rana?" Birkett said. "You can't be one of the Ranas that used to run this show, sir?"

"Yes, I am afraid I belong to that wicked family," the General smiled.

"I thought all the Ranas had been turfed out after the revolution."

"That fate was spared to those of us who had taken the precaution to support the winning side. After our victory His Majesty graciously consented to retain my services, and to restore me to my former residence."

"That's the little shack just across the road," Wilson said. "You wouldn't have noticed it without your glasses. It's not really much bigger than this place."

"Joke," Hobson said.

"Must be on the small side for that family, anyhow," Wilson said. "What's the score now, General?"

"Thirty-eight," the General said with a twinkle. "And a thirty-ninth on the way."

"What, babies, sir?" Birkett said.

"My oldest child is hardly a baby. He is sixty-two."

Wilson shook his head gloomily. "Sixty-two years, and still going strong. I don't know how you do it, General, unless it's the weather. I'd lost interest myself before I was out of my thirties. Mind you that was in London, after three bad years running—if it wasn't rain it was drizzle—and they were enough to dampen anybody down. Sorry, General, fill you up?"

"Since you insist, Mr. Wilson. But only a drop—not above here," He pointed half-way up the tumbler.

"There'll be no holding you tonight, General," Wilson said. "You'll be clocking up forty."

"I'm afraid that would require a feat of overlapping which nature does not allow. However, it is my cherished ambition to attain forty when opportunity permits. Then I shall retire and impose no further burden on womanhood."

Several Indians came in and Misra introduced then. They were all from the Embassy but Mathai was not amongst them. Birkett was chattering amiably with them when a big hand clamped down heartily on his shoulder.

"So you finally made it, old man? Jolly good show!"

Birkett looked round. "Ah, Potter."

The sight of the big grin stretched out under the airman's moustache, the eyes goggling behind the horn-rimmed glasses, the "near-miss" Guards' tie, caused him little enthusiasm. He felt the imminence of a dirty story.

"Heard you'd turned up today—bush telegraph, old man. And it's funny that you should have picked the Everest. The wife and I started at the Royal but we're switching to this place tomorrow."

Birkett's eyes fixed on the tie. Funny, a chap shouldn't need to fall back on a fake tie for a line-shoot, when he'd something as real to show for himself as that wound on his leg . . . He said, "I heard the Royal is pretty good."

"Quieter here, old man. I suppose you can find us a room, can't you, Wilson?"

"I might squeeze you in if we get a cancellation," Wilson said.

"I'm serious, old man."

Wilson shrugged. "Well, I only hope the Royal doesn't sue me for alienation of affection—just my filthy sort of luck."

Birkett moved away. A minute later Potter's hand clamped on his arm.

"Come over and meet the wife."

He steered Birkett across the bar. Mrs. Potter had blonde hair, big black curling lashes, and china-blue eyes whose affected look of childish innocence Birkett remembered from the photograph. She had a rather plaintive babyish voice.

"Major Birkett, I don't think I shall speak to you! I know you've been leading Potter astray. You're both terribly naughty boys!"

Naughty boys—God Almighty! Still, nice neat little waist no denying it. Not much bigger than What's-her-name's. (Ghosts from the past! It was the first thought he had given to Lakshmi Kapoor since leaving Delhi this morning.) He said curtly, "Sorry, must be mixing me up with someone else. Only met your husband once. Quick lunch in Delhi."

"Yes, Potter confessed how you both made eyes like mad at a pretty girl at the next table."

"Oh, rubbish," Birkett said.

"Oh dear, I believe I've said something awful," Mrs. Potter said plaintively. "Potter, did I say something awful?"

"You can't help it, old girl. Got to open your mouth sometime."

"I know I'm just so stupid!" The china-blue eyes settled on Birkett with a long steady look. She held the look for a fraction of a second, then her eyes dropped quickly and resumed their synthetic innocence—but it had been a fraction of a second too long.

Well, that was plain enough, he thought. That was just a little message to say, "Of course I'm just fooling around to amuse my silly husband, but you and I talk the same language." She couldn't have said it clearer if she'd used pen and ink, and sent it in a letter by registered mail.

He averted his eyes and looked past her with total indifference, knowing that it would only sharpen her interest. He said, "Excuse me, chap over there—must have a word," and moved to the bar, feeling her eyes still on him. Just then the telephone rang on the shelf behind the bar counter. Wilson picked it up.

"Hang on, I'll see." He took the receiver from his ear.

"Mr. Mathai here?" he asked one of the Indians.

"Krishna?" The Indian glanced round. "No, not yet."

"No, sorry, I'll get him to ring you," Wilson said into the telephone. He hung up and placed a cracked water jug upside clown on the counter.

Ten minutes later a young Indian entered the bar alone. Birkett knew at once that it was Mathai.

He was a tall, skinny youth with glasses. He had the gentle lost look often seen on the faces of Indian students far from their home in Bloomsbury. It was as though his body carried the burden of his country's mass poverty and undernourishment. His chest and shoulders were narrow and he did not look strong. He had long, fragile, shy hands with slender fingers: they were his best feature and rather beautiful. He wore a big ostentatious chromium watch. It looked awkward and cumbersome on the thin delicate wrist.

He paused a moment and looked round the bar. His big soft brown eyes contained hints of an eager nervous fire that was being guarded and withheld behind the glasses.

You can see he's an idealist, Birkett thought. You can smell that intellectual idealism a mile off.

The young man joined his Indian colleagues and accepted a soft drink—like several of the Indians and Nepalese in the bar who were already drinking lemonade, he had come for the social occasion and not for the whisky. Birkett paid him no further attention until presently Misra brought him over.

"Major Birkett, I wish you to meet my friend Krishna Mathai. He is one of our bright young stars from the Embassy. He was most excited when I told him. about you, for he is also a writer."

"No, excuse me, Mr. Misra, that is ridiculous, I have never published anything," Mathai said quickly, with smiling self-deprecation. His manner contained a rudimentary diplomatic poise that he was in the process of acquiring, but it no more than half-concealed the shyness and eagerness of youth. "Sir, it is a great privilege to meet you."

"Nothing like the privilege it is for me to meet a future ambassador."

"Oh, sir, I am still only a junior," the young man protested. "Sir, I am ashamed I have not read your books. But I have seen your book about India in our Ambassador's house."

"Bet your life it was a complimentary copy," Birkett said. "Always dish 'em out to important chaps like that. Best way to ensure they'll never read them and start tearing 'em to bits."

Mathai said quite suavely, "You have the true modesty of all great men, sir."

"Don't give me that stuff, young fellow!"

"You are the first real writer I have ever met, sir. It is a very special occasion for me. Who is your favourite author, sir?"

"Conrad."

"What is your opinion of François Mauriac?"

"Never read him. Not much time for reading—always seem to be on the move."

"I envy your travels, sir. It is also my ambition to see many countries and meet the different peoples."

"Chosen the right job for it."

"Yes, this is my first post out of India, but I am still young. I have plenty of time for my ambition to be fulfilled."

Not so much time as you think, laddie, Birkett thought. But then you won't need so much time for the new ambition that you're soon going to acquire. "Yes, lucky chap," he said.

"I hope also to achieve my ambition to become a writer. I have already started a novel."

The telephone rang again.

"Sorry, awfully sorry," Wilson said into the mouthpiece. "Filthy memory. And tonight we've such a bear garden . . ." He put down the instrument. "It's your wife, Mr. Mathai. Sorry, she rang before."

The young Indian hurried anxiously round the bar. Wilson gloomily removed the cracked water jug that he had placed upside down on the counter.

"Well, that's another black mark. I kept looking at this wretched thing, and knew I must have put it there to remind me of something . . . Fill you up, Major Birkett?"

"Thanks."

"She sounded very sharp, I'm afraid," Wilson said. "'I hope she isn't as sharp with Mr. Mathai. After all, he couldn't know that that wretched jug standing upside down meant 'ring up home'."

Mathai listened anxiously to the receiver. Then he hung up and came round the counter.

"I am sorry, sir, I must leave you. My son has earache."

"You've a son, eh?"

"Two, sir. I'm very proud of my sons. The eldest is four. The second, with earache, is a year younger."

So he's got a wife and children, Birkett thought. Funny, I never thought of him having a family. Well, too bad. Only wish I could have taken a single chappie instead—but I'm not in a position to pick and choose. So it's hard lines—but that's life.

He said, "Nothing serious, I hope?"

"No, the doctor says it is no cause for anxiety. But it is naturally upsetting, and my wife needs me." He hesitated diffidently. "Sir, I wish to meet you again, and also for my wife to meet you. It would be a great privilege to entertain you at our little house, though it is small and unworthy. Perhaps you would honour us for dinner tomorrow night?"

"Better consult your wife first, laddie."

Mathai said quickly, "Oh naturally, sir, I wouldn't have asked you without . . ." He hesitated, fearing to give the impression that he was not master in his own home. "I mentioned the possibility on the telephone, sir. My wife would be as honoured as myself."

"Well, delighted in that case," Birkett said.

"You are most gracious, sir." He slid a hand quickly inside his jacket. "I shall give you my card."

He took out his wallet. It was as ostentatious as his watch, with gold-protected corners and his initials in fancy gold letters. He fumbled through the warren of compartments with shy self-conscious hands.

He's ashamed of those hands, Birkett thought. He doesn't know they're beautiful. It's a weak point—always useful to know.

He took the card that the young man held out.

"Thanks, looking forward to tomorrow," he said. "And best of luck with that kid."

He slipped the card into his pocket and turned back, almost brusquely, to the bar, and did not look at the young Indian as he went out of the door.

Chapter Nine

The ancient car rattled to a stop outside the iron gates of the Royal Palace, flanked by the tall yellow pillars topped with icing-sugar.

The guards stood impassively, their rifles and bayonets at ease, making no move to open the gates.

An officer came out of the guardhouse and stopped smartly beside the car.

"Your name, sir?" he said in English. He referred to a piece of paper clipped to a board.

"Birkett. I've an appointment with Mr. Dixit."

"That's right, Major Birkett. His Majesty's secretary is expecting you. I will conduct you to the Palace, if you will permit me to ride with you."

The guards unlocked the gates and they passed between the yellow pillars. A large white building stood at the end of a drive.

That is the old palace, now used only for state functions," the officer explained.

Birkett nodded toward a white modernistic building in the formal gardens beside the drive. "What's the Odeon cinema for?"

The officer smiled. "Yes, exactly."

That's a ruddy silly answer, Birkett thought.

He said patiently, "That was just my joke. What's it for?"

"It is a cinema. It was built by His Majesty's late father. He had very progressive ideas."

The car swung off the main drive and pulled up before a large villa of angular modern style whose numberless counterparts might have been found anywhere from Cannes to Caracas. Two officers with A.D.C. armbands and revolvers in leather holsters stood outside. One of them, with a clipped moustache like Birkett's, stepped forward and saluted.

"Major Birkett? Good afternoon, sir. Please step this way."

He escorted Birkett into a reception room furnished in Western style. Four statuettes of girls holding out their skirts in sentimental poses occupied the corners. A large framed photograph of the King, in jewelled state robes and plumed helmet, hung on the wall.

"Please sit down, Major Birkett. You will smoke?"

The A.D.C. whipped a cigarette box from a table. It contained a choice of English and American varieties. He snapped the box shut, produced a lighter, and dexterously flipped it into flame before the tip of Birkett's cigarette as if performing military drill to numbers.

"Mr. Dixit, His Majesty's Principal Secretary, will be here shortly." He withdrew.

Birkett studied the portrait of the King. The photograph was hand-tinted with pale unlifelike colours that, together with the panoply of robes and headgear, divested the young clean-shaven face of character: it was the face of a wax dummy betraying no more of the man than the photograph of him in dark glasses that Birkett had seen in the newspaper.

And so much the better, Birkett thought. I don't want him brought to life, to know him as a person. It's quite enough that I must know Mathai as a man, and I'd rather the King became no more real to me than the wax face in that picture.

"Good afternoon, Major Birkett. I am Dixit."

A small beaming Nepalese, wax smooth round face, crossed the room extending a chubby hand. He wore a Nepali cap, polo-necked sweater with white spotless shirt-tails hanging out below, and white jodhpurs. He sank into the springs of an armchair with a movement of careless ease, and crossed his plump legs.

"I understand from Mr. Wilson's note that you are a writer, Major Birkett, You have naturally come to request an audience with His Majesty?"

Birkett flicked the ash off his cigarette into an ornamental ashtray with the glazed figure of a woman holding a borzoi dog on a leash. He shook his head. "No."

"No?" The secretary's bland manner, rubbed smooth like a pebble in a stream by the steady flow of visitors to the Palace, was momentarily ruffled. He derived much satisfaction from his power to produce the King for those who obtained his favour; and the failure to call upon him to exercise this power left him as deflated as a conjuror whom nobody had asked to produce the rabbit out of the hat. He was a trifle peeved. "Well, that's just as well. If you had requested an audience, I should probably have refused you. I could not put your name before His Majesty without good reason, and clearly you have no such reason. So I am sorry, I find it impossible to help you." He had stepped back comfortably into a familiar gear. "I wish I could hold out more hope, Major Birkett. But that is the position."

"Quite, I know His Majesty's a busy man. That's why I don't want to bother him."

"Then what can I do for you, Major Birkett?"

"I'm just trying to get an overall picture of Nepal and I reckoned I should begin with His Majesty—and I know that if there is one person who can tell me more about His Majesty than His Majesty himself, it's you, Mr. Dixit."

Dixit beamed. "I expect it will surprise you to know that His Majesty spends most of his time at his office desk."

"I gather he isn't seen much outside the Palace?"

"Rarely. His duties as head of state involve so much paper-work . . ."

I suppose it could take place in the Palace, Birkett thought. Easy as pie to trump up some pretext to get Mathai a royal audience. And they don't search you when you come in, so no difficulty about the gun. The King would probably receive him in here . . . Dixit's round beaming face momentarily faded and in its place he saw the wax tinted face of the King from the portrait; and he imagined Mathai slipping his hand inside his shirt, whipping out the gun and pulling the trigger, and the King slumping forward, knocking over the table, sprawling on the floor amongst the spilled cigarettes and shattered ashtray, the glazed fragments of the lady and the borzoi dog. And then Mathai turning the gun on himself as the A.D.Cs burst through the door . . .

No, no good. No witnesses—all thrown away on an empty room. Too easy for them to hush up the essential facts. They'd be on to the Indian Ambassador right away, who'd say, "Hold everything until I get round." And then, "I think that perhaps, in our mutual interests, a little discretion . . ."

In other words, identity and nationality of assassin with held pending investigations. Truth only revealed after interval, with pill carefully sugared for public gullet. India's position in Nepal totally unaffected. Plot fizzles out like a damp squib . . .

No, skip it. The Palace is out. It needs some public occasion, vast crowds to feel the emotional impact, show horror, hysteria . . .

"His Majesty's only relaxation is a quiet stroll in the Palace grounds," Dixit was saying. "My favourite picture of him is this little snapshot." He drew out his wallet. "I took the picture myself. Here you see—it has just caught His Majesty at his most gay and informal."

That's just why I don't want to see it, Birkett thought. And he stared at the photograph with his eyes deliberately out-of-focus, taking in only a blurred impression of a figure in grey flannels and open-necked shirt posing before a flower bed with shy boyish stance.

He handed the snapshot back. "Congratulations. You're a good photographer."

"You are too kind," Dixit purred. "Major Birkett, on second thoughts I feel that perhaps I was a little hasty in refusing your request . . ."

"Request?"

"For an audience with His Majesty—I shall put your proposal before His Majesty and I think you can take it that it will be favourably received."

"But as I explained, I had no intention . . ."

"Your case is more deserving than most. You cannot write a book about this country without meeting our beloved sovereign."

"Quite right," Birkett said. "But I think it might serve my purpose best at the end of my visit." And since by the end of his visit a royal audience would no longer be possible, this compromise disposed of the matter satisfactorily. He remained with Dixit a further fifteen minutes in the hope of learning of some royal activity outside the Palace that would offer the opportunity he sought. But no such information was forthcoming. And it was only when he had already risen to take his leave that Dixit mentioned the Tattoo.

"You'll be here for the Tattoo, of course? You won't be leaving before the end of the month?"

"Nothing fixed yet," Birkett said. "Why, something worth seeing?"

"The Tattoo is the finest spectacle of the year. You have heard of our Gurkha soldiers?"

"Not only heard of 'em but fought with 'em—thanks to your country's generosity in supplying troops for our wars."

"The Tattoo will therefore be of particular interest to you. Besides a magnificent display of drill, there will be a reconstruction of some historic battle."

"And won't His Majesty be there?"

"Oh yes, His Majesty will take the salute from under the tree in the centre of the maidan. It is a great joy to our people to see our beloved Sovereign on this annual occasion. They travel for many days from the farthest corners of our country to see the Tattoo. I am sure you will find it worth-while to attend, Major Birkett."

"Yes, I reckon you're right—very worth-while," Birkett said.

A Tattoo on the maidan, he thought. Crowds from all over Nepal and the King taking the salute. Yes, worth-while all right . . . And five minutes later, driving out through the icing-sugar palace gates, he ordered the driver to take him to the maidan before going back to the hotel; and as they cruised alongside the great open expanse of grass he could already imagine the forthcoming spectacle, with the packed spectators under the eucalyptuses, the marching troops, the King standing with hand raised in salute on the platform under the peepul tree. And then the sound of a shot . . .

By Jove, it was a chance that went beyond his wildest hopes. It was the luck of a lifetime. It was a gift from God.

2

"I've laid on the jeep, but I'm afraid it's in a filthy condition, Major Birkett," Wilson said. "It's thirty rupees a day."

"Thanks, any chance of a bath?"

"Yes, I'll get the boys to do you a brew."

An hour later the water arrived. It was brought by a procession of boys carrying old petrol cans. The boys filed through into the bathroom and emptied the cans into the tin tub. The water was agreeably hot. Birkett bathed, pulled on a clean pair of slacks, then took the suitcase from the bottom of the ward robe and removed the gun and harness. He strapped the gun under his arm and finished dressing. He locked the suitcase again, with the tin of heaven-helpers inside, and returned it to the wardrobe, and then went down to the waiting jeep.

The jeep's battered appearance was no worse than that of the general run of vehicles in Kathmandu, and it started promptly. He switched on the lights and shot off.

He found Mathai's house at the end of a rutted lane on the outskirts of the town. It was a small bungalow in a parched and neglected garden, surrounded by banana plantains with tattered fronds and puny misshapen bunches of fruit.

Birkett had hardly switched off the engine before Mathai was at the gate.

"Good evening, sir! Welcome to our little nest! It is a great occasion for us. It is the first time we have been honoured by such a distinguished presence!"

He conducted Birkett inside. The cramped living-room was cheaply furnished with upright wooden chairs and a hard settee. A commercial calendar hung on the wall, and a number of diplomatic invitation cards, mostly out of date, were displayed to full advantage amongst family snapshots on the mantelpiece. A bulky manuscript had been placed prominently on a table.

Mathai kept glancing at the manuscript, hoping that Birkett

would remark on it. He suddenly remembered something and opened a cupboard.

"You will have some Scotch whisky, sir?"

"My word, where did that come from?"

"I got it through the Embassy, sir."

He held the bottle like some precious unfamiliar object that he was frightened of breaking. It was evident that he had bought it specially for Birkett's visit. He poured him a large drink, and then a small one for himself.

"Well, good health, sir!" He glanced at the manuscript again. Impatience overcame him, and he said, "There is my novel, sir, such as it is."

"Looks plenty of it."

"It is only the first twenty-three chapters. They took me three years. But six months ago I encountered difficulties and could not get on. Now your arrival has made me eager to resume work. I believe a discussion of the difficulties with you would enable me to resolve them. After dinner I would like to explain the theme. It is a little complex. I would also like to read you a chapter aloud to give you an impression of my style."

A woman had entered silently and unobtrusively. She wore a sari of some drab colour and her face was without make-up.

"This is my wife, sir," Mathai said.

Mrs. Mathai dispensed an automatic greeting, bringing her palms briefly together and parting them again without speaking a word. She looked older than her husband. Her eyes were cool and watchful, without humour. There was a scuffle outside the door, and she turned and said something in Urdu.

"My wife allowed my sons to stay up to meet you," Mathai said, smiling in proud anticipation of their entry.

The door opened uncertainly and the two boys came in, clasping each other for moral support. They stood gaping at Birkett with big dark liquid eyes.

"I told them you were a famous man, so they are naturally very shy, sir," Mathai said.

"By Jove, that's a fine pair of kids," Birkett said. "They do you credit, Mathai. And that youngster looks in the pink—got over his troubles?"

"Yes, his earache is quite better, sir."

"They're a bonny pair."

"They are quite remarkable for their age sir. They both know many words of English. They will astonish you. You must please speak to them."

"I'm sure Major Birkett does not wish to be bothered," Mrs. Mathai interrupted. She spoke in a cool, expressionless voice that admitted no possibility of contradiction. "That is quite enough, Krishna. I shall take them to bed."

Mathai looked disappointed but made no protest. The children silently vanished at a word from their mother. Mrs. Mathai followed. Five minutes later she returned and sat on one of the hard upright chairs in silence whilst Mathai and Birkett continued to talk.

Yes, she's the one that wears the trousers all right, Birkett thought And Mathai's secretly proud of it. He's the sort that likes to be bossed. I reckon that calls for a hard approach for a start . . .

He knew the importance of being absolutely clear in his own mind about the kind of approach he intended to use—no use leaving it to the spur of the moment, squandering his resources as he vacillated between soft and hard. He had to play it one way or the other. He had been in two minds for a bit over Mathai. But now he'd got his answer . . .

They went into the dining-room. The dinner was an elaborate curry, and Mathai felt no reserve about drawing Birkett's attention to the efforts of his wife in its preparation. The curry was followed by a sickly sweetmeat encrusted with edible gold-leaf.

"It was very extravagant to use gold-leaf, sir," Mathai said proudly. "We usually consider even silver-leaf beyond our means but we wished to make the meal worthy of the occasion."

"I've eaten so much gold tonight I reckon I should get the local bank to lock me up in their vault," Birkett said.

"You will have nothing more, Major Birkett?" Mrs. Mathai enquired coolly. "Then I will let you and my husband talk alone."

"I am going to read Major Birkett a chapter of my book," Mathai glowed.

He ushered Birkett back into the cramped gentility of the living-room, impatient to get started. He picked up the manuscript, his long slender fingers jumping with nervous excitement as he turned the pages.

"Please sit down, Major Birkett. I shall remain on my feet—I find it easier to give expression to my reading." He prepared to begin, but noticed that Birkett was still standing. "Please sit down comfortably."

Birkett ignored the request. Mathai adjusted his glasses anxiously, suspecting that something had gone wrong.

"Right," Birkett said suddenly. "Now put that away." Mathai stared in perplexity. Birkett's peremptory manner, after he had sat at Mathai's table, partaken of his gold-leaf, seemed inexplicable. He wondered if it was a joke.

"I said put that away," Birkett repeated sharply.

"You mean my novel, sir?"

"What else?"

Mathai tittered.

"Stop that, and do as you're told," Birkett said.

Mathai put down the manuscript nervously.

"Don't you wish me to read, sir?"

Birkett ignored the question. He said, "Sit down." He paused only a fraction of a second. "Didn't you hear me? *Sit down!*"

Mathai dropped like a stone.

"Now, I'll tell you why I'm here," Birkett said. "We didn't meet by chance yesterday. I came to Nepal to talk to you. That's why I'm here tonight, not to hear you read your literary masterpiece."

Mathai said weakly, "I don't understand, sir."

"Why 'sir' and not 'comrade'?"

Mathai stared. He was speechless.

"Members of the Communist Party usually say 'comrade,' don't they?"

The blood drained from Mathai's face. It turned whitish-grey.

His lips moved but no sound came. He thought that Birkett had come to arrest him.

"It's a good thing I'm on your side, because otherwise you'd have given the game away without even opening your mouth," Birkett said. "Here, perhaps this'll cheer you up."

He took a folded sheet of paper from his pocket. He handed it to Mathai, who opened it, adjusted his spectacles, and scanned the lines of badly duplicated type. It appeared to be a circular letter from some religious society in Southern India, beginning "Dear Brother/Sister," and exhorting the reader to turn to Christ. His eyes came to a stop in mid-sentence in the fourth line. He carefully read over again the three words that had caught his attention, noting the comma dividing the first two, the transposition of two letters in the third. The colour crept back into his face. He looked up. "I understand now. I am very glad to know we have the same ideals, sir. I hold my ideals very dearly. I believe that Communism is the only answer for India. That is why I originally agreed to do special duty for our cause." He looked at the letter again uneasily. "I gather you have a duty for me now, sir?"

"Correct."

"There is something I must explain, sir. I have only once before been called upon to perform a duty. It was several years ago in Delhi, when I was required to procure the text of a certain secret foreign office document. I carried out the duty successfully, but I was very unhappy because I felt I had acted dishonourably and abused a trust. I suffered from keen pangs of conscience. I could not make a clean breast of it because that would have abused another trust. I could not even discuss my predicament with my wife, since I was bound to secrecy by the undertaking into which I had entered before our marriage. But I decided that in view of my position in the Indian foreign service, I would accept no further duties."

Birkett said nothing. His eyes were fixed upon Mathai. The young Indian shifted uncomfortably.

"I wished to announce my decision," he went on, but it was difficult to do so by message, and I feared my reasons would be misunderstood. Then, since I was not called upon again, it no longer seemed necessary. However, I feel I must stand by that decision now. I am sorry, sir. I trust it will not cause you great inconvenience." Birkett was still silent, and Mathai grew increasingly uneasy under the ice-blue stare. He repeated, "I am very sorry, sir."

There was another silence,

"Right, now we're going out," Birkett said suddenly.

"What for?"

Birkett ignored the question. He said brusquely, "Go and tell your wife I want some fresh air. Say we're going to take a spin in the jeep and continue the discussion of your book."

"Sir, since my mind is quite made up," Matthai said unhappily, "I feel it would only be wasting your time——"

"Do as you're told, Mathai."

Mathai found himself rising almost without conscious intention, under the authority of Birkett's tone that took obedience for granted. He started for the door.

"By the way, Mathai."

The Indian paused.

Birkett idly picked up one of the family snapshots from the mantelpiece and examined it. "Watch your step," he said carelessly.

Mathai left the room. After a minute he came back.

"Told her?" Birkett said.

"Right, off we go."

He walked past Mathai, across the narrow hall, and out of the bungalow, He went briskly up the path to the gate. He heard Mathai close the front door behind him. He got into the jeep, started up the engine, and Mathai got in beside him.

"Where are we going, sir?" Mathai asked.

Birkett did not reply. He switched on the headlights and the jeep shot forward. He turned left at the end of the lane in the opposite direction to the town. Soon they had left behind the last habitations. The headlights probed an empty countryside of paddy-fields, with an occasional shrine or pagoda beside the road.

Birkett drove in silence. He had not spoken a word since leaving the bungalow.

"Sir, I feel I am putting you to unnecessary trouble," Mathai ventured nervously.

Birkett said nothing. The jeep clattered and jolted on the rough dirt road. He continued for several miles: the farther he took Mathai from the security of familiar surroundings, from his home and wife, and the longer he maintained the unnerving silence and suspense, the easier would be his task.

At last he pulled up. He switched off the engine and lights and got out.

"Follow me."

He dropped down the bank into a paddy. The dry stubble crackled under his feet. The moon had just emerged above the mountain skyline putting the stars to retreat. He made for a dark shape across two or three paddies. He saw as he drew nearer that it was a small derelict pagoda. He stopped before the stone steps, whose niches sprouted weeds and tall stalks of rice. He heard the crackling of stubble as Mathai approached and came to a standstill behind him. He said without turning, "Ever been a soldier, Mathai?"

"No, sir."

"But you know what it means. A soldier is under discipline. He is a cog in a machine to whose interests his own are subservient. His actions are not dictated by his own free will, which he is obliged to surrender, but by the impersonal will of the machine, expressed through the orders of the officer elected to command him. Your position—and mine—are analogous. You are a soldier under discipline and obliged to obey my orders as your commanding officer."

"Sir, I have told you my decision."

Birkett whipped round. "'Decision?' A soldier does not decide. He obeys. I don't want to hear another word about your 'decision.' You understand?" Mathai was silent. "I asked you a question, Mathai. Do you understand?"

Mathai said weakly, "Yes, sir."

"Right, you have been detailed for a task by higher authority. You will carry it out under my orders. The task is perfectly clear and straightforward." He explained its nature. He spoke of the assassination in a blunt matter-of-fact voice as if it was a routine duty for which he detailed men every day.

Mathai stood in silence after he had finished, his glasses glinting in the moon.

"He is a good king, sir," he said at last.

"That is neither here nor there."

"Why must he be killed?"

"I don't feel obliged to answer that question. A soldier must carry out orders without regard to reasons. But I'll make an exception in this case, because I don't wish to deny you the satisfaction of knowing what service you are performing for your country." He explained how the assassination would lead to the overthrow of the present government in Kathmandu and the establishment of a Communist government, and how this bridgehead for Communism into India would vitally affect the future of the whole continent.

Mathai swayed a little at the foot of the steps.

"I have never killed a man, sir," he said presently.

"Nothing to it." He crooked his forefinger as though round the trigger of a gun. "A little pressure is all that's needed—easy as lighting a cigarette."

"But there are always guards near the King, sir. How could I get away without discovery?"

"Good God, you're a bloody optimist! You couldn't get away— not a hope. You'll have to shoot yourself after shooting the King."

Mathai's knees gave way. He dropped down on the steps.

"Stand up," Birkett said.

Mathai did not move.

"That is an order, Mathai," Birkett said.

Mathai rose unsteadily.

"You're behaving like an old woman," Birkett said. "What's the matter? Don't you like the idea of shooting yourself? All right, don't. Although personally I'd have thought it was infinitely preferable to the protracted miseries of imprisonment, public trial, and the hangman's rope." The young man swayed as if he was a little drunk. Birkett went on, "And I've got some heaven-helpers for you, by the way. They're always useful to have handy. You don't know what they are? Death pills. Same thing, different name. And much to the point, since I can assure you that they can render most efficient and valuable service in helping you into the hereafter, if you shouldn't have time to use the gun, or should make a bosh shot with it. All right, you can sit down now."

Mathai collapsed again on the step.

"Naturally the job requires a bit of guts," Birkett went on. "But you won't be the first to sacrifice your life for a cause. You'll be in the company of several millions who sacrificed their lives uncomplainingly in two world wars. Only you're a sight better off than them and should thank your lucky stars for it. They just disappeared ingloriously in the mud in the wholesale slaughter. But you're going to perform a duty of historic importance and your name's going to shine with glory. I only hope you appreciate the honour of being chosen for the task, and will prove yourself worthy of it."

Mathai, who had removed his glasses, sat with face buried in his hands.

"I'm sorry, sir, I can't do it," he said. "I must think of my family. It is impossible."

"I'll give you five minutes to change your mind," Birkett said.

He strolled off round the back of the pagoda. After a few minutes he came back. Mathai was still sitting on the steps, amongst the tall stalks of rice sprouting between the stones, his face buried in his hands. The moonlight gave the long slender beautiful hands the pallor of death. Like the marble hands of a statue, Birkett thought. The hands of a dead Christ.

"Well?" he said. "Changed your mind?"

"No, sir. I cannot do it. I cannot accept the duty,"

"Then stand up."

Mathai stood with difficulty.

"A soldier who cannot accept—or, more accurately, refuses to obey—an order is guilty of mutiny. And you know the penalty for mutiny?"

114

"I am an Indian subject, sir—a member of the Indian foreign service. They can't do anything to me."

"I don't know about 'they.' I only know what I can do—and intend to do without delay."

He unfastened a button of his bush-shirt, slid his hand inside, and drew the gun from the holster under his arm. He took three rounds of ammunition from his pocket and fitted them into the gun.

The click of the chamber drew Mathai out of his daze. He blinked and peered short-sightedly, and could not believe his eyes. He realized he must have taken off his spectacles. He put them on anxiously, and peered again at the object in Birkett's hand.

Birkett pulled back the safety-catch and pointed the gun at Mathai, his finger on the trigger. He lifted his other wrist to glance at his watch.

"I'm going to shoot you in sixty seconds unless you've changed your mind," he said. "Of course your family's going to lose you anyway, so it's simply a question of whether you prefer to leave them a legacy of glory or . . . Fifty seconds."

Mathai's throat was dry. He could not speak.

"Forty seconds."

Mathai closed his eyes and swayed.

"Thirty." He saw Mathai about to topple. "I'll shoot you at once if you faint. Quite unnecessary."

Mathai steadied himself.

"Twenty."

The perspiration on Mathai's forehead glistened in the moon.

"Ten. Five, Well?"

Mathai nodded and tried to speak, but no words came.

"Speak up," Birkett said. "What does that mean? You've changed your mind?"

"Yes, sir," Mathai whispered.

"You will obey my orders?"

"Yes, sir."

"You ran that a bit fine, laddie." Birkett clicked back the safety-catch again and shook the rounds out of the gun into his palm. He returned the gun to the holster and buttoned up his jacket.

"Right, that's all for now. We shall meet again on Sunday at six p.m. at the north-east corner of the maidan. Now, back to the jeep."

He turned and walked off briskly. He climbed the bank on to the road. He lit a cigarette and stood waiting beside the jeep. He heard the crackling of stubble and saw Mathai shambling across the paddy, weaving about like a drunk. He reached the bank and began a clumsy ascent, but missed his footing, sprawled on the slope and lay with his face in the grass, uttering little moans.

"Stop it," Birkett said sharply. The moans faded.

"Get up."

Mathai rose and renewed his dazed efforts to pull himself up."

"Pull yourself together and climb up properly," Birkett said.

Mathai resounded to Birkett's command automatically. "Now wipe the dirt off your face," Birkett said.

Mathai felt for his handkerchief.

"No, put that away—don't want your wife asking questions. Use this."

He held out his own handkerchief. Mathai took it, removed his glasses, wiped his face and put on the glasses again.

"Now get into the jeep."

Mathai got in obediently. Well, this is only the first round, Birkett thought. We've several more rounds to come. But I've won the opening bout hands down. He turned the jeep round on the narrow road. The sturdy engine responded to the pressure of his foot: as obedient as Mathai, as completely under his control. He was possessed by a sense of exhilaration and power—the power of the cheetah that was spare and trim and self-contained, whose strength and swiftness were unmatched, the perfect animal-machine, the ruler of the plain.

Chapter Ten

It was just midnight when he turned the jeep through the crumbling stone gateposts of the Everest. He swung round the bend in the drive, the headlights raking the white palatial facade, and came to a crunching stop.

The mood of exhilaration still possessed him. He entered the darkened hall, where the dusty old tiger snarled in the shadows, the crocodile wearily yawned and trickled sawdust from its side. He saw the lights on in the bar. Good, just ready for a nightcap.

He found Mrs. Potter alone, seated on one of the stools, drinking banana brandy. She fluttered her lashes at him.

"Major Birkett, you naughty boy, coming back so late! Now, you can't pretend you haven't been up to something naughty this time!"

He checked a wince and let his eyes fail to the neat little waist.

"What have you done with your husband? Moved over here by yourself and left him at the Royal?" He poured himself out a drink.

"Oh, you're forbidden to mention the horrible Potter! He's gone to the Ambassador's and I hate him!" She patted the stool beside her. "Don't you want to sit down?"

"No, prefer to prop up the bar."

"Now I've got it, it's Mr. Featherstone!" Mrs. Potter exclaimed. "I've been trying to think who you're exactly like, and of course it's Mr. Featherstone! He was a strong, silent Englishman just like you. He used to smoke a pipe and say in a delicious gruff voice, 'Mind if I prop up your mantelpiece?'"

"I was desperately in love with him, and he was just like you."

"Come off it."

She pouted. "Oh, you're being horrid. I can't help it if I'm stupid and say the wrong things."

"You're not stupid. At least not the way you pretend—though I'll grant you can't be very bright if you really think you're being clever with all that acting the fool."

She contemplated her empty glass, making rings with it on the bar. Suddenly the affectations were dropped and her voice lost its tone of childish plaint.

"I suppose I've got so much into the habit of acting the fool I no longer know when I'm doing it," she said. "I just do it for Potter."

"Potter's not such a fool as he sometimes likes to pretend either."

"No, but he keeps his work and everything serious shut away in a watertight compartment, and doesn't want me to share it. He just wants me to be silly and stupid and amuse him."

"By the way, what was your husband's line in the war?"

"Potter? Oh, he was something frightfully high up in the Guards."

"Never in the Ministry of Supply?"

"Goodness, what an extraordinary idea! No, of course not."

Birkett nodded. "I fancied that was a real Guards' tie. He told me it was only a 'near miss' and he'd never been in uniform."

"He's sometimes got rather a queer sense of humour."

"So I gather."

"He was actually frightfully brave in the war," Mrs. Potter said. "He was wounded in Normandy."

"Yes, I saw that thigh in Delhi when he was taking a swim—nasty time he must have had."

"He was in hospital for over a year. It still causes him bad pain."

"And what happened between you tonight? Bit of a tiff?"

She explained that while they were dressing to go to dinner with the British Ambassador, Potter had made some remark that she had thought unkind. She had begun to cry, and rashly announcing her intention not to accompany him, had gone and shut herself up in the bathroom, confident that he would come and apologize. However he had not done so, and at last, expediently deciding that she would have to initiate the reconciliation herself, she had left the bathroom—only to find that Potter had already gone.

She said unhappily, "I should have known he'd go without me sooner than climb down. You'd probably never suspect it from meeting him, but if Potter thinks he's in the right nothing in the world would make him give way. He can be quite merciless . . ." She told Birkett how once during the war he had put a man on punishment drill and kept him running round the barracks square with a heavy pack until he collapsed; and though he had been severely reprimanded afterwards by his colonel, he had been unrepentant. "Of course in some ways it's a wonderful quality. If he sets himself to do something he just goes on like a steamroller and nothing can stop him. But it also means he can be rather— rather a swine . . ." She made another sticky ring with her glass on the spillings of banana brandy on the bar. She added carefully, without raising her eyes, "That's why sometimes I think he couldn't blame me if I was unfaithful to him."

Well, that's what's called offering yourself on a platter, Birkett thought. And I can't say it'd be any hardship, just to round off the evening.

He finished his drink. "My God, this stuff's certainly firewater."

Mrs. Potter said, "You wouldn't like some proper whisky, would you?"

"What, Scotch? You don't mean you've got some real Scotch?"

"Yes, we got a ration from the Embassy. Shall I fetch it?"

"I wouldn't stop you. Only it's too gloomy down here—let's take it to my room."

She avoided his eyes. "Why not?"

They went upstairs. He waited in the corridor while she went into her room, and when she came out again she meekly placed the bottle in his hands with a kind of symbolic gesture of submission. They went along to his room where he poured out a glass for her, but she shook her head.

"I don't want any."

"I'm not so keen myself," he said.

"Then why did you suggest coming up here?"

"You know very well."

She said nothing.

"You're a bonny girl, you know," he said. He felt less interested in her now and wondered if it was worth the bother; he would have been happy to skip it and go to bed by himself. Still, now that he'd got her up here, he could hardly back out, so best foot forward. "Very bonny, indeed."

"We really shouldn't," she said.

"You're right. Better behave ourselves." He took her in his arms as if against his better nature, as if passion could no longer be withstood. She yielded without protest. But a minute later he suddenly became aware of a hard pressure under his left armpit— good God, the gun, he'd quite forgotten it. Just then her arm brushed against the hard bulk beneath his shirt. He instantly detached himself and moved to the bed. "Here, let's get this bedspread off. Neither of us are children, so let's stop beating about the bush. Get yourself into bed."

He retired to the bathroom, removed his bush-shirt, and unfastened the gun harness. She couldn't have guessed what it was, he thought. Still, not like me to overlook a detail like that. Black mark for carelessness. And don't let it happen again.

He reached up to a high ventilator and stowed the harness and gun out of sight on the ledge. He thought it was all to the good that she would be worried about Potter coming back; she would have to skip off quick. He didn't want her around all night. Any nonsense and he'd just tell her straight out that a roll in the hay was one thing and sleep another, and he liked to sleep alone.

He opened the bathroom door, stepped back into the room and stopped dead.

He saw that the bed was empty. The cover that he had removed had been spread over it smoothly, proclaiming its suspense from use as emphatically as a dust-sheet.

He looked round and saw Mrs. Potter at the dressing-table. She was still fully dressed. She had tidied her hair and repaired her make-up. Their eyes met in the mirror as she put a finishing touch to her lips.

"Sorry I'm afraid I'm being rather a disappointment to you," she said. She screwed the top on her lipstick and dropped it into her bag. She nodded to the whisky bottle on the dressing-table. "I'll leave that for you. Perhaps it'll be some consolation."

Birkett said, "What's the idea?"

"If you don't mind my saying so, I think you take rather a lot for granted."

"What d'you mean?"

"Because a girl lets herself be kissed, it doesn't necessarily mean she's willing to go to bed."

He felt that dangerous burst of rage. "You know ruddy well you were leading me on."

"I'm sorry, it was wrong of me. If you want to know, I've never been unfaithful to my husband. I'm devoted to him—I feel rather mean about some of the things I said tonight. And if ever I were unfaithful to him, it wouldn't be just out of spite after some stupid quarrel—or with so little feeling." She started for the door.

"You're not going yet."

He reached the door first. She came to a standstill, her way barred.

"Oh dear, you're not going to be difficult are you? I've said I'm sorry, so do please be nice." Her voice had returned to the tone of plaintive appeal as she reassumed the childish affectation, erecting it as a barrier for defence.

Birkett did not move. "You know what they call girls who do that?"

"Do what?" The black curled lashes fluttered innocently over the wide china-blue eyes.

"Come off it."

"Then stop being a naughty boy."

"Christ Almighty, 'naughty boy'! What do you think I am? A ruddy little kid?"

He grabbed her roughly. She struggled, but the struggling only provoked his violence and after a minute she desisted and abandoned herself, frozen and impassive, to his embrace; and soon his passion, with neither resistance nor response to feed it, began to lose its impetus, and then was gone.

He abruptly released her. Her face was drained of colour.

"Sorry," he said. "Ruddy silly of me. Sorry."

She went to the door without a word.

"Hang on, take the whisky," he said. "I don't want it."

She ignored him. She went out without looking round and closed the door.

Birkett stood without moving for a minute. Then he went to the dressing-table and poured some more whisky into the toothmug.

He drank the whisky carefully like a medicine, standing beside the dressing-table but not looking at himself in the mirror. He remembered the gun in the bathroom: he must put it away before he went to bed.

He finished the drink and poured himself another. He drank it slowly, and then put down the toothmug on the dressing-table and began to undress.

He went into the bathroom, washed and cleaned his teeth vigorously, and then returned to the room, switched off the light by the door and got into bed.

He remembered the gun again. He was tempted to leave it until the morning. But no, he had only forgotten it because he had been thinking about Mrs. Potter. And he was not going to get slack on her account.

He got out of bed and groped his way to the light-switch. He fetched the gun from the bathroom, locked it away in the suitcase, put the suitcase in the bottom of the wardrobe, and then switched off the light again and returned to bed.

Now, I'm going to sleep, he thought. I'm going to relax the tensions in my body and empty my mind, and fall at once into a deep sleep; and I'm going to remain asleep until six-thirty in the morning and then wake up with my head clear and my body refreshed . . .

He was dismayed to find that sleep did not come. He felt a deep-seated ache in his heart. It seemed to grow worse each minute.

He tried to put Mrs. Potter out of his mind. He reminded himself of his success with Mathai and his exhilaration as he had driven back in the jeep, trying to recapture the feeling of power and invincibility, of being like the cheetah at whose yawn every animal trembled, relaxed and self-sure, the Lord of the Plain . . .

The Lord of the Plain. My God, that was good. The Lord who spread such fear that a cheap little gazelle dared to laugh in his face.

No, skip the cheetah. The irony of that memory only made the ache worse . . .

He had just fallen at last into a doze when he heard the crunch of a car on the drive.

That must be Potter coming back, he thought.

He imagined Potter entering the room, and Mrs. Potter sitting up in bed to tell him about her ordeal, garnishing the story to amuse him with naive comical touches that made her self seem all the more innocent, Birkett all the more ridiculous. He groaned aloud. He wondered how he could face them at breakfast tomorrow.

He heard the clock near the maidan strike the hour. He heard it again an hour later. He was still awake when presently dawn crept into the room.

Oh, Mr. Middleton,
I've got such a pain . . .

2

He did not see the Potters at breakfast. He went down early to avoid them, then took his walking-stick and set out for a walk. The sun had just risen over the mountains. The shadows of pagodas pointed their parallel fingers across the Durbar Square. He made a circuit of the square, and then continued his walk along a dusty road leading out of the town.

The sun on his shoulders grew quickly hotter. He kept up a brisk pace for several miles until he reached the foot of a hill. A long flight of steps, flanked with stone Buddahs, led up the precipitous slope to the gold-encrusted Swayanbunath Pagoda whose four watchful eyes, at each point of the compass, surveyed the countryside. He started up the steps without pause. He felt the perspiration begin to prick. Damp patches spread quickly under his arms and across the back of his bush-shirt. Good, that's the way to get all that rubbish out of my system, he thought. The wetter the better. A good morning's walking, and I'll be able to see it in perspective—look anybody I like in the eye.

He reached the top of the steps. He made a smart tour of the pagoda and its attendant shrines, paused a few moments to take in the distant view of the town, and then descended the steps again and set off across country to another objective of interest.

He walked all morning and returned to the hotel soon after midday, then took a cold tub, put on fresh clothes and went down to lunch.

Potter and his wife were already seated at their table next to his own. Mrs. Potter, engaged in inconsequential chatter, saw him enter and was momentarily put off her stride. She attempted a smile, but it was strained and awkward. Potter followed her look. He grinned.

"Hello, old man," he greeted Birkett. "Well, what mischief have you been up to this morning?"

"Mischief? I've just been doing some rubber-necking." Birkett's voice lacked the lightness he had intended. He had persuaded himself this morning that Mrs. Potter would have discreetly refrained from mentioning last night's occurrence to her husband. Now Potter's words, as well as his manner, convinced him otherwise. They had been intended to needle him. "What mischief have you been up to this morning?"—after the mischief, he was saying in effect, that we all know you were up to last night.

He avoided their eyes as he sat down, dismayed by the tension that he felt in their presence. The morning's efforts had all gone for nothing. He fixed his gaze on one of the Rana portraits on the wall, then he glanced at the boy who was serving him—there was something like a smirk on his face.

Christ, had he been made the laughing-stock of the whole hotel?

"Oh, how scrumptious!" he heard Mrs. Potter exclaiming. "It's queen's pudding-gone-wrong! I must ask Mr. Wilson how he does it. Whenever I try to make it go wrong like that it always insists on going right."

She ought to be in a kid's high chair with a bib and tucker, Birkett thought. And that's the woman who thinks herself too good for me. Why, only last week I had a woman, right out of Mrs. Potter's class, risking her reputation for me, who'd have given her eyes to be in Mrs. Potter's shoes last night. And I'd only have to lift my little finger for her to come out here now . . .

It occurred to him that it might not be a bad idea at that. That'd show 'em. They'd laugh on the other side of their faces if they saw a pretty girl like Lakshmi sitting at his table, watching him with those big adoring eyes.

He wondered why he had not thought of it before. The idea alone made him feel better. By Jove, he'd do it. If he sent her a telegram this afternoon, she could catch the morning's plane. She could be here by this time tomorrow.

Now that he had made the decision, he could scarcely wait to finish his lunch to dispatch the telegram. He decided not to trust Wilson but to send it himself from the telegraph office. He skipped coffee and drove round in the jeep. He sent the telegram at the fastest rate, then returned cheerfully to the hotel for his customary after-lunch nap. But once more sleep escaped him, as he became increasingly possessed by anxiety that something would go wrong and Lakshmi fail to turn up. He imagined all the possible catastrophes that could occur: the telegram going astray, Lakshmi's hosts discovering her intentions and preventing her departure—or even Lakshmi herself deciding that after all the adventure was too foolhardy.

His telegram had been reply-paid and he had expected an answer by the evening. But it did not come and he passed another poor night. Doubts even assailed him, as he lay sleepless in the dark, about the sincerity of Lakshmi's extravagant declarations to him in Delhi.

He heard the maidan clock strike at one and two, and again at five. It was the second night running that he had been awake at five o'clock.

There was still no telegram for him in the morning. He drove to the telegraph office.

"No, nothing has come, sir," the clerk assured him. "If anything comes I will see it is delivered at once."

There was nothing by midday. He decided nevertheless to meet the daily plane, and drove out to the airfield. He found the reception building almost deserted. He had to go up to the control tower for information, and was told the plane would be an hour late. He walked up and down near the reception building, slashing with his walking-stick at the blue flowers growing in the tall grass beside the path, counting the fallen heads as he lopped them off. He had reached two hundred and thirty when a speck of silver glinted in the sky over the mountains. A minute later the aircraft dropped down over the paddies and hit the runway with a squeal of rubber, bounced into the air, and then settled down comfortably for its run in.

It taxied up to the reception building and came to a stop. The passengers began to alight. A tall grey-haired Indian came out, followed by two or three little smiling Nepalese, and then an Indian woman in a blue sari. He recognised Lakshmi.

Her face was radiant as she came up. Her eyes shone. She pressed his hand tightly. She could not speak for happiness.

"Well, nice to see you," he said. "Glad you could make it." He was astonished to find he felt awkward with her. It was as if she was not the person he had expected, but some stranger who had turned up in her stead. He felt none of the pleasure in her arrival that he had anticipated, but only a sense of anti climax. All the anxiety and suspense of the last twenty-four hours suddenly seemed absurd. He resented her for being the cause of them.

They went into the building.

"Must have given you a bit of a surprise to get my telegram yesterday, didn't it?" he said, to make conversation.

She shook her head.

"No, I knew it would come," she said radiantly. "I knew all the time."

He felt a burst of annoyance at this presumption. She evidently supposed that he had been driven to send for her by some irresistible compulsion. He felt tempted to disillusion her, and point out that he had only done so because of circumstances that had nothing to do with her, and he only prevented himself by abruptly changing the subject, saying, "Now, where's your passport?" and occupying himself with the formalities of the customs; and by the time these were concluded and they were ready to depart in the jeep, he had his feelings under control again.

"Well, what yarn did you spin your friends in Delhi?" he asked as they drove off. "Don't tell me old Phantom Fanny's been put to work again?"

"No, I told them the truth," Lakshmi said.

"What, you didn't tell them you were going off to Nepal for some high jinks?"

"Yes, I knew it was hopeless trying to pretend—only I didn't say Nepal but Darjeeling, and I didn't say who you were. If they want to tell my husband, I don't care," she said, glowing. "I don't care about anything except that I'm here."

"You were lucky to find me at the airfield," he said. "I only went on the off-chance. Your telegram must have gone astray."

"I didn't send a telegram."

"No?" He had guessed as much, but affected surprise. He felt a fresh access of annoyance at the lack of consideration that had caused him so many hours of unnecessary nervous stress. "Well, that was good money down the drain. Didn't you realise my telegram was reply-paid?"

"Yes, but it didn't arrive until nine o'clock last night, and I didn't have a chance to send a reply. And this morning it seemed pointless since I thought it would arrive no sooner than mine."

"It would have arrived a good bit sooner, especially as your plane was held up," Birkett said. "Anyhow, never mind."

They arrived at the Everest and Wilson, whom Birkett had tipped off about the possibility of Lakshmi's arrival, had given her the double room next to his and decorated it with a vase of flowers.

"I thought they might help to take the blight off the place, but I'm afraid it would have been asking too much of any flowers, never mind these filthy little weeds from our garden he said. "Anyhow, there are two of you now so perhaps you'll be able to console each other."

He retired and left them alone.

"Nice to know we're not going to have the Purity League banging on the door," Birkett said. His temper had improved since entering the room, as Lakshmi's physical attractions had impressed themselves upon him again. "Well, let's look at you. You know, you're still looking very bonny my dear."

She tentatively abandoned her packing and entered his embrace; but soon detached herself again and returned to her suitcase, keeping her face averted.

"What's up?" he asked.

"Nothing, why?"

"Come off it, what's the matter?"

"I don't know, I just have the feeling that you aren't really pleased to see me. You sounded in the jeep almost as if you hated me."

"You don't think I'd have asked you to come if I didn't want to see you?"

She shook her head. "I don't know, I expect it's just getting used to each other again." She took a little packet from her case and handed it to him. "Just a tiny present—I remember you said you'd lost yours in China."

It was a gold pencil engraved with his initials.

"Thanks, that's very nice," he said. "Nice of you to think of it—can't have had much time for shopping since last night, can you?"

"I got it the day you left at the same time as my visa. I wanted to have them ready."

He took her out for a walk round the bazaar. The present of the gold pencil displeased as much as it gratified him, because it placed him under a moral obligation to give her a present of at least equal value in return. He did not believe in giving women presents on principle: they were most of them spoilt enough already by men pandering to them, and if their favours could only be won

128

with bribery, so far as he was concerned they could keep them—
and though circumstances had occasionally obliged him to make
an exception, it had never been to the extent of more than some
little trinket. He reckoned that the pencil would have been cheap
at a hundred rupees. And he had never given a present costing a
hundred rupees in his life. The problem gnawed at him as they
strolled through the bazaar. The shopkeepers, squatting in their
little open-fronted shops with carved wooden pillars, importuned
them with appeals to pause and inspect their wares. He urged
Lakshmi on.

"They're all tourist traps in this street," he said.

"I don't want to buy anything—only to look."

"You don't know these robbers, once you stop you've had it."
He kept her moving until presently they came to a curio shop piled
with junk that looked less like a snare for artless Europeans. The
fat proprietor's indifference to them was an added reassurance.
"Now, this is the sort of place to find the real genuine stuff."

They paused before the shop and Lakshmi's eye fell on a rusting
tin containing Tibetan jewelry. She pulled out a necklace of green
jade Buddhas. Her eyes shone with appreciation. She was about
to exclaim over its beauty when she realized that Birkett might
think she was hinting, and she dropped the necklace back in the
box.

"Do you fancy it?" All that Tibetan stuff came over by the
cartload and was as cheap as dirt. The necklace couldn't cost more
than ten or twenty rupees, but the fact that she'd picked it out
herself gave him an excuse to buy it and call it quits.

He poked the necklace with the end of his walking-stick and
asked the shopkeeper, "How much is that bit of trash?"

The shopkeeper pulled the necklace out of the box and tossed
it on the floor.

"Three hundred rupees."

"Come off it, you're kidding." Three hundred rupees was about
twenty-five pounds. "You mean thirteen, don't you?" The shopkeeper
opened another tin and took out three hundred-rupee notes. He
waved them at Birkett and put them back in the tin.

"Christ, what, for this thing?" He poked the necklace with his stick again. "You ruddy old robber, you must think we're daft." He pulled Lakshmi away in disgust. They continued up the street. "Sorry, but these people think we're made of brass, and they've got to learn their lesson. Pity, I'd have liked to get it for you. I'd expected him to say a hundred rupees, and then I wouldn't have hesitated."

This declaration of intention satisfactorily solved the problem, and he decided that no present was now needed. Perhaps some little token when she pushed off, if he felt it was called for.

Their mutual preoccupation with the bazaar had obscured the awkwardness between them; but returning along the empty road to the hotel, obliged once more to make conversation, it was again apparent. They turned through the hotel gates and started up the drive. Just then Mrs. Potter came down the steps with her husband. A good hundred yards separated the two couples so that they remained face to face for what seemed to Birkett an uncomfortable length of time. He could see the Potters' restrained curiosity about his Indian companion, but he decided to leave introductions until dinner and meanwhile to keep them guessing. They drew nearer. He gave a brief nod and said, "'Evening."

"Hello, old man," Potter grinned. Mrs. Potter smiled brightly. They passed by.

Lakshmi was silent for several moments and then asked, "Who were those people?"

"Just a couple staying at the hotel." He had noticed something more than casual interest in her tone. "Why?"

"I only wondered."

They entered the hotel and he said, "Well, I expect you'd like a bath before dinner. I'll get the boys to lay it on."

Dinner passed in an atmosphere of subdued formality. Birkett noticed that Lakshmi's attention was concentrated on Mrs. Potter, whom she was submitting to that particular form of appraisal that a woman reserves for other members of her sex.

After dinner they took a stroll in the garden before turning in. Lakshmi said evenly, "I'm still not sure why you sent for me."

"Look, why do you think? You think it was just for the fun of sending a telegram?"

"I don't know, but you're quite different from what you were like in Delhi. I knew you weren't in love with me and I was nothing to you but a rather pleasant distraction. But you didn't resent me like you do now."

"You're imagining it."

She was silent. After a while she said, "It's nothing to do with that woman, is it?"

"What woman?"

"That lovely fair woman with the blue eyes at the next table— Mrs. Potter."

"Lovely! Good God! What on earth could it be to do with her?"

"I don't know, but it was impossible not to notice how it disturbed you when we passed her on the drive and then again when you saw her at dinner. I wondered if there'd been anything between you."

He knew that half-truths were always safer than outright denials, and he laughed and said, "Good for you. Full marks for powers of observation. Yes, she had a row with her husband the other night, drank too much of the local firewater, and gave me the works. She flapped her eyelashes at me, and suggested polishing off her husband's bottle of Scotch whisky upstairs. I was all for that! Only I'm afraid I drew the line at providing further entertainment, so I gave her a pat on the bottom and sent her home. And of course a woman scorned . . . Well, I've been giving her a wide berth as much as possible, but another couple of days and it'll all be forgotten. Anyhow, it had nothing to do with my sending for you."

"I just wondered. Anyhow, I must go to bed. I didn't sleep at all last night and I'm terribly tired."

He said goodnight at her door and went along to his own room. But the absurdity of finding himself alone when the woman who only a few days ago had given herself to him passionately, and who had flown here from Delhi for the specific purpose of doing so again, was only a few feet away on the other side of the wall dividing their rooms, made him regret that he had not taken more trouble to smooth her down with a few reassuring words. Well, the night was still young.

He left his room and tapped lightly on her door.

"Can I come in?"

"Just a minute."

He heard her opening the wardrobe, shifting some hangers on the rail to find some garment. He felt newly irritated at being asked to wait as if he had been Wilson or the roomboy.

"What's up?" he said "I'm an informal chap, you can skip the full evening dress."

"You can come in now."

She was wrapping herself round with a dressing-gown. She showed no pleasure or otherwise at his reappearance.

"I was taught never to go to bed on a misunderstanding," he said. "And I fancied you might sleep easier if we cleared things up a bit."

She shook her head. "There's nothing to clear up, is there?"

"I know I've been a bit short with you once or twice and given you the idea I wasn't glad to see you. My fault entirely, though in fact it was more of a compliment than you thought. My nerves had been so keyed up for twenty-four hours, fretting that you wouldn't turn up, that when you actually arrived they just started to snap like piano strings. That's all it was."

"Of course," she said. "I'm sure we'll both feel quite different in the morning. Now I just want to sleep."

"All right, I'll be off. I only wanted to make sure you weren't lying here regretting you'd come."

"Thank you. It was very thoughtful."

He returned to his room. Well, at least he'd had the good sense to recognize a brick wall when he saw it, and not repeat the dismal spectacle of the other night. Nevertheless he felt disturbed, and there was that ache under his heart again. And once again, for the third night running, the more he tried to induce sleep the more it evaded him, and he heard the clock strike every hour from eleven until three—and then did not hear it again or remember anything more until he awoke to find himself sweating in the hot yellow light of the sun slanting through the window. He looked at his watch. It was five minutes past ten.

He felt as shocked and guilty as if he had caught himself in the midst of some unspeakable crime. He had not slept until ten o'clock for as long as he could remember. Sleeping late in the morning was a self-indulgence of which he had always felt a peculiar horror. It was the first concession to softness. He wondered how he could have let himself slip so far.

Then he remembered it was Sunday. It was today that he was meeting Krishna Mathai on the maidan.

I need all my equipment in perfect working order today above all days, he thought. I can't afford to miss a trick, or young Mathai will slip through my fingers. And that'll be so much for the job— and so much for me.

He got out of bed and opened the door.

"Boy! Bring me some cold water! Quick sharp!"

He felt better after the cold tub. It removed some of the guilt of the late rising.

It's those two women who've messed me up, he thought. And it's my fault for forgetting all the lessons I've learnt— forgetting that whatever guise women wear they're all out to destroy you, whether it's with the swift stroke of a dagger or the slow insidious poison that softens and conquers you by degrees—like that woman in the next room who last night began injecting me with the poison of her moods. Well, I've caught myself just in time, and she'd better watch her step because any more of her tricks and I'm packing her off home on the next plane.

Chapter Eleven

He found Lakshmi at breakfast in the dining-room. She greeted him cheerfully as he sat down. "Sleep all right?" he asked her.

"Yes, I feel marvellous this morning."

A boy approached the table with a brown paper bag. He placed it beside Birkett. "Your sandwiches, sir."

"Sandwiches? I didn't order any sandwiches."

"No, I did," Lakshmi said. She thanked the boy who went off. "I thought it would be nice to have a picnic."

He said sharply, "You did, eh? Well, supposing I didn't?"

"But they're only for me—the boy made a mistake." She took the brown paper bag and put it beside her chair. "I'm just going to browse around by myself."

He was mollified—evidently she'd seen which way the wind was blowing and wisely decided not to hang round his neck. "I see, that's different. Yes, I'll be glad of a chance to catch up with a spot of work."

"You have started a new book?"

"No fear, I haven't been here long enough for that—just notes to write up."

He took a short brisk walk after breakfast and then returned to his room. He devoted the morning to exercises, learned in the yoga ashram near Madras, to bring himself up to pitch after the disruptive effect of the last few days.

He first spread a blanket on the floor and, wearing only a towel round his waist, lay down on his back. He relaxed his muscles, giving attention to each part of his body in turn, dealing separately with each lingering point of tension. Then, satisfied that his body was at rest, he relaxed his mind making it to all intents and purposes a perfect blank.

He maintained this state for twenty minutes. Then he sat up cross-legged and devoted himself to breathing exercises. He followed these with an exercise in concentration upon various states of mind, experiencing in turn grief, joy, anger, amusement, ringing the changes at ever decreasing intervals so that one moment tears seemed on the point of flooding from his eyes, at the next he was shaking with mirth. He repeated the exercise with convictions instead of emotions, now becoming an ardent opponent of Communism, now its supporter; now a violent defender of racial segregation and white superiority, now a fanatical religious believer exhorting an audience of atheists to turn to God. He knew that this power to simulate conviction—or momentarily acquire it—was the most important instrument at his disposal. For the majority of mankind, lacking convictions of their own, were drawn to men of strong conviction as though to a powerful magnet: and there was nothing, however demonstrably false, however much opposed to their own interests, that they could not be persuaded to believe was the truth. They would readily believe that black was white, that their enslavement by tyrants was an enviable state of freedom, that a glib over-sexed madman in a nightgown performing moonlight love-rites in the New Forest was the new Messiah—that death in battle, from which no conceivable benefit could come for the multitude who gave their lives, was a glorious sacrifice for the common cause.

Lastly he set about performing an exercise to measure the effect of the morning's work. It consisted of sitting cross-legged in the "lotus" position, and imagining two cords—one attached to each wrist—passing over pulleys on the ceiling, with baskets dangling from their opposite ends to balance the weight of his arms—and then pebbles being added one by one to the baskets, each pebble imperceptibly increasing the tension on the cords until at last his wrists—if his concentration had achieved sufficient intensity—would be pulled away from his sides, and his arms, without any conscious effort on his part: lifted to an outstretched position. If, on the other hand, concentration was lacking, his arms would remain inert at his sides. Now, as he mentally added pebbles to the baskets, his arms rose slowly as though in response to an irresistible pull, and in a few minutes they were outstretched at the level of his shoulders.

He let his arms remain at the outstretched position for ten minutes, the support of the imaginary cords giving him the same immunity from stress and pain as a person under hypnosis, and then dropped them slowly as clockhands as he imagined the pebbles in the baskets gradually being unloaded. The morning's efforts had not been wasted. He rose with satisfaction from his hard seat on the blanket, dressed, and went downstairs for a light lunch.

He returned to his room after lunch, lay down on the bed, and with a return of his old facility fell promptly asleep. He woke after exactly twenty minutes and spent the afternoon repeating the exercises of the morning, increasing the length of time devoted to each. He continued them without interruption until five o'clock when he took a cold tub and a cup of tea, and a few minutes' relaxation on the bed. A glow of satisfaction possessed his body. He felt like some musical instrument that had been repaired and tuned and brought back to a state of perfect precision, and now calmly waited the demands to be made upon it, knowing that whatever chords might be struck it would not fail with its prompt and harmonious response.

Thus, shortly before six, he set off in the jeep for the meeting with Mathai.

2

He parked the jeep at the north-east corner of the maidan, took his walking-stick, and strolled on to the open expanse of grass. His whole being proclaimed his enjoyment of the pleasant surroundings, the crisp air of late afternoon that bore the tang of distant mountains. He saw a figure in a white suit waiting under the fringe of eucalyptus trees, but gave it only a casual glance.

Presently he heard footsteps behind him. He looked round as the white-suited figure hastened up.

"Hello, it's young Mathai! Just out for a breather, eh?"

Mathai burst out, "Sir, I have come to tell you I cannot carry out the duty. I have absolutely decided." His tense aggressive manner showed how desperately he had been screwing himself up for this moment. "I am sorry, sir, but I am not afraid—"

"Steady on, steady on," Birkett laughed good-naturedly, raising his hands in mock-surrender. "Take it easy, old chap."

"I am not afraid of the consequences. I cannot carry out the duty because I have responsibility to my family. You can do what you like but it will make no difference, and I advise you to be careful—because if necessary I shall sacrifice my career and report everything to my Ambassador."

"My dear chap, I'm afraid I haven't taken in a single word," Birkett said. "Good Lord, I hope you don't make a habit of pouncing out like that on poor old fellows taking an evening stroll. It could give one a real turn in the dark." His apparent surprise at seeing Mathai was so convincing that Mathai himself paused momentarily, wondering if something could have gone wrong. Birkett continued in the same light manner, "Let's take things quietly for a moment or two. By Jove, what a grand evening, eh! Look at that sky, Mathai! Doesn't that make you wish you were a painter? Or perhaps you are, you're an artistic-looking chap. I mean, take your hands . . ."

Mathai glanced at his hands and removed them from sight.

"No, sir, I have never painted," he said.

"No, of course, you've chosen writing as the best means to express yourself—and much wiser to stick to one thing and not disperse your talent." He took Mathai's arm paternally. "By Jove, that's a nice sight! Look, that little chappie with the kite!"

He paused, his arm still linked affectionately with Mathai's, watching the small Nepalese boy in jodhpurs and woolly cap run across the turf, pursued by the kite bobbing and dancing on the end of a string.

"You know, that's the best sight in the world, Mathai—a youngster having a bit of fun!" Birkett exclaimed with enjoyment. He watched keenly as the kite swerved into the air, dived abruptly to earth again. "Bad luck, young fellow . . . By the way, how are those bonny youngsters of yours, Mathai? That poor little chappie quite got over the earache?"

"Yes, sir. Sir, I wish to make quite clear—"

Birkett suddenly chuckled and squeezed Mathai's arm. "You know, I like you, Mathai! Blowed if I know why, but dammit, I like you! Let's sit down, shall we?" He stretched himself on the grass, and Mathai squatted reluctantly beside him.

"Sir, I have told you my decision."

"Oh yes, your decision. Don't worry about that, Mathai," Birkett said absently, his attention still fixed on the youthful kite-flyer. "You can forget that whole business. I've got another chap for the job . . . There she goes!"

"I beg your pardon, sir?"

"I said there she goes—the kite. My word, look at it!"

"What did you say about the job, sir?"

"I said I've got this other chap now. Everything buttoned up, so don't give it another thought . . . Watch out, laddie, it's going to have you off your feet!"

Mathai stared at him incredulously. "Who is the other man you have chosen, sir?"

"You ought to know better than to ask me that, Mathai."

"But he is with the Embassy, sir?"

"No, I regret not." Birkett paused briefly in troubled thought, but then abruptly dismissed the worry and said confidently, "But I'm not bothered, he's got plenty of fine qualities to make up for it. He's my chappie all right, there's no doubt about that."

Mathai was clearly trying to adjust himself to the momentous thing that had happened. Birkett's few casual words had suddenly turned his whole world upside down again. It was not only that for three days he had been totally pre-occupied with building up a gigantic edifice of courage, argument and threat with which to confront Major Birkett; it was also that for three days his head had been filled with bitter hatred for him. He had prayed for disaster and sudden death to befall him, seeing him in his mind's eye as such a monster that on first catching sight of him on the maidan it had come as a little shock to discover that after all he was no more than human size, and not breathing fire. And there had been further surprise in his cheerful and friendly manner, and he had suspected a trap.

But was it a trap? Was it not possible that Major Birkett had of his own accord released him from the terrible duty, had spared his life, simply because he, Major Birkett, liked him?

"Watch out! Oh, hard lines!" Birkett shared the little Nepalese child's dismay as his kite came to grief in some telephone wires, already festooned with the tattered remnants of kites like last year's bunting. He called out, "Here, young fellow-me-lad!"

The boy turned from his sorrowful contemplation of the stranded kite. Birkett beckoned, and he approached with little wondering blackberry eyes.

"Here, get yourself a new kite, sonny." Birkett held out a five-rupee note. The boy took it with studied aplomb, trying to conceal his lack of ease. He pushed it into the pocket of his jodhpurs with the black little eyes fixed on Birkett's, retreated a few paces, then suddenly turned and scuttled off like a rabbit.

Mathai felt foolish and ashamed. He only wished that there had been some way of wiping out all his evil and malignant thoughts of the last three days.

"He did not say thank you, sir," he said, pained that yet another injustice to Major Birkett should be added to his own.

"Good Lord, I should hope not!" Birkett said. "I don't want gratitude. I ought to thank him—there's far more pleasure in giving than receiving."

The evidence of goodness in a person always moved Mathai profoundly, and Major Birkett's charity made him feel the prick of tears. He was the sort of man he had always dreamed about as a father. His own father had died when he was a baby and he had partly made up for the lack by creating for himself an imaginary father, whose qualities had included physical courage, goodness of heart, and progressive social ideals.

Now it occurred to him that he had never before met a man who personified these qualities in such marked degree as Major

Birkett. And it filled his heart with joy to remember Major Birkett's expression of liking for him.

Then a sudden anxiety clouded his gladness. He said, "Major Birkett, may I ask a question? Why did you release me from the duty? Am I right in supposing it was consideration for my family?"

Birkett hesitated. He said uncomfortably, "I'd rather not answer that, Mathai."

This evasion seemed to confirm Mathai's fears—that Major Birkett had suspected that he was a coward and weakling and inadequate for the task, and had not released so much as rejected him. He said, "The man you have chosen, he is not married?"

"Yes, wife and son. Lost his young daughter of six last year. Typhus."

"And now his wife must bear another loss. . . . She must lose her husband. That is terrible."

"I'm afraid that's the way it goes."

Mathai was silent. After a while he said, "Sir, I wish to make quite clear that my decision to refuse the duty was made entirely on account of my family."

"It makes no odds now, Mathai."

"It was not because I was afraid, sir."

Birkett said nothing.

"I assure you I was not afraid, sir," Mathai went on. "I have many bad weaknesses, but fortunately cowardice is not amongst them." He realized miserably that his voice had not rung true. Of course he had been greatly afraid. The idea of firing a gun was alone enough to frighten him: he hated loud bangs and obviously, if he fired the gun himself, he would not be able to put his fingers in his ears. He had never fired a gun in his life, and his youth had been over-shadowed by the fear that he might one day have to serve in the army. He repeated, trying to give his voice more conviction, "No, my decision was made solely on account of my family. I had no fear."

"Lucky chap," Birkett said. "I'd have thought that job was enough to put the wind up anybody. This other chap admits he's scared stiff. And so should I be, I can tell you!"

"I do not believe it, sir. You are a soldier and a man of courage."

"Courage doesn't mean the absence of fear, but the ability to beat it."

Mathai perceived the utter stupidity of his lie. It was not only unbelievable but also proof in itself of the cowardice it had been intended to conceal—whereas if only he had had the sense to admit to being afraid he would have won Major Birkett's respect. Yet it had been no more than a partial lie, for it was perfectly true that he had mc1de the decision because of his family and not because of his fear: and he had only denied feeling fear in order to avoid confusing the issue. He would have liked to explain this to Major Birkett now but decided that it was too complicated to put into words, and he would probably confuse .the issue more than ever. And he remained silent, sunk in his shame.

"Cheer up, old chap," Birkett said with an amiable laugh. "Of course you were afraid, but I don't blame you a bit for saying you weren't. Nothing more natural."

"It was foolish to tell a lie, sir."

"Good Lord, we all tell 'em by the dozen. It was only a white lie, anyhow. And it doesn't alter the fact that you were thinking primarily of your family. You quite naturally wanted to make that clear, in case I got hold of the wrong end of the stick. That's all it was, wasn't it?"

Mathai stared in amazement. He thought that Major Birkett must have been reading his mind. "You have put my own thoughts into words, sir. I wanted to explain but was afraid you would not understand."

"Why on earth not? My dear chap, I'd have done exactly the same in your shoes. We're all pretty much alike under the skin, you know. You're not half such a bad fellow as you like to think."

Mathai was possessed by a great happiness at being so well understood. He had never before met anybody of such great understanding and compassion, who could have so readily forgiven a falsehood and relieved his sense of guilt. And he felt a great flood of warmth—of something almost like love for Major Birkett. He said, "You are a wonderful person, sir. You have truly remarkable insight."

"Nonsense, nothing remarkable about it," Birkett said. "Anyhow, I've been through all this before. The other chap's reactions were exactly like yours. He started off by turning the duty down flat. Nothing to do with being afraid or anything like that, just on account of his family. I was about to get tough with him, and then remembered the lesson I'd learned with you. I'll tell you frankly, Mathai, I've always flattered myself on being able to manage people, but after our meeting the other night I was filled with such bitter self-reproach for the clumsy way I'd handled it that I nearly turned the gun on to myself, and I'd like you to know I'm sorry."

"Sir, there is no need—" Mathai protested.

"Oh yes there is, I can't easily forgive myself for it. Anyhow, this time I'd more wisdom than to use threats and I just told this chap, 'Too bad, but let me know if you change your mind.' And of course the next day he was back. He'd begun to see into the thing a bit deeper, just as you'd have done sooner or later with that keen brain of yours."

Mathai beamed, and began to protest modestly, "Oh, sir . . ."

"Don't 'oh sir' me, you've plenty of grey matter, Mathai, so don't try and kid me you're a numskull. You'd have seen just as clearly as this other chap that it's nonsense to say you're prepared to make a sacrifice on your own behalf but not on behalf of your family: because, taking a wider view, your family is simply an extension of yourself, and your family's honour is in your hands. In fact, as this other chap put it to me, 'It's precisely because of my wife and child that I must make the sacrifice, because my failure to do so would dishonour them, betray them—and they could never look at me again without contempt.'"

"But they need not have known, sir," Mathai said. "I had not intended to tell my family of my refusal of the duty."

"No, but even so . . . I'm rather surprised you should feel that makes all the difference. The attitude seems to me a little superficial." He cast Mathai an uneasy glance, as though perceiving for the first time some flaw in his character. "Still, I suppose some people are tougher than others, and provided you felt that, so long as they didn't know about the betrayal, you could look them in the eye—then well and good."

Mathai wondered miserably how he could have made so foolish and shallow an observation, and tried quickly to make amends and retrieve Major Birkett's good opinion of him, saying, "I only meant, of course, that it would make it easier for them if they did not know, sir. Naturally, one's own conscience would still suffer."

"Ah, that's better!" Birkett smiled with relief. "Sorry, I was letting myself doubt your integrity. Yes, I didn't think you were the sort of chap to be satisfied with mere appearances. In fact, I fancy you'd have had just as bad a time with your conscience as this other chap, who went so far as to say that his self-contempt would probably have driven him in the end to take his own life."

"I do not think I would have the courage for that. I now admit frankly, sir, I am a coward."

"You talk as if being a coward was an unalterable fact—like being an Indian or having black hair. Rubbish, it's nothing of the kind. Cowardice and courage are simply attitudes of mind that can be acquired or lost. You're no more a coward than anybody else."

"You are very generous, sir." He hoped that Major Birkett really believed it, though he knew it was not true.

"Anyhow, that's the other chap's worry now. You can forget the whole thing and get on with your book. What about the book, by the way? I want to hear about it."

"It is not important, sir," Mathai said evasively.

"It was important enough to you the other day."

"I will tell you about it another time, sir." He wished Birkett had not mentioned it. The events of the last few days, with the extraordinary demands they had made upon him, had revived a feeling of shame about his literary activities, which he knew had their origins in his weakness of character-for they had been part of the intellectual façade that, like his pacifist beliefs and the myopia that had obliged him to wear glasses, he had developed with certain deliberate intent in order to prove himself unsuitable for military service. And it was not as a writer that he had seen himself in his most secret dreams of success—for literary success could be attained even by cowards and weaklings—but as a great soldier achieving glory and renown by courageous military exploits.

"I want to hear about it now," Birkett said. "What's the theme?"

Mathai reluctantly explained that the story concerned an Indian civil servant, married with two children, who was wrongly convicted of embezzlement and sent to jail. He suffered many months of hardship. Then one day, whilst working with a convict party outside the prison, he managed by a spectacular feat of strength to overcome the warders and escape. And with freedom thus regained, he was able to obtain evidence to prove his innocence and win back domestic love and respect.

When he had finished, Birkett said, "Well, by Jove, he sounds a tough fellow, the way he overpowered those guards and risked a bullet in his back."

"Yes, sir, I have explained that he is a man of strong physique, besides great prowess and courage." He added quickly with a blush, "It is not intended as a self-portrait."

"Nevertheless, it is a self-portrait. There are few first novels that don't contain a self-portrait somewhere, even though, like yours, it's in disguise and highly idealised."

"I have never embezzled money, sir."

"No, the crime stands for something else—perhaps that cowardice you're so worried about."

Mathai felt his cheeks burn again. He said, "But he did not really commit the crime, sir."

Birkett smiled. "No, wasn't that convenient? Nothing like reassuring ourselves that we're misjudged—misjudged by ourselves, if you like—and that we aren't really guilty at all but are going to justify ourselves to the wife and kids, and end up with that love and respect that we're so afraid of losing. Yes, I'm sure you'll write that story with great feeling, Mathai, and best of luck to you . . . Now, let's stroll a bit, shall we? It's getting parky."

The sun, long since gone from the valley, still lingered on the white frieze of mountains above the eucalyptus trees, which seemed to have moved quite near and stood out in sharp definition like a jagged paper cut-out against the sky, with every rockface, every crest of snow, depicted with perfect clarity. It faded to a last warm glow and then was gone; the mountains turned a cold grey and retreated. Dusk dropped quickly, and the shadows darkened under the great leafy branches of the peepul tree in the centre of the maidan.

They approached the tree and paused beside the platform surrounding its trunk, on whose perimeter four stone figures of Gurkha soldiers with rifles and packs—one at each point of the compass—stood gazing out across the grass.

Birkett said, "So this is where His Majesty will take the salute at the Tattoo."

"Yes, I am lucky, sir, there are seats on the platform allotted to all the Embassies, so I shall have a good view."

"It'd have been very convenient. I don't know how we're going to get this other chap a seat on the platform, but we'll find some way or other."

Mathai stared at him. "You mean—it is to happen at the Tattoo, sir?"

"That's the idea."

Mathai was speechless. He turned his gaze from Birkett to the dark shadows on the platform. He had never thought of it happening on such an occasion. He had pictured it against the background of the Royal Palace when the King was alone. It had seemed terrible enough to him even then, but now he was filled with new awe at the thought of it occurring here at the great public event before the distinguished assembly of Nepalese and foreign officials in colourful regalia on the plat form, the massed troops, the vast crowds of townsfolk and villagers from every part of the valley, the Sherpas and peasants down from the hills . . .

"Yes, it'll be quite an event," Birkett said. "We're going to see history in the making. Take it from me, ten years from now it'll be in all the books, and that chap's name will be a household word. Funny to realize it: he'll go up on to that platform as an ordinary insignificant chap like hundreds of millions of others whose names are unknown, whose lives are meaningless, whose deaths are unmourned—and then with one supreme act of selfless courage he's going to bring himself before the eyes of the world in shining glory! Just think of it, Mathai! He'll be enshrined amongst the great heroes of the revolution! There'll be statues raised, streets named after him and songs composed in his honour—the kids'll be singing 'em in every school! And what joy and pride for his son, who'll be feted as a hero and shine with his father's glory—and feel closer than ever before to his father, whose spirit he'll find kept alive wherever he goes on the face of the globe!" Birkett's eyes shone with inspiration at the vision of greatness that man could achieve. Then he came abruptly back to earth. "Anyhow, time I was off."

"Sir, you did not answer my question," Mathai said. "I wish to know, why you decided to release me from the duty."

Birkett said awkwardly, "My dear chap, what difference does it make now? Let's skip it, there's no point . . ." His eyes had fallen as if by accident on Mathai's delicate hands with the slender beautiful fingers, which held him in some momentary distraction; then quickly, tactfully, he switched them away. "No point in raking all that over now."

"It was because you thought I was a weakling, wasn't it, Sir?" He held out his hands and looked at them unhappily. "I have noticed you keep looking at my hands. It is true, they're like a girl's."

"Oh, my dear chap . . ." Birkett stood uncomfortably for a moment. His face was deeply pained. Suddenly he reached out with an impulsive movement and seized Mathai's hands in his own. "My dear chap, they're beautiful hands. They were never meant for holding a gun. They're the hands of an artist, a writer . . ." Thus might a saint seize the gnawed stumps of a leper's hands.

It was a gesture of infinite compassion. It was a gesture for whose achievement he had spent the morning and afternoon cross-legged on the blanket working assiduously at his exercises. And it was a gesture that seemed to Mathai the most tender and beautiful that he had ever witnessed; and his eyes filled with tears.

Major Birkett is a true Christian, he thought. He is the only Christian I have ever met who truly follows the teaching of the great Christian Messiah. He is one of the few true Christians alive today, and I feel towards him a great love. I would do anything in the world for him. I would even lay down my life. It occurred to him that perhaps the way to do so was still open, and elation possessed him as he was seized by the notion of declaring a reversal of his decision, and entreating Major Birkett to consider the advantage his position in the Embassy gave him over the other man, and accept him for the duty. He was about to break out eagerly with this proposal, when the sobering thought occurred to him that perhaps he was acting a little hastily. The elation passed. He decided that even his great love for Major Birkett could not sufficiently swell and sustain the dismal little stock of his courage. And feeling unworthy of Major Birkett's beautiful gesture, he withdrew his hands and said lamely, "I hope we may meet again, sir."

"Not much point, Mathai."

"I would like to think it over again, sir." He had not intended to say this but he could not bear that their parting should be final. "I mean, in case anything happened to the other man—if he was ill—"

"It would take more than illness to stop a chappie like that! No, sorry, Mathai, I've given him my promise and can't go back on it. Still, I'd be glad to meet you for another chat. Make it Friday, same time, the bridge over the Bhagmati on the Tahachal road. Now, good-bye, Mathai—and good luck with that book."

"Good-bye, sir." He tried to make his hand hard and strong as he extended it to meet Major Birkett's, but it collapsed in the iron grip and was crushed into flabby passivity. And as he watched the erect soldierly figure turn and walk briskly away, merging into the darkness of the maidan, his heart was stabbed with new pain.

He must despise me, he thought. I would like him to love me like a father, but he must despise me because I can't even shake hands like a man.

He lifted his hands and gazed at them miserably. I couldn't do it, he thought. I haven't the courage. I am a weakling. My hands are like a girl's and you can count my ribs like a piedog's. And my nature's as cowardly and contemptible as a piedog's—you've only to reach for an imaginary stone and I cringe, and before you can lift your arm and pretend to throw, I've turned my mangy drooping tail and slunk away.

Chapter Twelve

Birkett returned to the Everest in a good mood. Things were shaping up nicely, he thought, very nicely indeed. And he looked forward to the evening with Lakshmi. After all, she was a bonny girl, and he'd earned a bit of recreation. He quite fancied a rough-and-tumble tonight.

She was not in her room. He found her down in the bar, the centre of a circle of men that included the red-headed Hobson. They were all very jolly and making much of her. Her eyes shone as she basked in their admiration.

"Hello, here's the man himself," said Hobson. "Here's the gallant Major."

Birkett felt the dampening effect that his arrival had on them. Even Lakshmi's eyes lost some of their brightness.

She's getting above herself, he thought. I didn't bring her out to Nepal to make an exhibition of herself.

He felt all the more annoyed because a minute ago he had been in such a good mood, full of the most generous intentions towards her.

"Well, we are looking pleased with yourself tonight," he said.

"Been enjoying ourselves, haven't we, my dear?" Hobson said. His tone was patronizing, and he stood proprietorially beside Lakshmi. "I found her poking around the bazaar on her own. Couldn't allow that, could we, my dear? Might have fallen into the hands of a big, bad Nepalese wolf. So I took her under my protective wing."

"Very nice of you, I'm sure," Birkett said indifferently.

"Well, have a drink on it."

"No, thanks. Ready for dinner?" he asked Lakshmi.

"You don't mind Mr. Hobson joining us?" she said. "He's really been so wonderful—he's given up practically the whole day for me."

"Obviously a great hardship," Birkett said. "No, I don't mind. He can eat where he likes."

They went into the dining-room. Hobson carried on a half-joking flirtation with Lakshmi throughout the meal, making humorous pretence of sharing some naughty secret with her. After the pudding Lakshmi took the little silver box from her handbag and began to spread a pan leaf with lime.

"Christ, you're not up to that game again?" Birkett said. "I don't like it."

"I'm sorry, I just did it from habit," Lakshmi said sweetly, and began to put the pan away.

"You can do what you like so far as I'm concerned, my dear." Hobson said.

"I can see you'd be better off with me out of the way," Birkett said. He pushed back his chair. "I'll say good night." He rose abruptly and left the dining-room. He fetched his stick and took a brisk walk. On his return he saw two shadowy figures strolling across the lawn. He fixed his gaze firmly ahead and continued up the drive.

The cheap bitch, he thought. I'm not going to be messed up by a cheap bitch like that again. I'm going to shut her from my mind.

He fell asleep easily enough. But an hour later he woke from a nightmare, convinced that Lakshmi and Hobson were at that moment in bed together and making love. He listened for sounds from Lakshmi's room. He could hear nothing. But the wall was thick—and anyhow they might have gone to Hobson's room. He told himself that he didn't care a hoot. But the words were belied by the pain gnawing into his heart.

The next morning he was already at breakfast when Lakshmi entered the dining-room. She sat down smiling.

"Well, I'll always be grateful to you for bringing me to Nepal," she said. "Even if it didn't work out quite as we intended, I've had a lovely time. I can hardly bear to leave it—but I think I'd better take this afternoon's plane."

"Why?"

"There's no point in staying as you obviously don't want me."

"What about what's-his-name? That overgrown schoolboy? Doesn't he want you?"

"Yes, he's begged me to stay. He said he'd thought he could never fall in love with an Indian woman—but now he's met me he'll never be happy with an Englishwoman again."

"You're better than a ruddy missionary. How can you drag yourself away?"

"I'll manage."

He looked at the red spot in the centre of her forehead. He was suddenly beset by an intense physical yearning for her—infinitely more intense than any yearning she had ever provoked in him before.

He said abruptly, "Hang on another day."

'Why?" she said.

"Let's have a day out in the country. Take a picnic."

She was silent for a moment. "All right, if you really want to."

They set off after breakfast in the jeep. He could not get Hobson out of his mind. He said suddenly, trying to mask his anxiety with a pretence of humour :

"What was old Copperknob like in bed?"

"In bed?"

"Yes, I saw you getting steam up in the garden. You must have ended up in bed, didn't you?"

She laughed. "I couldn't have gone to bed with him in a million years. But I'm rather touched and pleased—you couldn't possibly have believed it of me unless you'd been jealous."

"Jealous? Me? Look, you don't honestly think I could get worked up about a woman who'd go for a man like that Copperknob, do you? If you want him, you're welcome to him. But jealous? Not on your life. You could have had a rough-and-tumble with him right out there on the lawn, or gone at it all night in the bushes like ruddy rattlesnakes, and I assure you I wouldn't have given a hoot."

Lakshmi smiled to herself and said nothing. They were crawling along in the jeep at a few miles an hour. It was impossible to go faster because of the multitude of pedestrians streaming out of Kathmandu. Evidently it was a public holiday in celebration of one of the numerous Hindu festivals that in Nepal, as in India, seemed to follow each other in such remarkably quick succession.

The stream continued unbroken for mile after mile until it seemed impossible to believe that the little town could ever have contained so many people.

They came eventually to the goal of the pilgrims—a collection of temples and shrines covering the area of a small town. The pilgrims milled round the sacred buildings, propitiating the stone gods with offerings of flowers and fruit and sweetmeats, scattering scarlet powder, dribbling a few grains of rice into the piles accumulated by squatting beggars.

Birkett parked the jeep and they joined the throng, looked inside one or two temples, and emerged at last on the bank of the sacred river astride which the town of temples was built. A wide flight of steps led down to the water, which was crowded with bathers.

"It's like Benares," Lakshmi said.

"Or Blackpool," Birkett said.

"Where's Blackpool?"

"It's where I had a couple of holidays as a kid. It's just like Benares—pilgrims coming from all over for a dip in the holy water."

"The water is really holy?"

"You'd think so by the way they stampede to get into it, just like these chaps. The only difference is that they don't stand there saying their prayers. It's too ruddy cold to stand around praying at Blackpool."

They stood at the top of the steps watching the bathers patiently and greedily seeking, by every possible means, to make the water impart its magic to their bodies—washing themselves frenziedly from head to foot, scooping it to their faces and into their mouths, drinking it, throwing back their heads and gargling with it. Others stood chest-deep, facing upstream with hands together before their faces, paying homage to the deities at the river's source. An insistent voice blared forth from a loudspeaker with ear-shattering din. It sounded like some ritual intonation.

"What's he nattering about?" Birkett said. "Is he reading the scriptures?"

"I expect so," Lakshmi said. The voice was speaking in Nepali, which was as strange a tongue to her as to Birkett.

"No, excuse me, it is an advertisement," said a little Nepalese behind them. He had a round happy face with a few grains of rice stuck on his forehead in a smear of greasy yellow ochre. "It is advertising toothpaste."

"Well, I'm blowed," Birkett laughed.

"Yes, we have made great progress in Nepal since the revolution," the little man said happily. "We are advancing in great strides. We not only advertise toothpaste by the most modern methods, but our country has also become a member of the United Nations Organisation." He pointed to a row of stone platforms set at intervals along the bank of the river. "Those are for the burning of bodies. You may see great burnings here at Pashupati. Please see the third stone from the left. It is of special interest."

"It looks no different from the others," Birkett said.

"It is the stone upon which the body of our last sovereign was burned. It is also where the body of our present gracious and beloved sovereign will eventually be burned. But of course His Majesty is still a young man. The event may not be expected for many years and I shall doubtless not live to see it. I shall be sorry in some ways."

Well, you can cheer up, because if you can hold out for another week or two you'll see it all right, Birkett thought. You'll be back here amongst the crowds with the result of my handiwork—the finished article, as it were—lying down there on the stone slab. The ashes drifting away upon the sacred waters, the curtain coming down, and then it will all be over . . .

He gazed down at the stone platform. It was the first time he had thought about what would happen to the King after the assassination. He wondered whether he would attend the burning. Christ, no, there'd be no need. The only point in attending would be to prove to himself that he wasn't too squeamish, that he could coolly face it. But if he'd already faced the shooting itself, he'd have all the proof he needed . . .

He said, "Most interesting. Thanks. Well, we must be pushing off." He thrust the imaginary scene of the cremation from his mind, the imaginary smell of burning flesh from his nostrils. He was on holiday today—he didn't want to think any more about the job. He asked Lakshmi, "Seen everything you want?"

"Yes, I'd be glad to get out of the crowds."

"Then let's skip off quick—find some quiet spot for lunch."

They found a track that took them up into the hills above the plain. They ate their picnic in the crisp sunshine, looking down upon the mosaic of paddy-fields, the brown muddy serpent of the Bhagmati River, the sprawling wooden town with the gold roof of a temple in the Durbar Square glittering in the sun, standing out amidst the clustered brown rooftops like an old man's gold tooth. Birkett had no difficulty in forgetting his job up here, where the height and the crisp atmosphere gave him a sense of detachment from the world below-made him feel almost light-headed. And he was so full of good spirits that Lakshmi kept staring at him in delighted amazement and marvelling at the change that had come over him.

After the meal he said, "Now, let's play the Picnic Game. I've not played it since I was a kid—must have been talking about Blackpool that brought it back. We make up a story together, adding one sentence each in turn. Go on, you start—anything that comes into your head."

Lakshmi said, "*Mr. Wilson came out of the Everest Hotel.*"

"That's the style, I can see you're hot stuff. *And met a fat lady from Birmingham.*"

"*She said, 'Marry me and come back with me to America.'*"

"Why America, if she was from Birmingham?"

"Isn't Birmingham in America?"

"God, of all the ruddy ignorance! You're not serious?"

154

"Then where is it?"

"There may be *a* Birmingham in America, but *the* Birmingham's in England. Honestly, I'm surprised at you. I could understand you not knowing about Blackpool—but Birmingham!"

"I've never been to England," Lakshmi said. "I don't suppose you'd heard of Lucknow before you came to India."

"Never heard of Lucknow? My dear girl, I knew all about Lucknow when I was still at grammar-school, before you were even a gleam in your mother's eye. I can hear old Peg Leg now—he was the history master—telling us about the siege of Lucknow when those dastardly Indians had stabbed us in the back again. No sense of loyalty, those native fellows—couldn't trust 'em an inch."

"All right, don't bite my head off. I'm on your side. I'm only quoting."

"I'm sorry, it was just habit. I grew up learning to hate the British, who used to call us 'wogs' and despise us. I was forbidden to speak to them except to shout 'Quit India.' Of course I also secretly envied them, and I suppose it's all mixed up with what I feel about you. I still get a sort of kick out of being accepted on equal terms by the mighty conquerors." She rummaged in her bag and took out the silver pan box. "You don't mind, do you?"

"No, go on. You've got your independence now."

"I know, but if it really offends—"

"Go on, enjoy yourself."

"I can't make out what's come over you today. You're being so warm and nice."

"Must be a catch in it somewhere. Maybe I'm aiming to get something out of you."

"What?"

Birkett grinned. "Look, we'd better get back to Wilson and the fat lady from Birmingham. We can't just leave 'em standing there in the drive."

Later he closed his eyes for a nap and when he opened them again Lakshmi had gone. Fifteen minutes later she had still not returned. He walked about impatiently, peering in one direction and then another. She might have fallen over a precipice. He imagined her lying dead. He felt an access of tenderness.

Then the idea suddenly occurred to him that she'd slipped off for a secret rendezvous with Hobson. Despite its absurdity, the idea alone was enough to reopen last night's wound—to cause him an ache of dismay.

Of course she's right, I'm jealous, he thought. Last night I was fairly eaten up with jealousy.

Just then he saw her returning. She carried a bunch of wild flowers. He felt a burst of anger at her thoughtlessness in causing him unnecessary anxiety. He was about to give vent to it when it occurred to him that it would only betray how ridiculously concerned he had been about her. Better not let her think he'd been anxious at all.

He said, "Hello, I wasn't expecting you back for another fortnight; I thought you'd probably decided to have a crack at Annapurna."

"I'm sorry, were you worried?"

"Not a bit. It did occur to me that you might have been raped by an Abominable Snowman. But I decided the experience would be of sufficient scientific interest not to interfere."

"You are not a bit gallant."

She lay down in the grass, kicking off her sandals and wriggling her toes in enjoyment of their freedom. The contrast between the darkness of the upper part of her feet and the paleness of the soles reminded him of her suffering on account of her complexion. A sudden new wave of tenderness swept over him. It was accompanied by a resurgence of physical desire for her. He turned his eyes to the segment of bare waist visible between the folds of her sari. The sight of its slenderness and honey-brown smoothness further provoked his desire so that it became almost intolerable.

By Jove, I've never wanted a girl so much in my life, he thought. I suppose it's because now I don't know if she's mine for the asking, like I did in Delhi, and because there's another man after her.

He said, "You're a bonny girl, you know. By Jove, you're bonny."

She just smiled. It was a lovely radiant smile that he had not seen since her arrival at the airport, and as she smiled she held his eyes with her own.

"And I missed you when you were away just now," he said. He hadn't meant to tell her, but it didn't seem to matter now that he had said it. "It seemed such a waste of time—I mean we've wasted so much time avoiding each other since you came that we don't want to waste any more."

"No," she said.

"And I tried to hide it just now, but I'd really got the wind up. I was afraid you'd fallen over a cliff. Now look here, young lady, you're not to go wandering off like that again, d'you hear? You can consider that as a Queen's Order and Regulation—which means that if I catch you disobeying it, I'll turn you straight over my knee."

That night they made love and it went better than it had ever gone in Delhi. And afterwards Birkett said, "Well, I'll say this for you—you're certainly a giver. You don't hold anything back."

"Why should I?"

"There's few that know how to give themselves like that. No, you're the best giver I've ever known." He patted her. "Well, now I'll be getting along."

They were in Lakshmi's room and she had not expected him to go. She said, "Don't you want to stay? You can if you want."

"We'd neither of us get any sleep in that bed. It's too small."

"We could put the two beds together."

"No, too many boys around the corridors in the morning. We don't want 'em to see me coming out of your door."

He returned to his own room. He had purposely suggested using Lakshmi's room earlier in the evening because he had foreseen that it would be easier to leave her like this than to turf her out of his own bed, send her packing. No, he wasn't going to start any of that all-night business. Making love was one thing, and sleeping was another, and he saw no reason why women always wanted to confuse them. He hated sleeping with a woman. She entwined you with her arms so that you were like a kitten entangled in the knitting, and every time you moved it was like playing spillikins—

you needed the knowledge of a constructional engineer, combined with the delicate touch of a watchmaker and the patience of a saint, to achieve your objective without disturbing the whole complicated pile. Besides, it was too ruddy sweaty and unhygienic. No thanks, he'd stick to his rule of sleeping alone.

He got into his bed between the cool empty sheets. By Jove, it was bliss. There was nothing like another person's bed for making you appreciate your own. Still, it had gone very well with that girl today—no doubt about it. And he was already looking forward to tomorrow.

The next day they took another picnic and made love in the hills. They could hardly bear to break off for lunch. Birkett was astonished by the swift and repeated recurrence of his desire. It was unprecedented in his experience. He seemed no sooner to have possessed her than the need was once more upon him to possess her again. Perhaps it was something to do with that remarkable capacity of hers for giving—for total abandonment—which afforded him not only intense physical satisfaction, but also the sensation of total possession and domination.

"You know we should be ashamed of ourselves," he said. "We're getting one-track minds."

"I don't care." She was in a dream. She had never made love in the open-air before, and the discovery that it was possible—that they could stop the jeep almost anywhere in the deserted hills and accept the hospitality of the nearest grass made her feel she was losing all sense of responsibility and reality, so that she could believe herself now almost capable of abandoning herself blithely in some crowded square in Kathmandu. She could not bear to lose physical contact with him. She melted against him in the jeep; and when they got back to the hotel in the evening, and he urged her to keep her distance at least until they got upstairs, the strain of doing so became so intolerable that before they had reached the upper landing she had let her fingers steal out to his hand for a brief reminding touch, her shoulder brush as if accidentally against his arm.

He went into her room with her, though he was now beginning

to feel distinctly surfeited with her embraces, and his thoughts were soon wandering elsewhere. He would have preferred to spend the evening by himself, not see her again until tomorrow. And he was considering how this might be achieved when he heard a knock on the door of his own room just down the corridor, followed shortly by a knock on the door of Lakshmi's room.

He said, "Yes, who is it?"

"I'm sorry, it's Wilson," came the voice from outside.

"Nothing to be sorry about," Birkett called out cheerfully. He was glad to be in contact with another human being. It relieved his growing feeling of suffocation. "What's up?"

"You're wanted on the telephone. It's a gentleman called Mr. Kensington."

"Never heard of him."

"I'm afraid that's what he said. It sounded like an Indian to me. I'd know that Indian accent anywhere."

"I'll be right down."

It can't be Mathai, he thought. He surely wouldn't be such a fool as to ring me at the hotel. But then who else? He went downstairs, hoping that in case it was Mathai the bar would be empty, since otherwise the conversation would inevitably be overheard. But it was after seven and, besides Wilson himself, he found Hobson already installed at the bar drinking banana brandy with Mr. and Mrs. Potter.

Wilson jerked his head towards the telephone. "It sounded to me like Mr. Mathai."

"Mathai?"

"Yes, I felt certain it was Mr. Mathai. But he distinctly said his name was Kensington."

"Probably one of the South Kensingtons," Potter said. "Very good family. Of course they won't have anything to do with the West Kensingtons."

"Potter, don't be ridiculous," Mrs. Potter said. "Those are Underground stations."

Christ, I'll murder young Mathai, Birkett thought. It's bad enough to ring up at all, but to try a trick like that he must be insane.

He picked up the receiver from the shelf behind the bar. "Birkett here."

"Major Birkett, this is not really Mr. Kensington. I thought it safer not to use my own name on the telephone. But I am your friend—"

"Yes, hello, Mathai," Birkett said. Best to cut your losses when your pretence was found out, and pretend you'd never been pretending.

"Oh, Major Birkett . . ." Mathai was temporarily taken aback by Birkett's apparent indifference to matters of security, to which he had paid such careful attention. "Major Birkett, I cannot keep our appointment for tomorrow. I'm very sorry, Major Birkett. I am prevented by duties at the Embassy."

"Oh, pity," Birkett said. "Never mind. What about the next day?"

"No, that is also impossible."

My God, the young puppy's doing the dirt on me, Birkett thought. He's running out and leaving me in the dirt.

He felt the blood drain from his face. He'd thought he had tied him up as neat as a parcel at that last meeting on the maidan, but evidently he'd miscalculated—blundered. It meant he'd have to chuck it, admit failure on the most important job of his career.

He said, "Well, can't be helped. Another time. I'll be in touch with you, Mathai. Don't worry, you can count on it. We shall certainly meet for another chat."

"Yes, sir. I thought tonight—"

"Eh?"

"I wish to speak to you urgently, sir. I wish to meet you tonight."

The blood came slowly back into Birkett's face. By Jove, that had been a bad scare. "Yes, sorry. Didn't quite follow."

"I could be at the meeting-place we arranged in twenty minutes, sir."

"Fine, I'd enjoy it. Looking forward. I'll be along." He put down the receiver.

"I knew I was right," Wilson said. "I've always been good at voices. Of course I would be—there's nothing anybody could think of to be good at that could possibly be more futile."

"I don't know, must come in handy sometimes, old man," Potter said. "I mean, personally I'm fascinated to learn that Mathai's alter-ego is Mr. Kensington."

"Fancy pretending to be an Underground station," Mrs. Potter said. "I think it's silly. I'd sooner pretend to be a proper railway station like Euston."

"I suppose it's his idea of a joke," Birkett said. "Anything for the sake of a laugh. Well, I'm just off for a drink with him. He's trying to pick my brains about how to write a best-seller, By Jove, he must really be round the bend!"

He told Lakshmi the same story and set off in the jeep. It took him ten minutes to reach the Bhagmati. He parked the jeep and walked to the middle of the long wooden bridge, and leaned on the rail. The river moved soundlessly below him, refuse drifting on its surface. Its wet muddy smell filled his nostrils. Dim lights were beginning to appear in the windows of the wooden houses scattered along the bank. There was a sudden deafening clatter as an ancient lorry with a flickering headlamp crossed the bridge, rattling the loose boards. Silence returned as it disappeared up the road. Presently a bicycle with a bright lamp appeared from the direction of the town. The boards rumbled softly under its wheels. It came to a standstill beside Birkett and Mathai dismounted.

"Good evening, Major Birkett!" He was in a state of great excitement. His eyes shone with elation. "Sir, I have changed my mind about the duty, and I wish you to reconsider—"

Birkett said sharply, "Your light's still on, Mathai."

"Oh, thank you sir." He switched off the lamp. He was very proud of the elaborate chromium lamp which, like the gold leaf decoration on food, satisfied his need for ostentation. "Sir, I beg you to accept my new decision."

"For God's sake, Mathai! You've got to learn self-control. Now, we'll walk along together."

They dropped down on to the river bank from the far end of the bridge. Birkett maintained a frigid, disapproving silence. He had to make sure of destroying any idea that Mathai might have that he was doing Birkett a favour, that Birkett was going to throw his arms round his neck. That would only weaken Mathai's resolution, and he had to harden it. He had to make it as hard as steel.

Fencing blocked their path, and they dropped down to the wide expanse of mud below the bank. The mud looked hard enough to support them; but after a few steps Birkett's foot sank through the sun-baked crust into the wet mud below.

"Damn and blast." He withdrew his foot, tore a handful of grass from the bank, and began to clean up his shoe. He took his time. Mathai waited, bursting with impatience. At last Birkett threw away the grass.

"First of all, Mathai, I want an explanation from you. How dare you take it upon yourself to ring me up at the hotel, ignoring all considerations of security?"

"Sir, it was for reasons of security that I called myself Mr. Kensington."

"Of all the ruddy silly names!"

"I tried to think of a common English name, sir. I thought Kensington was a common name. I am sure I have often heard it."

"Well, you couldn't have drawn more attention to yourself if you'd called yourself Pandit Nehru. In any case you should never use tricks of that kind unless you're sure of not being found out— and unless you're competent to carry them through." He continued to give him a severe dressing-down. When he was satisfied that Mathai was sufficiently deflated, he said, "All right, what did you want to say to me?"

"It was about the duty, sir," Mathai said miserably.

"You're wasting my time, Mathai. First, the matter's already settled, and second, even if it weren't—would you honestly consider yourself worthy of it?"

Mathai said weakly, "I thought that since the other man is not in the Embassy, sir—"

"No, but he's a match for the job—and worthy of the honour of performing it. I don't think you're either, Mathai. Though even if you were, I still couldn't go back on my promise to the other chap. So no more to be said. Let's get back to the jeep." He turned briskly away and climbed up the bank. Mathai followed after him unhappily. They had covered half the distance to the bridge when a hesitation began to appear in Birkett's pace, and then he came to a standstill.

"What's the matter, sir?" Mathai said.

Birkett did not reply. He was lost in thought. He turned aside and stood looking out over the sluggish river. Presently the silence was broken by the rattle of the bridge, like a distant machine-gun. The noise ceased as suddenly as it had begun. Birkett's silent meditation continued another few moments, and then he turned back to Mathai.

He said, almost as if he was asking Mathai for advice, "You know, Mathai, I wonder if I'm making a most terrible mistake? I wonder if I'm not allowing the personal obligation that I feel towards the other chap to influence my judgment . . . ? Well, I should be very ashamed of myself if I am. Of course neither my feelings nor his feelings matter a hoot: the only consideration is the job. And so far as the job goes-well, it's no use pretending it isn't a terrible drawback—I mean, not being in the Embassy . . ."

He let his eyes dwell on Mathai, as if seeking qualities in him that he might have overlooked, wondering whether after all he dare take a risk. And Mathai drew himself up and tried to look straight and strong like a soldier.

"If only I knew you better, Mathai. If only I felt more sure."

"Sir, may I speak?"

"Certainly, go ahead."

"Since our last meeting I have become a changed man, sir. I have become inspired. I have realised that few men are given such opportunity to serve their cause. It is a wonderful privilege, and will bring honour and glory to my family that will make up many times over for their personal loss. I beg you to accept me for the duty, sir, and I promise you will not regret it."

"But it's going to need guts, Mathai. And you said yourself on the maidan that you were—well . . ."

"A weakling and a coward. And it was true, sir. But it is no longer true."

"You think you've changed so much in a few days?"

"It is not me that has changed, sir, only my attitude. Now I have courage because I am inspired. I know that however great my fears: I can overcome them. I still have the body of a weakling, but it is possessed by the spirit of a lion."

"By Jove, I never thought I'd hear you talk like that Mathai." Birkett gazed at him with twinkling appreciation. "I honestly never thought it." He gazed for another moment, then turned away and once more stood pensively looking at the river. After a minute he seemed to come to a decision, and turning back smartly he said, "Right, young fellow, I'll take a chance on it. The job's yours. God knows how I'm going to break it to the other chap—but that's my lookout and needn't worry you. Its just up to you to show me I've done the right thing."

"I shall not let you down, sir." Mathai knew now that he could have been a soldier after all, could even have faced bayonets. He only wished he had made the discovery sooner and become a soldier instead of a diplomat—he felt his life had been wasted. But now he had been given the chance to redeem it in the single glorious moment of his death.

"Very well, the Tattoo's a week on Saturday," Birkett said. "We'll meet again on the Wednesday beforehand, when I'll give you equipment and briefing—same place as before, northeast corner of the maidan, five-thirty in the afternoon. That's all now. We'll separate here. Goodbye, Mathai—and congratulations."

"Sir, I wish to say another word. I wish to say how happy I am to work under such a fine man as yourself. You are the finest man I have ever known. You make me feel a great humility—but also great happiness and pride."

"Come off it, Mathai. None of your ruddy soft soap."

"I look upon you as a son looks upon his father. I feel you are a father, sir, and I would like you to think of me as a son."

"I'd be proud of a son who spoke as you've spoken today," Birkett said gruffly. He clapped Mathai's arm, turned abruptly, and walked away.

He'll have me changing his nappies next, and calling me Daddy,

Birkett thought as he reached the jeep and climbed into it. Still, such sentiments aren't to be discouraged. You have to show Daddy what a big brave boy you are. You don't let Daddy down.

He drove back across the bridge with an ear-shattering clatter. Ten minutes later he was back at the hotel. He parked the jeep in the drive and started up the stairs.

"Well, how was Mr. Kensington, old man?"

Birkett paused and looked up. It was Potter. He was leaning over the marble balustrade, grinning.

"Mathai? He was fine," Birkett said.

"Catch any fish?"

"Fish?"

"Down at the river, weren't you?"

Without a flicker of muscle, without the least hesitation of his foot on the stairs, Birkett said, "The good old bush telegraph, eh?"

"Your shoes, old man."

Birkett glanced down. His right shoe still bore streaky traces of mud.

"No mud in town old man. Hasn't rained for weeks. Only place it could have happened is down at the river." Potter grinned, "I know, quite uncanny, isn't it, old man?"

"Yes, you're a real Sherlock Holmes—just took a turn along the river on my way back from Mathai's." Birkett's voice was light and dry. "I must go and get cleaned up."

"That's the stuff, old man. Must remove the evidence." With a flick of the hand, Potter moved past and down the stairs. Birkett stood looking after him. That was certainly pretty smart work, he thought. He's certainly not the grinning buffoon he looks. But then he doesn't even quite look it. He remembered the man whom Potter had kept running round the barracks square with loaded pack until he dropped. He also remembered the wound that had removed half of Potter's thigh. He couldn't reconcile what he seemed to be with what he was. Then the idea occurred to him that Potter might only be using the Embassy job as a cover—that he had come out to Nepal to tail him.

Except that it was really absurd. Potter might well be less of a fool than he wished to show himself—he might have all sorts of reasons for wanting to hide behind the disguise—but a professional agent didn't go around baldly announcing his presence like that. He didn't say, "See what a clever spy I am. I've just caught you with mud on your shoes." It didn't make sense.

Chapter Thirteen

Birkett stooped under the low-carved lintel of the shop. The proprietor squatted on his piece of matting.

"I'd like another look at that trinket we saw the other day," Birkett said.

The fat Nepalese, without moving from his squatting position, reached for the tin and took out the necklace that Lakshmi had admired and that Birkett had found too preposterously expensive even to consider. He was only astonished that it should have occurred to him to consider it now. Still, he was going to enjoy surprising her with the present, if only he could get the necklace at a reasonable price. He proposed to offer two hundred rupees, and settle for two hundred and twenty-five. Otherwise he'd skip it.

He examined the necklace indifferently, as if it fell short of his expectations. He tossed it carelessly aside on the matting.

He said, "What did you say you were asking for it?"

"Four hundred rupees."

Birkett looked at him sharply. "Eh?"

"Four hundred."

"It was three hundred last time and that was already a sight too much."

The man explained that three hundred was the price for the English and four hundred for Americans—and since an American woman tourist was interested in the necklace, and was coming back this evening to pay him the full sum, he was not prepared to let it go cheaper.

"You'll never get four hundred for that trash, not even from an American," Birkett said. "I'll give you two fifty."

The Nepali did not even bother to reply. He smiled with faint scorn and returned the necklace to the tin.

"All right, you're a ruddy old scoundrel, and I know you're doing me in the eye, but here's your three hundred." He dealt the notes on to the matting beside the proprietor's plump crossed feet.

The proprietor ignored them.

"Now look, come off it," Birkett said. "What's your rock bottom price?"

"Four hundred."

"I don't believe it. There's no such thing as an Oriental who won't bargain."

The proprietor stuck firmly to his price and Birkett felt sure that the story about the American woman must be true. It made the necklace all the more attractive to know that someone else was after it; and he was already so appalled at his own recklessness in offering three hundred that a bit more could hardly make it worse. He added another note to the three on the floor.

"Well, I take my hat off to you," he said grimly. "I'm pretty hard-headed when it comes to money, and you're the first man to get the better of me for many a day."

The fat proprietor screwed up the necklace in a piece of newspaper as if it had been threepennyworth of chips, and Birkett stepped out into the street.

Four hundred rupees, he thought. Four hundred ruddy rupees. That's thirty quid—for a bit of frippery for a woman.

And it's not even for her birthday, he thought. It's for nothing at all.

He found Lakshmi in her room. Her excitement and joy over the present was like a child's—it made him grin with sympathetic pleasure, and helped to ease his lingering hurt over the expenditure. He was only irked by the thought that she must inevitably suppose the necklace had cost him no more than three hundred rupees; and the urge to tell her that he had paid four hundred became so strong that he only managed to resist it with a struggle.

He watched her take out a dozen bright diaphanous saris and drape them one after another round her shoulders, trying to decide which best showed off the green jade of the necklace. She kept exclaiming how she loved presents that came, like this, as a complete surprise.

"I'm afraid it wasn't a real surprise, as you'd picked it out yourself," he said. "Only I'm not much of a hand at choosing presents—not that I've ever really tried."

"Didn't you give your wife presents?"

"For birthdays and Christmas, of course—but I always gave her cash and let her buy them herself."

"Didn't you ever bring something home as a surprise?"

"No, I'd only have got some useless thing she didn't want."

"Still, sometimes even useless presents are rather nice . . ." She was pensive for a moment, then her happiness burst out again as she tried on another sari before the mirror. "Look how marvellously it goes with this pink! I'm sure people will think I've been stealing the crown jewels—it looks so precious!"

And then it was suddenly coming out before he could stop it: "Well, it almost might have been the crown jewels, the price I was asked for it. I'm afraid I got done. I had to pay four hundred rupees."

"Four hundred? Oh, but you really shouldn't!"

"Never mind. So long as it's what you really want, I'll feel I've got my money's worth."

That night he found himself reluctant to leave her bed for his own. He said, "Look, I reckon I'll stay here tonight. Even if I'm seen leaving your room in the morning, it's not going to tell anyone anything they don't already know, It must be bazaar-gossip by now that you aren't here to type my letters."

It was the second joy for her in one day. She happily pulled the two beds together and arranged the sheets to make the beds into one. She said anxiously, "You think you'll be comfortable? You'll be able to sleep?"

"Don't worry. I'll be out like a light as soon as my head hits the pillow."

But, oddly, the expected sleep did not come, and the longer it eluded him, the further it retreated from his grasp. Lakshmi, as he knew from her breathing, had fallen off quickly. He heard the clock near the maidan strike midnight. He tried to induce sleep in his customary manner by an effort of will, but could not empty his mind. It was possessed by one gnawing obsession after another. He remembered the sum he had paid for the necklace; he was convinced now that the shopkeeper had been lying to him about the American woman—that the story had been sheer fabrication. He had been outwitted and cheated. He felt anger and hatred for the plump little man with the soft plump feet. And he thought of one vindictive scheme after another to force him to refund part of the money.

Then he began to feel the room become increasingly suffocating. He seemed hardly able to breathe. Lakshmi must have forgotten to open the windows. He got up, deeply resenting her oversight, only to find that both windows were open wide. He returned to the bed.

The clock struck two. Presently he fell asleep and dreamed that he was on a steep slippery slope, at the top of which was a house whose safety he desperately wanted to reach. There were various excrescences on the slope that might have served as handholds, but his body was paralysed. He began to slip downwards towards a black bottomless abyss. There was only one hope left to him, to grab the slender trunk of a lone tree just below him. He tried to move his arm in preparation for the required moment. He discovered that it was held to his side as if bound by rope. Suddenly the slope seemed to tilt to a steeper angle and he began to fall swiftly. His arm still would not move. Terror seized him by the throat as he dropped into the hot, suffocating blackness. He woke with a violent start, gasping for breath. He scrambled out of bed, grabbed his clothes from the chair, and escaped from the room. He went along the empty corridor to his room, took his walking-stick, and set out for a walk.

He returned after an hour. The feeling of suffocation had left him and he felt himself again. He went back to his own room and got into bed. He was soon asleep.

The next morning he was at breakfast when Lakshmi joined him. They did not mention the night before. He excused himself before she had finished her meal, saying that he must devote the morning to work.

He met her again in the garden just before lunch. The atmosphere was constrained. She was waiting for him to explain his abrupt departure from her room, but again he did not mention it.

Why should I? he thought defensively. I'm under no obligation to give her an account of myself every time I move from A to B.

At lunch they hardly spoke.

He returned to his room in the afternoon and did not see her again until about five o'clock, when she knocked and came in. She said, "Please tell me what is the matter? What happened last night?"

"Last night? I got too hot and went out for a walk, that's all. I went back to my room afterwards so as not to wake you."

"Then why have you been so strange all day?"

"Strange? Who's strange? I'd say you've been strange, if anybody."

She said, "I don't think you left because it was too hot."

"Really? Then why did I leave? I'd be interested to know."

"I think it was for the same reason that you so often keep suddenly freezing up. I remember the first time it happened—when you were kissing me on the terrace of that tomb outside Delhi. You suddenly went dead. It was awful. I could feel you hating me. Just as you're hating me now."

"Rubbish."

"It's not rubbish. And if you hate, it means you're afraid. And I think I know what you're afraid of—getting lost."

"What's that supposed to mean? Lost where?"

"Wherever you might find yourself if you went too far and found you couldn't get back."

"I wish you wouldn't talk in riddles."

"It isn't a riddle. If you spent the whole night in my room, that might be going too far. You might find you'd want to spend the next night, too. You might find you couldn't do without me. And that's too terrible even to think about because you'd be dependent on me—you wouldn't even by yourself any more. You'd be completely lost. No, it's much better to hang on fast to something safe and known, and not let yourself get carried away."

Hang on fast . . . The phrase all at once brought back his dream of the night before—the steep slope, the sudden swift sickening fall, the paralysed arm at his side unable to grab for the tree.

He abruptly dismissed the memory. "Look here, what do you think I am? A ruddy clock to tinker about with and take to bits? I call it ruddy impertinence."

She was at once contrite. "I'm awfully sorry, I didn't mean . . . Of course you're right. I was being terribly impertinent."

"Never mind. Skip it. Come on, let's take a stroll before the sun goes."

But it was not until the next day, as they picnicked again at their favourite spot in the hills, that their former ease together returned. And now, suspended on the green shelf between snowy peaks and patchwork plain, in the clear crisp air, Birkett once more felt that sense of light-headed detachment. He brimmed with good spirits. They played the Picnic Game again.

"My turn to begin," he said. "*There was once a crafty old fellow called Major—I forget his name, but anyhow he was really a terrible old ram, especially when he was on a picnic with this Indian girl he was toting around—can't remember her name either but she was a nifty piece—and really, the pair of 'em they certainly had a high old time.*"

Lakshmi picked it up. "*And the higher they went in the mountains the nicer he became—though even down on the plain he could be very nice too, and sometimes gave her wonderful presents. The only thing he never gave was himself.*"

"*Yes, he was a proper lone-ranger, this chap, and the minute he felt his independence threatened, he'd blow his top. It used to drive this Indian girl nearly mad.*"

"*She didn't really understand it, that's all. Of course it was probably because she was a woman and she hated being alone, she just wanted to sink her life into somebody else's. But she thought that sometimes a man, too, must feel insufficient by himself and want to share things, and have somebody to stand by him—that even a cheetah must occasionally feel lonely as it prowls across the plain. That's why she was—puzzled."*

"Look, not admitting that I'm this ruddy old ram under discussion," Birkett said, "I'll give you the plain answer to that one. When you're alone there's nobody who can muck you up. You're self-contained. You're armour-plated. And you can't get hurt. Yes, there's your answer—you can't get hurt."

She said, "You must have been terribly hurt once to feel like that. Was it because of your wife?"

"No, I'd got the hang of things long before that. There were those schools I went to—then going back even further, there was my sanctimonious father. And then there was my mother."

"You mean your mother didn't love you?"

"Love me? My mother? Of course she did. I was her sun and her moon and her stars, and her whole bloody Milky Way. I can see her now, coming down Mostyn Road with her shopping-basket, past the ugly Edwardian little villas with their donkey-stoned steps, in her ridiculous hat held on with a hat-pin, her cheap ill-fitting dress, her shabby shoes. I remember those shoes, one of them had a split seam at the back, and she'd clumsily stitched it herself to save sixpence . . ." He broke off. He had suddenly, astonishingly, felt himself on the point of tears. He put his hand to his forehead to hide his eyes. Lakshmi waited in silence. It was several minutes before he felt sufficiently sure of himself again to go on.

He said, "Sorry, it was just the thought of those shoes."

"You must have loved her very much."

"Yes, and that's when I first learned that loving means getting hurt—that loving means losing. Because if you love, you put all your chips on one number—and you may get a good run of luck, but the number's bound to stop coming up in the end. A lover's a loser—sooner or later he'll be let down. And how can he expect other women not to let him down, if he's even let down by his mother?"

"What do you mean?"

"Not on purpose, of course. Not even avoidably, but just in the course of being a mother. Yes, at nine years old, when you've scarcely grown out of your teddy-bear, you're bundled into your little schoolboy's overcoat and whipped off to the station, and you cling desperately to your mother behind the platform poster with a great aching hole in your stomach. And this time you've finally had it. Wham! Down comes the knife in the dirty yellow fog on the London Road platform, and then you're getting into the train full of the cruel little boys planning dormitory tortures, and masters with jolly end-of-holiday veneers looking you over to see how much they'll enjoy whacking you. Your first woman, who had protested so much love for you, has finally abandoned you, her face is fading in the fog, and you're being carried away through the squalid little back yards of the Manchester slums . . . Christ, you'd see you never went through that again as long as you lived. If that's what attachment meant, you'd stay independent—run a one-man show."

Lakshmi said, "But you didn't stay independent. You got married."

"Yes, I ought to have known better. I let myself forget the lessons I'd learnt. But at least Dorothy did one good thing for me—she made sure I never forgot them again."

Lakshmi said thoughtfully, "But why did you marry her? Did you really love her?"

"Of course I loved her!" Lakshmi was silent, and he said angrily, "Why, don't you believe it?"

"I had the feeling that perhaps you didn't—that perhaps, except for your mother, you'd never really loved anybody in your life."

"I just know where to draw the line, that's all."

"But when you're in love you don't draw lines. I was wondering if it wasn't partly your fault that your wife—"

"Now, come off it! If a chap's been away for a year, fighting a war, and comes back and finds his wife in the family way, and not even ashamed about it but fairly blooming—well, you can't blame the husband."

"You could do—if she'd given up hope even before he went

away. If she'd been giving herself for so long, and found nothing coming back."

"Look, if you're trying to convince me that Dorothy wasn't a ruddy little bitch, you're wasting your time—so let's just skip it, it makes me sick to think of her."

But he kept thinking of her after that, and was still thinking of her that night in bed. The fact was, of course—he was forced to admit it to himself—he had never been in love with her. The marriage had been a drastic mistake for which he had despised himself. It had been in his social-climbing days, and he had already succeeded by dint of hard application in acquiring a certain man-of-the-world veneer—but he was still self-conscious of the Lancashire lad that lay beneath, still felt the grammar school and the little villa in Mostyn Road, the ecclesiastical penury, the margarine-on-weekdays and the patched clothes, sniffing close at his heels like a pack of old disreputable unwanted dogs; and Dorothy, with her la-di-da voice and retired naval-officer father, had at first seemed a goal beyond his reach. He could not hope to compete with all the admirers who surrounded her at her cocktail parties—the rich idlers, the stockbrokers, the young men in striped trousers who were "in Lloyd's." He'd let her take most of the initiative for fear of a rebuff; and after the marriage he had felt inflated to twice his former size. "By Jove, I've done it," he had thought. "I started as a grammar-school boy in Mostyn Road—and I've married a Kensington girl with an upper-class voice and her own fur coat!" At the same time he had felt trapped and resented her, and had refused to consider having a baby. He had protested that they were too young, that they couldn't afford it—but in fact it was because a baby was the final death-knell of independence, the ultimate tie. A baby meant giving too much of yourself away—it meant a loss of manhood and strength, of perfect self-containment. Of course there had been tears and scenes. And then Dorothy's gradual withdrawal from him, the moodiness, and the tears that would suddenly start gushing for no reason at all . . .

He'd always tried to keep those particular memories away: he supposed he felt guilty about the baby.

Well, perhaps it was true that the failure of the marriage had been his own fault. If he'd loved her, given her a baby, she might not have slipped into bed with another man the moment he'd gone off to France. But you couldn't be sure. Once he had let her feel she had conquered him, once he no longer presented a challenge, she might have lost interest, dropped him overboard, blithely left him to drown.

No, he'd never loved her—and it was probably true, as Lakshmi had said, that he had never loved anybody in his life. Not in the way that Lakshmi loved, yielding her body and soul in utter abandon. He could not help admiring her for it—for the sheer foolhardiness, the complete indifference to the risks of leaping into the yawning chasm, of being swallowed up, lost. It was an act of self-destruction.

He had said something of the kind to her coming back in the jeep: that loving was self-destruction. She had said, "No, it's the opposite—it's by not letting yourself love that you destroy yourself. You keep yourself alive without living."

"I'm living," he said.

"I'm not sure . . . You've so many locked doors that I've never seen behind."

"I've been opening doors for you all day."

"Yes, you always begin to open them in the hills—you become so different."

He had never in his life talked about himself before. He had never wanted to do so—but now that he had started he could scarcely wait for the next opportunity to tell Lakshmi the latest thoughts that their talk had provoked; and the next day at breakfast he suggested another trip to the hills.

"Come on, let's skip off quick," he said. "We're wasting the best part of the day."

She laughed. "But I haven't finished my coffee yet."

"Well, hurry up."

And they had no sooner set off in the jeep than he said, "You know, I reckon you were right—I mean about the mess-up with Dorothy being partly my fault. The blunt fact is that I only married her because she'd got a plum in her mouth . . ." It gave him remarkable relief to get this off his chest. He could see that those Roman Catholics, for all their fairy tales, their Immaculate Conceptions, their little adolescent saints who'd seen Our Lady in the clefts of rocks, had really got a point when it came to the confessional—the unloading of guilt like refuse through the little grille, with the priest conveniently sitting inside to cart it away. He realized now how his shame over the marriage must have burdened him. He had expected Lakshmi to be profoundly shocked. But to his astonishment she took it almost as a matter of course— after all, she was Indian and in India expedience and not love was the accepted basis of marriage.

"Still, that doesn't excuse me in England," he said.

"There must be plenty of calculated marriages even in England. I think women are the same everywhere—they are very realistic."

"Yes, but I don't think they pretend to be in love like I did."

"You sound as if you're afraid I'm trying to take something away from you. You enjoy feeling bad about it, don't you?"

"Oh, rubbish! That's ridiculous. I'm afraid you're not a very reliable markswoman. You'll score a bull's-eye one minute, and then not even hit the target." He was silent. After a minute or two he said grudgingly, "Well, there may be something in it. I suppose we do sometimes tend to cultivate our sores—they become old friends in the end. But 'enjoy' wasn't the right word. No, I'm afraid you were right off the mark there . . ."

Later, when they had finished lunch up on the green shelf above the plain, in the pure crisp air, he said suddenly, light-heartedly, "By the way, I'm a Communist."

"Really? Since when?"

"I've been a Party member for years."

"Well, I'm afraid I don't really know much about it—I'm so ignorant about politics."

He realized with astonishment that she had scarcely bothered to take it in—that her mind had already switched to other matters. He said, "But don't you mind?"

She shrugged. "You know, India isn't America. Communists aren't regarded as monsters of evil. They're quite respectable."

Her interest suddenly took fire, and she sat up, "Oh, but I know what you can probably explain to me. Why do the Communists have such terrible taste? I'm sorry, I suppose I shouldn't say that, I mean as you're a Communist, but at the Trades Fair in Delhi both the Chinese and Russians had enormous pavilions, but honestly, their dresses and fabrics all those dull colours and horrible flowery designs—well, it wasn't much of an advertisement . . ."

It was not until much later that she was struck by a new aspect of the matter that puzzled and worried her. She said, "You know the evening we met in the Club? Well, I've just remembered you talking to that young Sikh—of course I was eavesdropping—and telling him you hated Communism and brainwashing. In fact, you once started running down Communism to me . . ."

"I have to keep it under my hat. If it got round that I was a Communist I'd lose a market for my books, even if I could find a publisher to touch 'em."

"But surely you say what you think in your books?"

"No, I avoid politics as much as possible—and when I can't, I stick to the middle of the road."

"That doesn't sound very—well—honest."

She didn't mind that he was a Communist, but this disloyalty to his true beliefs, this wearing of a false face in public, deeply disturbed her. Birkett smarted under her disapproval, and was beset by the temptation to hint at the truth—that so far from being disloyal, it was a passionate and active loyalty to his beliefs that accounted for the falseness. Down on the plains such a transgression would have been unthinkable. But up here in the hills, detached from reality, all his guards were down, and he had to struggle hard with himself to keep silent. Lakshmi was also silent, exploring this new and disturbing discovery about him—trying to understand it, so that she could justify it to herself and save her respect for him.

She said, "But now I come to think of it, it seems so strange that you should be a Communist. Not just because you're English, but because there are things about you that don't seem to fit in. Why are you a Communist?"

"Because I believe it's the best system for the majority of people."

"But do you really care about 'people'?"

"Of course I care about them!"

"That's what I find so hard to believe. You talk as if you hate people. And you purposely cut yourself off from them. How could you do that if you really cared about them?"

"You don't have to throw your arms round people's necks, slobber over them, to want to see them getting a square deal, and living in a world that's efficiently and realistically run."

Lakshmi was not convinced. She said, "I once wanted to be a dancer—not because I wanted to make people happy who watched me, but because it would have satisfied a secret longing to show off. I think it's often the same with politicians. They're not really concerned with making people happy, but only with satisfying something in themselves. I don't believe many of us really care about all the millions of people we don't know—really 'love humanity.' We've scarcely enough love for the few people around us, and you've admitted yourself that you've never really loved anybody . . ."

"I was talking of women. That's a different sort of love."

"Yes, but if you can't love a woman—if you keep your heart locked up—I don't think you're capable of unselfish love for strangers. I'm sorry, I suppose I shouldn't really say—"

"You can say what you like," Birkett said. "It's not so easy to get my goat up here. You can pull me to bits all you like, and you can come to what conclusions you like. But it won't make any difference, because whether I love humanity or hate its ruddy guts, the fact remains that I believe in Communism, and nothing in the world's going to shake that belief. I'm a Communist to the core. I've been a Communist for the last ten years, and I'll be a Communist for the next ten years—and I'll still be a Communist when I die. And if you happen to be around at the time, you can tell 'em to skip the marble urns. They can just mark the spot with a hammer and sickle, and if they want to give me an epitaph they can say, 'Here's Birkett. A ram, and—God help him—a ruddy Red'."

Chapter Fourteen

Two days later—it was the day before he was due to meet Mathai again—a disturbing thing happened. He had been for a walk before lunch, and on his return to the Everest found Lakshmi in a deck-chair on the lawn. She held up her book.

"I hope you don't mind. I wanted something to read, and took this from your room."

"Take any of my books you like."

"I got rather a shock when I went in. There was somebody there."

"You mean the roomboy?"

"No. Mr. Potter."

Birkett stared at her. He had somehow guessed a second before she had spoken that it was going to be Potter. He said, "What was he doing?"

"He wasn't doing anything—just standing by the chest-of-drawers. He said he'd heard that your room was the nicest in the hotel, and he wanted to see it so that if he liked it he could take it over when you leave."

"He might have asked me first."

"I know, I thought it rather odd, but I couldn't think of any other reason why he should have gone in, except to steal something. And Mr. Potter doesn't look the sort of person who'd steal."

"Nothing much to steal anyway. No, shouldn't worry about it. I expect he was telling the truth."

He went up to the room. There were various letters and papers on the table, but the roomboy had tidied up while he had been out and it was impossible to tell if they had been disturbed. Anyhow, they were of no importance. The only important articles in the room were the gun and the tin of heaven-helpers. He opened the wardrobe. The suitcase stood in the bottom where he had left it. He carefully lifted it out, looking for any dust marks that might show if it had been recently moved—but there was no dust or any other means of telling. Next he examined the locks for evidence of tampering—nothing. But of course if Potter was what seemed disturbingly possible, a couple of suitcase locks would have been child's play. He'd have had them open in a jiffy, leaving no traces—and not omitting to note any hairs or other little traps laid to catch the unwary, and taking care to replace them.

He unlocked the suitcase. The gun and throat-pastille tin were safely inside. He examined the gun and ammunition. All in order. Lastly he opened the tin. The pills rested like eggs in a nest of cotton wool. There had been only a few, but now he felt sure that there were fewer than before. He counted them. There were five.

He tried to remember the pattern in which they had previously lain. He could not be absolutely certain, but he was almost certain that one pill at least was missing.

He closed the tin. Anyhow, whether there's a pill missing or not, he thought, I don't believe that cock-and-bull story about taking a prospective look at the room. I'm afraid friend Potter's up to no good.

He locked the suitcase and returned it to the wardrobe. He went downstairs. He met Potter passing through the hall.

"Ah, I've been waiting to speak to you, old man," Potter said.

He drew Birkett confidentially aside. Birkett waited, supposing he was going to repeat his improbable story, but to his surprise Potter said, "I feel a perfect idiot, old man. Mrs. Kapoor caught me in your room this morning, and I had to make up some excuse for being there on the spur of the moment. I began to act like a schoolboy caught stealing the tarts, and of course she knew it was just tommy-rot."

"Well, what *were* you doing in my room? Why couldn't you tell her the truth?"

"I wanted to stand by you, old man. I didn't want to let you down."

"Let me down? I don't get it."

"It's like this, old man. You see, my wife doesn't keep any secrets from me, and she told me all about that night when you two had your little flutter."

Birkett felt the blood burn in his cheeks. "She did, eh? Yes, both of us as high as kites. Damn' silly escapade—sorry, Potter."

"Don't mention it, old man." He winked an eye, and pulled roguishly at his moustache. "I don't blame you—I'm the first to know what it does to a chap when Betty flutters those eyelashes."

"So you weren't waiting up in my room to horsewhip me, eh? Then what was the idea?"

"Well, last night Betty missed her ruby brooch—remembered she'd left it in your room. Didn't want to bother you about it—bit embarrassing, what?—so she asked me to slip in and pick it up for her. And when your lady friend caught me in the act, I naturally tried to cover up for you."

"Well, did you find the brooch?"

"No, I'd no time to look before Mrs. Kapoor came in."

"All right, we'll go and have a look together."

They went upstairs. Potter's second story seemed to Birkett as improbable as his first, and he felt certain that there was no brooch to be found—that after going through the motions of looking for it, Potter would have to pretend to think it lost. They entered the room.

"If she'd left it here, I'd certainly have found it by now," he said.

"I'm inclined to agree, old man. Not much hope. She thought she'd left it on the shelf of the pedestal table by the bed—but she's such a scatterbrain, that's the last place it'll be."

Birkett went to the pedestal table and slid his hand into the deep shelf. His fingers encountered a small object at the back. He pulled it out. It was the ruby brooch that he now remembered Mrs. Potter had in fact been wearing on the night of her unfortunate visit.

"By Jove, here we are!"

"Good show, old man," Potter said. He pocketed the brooch.

"Well, I think we can now consider that little incident closed. So keep the flag flying, old man—and no doubt see you at lunch." And he was gone.

Well, thank God for that, Birkett thought. So Potter's story was true—he was really looking for the brooch. And of course I must have been mistaken about the pills. I've been letting my imagination run away with me . . . And thus relieved of the heavy burden of apprehension, he went cheerfully downstairs to rejoin Lakshmi.

But during lunch he was silent, his apprehension returning. The brooch really proved nothing. If Potter was what he feared, and had gone to search the room for evidence of what Birkett was up to, he would naturally have prepared some story to cover himself in case he was caught in the act. And he would have known that there was nothing like concrete evidence to make a story convincing, and would have brought the brooch along with him and slipped it into the shelf as soon as he entered the room.

The more he thought about it, the more certain he became that this was what had happened. And the more certain that after all he had been right about the pills—that there was one missing.

Yes, Potter's on my tail, he thought. He's been tailing me from Delhi.

"What are you doing this afternoon?" Lakshmi asked him.

"I think I'll take a snooze."

She reminded him that in the evening there was a big reception given by the American Ambassador to India, who also represented his country in Nepal and was paying one of his periodic visits. Mr. Wilson, who had been asked to supply snacks for the occasion, had arranged for all his guests to be invited.

"All right, we might take a breather in the jeep first," he said. "See you at tea."

He went upstairs. He did not want to sleep but to think about Potter. He paced the room. He saw now that his meeting with Potter in the hotel in Delhi had been no accident. It had been carefully planned. They had probably decided to put someone on to him as soon as he had come out of China into Hong Kong.

They had sent out Potter. Probably Potter had gone to Hong Kong, missed him, and followed him to India and then to Kathmandu.

Potter, in fact, had arrived in Nepal ahead of him—a clever move to avert suspicion. Birkett only wished he had told Potter he was going to Iceland. He'd have enjoyed sitting here in Kathmandu and thinking of Potter kicking his heels in Reykjavik. He also saw that Potter was not past making use of his wife—that her visit to his room had been a put-up job. Quite a Mata Hari, our little blue-eyed doll, he thought.

Still, if it hadn't been for Mrs. Potter, he would never have sent for Lakshmi. He was grateful to Mrs. Potter for that.

He remembered Mrs. Potter feeling the gun-holster under his arm. Well, that had been a nice little titbit to take home to hubby.

On the other hand, he was certain that Potter could not know what kind of job he was planning. No, it was impossible—neither the meeting with Mathai nor the gun, nor the heaven-helper he had taken from Birkett's room, could have enabled him even to hazard a guess. He wouldn't know until the job was carried out. Then, of course, he would know in retrospect what they had been up to; and since it had been carried out by Mathai, he would know that Birkett had been behind it. But he would have no evidence against Birkett—not a shred.

No, he won't be able to touch me, Birkett thought. It's the biggest job of my career, and I'm not going to lay off because of Potter. I'm going right ahead. And he can't lay a finger on me.

All the same he was uneasy. Because no matter how much you told yourself that you were in no danger, a man on your tail made you feel the lurking presence of danger—made you jump at unexpected sounds, imagine figures crouching in the shadows, and even in an empty room feel pursued by some nameless fear. He remembered vividly the fear that had pursued him during those days on the Island of Arran, on the only other occasion that he had been tailed—or had at least been warned that he was going to be tailed, and was waiting for it to happen. He had been up to Glasgow on a job, and then had gone over to the island for a few days' holiday, and had got the warning by telephone from a contact on the mainland. The fear had pursued him even up into the mountains amongst the screes and bogs, where he had gone for a day's walk in the mistaken belief that he could shake it off. And he remembered descending the steep mountainside at dusk, feeling certain that danger awaited him in the village below—that he would find the man who had been described to him waiting at the little hotel to make the arrest. But there had been nobody—and when at last on the quay, just before his departure, he had seen the brown belted tweed overcoat, the yellow scarf, the green felt hat with the fisherman's flies stuck in the band, he had felt almost relieved that the suspense was over. The man had followed him up the gang-plank on to the *Maid of Islay*. It was like mounting the steps to the gallows. "When my feet touch dry land again I'll no longer be a free man," he had thought. And as though to confirm this thought the man had suddenly come abreast of him and bared his teeth in a frigid grin. Birkett had supposed that they would be waiting to arrest him as he came ashore at Glasgow. It had been like waiting in the Big Schoolroom all over again to hear his name called, knowing there was no possible escape from the summons to the rostrum, to the wooden chair, to the public humiliation . . .

But then on the *Maid of Islay*, just as in the Big Schoolroom, nothing—incredibly, inexplicably—had happened. And just as he had watched the Headmaster in mortarboard and gown sweep off down the aisle, so had he watched the man in the green felt hat and the Harris tweed sweep away down the gangplank. And his feet had touched dry land again in disbelieving freedom. And he still didn't know why . . .

Well, that time he had thought they'd really got something on him—there'd been plenty of excuse for getting the wind up. But there was no excuse this time.

And Potter must be a poor hand at his game if he gives himself away like he did this morning, he thought. So the devil take him.

He began to feel better, and was in a cheerful mood again when he set off with Lakshmi after tea for a blow in the jeep. They returned later than they had intended, and by the time they had bathed and changed, and driven round to the old Rana palace that the Americans had taken over for the occasion, the reception was in full swing. The enormous room was crowded with guests, who stood chattering amongst the marble pillars, and under the great painted wall-panels depicting spectacular big-game hunting episodes in the lives of notable Ranas. The British and Indian Ambassadors were present in their diplomatic regalia, as well as the rest of the diplomatic corps with their wives, prominent members of the Nepalese government in jodhpurs and shirt-tails, and many other Nepalese brilliantly displaying a variety of exotic uniforms. There was a terrific hubbub. Wilson came up to them.

"I'm afraid it's an awful bear garden," he said apologetically, as if he were personally responsible for the noise. "I hope you're good at lip-reading, because it's your only chance of understanding what anybody's saying. Of course it's only just started like this. You could hear a pin drop until ten minutes ago, when His Majesty left."

"So he was here, eh?" Birkett said. He felt intense relief at having avoided an encounter with the King.

Two servants paused beside them with trays of drink and snacks.

"That's real Scotch," Wilson said. "The Yanks flew in a plane load, but I'd snaffle as much as you can as quickly as you can—there are so many people here with hip flasks that it will all be gone in an hour."

Birkett saw Mathai approaching. His eyes shone with eager devotion.

"Good evening, sir!" He put his palms together before his face. His long beautiful hands made the gesture more than ever touching.

"Evening, Krishna."

"Thank you, sir."

"What for?"

"I'm very moved that you should use my first name, sir."

Good God, did I? Birkett thought. Yes, I believe I did—without thinking. I called him Krishna without thinking.

He was appalled at himself. He turned abruptly to introduce Lakshmi. He said, "Mrs. Kapoor—Mr. Mathai. Now excuse me . . ."

He moved briskly away. Good God, Krishna, he thought. Krishna. As if he was my bloody son.

He saw the tiny General who had been at the bar of the Everest on his first night. He was in uniform, with little black pointed polished shoes. His face was swamped by a peaked cap that was several sizes too big and rested on his ears.

"Evening, sir," Birkett said.

The General had to tilt back his head to see Birkett's face from under the brim of the enormous cap. His little elephant's eyes twinkled. "Ah, Major Birkett."

"Puts me to shame, sir. I'm afraid I never took in your name properly, except that you are a Rana, of course. You've nearly as many names as children—if I remember correctly."

"Yes, but the number of my names is static, whilst the number of my children is in constant flux."

"When's the next one due, sir?"

"My wife will present me with my thirty-ninth in about two months' time. I hope to see my fortieth smile upon the world not more than one year later. I have promised my wife that she shall then have a holiday, strictly without me. I would like you to meet her, Major Birkett. Perhaps you would honour us with your presence for lunch on Sunday?" Then, with an appreciative glance in Lakshmi's direction, "Your friend is also welcome, of course."

Sunday, Birkett thought—I fancy we'll none of us be in a mood for luncheon parties by then. But he said, "Thanks. Very nice of you, sir."

"Good, we shall be looking forward." He moved away. "Good evening, Major Birkett."

Birkett turned and saw Mrs. Mathai. She touched her fingers in greeting. He responded crisply. Blast her, he thought, she's the last person I wanted to meet. He said brusquely, "Evening. Kids all right?"

"Yes, they are very well," she said, her manner surprisingly warm. Major Birkett, I wish to thank you for what you have done for my husband."

"Eh?"

"You have given him new faith in himself—and inspiration. He will now be able to finish his book. He does not speak about it, but I know he is full of confidence. He keeps saying how proud we shall be of him—how he will bring honour to our name."

"No doubt." He looked away across the room, trying not to listen to her, to think about her—trying to screen himself off from her.

"I also have great confidence in his success. His character is sometimes weak, but I have a strong character and he will always have me behind him." She looked over towards her husband, who was still talking to Lakshmi. "I shall urge him to finish the book when we go on leave."

"Leave?"

"Yes, my husband's leave is due in a month's time. He says we must not count on it, in case something unexpected should happen, but I have made all our plans. We shall go back to India. The children are so excited."

"Excuse me—glass empty. Just going to grab . . ."

He made off. He wanted to get hold of Lakshmi and get out of this heat and noise, but he could not approach her because of Mathai. He wasn't going near Mathai again—he couldn't stand any more of those looks of Daddy-worship and devotion. He took another glass of whisky from the tray and stood looking up at one of the painted panels on the wall.

He finished the whisky in a couple of gulps. He put down the glass. He looked round for Lakshmi. God Almighty, still nattering with Mathai. Well, he'd just have to go and grab her.

He made his way towards them. He ignored Mathai. He said, "Getting thick in here—let's push off." He could feel Mathai's hurt eyes on him.

"Yes, I suppose it is getting a bit stuffy," Lakshmi said. "I hadn't noticed. I've been having such an interesting talk with Mr. Mathai."

Mathai began eagerly, "Yes, we have discovered we are both from Lucknow, sir. We were both born within—"

"Come on, then. Let's skip off quick."

Mathai looked deeply pained at the interruption. Lakshmi noticed it. She tried to make amends for Birkett by putting extra warmth in her voice as she said goodbye.

Mathai said unhappily, "Goodbye, Mrs. Kapoor. Goodbye, sir."

Birkett snapped, "'Bye," and turned away. Lakshmi followed him. He went off to fetch the jeep, which he brought to the steps to pick her up. She got in, tying a silk scarf round her head to protect her hair from the wind.

She said, "I don't know whether you realized it, but you were terribly rude to Mr. Mathai just now."

"I was suffocating—I didn't want to get caught."

"I felt rather awful about it. He'd been saying such wonderful things about you. He said you were the sort of man he'd have liked as a father."

He noisily changed gear. He said, "Eh? Who, Mathai? Very nice of him, I'm sure."

"You don't sound as if you think much of him. I thought he was rather nice. And he's got such beautiful hands. Have you noticed?"

"Hands?"

"Yes, I couldn't keep my eyes off them. And then—wasn't it funny?—I found I'd met his mother. Of course his father died soon after he was born, and he was her only child, and I can remember she never stopped talking about him. She simply doted . . . Are you listening?"

"Sorry, thinking of something else. Look, frankly I don't care two hoots about young Mathai, so you might as well skip it!"

2

Mathai was waiting at the corner of the maidan when he drew up in the jeep at the appointed hour the next day. He made the young man get in beside him and they drove out of the town. Birkett did not speak until they had pulled up beside a quiet track amongst the paddy-fields. Then he said abruptly, "Right, Mathai. Now for your briefing."

He avoided the young Indian's eyes. He had begun to feel something like hatred for Mathai. The feeling had increased steadily all day. I hate his softness, his weakness, his hysteria, he thought. I hate his skinny wrists, his girlish hands . . . He let these reasons satisfy him, suppressing the sneaking doubt that they were enough to account for such intensity of feeling, such a bitter rankling. He had seldom experienced such personal hatred. It reminded him of the hatred he had felt for the boys at his prep school who had so cruelly bullied him. But they had had power over him and his hatred had sprung from fear. It was not as though Mathai had any power . . .

He said, "We've a lot to get through, so let's keep this meeting business-like and stick to the point." He talked as coldly and as impersonally as a machine. It took half-an-hour to give Mathai his instructions and make sure that he had memorized them. They covered almost every move he would make from the time he got up on the day of the Tattoo, and were carefully numbered and divided into sections, so that by knowing the total number of orders in each section he could make periodic checks on himself to make sure none had been forgotten. For in the stress of such an occasion even an experienced operator could suffer disastrous lapses, and would usually take such precautions.

The orders also covered every conceivable change of official programme or other eventuality that might occur. He warned Mathai to keep his mind cool and flexible-to expect the unexpected, so that he would on no account lose his head.

After giving the orders he took out the gun and harness. He asked Mathai if there was anywhere that he could keep the gun at home where there was no possibility of its being found by his wife.

"Yes, sir, there is a chest in our bicycle shed for which I have the only key," Mathai said. "I can also lock the shed."

"Good, because I'd prefer us not to have to meet again before the event. Now, have you ever used a gun before?"

"No, sir."

"Right, hold it. Go on, it's not going to bite you. Grip it. Get the feel of it. Get used to it, so that it doesn't just feel like a great clumsy weight in your hand, but like part of your hand, and that you've complete control of it."

They spent a long time on the gun. Next Birkett said, "Now, for the heaven-helpers."

"Sir, I wish to kill myself with this gun. It will be more brave."

"Right, but you've got to carry one of these in your mouth as well in case anything should prevent your using the gun. And even if you can use it, you've got to swallow the pill before pulling the trigger, otherwise you may wake up in clink, and find that you've made a bosh shot of it and only grazed your forehead—and that the State has considerately patched you up again, so that you will be in good condition to take that little walk to the gallows. And you don't want that, do you? Right, that's all. Now repeat your orders once more." Mathai repeated them.

"Right. Any questions?" He waited. Mathai was silent. "Well?"

Mathai said diffidently, "Sir, why do you not look at me today? Why do you avoid my eyes as if I was something offensive and dirty?"

"I'm not avoiding your eyes." He returned his eyes towards Mathai, but they were glazed and did not see.

"You are still not looking at me, sir. I think you hate me."

"Yes," Birkett said.

"Why, sir?"

"For Christ's sake, man," Birkett said, letting himself go. "Use your bloody nut, if you've got one. How d'you think I could sit here giving you a gun to blow your brains out, and pills to knock you out cold in ten seconds flat, if I didn't bloody well hate you? Do you honestly think that if I was really your beloved Daddy . . ." He broke off. He got abruptly out of the jeep and walked away up the road. He stopped and stood with his back turned, looking out over the paddy-fields.

Mathai sat without moving. Major Birkett was nearly crying, he thought. The fine, strong soldier was nearly crying because he loves me like a son and must send me to die. His emotions are truly noble.

Presently Birkett came back. He had regained control of himself.

He no longer avoided Mathai's eyes. He smiled wrily. "Sorry, Mathai. Poor show. Behaving like a ruddy prima donna."

"It doesn't matter, sir."

Birkett got back into the jeep.

"Good God, look at that petrol gauge. Has it stopped working, or are we out of ruddy juice?" He started the motor.

"You are a fine man, sir. You have true nobility."

"Now that's enough, Mathai. Mustn't behave like babies. Let's try and remember we're grown-up and keep our minds on the job."

Chapter Fifteen

He sat cross-legged on the folded blanket, his arms at his sides. He closed his eyes.

There are cords attached to my wrists, he thought. The cords pass over two pulleys on the ceiling, and baskets hang from their opposite ends. The weight of the baskets keeps the cords taut but is not enough to lift my arms. There is a man standing by each of the baskets. Now each man puts in a pebble. I can feel the increased pressure on my wrists. The men put in more pebbles. Now my arms are lifting . . . lifting . . . lifting . . .

His arms remained limp at his sides.

It's not working, he thought. I must concentrate harder. I must concentrate with my whole being upon the pressure of the cords . . . Now the men are putting in more pebbles. The pressure on my wrists is becoming irresistible. I am not thinking of anything else but the pressure. The trouble before was that half my mind was wandering. I kept imagining that I was on a picnic with Lakshmi and Mathai was with us, only he was a child, and we were married and he was our son, and we were discussing his future career, and I was saying, "I agree with your mother, Krishna," and Krishna was—

God, I'm wandering again, he thought. Now I'm really going to concentrate. The baskets are full of pebbles. The cords are pulling harder . . . harder . . .

His arms did not move. He finally gave up. He was in despair.

I don't know what's been the matter with me, he thought. I've gone completely to pieces. And the Tattoo's the day after tomorrow. I must pull myself together before the Tattoo . . .

He had been like this since yesterday evening, since his last meeting with Mathai. He had kept feeling strange and disturbing emotional stirrings that seemed to bear no relation to his thoughts—that he could no more account for than if they had been happening to another person. They had kept returning at intervals, threatening to overwhelm him like a tidal wave. It was extraordinary. Nothing of the kind had ever happened to him before.

It must be because of Mathai, he thought. Because I've grown fond of him. And because fondness is an attachment that destroys and corrupts. It is a carcass that breeds fat maggots of doubt . . .

I'm beginning to doubt the rightness of what I'm doing. I'm beginning to question my own faith. But the doubt is only weakness. It is right for Mathai to die, for his death is essential to our cause. His death is justified because it will bring to millions the hope of a better life . . .

It appalled him and terrified him to think of losing his faith. His faith was like a great iron pillar. It was the source of his courage and strength, the centre and the purpose of his existence. Deprived of it . . . But he dare not even imagine such a condition, it would be like falling into a great yawning abyss.

The compulsion to tell Lakshmi about Mathai, about the job on which he was engaged, increasingly possessed him. He wanted her reassurances, her blessing. He was convinced with one part of himself that he could make her understand. But with the other part he knew that it would be madness. Women became bogged down in trivial details and failed to understand the larger issues. The harsh realities of politics were outside their comprehension. They were too soft and sentimental to grasp that it was a battle of life and death, and that you'd got to fight tooth and nail with no holds barred—because otherwise you'd go down the drain.

And even supposing she could have grasped it, it would still have been an unspeakable transgression to tell her. A breach of discipline that could bring an end to his career in shame and dishonour. No, it was unthinkable.

Yet the dangerous, irrational compulsion remained. And that night, lying beside her after making love, he was horrified to hear himself break their long silence by suddenly exclaiming, "By the way, I never told you before—I used to be a Communist agent. I used to do underground work—cloak and dagger stuff."

"Used to" makes it all right, he thought to excuse himself. It doesn't matter so long as I don't tell her that I'm doing the work now.

"Really?" she said. "I didn't realise you'd been so deep in it as all that. What sort of things did you do?"

"All sorts—sometimes above-board, sometimes not. Often a job would go against the grain. It wouldn't be easy to square your conscience. But you'd realise in the end that you couldn't apply ordinary day-to-day standards when such big issues were at stake— and when those standards were ignored by the other side. For instance, once I had the job of organising an assassination."

"An assassination? You mean killing someone?"

"Yes, it was years ago now. South America. The chap they wanted bumped off was a—a leading figure in the government. Quite harmless—nobody had anything against him personally. But his assassination, according to our calculations, would have certain repercussions that would benefit thousands—millions—of people, improving their lives and saving many from famine, disease, and death. That was the equation. One life—or rather, two lives—against millions."

"You were supposed to kill the man yourself?"

"No, the result could only be achieved if the assassination was carried out by a certain young chap who would be obliged to kill himself immediately afterwards—hence the two lives involved. My job was to persuade him to make the self-sacrifice, which meant discovering his weaknesses, exploiting them, and tempting him with the promise of honour and glory. Pretty immoral on the face of it—and not made any easier by the fact that I liked the chap. But then I would think of those suffering millions . . ." He explained that power politics weren't played with kid gloves. You couldn't afford to be a dreamer, an idealist, a Gentle-Jesus-Meek-and-Mild. You'd got to be a realist. You'd got to face the fact that freedom and justice could only be won by kicking people in the teeth. And he finished, "So I carried out my orders, and saw the job through."

Lakshmi was silent. She said at last, "Why have you told me all this?"

"Because I don't want to hide anything from you. I want you to know what sort of chap I am."

"But that was a long time ago. You've changed."

"No, I've not changed. If I was given the same job today, I'd still think it right to carry it through. And I'd like to know that you'd understand and think the same. Well, would you?"

"Do you honestly want to know my opinion?"

He turned to look at her. She lay beside him, her head on the pillow and her long hair loose about her shoulders, her huge brown liquid eyes staring up at the ceiling. She said quietly:

"I think it was murder."

Birkett was silent for a minute. Then he swung his legs out of the bed and got up without looking at her.

"Where are you going?" she said.

"If that's the way you think, there's nothing I can do about it. You don't want a murderer in bed with you." He began to dress.

"Whatever you did, I'm sure you were being true to your own lights," she said.

"Jack the Ripper was probably being true to his own lights. And so far as you're concerned, I'm on a par with him."

"No, it's just that I don't believe that what you did can really have brought more good to people than harm. Perhaps it did bring some material benefits—I don't know. But we've got a saying in India, 'If the river is poisoned at the source, it will be poisoned at the mouth.' If you start by solving your problems by bad means, you will always solve them by bad means—if you start by killing, you will go on by killing. And it won't only be yourself that's corrupted, there'll be others who will follow your example."

He said, still not looking at her, and his voice hard, "And you think if you turn your other cheek, they'll follow that example too, and you'll all be palsie-walsies? Don't you believe it! They'll kick you in the groin and push you down the drain." He buckled his bush-shirt.

"Please don't go."

"Why not? Don't tell me you'd go to bed with Jack the Ripper?"

She was on the point of tears. She said, "I don't know who he is, but I suppose I would if I was in love with him."

"Well, I don't like going to bed with a woman who thinks I'm a murderer. I'm sorry. Goodnight."

He felt that tidal wave of emotion threatening to overwhelm him again as he returned to his room. It beat at the bottom of his throat, trying to force its way upwards. He was tempted to throw himself on his bed, give way to it. But no, that was a road down which there was no return. If he once abandoned control, he would never regain it.

He got into bed. I was out of my mind to tell her, he thought. It was obvious that she wouldn't understand—that I was only submitting myself unnecessarily, like Ulysses, to the beguiling song of the sirens that would lure me to destruction on the rocks. Well, as Ulysses was bound to the mast to save him from becoming their victim, so am I bound to the iron pillar of my conviction. She's a woman, she has no more idea of the world than a romantic kitchen-maid, and her head is as full of pretty dreams. And she can call it "murder" all she likes, but I'm lashed tightly to my pillar, she won't get me on those rocks . . .

The next morning he woke about seven o'clock. He remembered that it was Friday.

And tomorrow's Saturday, he thought. Only one more day of suspense . . .

Lakshmi was as cheerful at breakfast as if nothing had happened, and he suggested another picnic—the detachment he always felt up in the hills would ease the suspense and make the day pass quicker. They went to their favourite spot on the green shelf between snow peaks and patchwork valley. The sparkling air went quickly to Birkett's head and he began to laugh. "By Jove, I'm happy! By Jove, we've had some good times up here!"

His laughter continued. The tears began to roll down his face. She stared at him in astonishment.

"What's the matter? Are you all right?"

"Me? Yes, fine. Haven't you ever seen a chap laugh before?" He controlled himself and wiped away the tears. "Don't worry, it's only the altitude. It always makes people dotty. Never been to Kenya, have you? No, of course you haven't. Anyhow, they're all dotty up in the Kenya Highlands—every man Jack of them, right round the bend . . . Now, come on, the Picnic Game—it's time we made up a story about you. I'll start. *Well, my dear, there was this bonny little Indian slip-of-a-thing called—well, as a matter of fact her friends used to call her just Slip-of-a-Thing, because her waist was the slippiest little waist in the whole of India and you couldn't help wanting to slip your hand round it—and one day she was lying in bed when the door began to open slowly, and she looked up and stared in horror as she saw . . .*"

"What?"

"I don't know. It's your turn."

"You can't stop in the middle of a sentence."

"Go on, you know what would horrify her better than I do."

"Instead of her lover whom she had been impatiently expecting, she saw a horrible ugly monster entering the door."

"Nice of you to make the distinction . . . *Her amorous sigh gave way to a stifled though ladylike cry, and seizing a knife she prepared to defend her honour.*"

"*She was about to plunge it into the monster's heart when she suddenly stopped.*" Lakshmi was sitting cross-legged on the grass. She had become carried away by her little fantasy, imitating the action of the interrupted stab. She gazed at the imaginary monster, her expression changing from horror to tenderness.

"*Because after all, she thought, it can't help being a horrible ugly monster, and it's probably terribly unhappy because nobody loves it, so she said: 'Oh, how beautiful you are! All my life I have dreamed of meeting such a beautiful monster! Please forgive the swift thumping of my maidenly heart, and come in for a cup of*

tea! Let me take off your shoes, Mr. Monster! Let me stroke your
lovely forehead, and smooth away the pain!"

She stroked the monster's forehead. Her expression was filled with tenderness and pity, and as he watched her, Birkett felt once more that emotional stirring.

"By Jove, I believe it's just what you would do, too!" he said.

She came to earth. "I wouldn't. I'd just scream and run."

"I don't know. It's more or less what you did last night when you found you'd got a monster in bed with you."

"Oh, nonsense! Come on, let's get on with the game. It's your turn."

"You're looking so bonny, I reckon it's time we switched to the other Picnic Game."

"What other?"

"Well, that's a funny question coming from you. You're usually the first to suggest it."

She understood. "I'm not! I've never suggested it!"

"There are more ways than one of suggesting. And you can stop looking at me with that wide-eyed innocence, like Mrs. Potter, because there's nobody who knows better than you how to give a man ideas with a flick of an eye."

And it went so well this time that in the midst of making love she cried out to him, as she had often come near to crying out before, to let her have a baby.

Her demand filled him with momentary fear—fear that he could not resist the temptation to indulge her. But then he thought of tomorrow, and how tomorrow she would think of him as a murderer, and he said, "No."

"Please!" she cried, as one who pleads for her life. "Please!"

"No."

And so, her wings clipped at the very zenith of her flight, she plummeted to earth in tears. She felt as if her heart had been torn out of her breast, thrown on to the rubbish dump. She lay sobbing. "Why didn't you let me?" she cried. "Why were you so cruel?"

"It would have been lunacy," he said.

"It would have made no difference to you. I'd never have troubled you."

"You're going to have a hard enough time explaining things to your husband when you go home, without having to explain away a kid."

"I'm not going home."

"Eh?"

"I was just a beast of burden before I met you. You've seen those oxen we use for grinding corn, walking round and round all day with hanging heads and empty eyes? I was like that at home—but now I'm a real person with a soul, and you've given it to me, and that's why, if you'd really understood what a man means to a woman he's brought to life, you wouldn't have left me last night. You'd have known that what you told me could make no difference."

"I reckon that the way you look at what I did, there is a lot to forgive."

"Forgive? That shows how little you understand, if you can say 'forgive.' Do you think a mother has to forgive a child? Do you think that a person in love has to forgive the loved one? No, you accept what they've done just as if they were a part of yourself."

Birkett said, "Anyhow, what were you saying about not going home?"

"If I go back I shall just wither and die again. I can never go back after this."

Birkett said uneasily, "I reckon I'm not much of a catch for any woman. I'm a real lone-ranger."

"Don't worry, I'm not trying to blackmail you. I shall go back to my parents for a bit. Then I shall go to Calcutta or Bombay and find a job."

"You'd have had a hard time with that kid."

"I'd have managed. I wouldn't have worried you."

He was silent. He felt all the more moved that she wanted his child after what she had learned about him last night. He felt those dangerous stirrings of emotion again, those first hints of the threatening wave.

Lakshmi said, "By the way, I realised last night after you'd gone how perfectly everything that you told me fitted into the picture. I mean, that lone-ranger you've always wanted to be, that cheetah prowling alone—I imagine no one could be more alone than a secret agent. Nobody to confide in, nobody with whom to share the truth about yourself—you're sealed right off, in perfect isolation. It must have made you feel so safe."

"Safe? Don't you believe it. I'd say there are few more dangerous games. You need a steady nerve for it—especially when you've someone sitting on your tail."

"Yes, but the physical dangers were nothing like so terrible as those other dangers you'd always been running away from. I mean, the dangers of losing your independence, of making attachments—of loving. And you were safe against those."

He said, "Perhaps not so safe . . ."

"You're still safe. You still don't know what it's like to be in love—to feel everything inside you melting at a glance, a word, a touch of a hand—one minute feeling your heart leap with joy, the next wanting to burst into tears."

I want to burst into tears, he thought. Am I in love?

He said, "If I've changed you, I reckon you've changed me a good bit, too."

"Yes, it's true you've changed. You've begun to open doors that you'd always kept locked."

"And it's surprising what queer things have come rushing out."

"What sort of queer things?"

"I mean, feelings. You've no idea what you've stirred up. A regular hornets' nest."

"A hornets' nest," she smiled.

"What's the joke?"

"Because that's just what it is for you—a hornets' nest. You're still as much afraid of the feelings as if they were hornets with stings."

"I'm not afraid."

"Of course you're afraid. For instance, you're so afraid of feeling anything for me that you never even dared say 'I love you' just to please me. The idea is so horrifying to you that you're afraid even of the pretence."

"You don't want me to pretend, do you?"

"Yes, I'd love to hear you say 'I love you,' even though you didn't mean it. But you couldn't do it."

"Oh, rubbish."

"Then say it. Go on. Say 'Lakshmi, I love you'."

"I don't say that sort of thing to order."

"There you are! You're afraid!"

I believe I could say it if it wasn't for tomorrow, he thought. I believe I could say it—and almost mean it. I felt a real pang when she talked of going back to her parents just now. I've become so used to having her around that I'm going to miss her. He watched her open her little silver box and prepare some pan. The homely familiarity of what she was doing made him feel a sudden burst of tenderness. It was as though she had taken out her mending, switched on the radio, poked the fire. If it hadn't been for tomorrow, I might have thought of setting up shop with her, he thought. There's no doubt about it, we fit each other. And I'd like to know she's always going to be there to talk things over with.

But I cannot contemplate a future with her because of tomorrow. Because tomorrow young Mathai is going to shoot the King of Nepal and then shoot himself, and Lakshmi will know who has caused the two men to die. And she will know that I was planning their deaths all the time we were together—that murder was in my mind as I lay in her arms.

Yes, she will call me a murderer, he thought. And today is our last day together, and tomorrow it must end.

But I'm not a murderer yet, he thought. There's still time to call it off. And if I call it off I can marry her, we can have kids . . .

He felt a sudden new uprush of emotion. It caught at his throat. Tears stung in his eyes.

Christ, what's happening to me? he thought. Call off the job? Betray the cause? It's unthinkable. I must get a grip . . .

He jumped up. He said abruptly, "I'm off for a walk."

"I'll come with you."

"No. I'm going alone."

She recognized the voice—the resurrected hate. She stared after him in astonishment and dismay.

He walked briskly along the hillside. The waves battered at his throat. He fought them until they subsided. By Jove, that was a near one, he thought. That was touch and go. I mustn't let that happen again.

He came to a solitary tree on the slope. He stopped in its shade. He stood erect, one hand against the trunk. He closed his eyes. He must make himself strong again before he returned to Lakshmi. He concentrated his thoughts. He imagined that he stood on the African plain and that the tree under which he stood was and that he was the cheetah. Spare and trim and self-contained. Spare and trim and dedicated. Swift-limbed and strong and a stranger to doubt. The King of the Plain out on the prowl, dedicated to the kill . . .

He remained standing under the tree until the words that he repeated to himself carried conviction. And when he started back along the hillside, he felt strong again.

He still felt strong as he rejoined Lakshmi—strong enough to remain indifferent to her hurt look.

He said, "Let's pack up. I've had enough of this place."

"What happened?" she said miserably. "What made you suddenly go like that?"

"Go like what? I wasn't aware that I'd 'gone like' anything."

She saw that it was no use questioning him further. All contact between them was severed. They were isolated like islands in a gale. They climbed silently into the jeep. The silence continued as they drove down the steep track and along the straight flat road between the paddies towards Kathmandu.

Spare and strong and dedicated, Birkett thought. Like the cheetah.

Each repetition was another stone added to his fortress. And he was still strengthening the fortress as they approached the outskirts of the town—and something happened that made it collapse like a house of cards.

2

It was not Birkett's fault and they did not know at first what they had hit. They had been passing a wayside shrine and had seen a little boy nearby throw a stone at something hidden behind it, and then had caught only a glimpse of some black animal as it charged out from behind the shrine—and then there was a thud and a jolt as it was struck by the jeep and went under the wheel.

Birkett braked abruptly. The jeep skidded to a stop in the dust. They could hear the animal squealing on the road behind them.

"That ruddy little brat, I'll wring his neck!" Birkett exclaimed. He jumped out. But the boy, seeing the consequences of his mischief, had already taken flight and vanished.

Lakshmi had also got out of the jeep, and they hurried back along the road. The animal was twisting and bouncing in the dust.

Lakshmi exclaimed, "It's a goat. Oh, how awful!" She drew back in horror as she saw the gash on its breast where a piece of hairy flesh, peeled off like fruit rind, hung down in a loose flap. Both its forelegs were broken. It kept rearing its hindquarters, its head ploughing in the dust.

"Well, I'm afraid that's done for," Birkett said. "There's no saving that."

"What can we do?"

"Nothing, unless we can find the chap who owns it."

They looked round but there was nobody about. The animal's shrill squeals continued unabated. Lakshmi had turned pale. She said in anguish, "Can't you put it out of its misery? Can't you kill it?"

"Not without a gun. Come on, better leave it."

"No! Please do something! I can't bear it!"

Well, it's only a ruddy nannygoat, he thought. I'm not going to let her think I'm afraid of killing a goat.

"Very well," he said. He went back to the jeep and looked through the tool-box for a suitable instrument. He took a wrench and returned up the road.

"Please be quick," Lakshmi pleaded.

"Don't worry, I'll soon finish it off."

He grabbed hold of the goat and brought down the wrench on the hard little nodule between the ears. The animal struggled more frenziedly than ever. Lakshmi buried her face in her hands. He raised the wrench for another blow, but as he brought it down the animal wriggled from his grasp and the wrench glanced off its head. He struggled with it, managed to straddle it and grip it between his knees. "Christ," he said. He struck again. "Oh, Christ."

He suddenly became aware of people watching. There were at least half a dozen who had appeared silently out of nowhere as they always did in the country as soon as you stopped the jeep. They stood in a semi-circle at sufficient distance to proclaim their detachment. They gazed in silence and without expression, suppressing any sign of emotion that might have appeared to commit them, to identify them in any way with the affair.

It occurred to Birkett that since they had not seen the accident, they would not realize that he was trying to kill the goat to put it out of its pain. They must suppose that he was slaughtering it to steal the meat, or for some other obscure purpose of his own—that he was willfully murdering it.

That's it, they think I'm a murderer, he thought. Everybody thinks I'm a murderer—a murderer of goats, a murderer of men.

And he began to attack the animal with renewed violence in order to kill it quickly. Christ, why didn't it die? Why didn't it die? Suddenly he could bear it no longer and he released his hold on the goat, letting it fall back into the dust. He dropped the wrench beside it, and without looking at Lakshmi, walked off down the road and got into the jeep.

Lakshmi stared helplessly at the goat. It lay without moving, uttering weak little cries. Its body trembled. Finally one of the onlookers took a curved Gurkha knife from a sheath lifted the goat's head from the ground, and slashed at its neck as casually as at a bunch of bananas. Its cries ceased.

Lakshmi returned to the jeep. Birkett sat stiffly behind the wheel looking straight ahead. His face was set. She got in beside him. He did not look at her.

"I'm sorry," she said. "It was awful. I'm sorry."

He did not reply. He started up the jeep and they moved off. He remained tense and rigid. Soon they were back in Kathmandu, passing the maidan.

Five more minutes, he thought. We'll be back in five more minutes. I must hold out until then.

He knew that this time there was no saving himself. It took all his strength to hold the dam against the great bursting pressure inside him, and he could not hold it much longer. Five minutes seemed an eternity.

At last they were turning into the gates of the Everest. He drew up near the entrance and got out delicately, nursing himself like a basket of eggs.

Lakshmi said, "Is there anything I can do?"

He shook his head. He went stiffly up the steps and into the hall. It was more difficult to hold the dam when he was moving and he was afraid he would not make it. He called upon his last reserves of strength to get upstairs, go down the corridor, open the door of his room, close the door again carefully behind him. And then the moment it was closed the dam burst, and the great waves broke over him as he threw himself on to the bed and buried his face on the pillow, and gave himself up to the cataclysm.

He cried for two hours.

Once Lakshmi came in, and he did not even mind that she should see him lying there sobbing like a child.

She asked if there was anything she could do. But he shook his head, and she went away.

Later the sobs began to subside. At last they stopped altogether. He lay still on the damp rumpled bed. He was drained of all thought and feeling.

Presently he got up and went over to the dressing-table. He stared in the mirror, at the bedraggled unfamiliar figure with the rumpled trousers and rucked-up vest, the blotched tear stained face, the moustache with damp crushed bristles like an old disreputable toothbrush. He had never seen a sadder bit of human wreckage.

Well, there you are, he thought. There's the cheetah for you.

Spare and trim and dedicated—the perfect animal-machine. The King of the Plain.

Well, that's the end of that little game. No more playing at cheetahs. No more fever trees. My fever's over. My temperature's down.

His head was dear now and he saw quite plainly what he must do.

He went into the bathroom and washed away the stains of his tears as best he could. He put on clean clothes and had just finished dressing when Lakshmi came in.

"I'm going out," he said.

"Out? Where?"

"I've got a job to do. I'll explain later."

"Won't you have dinner before you go?"

"No, perhaps when I come back."

He went down to the jeep and drove round to Mathai's bungalow, but Mathai was not there. Mrs. Mathai told him that he was still at the Embassy.

"He warned me he was going to be late tonight," she said. "He wanted to dear up a lot of work so that he needn't go to the office tomorrow."

He thanked her and got back into the jeep and drove to the Indian Embassy. He drew the jeep up beside the road some distance from the Embassy gates and sat waiting. He was still waiting after an hour, but he did not mind so long as Mathai eventually came. He sat without moving and scarcely noticed the passing of time. Once he was surprised to find himself crying again gently—it was odd how tears came without any apparent thought to provoke them. He did not try to stop himself crying and after a while the tears passed. A bit later a bicycle came down the Embassy drive. He recognized the powerful white beam of Mathai's chromium lamp. He flickered the lights of the jeep several times as Mathai approached, to draw his attention. Mathai dismounted.

"Major Birkett!" He glanced back anxiously towards the Embassy gates. "Sir, you are sure it is safe to speak here?"

"Yes, it's quite safe, Mathai."

"We must take no chances, sir. We have a great responsibility."

Birkett wrily noted the new self-assurance, the new hint of arrogance. Mathai even held himself more proudly, more like a hero.

"Don't worry. I've good news for you, Mathai. There's been a change of plan. The match is scrubbed."

"I beg your pardon, sir?"

"Our little game tomorrow—I decided that I'd already backed enough shins, and I've scrubbed it. So you can go home and finish your book, Mathai. You can become a famous writer after all. The operation is cancelled—it's all off."

.

Part Three

Chapter Sixteen

And then he found that it wasn't off after all—that the match wasn't as easy to scrub as he'd thought. Because he'd done his job too well. He'd sold Mathai the idea of martyrdom so successfully that now he wasn't going to be done out of it.

Mathai stood beside the jeep holding his bicycle. He regarded Birkett complacently.

"I think you must be ill, sir," he said. "I think you look ill."

"I'm nothing of the kind," Birkett snapped. "I'm in extremely sound health, as it happens—sound enough to have come to my senses, and realise that however excellent our ideals, this is not the way to achieve them."

"But only two days ago you held quite the contrary opinion, sir. Such vacillation is most uncharacteristic of you. I therefore conclude that you are ill, and feel sure you will revise your opinions again when you are better."

"That's confounded cheek, Mathai!"

He was dismayed by the petulance of his own voice. Gone was the old iron, the old authority, the old self-assurance—it must really sound as though some illness had undermined him. He must get a grip on himself.

"Now, look here, Mathai," he said. "I didn't come here to argue with you. I came to give you a new order. Your previous orders are cancelled. The operation for which you were detailed will not take place. I shall now return to your house with you, and you will give me back the gun and the box of pills."

But the authority was still lacking, and Mathai's complacency was unshaken.

"Sir, you once told me that I must regard myself as a soldier and that my failure to obey the orders of a superior officer would be an act of mutiny."

"Yes, exactly," Birkett said. "And I'm glad to hear you took it to heart—because you're coming pretty close to mutiny now."

"No, sir. In this instance it is not myself but the officer who is failing to obey superior orders, and who is therefore guilty of mutiny. And under the circumstances, my own duty is clearly to continue to carry out the superior orders on my own initiative."

Birkett tried switching to a different key. He dropped the impersonal military approach and became more paternal.

"Oh, come off it, Mathai, there's a good chap. I'm sure we can work this thing out somehow between us. Look, we can't possibly talk properly like this—put down that bicycle and come and sit here beside me in the jeep." Mathai remained stubbornly unmoving, and he went on. "After all, we always got on pretty well in the past, didn't we? You were once even disposed to look upon me as a father. Can't you think of me like that now?"

"No, sir. It is no longer possible."

"Well, that's a pity, because I'm bound to say I should be very proud to think of you as a son."

"I prefer you not to do so, sir. I would not wish to see my father betray our cause. Now, excuse me." He switched on the big chromium lamp on the handlebars of his bicycle and spun the pedals ready to mount.

Birkett's patience snapped.

"You're behaving like a ruddy little idiot, Mathai. You can't go ahead with that business alone. If you'd think for half a second, you'd realise that I could stop you as easy as pie. I've only to lift up the telephone and tip off the police—and then you'd be dished good and proper."

Mathai paused with his foot on the pedal. "I don't think you will tell the police, sir," he said calmly. "I think that, despite your change of opinion, you have too much honour to betray a colleague."

"I shouldn't count on it. Anyhow, I'll tell you another thing. You think you're going to get martyrdom out of this job. I made it my business to make you think so, because I saw from the start that you were the sort who'd fall hook, line, and sinker for the idea of a bit of glory. But it was sheer eye-wash. You honestly think they're going to make a hero of you? Stick up your statue in Red Square? Have the kids singing songs of praise about you? Stop fooling yourself, Mathai. They're going to throw up their hands in hypocritical horror and disown you. They're going to spit on your name."

"I have considered that possibility, sir. And although I should welcome fame and honour for my family, I have realised that without the promise of such reward the act would be more disinterested and therefore the true glory all the greater."

Rage seized Birkett. "All right, Mathai! If you want to make a fool of yourself, I don't care. Go ahead and do the ruddy job. But remember the responsibility is yours."

"I'm ready to accept it, sir."

"Then I've nothing more to say to you, Mathai. Get on that ruddy bicycle and go and win your true ruddy glory—but just remember I've washed my hands of it! I'm right out of it now!"

He watched the red tail-light of the bicycle disappear down the road. Well, I did all I could, he thought. So good riddance. It's his own affair now, it's nothing to do with me . . . And he abruptly started the jeep and drove off. He shot past Mathai without a sideways glance, leaving a contemptuous trail of dust.

He went straight up to his room at the hotel and threw himself on the bed. Presently Lakshmi came in.

"I saw the jeep was back," she said. "I'd asked the boys to keep some dinner for you. Don't you want it?"

"No, thanks."

"You said you would explain everything when you came back," she said.

"I'm too tired now," he said. "Skip it."

"It's not something to do with what you were talking about— that secret underground work you were doing? You're not still involved in it?"

"Skip it, I'm all through."

"You don't want to come to my room tonight?"

"No, I'd be a dead loss tonight. Better leave me alone."

She went away and he got into bed. He heard the clock strike near the maidan, and imagined how the maidan would look tomorrow, with the dense crowds, and the parading soldiers, and the King on the platform taking the salute. And then a sudden scuffle behind him, a shot . . . well, it was nothing to do with him now, He'd washed his hands of it. The responsibility was all Mathai's.

He kept waking during the night, and thinking of the Tattoo, and reminding himself that the responsibility was all Mathai's—that the blood would all be on Mathai's hands. He was still reminding himself when dawn came. But now, in the remorseless grey light, he knew that he did not really believe it, and that the responsibility remained his own—for you could not disclaim responsibility for the consequences of something you had started yourself. Supposing you had put a time-bomb on an aircraft and then changed your mind and hurried back to remove it, only to find that the aircraft had taken off? Could you have disclaimed all responsibility when it crashed? You'd have certainly looked a fine sight, he thought, standing amongst the twisted wreckage and charred human remains, wringing your hands and wailing, "It wasn't my fault—I washed my hands of it . . ."

No, he'd got to tackle Mathai again—stop him somehow. And if he had no success with Mathai himself, he could tip off his wife: Mrs. Mathai would soon make short work of those heroics, and bring him into line.

He rose at once and drove round to Mathai's bungalow.

The door was opened by Mrs. Mathai. She said that her husband was out.

"Out?" He glanced at his watch—it was not yet seven o'clock.

"He's gone for a walk," Mrs. Mathai said. "He often goes out early now. He finds it the best time to think clearly."

Birkett said tersely, "Only wanted a word. I'll come back later."

He went back to the hotel for breakfast and returned to Mathai's bungalow about eight-thirty. The door was once more opened by

Mrs. Mathai. The two boys clung shyly to her skirts. They watched Birkett with their huge brown eyes. "I'm sorry, my husband's gone out again," she said. "I told him you were coming back, but he said he was sure you would understand that this morning he wanted to be by himself. He just took his bicycle from the shed, without even waiting for breakfast, and dashed off."

"What time'll he be back for lunch?"

"He's not coming back. He said he'd eat something in the bazaar and go straight on to the show this afternoon."

"You mean the Tattoo?"

"Yes, he seemed very keen not to miss it this year, although he usually avoids anything military, and we both disapprove of that sort of thing for the children. I shall stay with them here."

He must have foreseen the danger of my bringing some new pressure to bear, Birkett thought, and decided it was safer to skip off. Well, he's certainly scotched my little game—no use tipping off his wife if she's not going to see him again before the event.

"Never mind, I expect I'll run into him at the Tattoo," he said. He brought his hands briskly together under his chin, and Mrs. Mathai returned the gesture, and the two liquid-eyed boys at her skirts did likewise, shyly and inconspicuously touching their palms as if they hoped not to be seen.

He turned abruptly and went up the path, and then, as soon as he heard the door close, diverted his steps to the wooden bicycle shed amongst the tattered banana plantains in a corner of the garden, where Mathai had told him he would keep the gun and the pills. The door of the shed was ajar and he went in. Mathai's bicycle was missing. On the floor, amongst the garden tools and oddments, there was an old battered tin trunk. The key was in the padlock which hung open. He lifted the lid. Inside there was a tin of weedkiller, a puncture outfit, a few bicycle accessories. The gun and pills had gone.

So that confirmed that Mathai had no intention of returning before the Tattoo, and that he still meant to go through with it— no good hoping that since last night he'd changed his mind.

He returned to the jeep and drove back into the town. He spent the next hour or two cruising through the streets of the bazaar, keeping his eyes skinned for Mathai, or for his bicycle with the big ostentatious chromium lamp, and stopping at every likely cafe and public building to look inside. Then, meeting with no success in the town, he carried the search out to the countryside, and spent the rest of the morning jolting along tracks and lanes, and halting the jeep to investigate shrines and pagodas whose cool shady interiors offered the likeliest refuge for anyone wanting to while away a few hours. He worked systematically, covering all the country roads that lay within five or six miles of the town, but with no more success than before. Finally he gave up and drove back to Kathmandu. The road took him over the bridge where he had met Mathai, and he stopped the jeep on a sudden hunch that he might have chosen to spend the morning at the same spot along the river bank where they had stood and talked. He made his way along, floundering in the mud, but the place was deserted.

He got back into the jeep, weary and dispirited, and looked at his watch—twelve-thirty. Only a couple more hours to the Tattoo.

There wasn't much he could do even if there had been more time, he thought. Mathai was clearly taking no chances. It was no use counting any longer on finding him before the show began . . .

All right, if the assassin couldn't be kept away from the victim—couldn't the victim be kept away from the assassin? Wasn't there some way of preventing the King's appearance at the Tattoo?

An anonymous communication would do it: a note in disguised writing, a telephone call. They might suspect a hoax, but would not dare ignore it. Of course Mathai, once arrested and put in irons, would give away the whole bag of tricks. But there was nothing to fear. Birkett would have shaken the dust of Nepal off his heels by then—and anyhow, they'd only have Mathai's word for it, no proof. No, Birkett would be all right—only Mathai would go down the drain. And he couldn't blame Birkett, he couldn't say he hadn't been warned. But of course Mathai had been right—he couldn't do it. A week ago it would have been different, for he had always regarded honour as a luxury, and prided himself on the conviction and strength of mind that had enabled him to put expediency first and to dishonour himself for his cause. But now he had no conviction and no cause, and no strength to eschew honour.

No, he could not do it. He must stop Mathai himself. And if he couldn't find Mathai until it was too late to use persuasion, he would simply have to use force—catch him the minute he turned up at the Tattoo and stick to him like a limpet, and then if Birkett's presence alone wasn't enough to keep him from pulling the gun, get on to him at the first move of a finger towards it and physically stop him.

Yes, it should be easy as pie, provided he could find Mathai on the maidan. And he'd find him all right, because there was one place where sooner or later Mathai was bound to be—and that was near the King.

His confidence grew as he turned the plan over in his mind. He started up the jeep and drove back to the hotel. He paused on the steps to scrape his muddy shoes. He heard a car come smartly up the drive. It halted alongside him with a crunching skid on the gravel, and he looked up and saw that it was a British Embassy Land-Rover with a uniformed Nepalese driver, and Potter seated beside him. Potter stared into his face and grinned, and said, "I see the river's still got its fatal fascination for you, old man."

He held his gaze firmly on Birkett's face, carefully avoiding a downward glance at his feet. It was one of Potter's little tricks that were meant to disconcert.

Birkett took good care not to appear disconcerted. He lifted a foot and poked at the sole with the stick, saying, "Yes, it was certainly fatal to my shoes."

"I wonder what's the connection this time?"

"Connection?"

"Well, take your last visit, old man. The connection there was with the telephone call from Mr. Mathai—sorry, Mr. Kensington. So I'm wondering if it connects up with him again this time---or just with the fact that today's your big day."

"What's big about it?"

"I was thinking of the Tattoo, old man. I know what a Tattoo means to you old soldier types."

Birkett smiled as he continued working on his shoes. "By Jove, I was forgetting it was today. Yes, you're right, nothing I enjoy more than a good bit of drill."

He's only guessing, Birkett thought. He may have hit on the truth, or something like it, but only as one possibility amongst many. And the whole joke, of course, is that it isn't the truth any longer, that he doesn't know I've changed sides . . . Only it might turn out to be a rather bad joke if he ever got his hands on me. Because he wouldn't believe it—and it wouldn't make much difference even if he did, for I'd still be the chap who'd put the time-bomb on the plane. And so far as Potter is concerned, trying to take it off again wouldn't cancel out the original act of putting it on. So I must watch my step—Mathai may see me now as being on Potter's side, but I must remember that Potter sees me as being on Mathai's.

He said, "And so far as that goes, it's a big day for you, too."

"No, I'm afraid soldiering was never old Potter's line. I told you how I spent my war."

Birkett glanced up at him. He said, "Yes, exactly. I was thinking of all the uniforms and equipment there'll be on display. By Jove, what a sight to stir the heart of someone who once worked in the Ministry of Supply!"

"One up to you, old man!" Potter grinned. "Yes, you're right. I can expect some big moments, too—of one kind or another."

The humour drained out of his grin and it hung there stiffly as if maintained by wires, a frozen and hostile baring of teeth. It made the big airman's moustache, the horn-rimmed goggles, seem as incongruous, and as tastelessly flippant, as a false nose and paper hat worn by a hangman making ready his gallows. Birkett was overtaken by sudden uneasiness. It was not the menace of the grin that disturbed him, but the feeling of something familiar about it, something that remained as elusive as a word on the tip of the tongue.

And then there was a sudden violent stirring, and he knew where he had seen Potter's frozen smile before. Seen Potter before . . .

Momentarily the memory held him and he was no longer in Nepal but in Scotland, no longer in the Everest Hotel but on the *Maid of Islay* bound for Glasgow from Arran . . . A big man in a green felt hat and a brown tweed coat: the direct gaze, the sudden icy grin . . . Birkett knew now that it had been Potter on the *Maid of Islay*. Potter who, for reasons unknown, had let him go.

Except that Potter never let go. He had Mrs. Potter's word for that.

He abruptly pulled himself together.

"My word, must get into that bath, or I'll be late for lunch."

"You look as white as a sheet, old man. Are you all right?"

"Quite."

Birkett dodged past and made quickly for the stairs.

Perhaps I'm mistaken, he thought. That man on the *Maid of Islay*—perhaps it wasn't Potter after all. Still, it's uncanny how that grin . . .

His cold muddy shoes squelched on the marble steps. He gripped the banister rail. He felt weak at the knees.

Chapter Seventeen

General Ranju Shamsher Jang Bahadur Rana, eighty-four years old and father of thirty-eight children, unaccompanied by his young wife owing to the imminent arrival of the thirty-ninth, stepped delicately from the back of the car.

He crossed to the steps under the peepul tree, tottering a little under the weight of his sword and hefty gold epaulettes. His peaked cap was several sizes too big and rested on his ears. He picked his way up the steps, moving his tiny pointed polished shoes as carefully as chessmen, and gained the platform.

His car moved off and another took its place. The sun blazed down on the heads of the patient crowds watching the distinguished arrivals. The feathery tips of the eucalyptus trees round the maidan were motionless in the afternoon heat. The long white frieze of mountains stretched away over their heads to the corners of the sky.

The band of scarlet-uniformed Gurkhas struck up "The Daring Young Man on the Flying Trapeze." A carriage drawn by four grey horses approached across the open expanse of grass.

"Is this the King?" Lakshmi asked.

"Potter will know," Mrs. Potter said. "Potter, where are you? Quick, we want to know if this is the King!"

"Hang on, old girl." Potter clamped an enormous pair of field-glasses to his eyes.

"Major Birkett, who is your favourite author?" The young Nepalese journalist stood with pencil poised over his notebook, head turned half-way from Birkett to peer at him better with his left eye. He had lost the right eye and the lid was permanently sealed.

"Conrad," Birkett said.

"No, that's the Prime Minister in the carriage," Potter said.

"Major Birkett, you write with a pen or a typewriter?"

"Ah, I was waiting for that one," Birkett said. "The hardy old perennial."

The Prime Minister alighted from his carriage and mounted the steps under the peepul tree. He was lanky and ascetic-looking, dressed in white jodhpurs, European-style jacket, and flapping shirt-tails.

"He looks just like a sexton," Mrs. Potter said.

The tiny old General, tottering a little on the small pointed black shoes, came towards them across the platform. "Good afternoon, Major Birkett." He peered up at Birkett, straining back his head in order to see under the obstructing brim of the enormous cap resting on his ears. "I have been very remiss not to confirm my invitation to you and your lady in writing for luncheon tomorrow. But I trust that you have not forgotten your promise to give us the pleasure of your company?"

"The pleasure will be entirely ours, sir."

"Mine, I assure you."

"Hello, here come the Lancers."

"The Lancers?" the little General said anxiously. "Then His Majesty must be arriving. So you will please excuse me? His Majesty has graciously honoured me with the privilege of receiving him!" He went off, delicately picking his way amongst the rows of chairs to the centre of the platform. "Potter, quick, give me the glasses! It's the King!"

"Here you are, old girl."

"Potter, I can't—oh, that's better, I was twiddling the wrong knob! Oh, look, what a sweet little King!"

The column of riders came cantering across the grass with pennants fluttering from their lances. They peeled off in pairs and formed a rank facing the peepul tree. Behind them, with more lancers following, came an enormous open Cadillac. It was bright puce with white leather upholstery. The King sat in the middle of the back seat. He looked very small and alone with a white empty expanse on either side of him, like a little boy of rich parents being driven to school by a chauffeur. He wore khaki uniform, and the big sun glasses that protected him from the glare of the sun and the people.

The car drew up before the platform. General Ranju stood at the foot of the steps, his shoulders held bravely square under the burden of the epaulettes, his face swamped by the enormous hat resting on his ears. He saluted carefully and with intense concentration. His hand quivered with tension. The King gave a rather nervous salute in acknowledgement as he alighted from the car.

A movement swept through the crowded platform like wind through corn as the spectators, bringing their palms together in an attitude of prayer, inclined their bodies in a low bow. The King mounted the steps, bowing to one side and then the other, his hands meeting and parting before his chin in soft quick little claps. The spectators, curiosity in conflict with protocol, craned their necks from horizontal bodies to catch a glimpse of the sovereign.

The King turned at the top of the steps and stood at the salute while the band played the National Anthem. He looked rather crushed and unhappy as if he had long been weighed down by the dread of this ordeal, and now longed only to be back alone with a book by the lily-pond in the Palace garden.

Birkett looked round the platform and scanned the faces of the nearby crowds, but there was still no sign of Mathai. He saw that Potter's gaze was fixed on something further along the platform, passing him at a tangent, yet near enough to include him in the field of vision while his attention appeared to be absorbed elsewhere. He knew that since their arrival Potter had not missed the smallest movement he had made.

The anthem came to an end and the King took his seat on a big carved gold chair with a red cushion.

All at once Birkett leant close to Lakshmi's ear and whispered, "Come with me."

He took her arm. She yielded in puzzled silence as he steered her quickly along the row to the gangway. They reached the back of the platform and he stopped and said, "No time to explain now. You must trust me and do as I tell you. Remember Krishna Mathai?"

"The young Indian at the reception?"

"Yes, he's loose with a gun—means to use it."

She stared in bewilderment. "You don't mean shoot——?"

"The King—unless I catch him first. I'm going to watch out on the other side of the platform. I want you to keep your eyes skinned on this side, and if you see him, make some signal from over there at the back of the tree where I'll be watching out for you. Now, go back to your seat, and if Potter or anybody asks where I am, say I've gone back to the hotel—stomach-ache after Wilson's ruddy lunch. Got it?"

She nodded uncertainly.

"Right, I'm off," he said.

He vaulted down from the platform and pushed through the crowd towards the road until assured that he was safely lost from view of the platform. Then he circled back to the other side of the tree. An official stopped him as he ducked under the cordon at the back of the platform. He showed the numbered seat ticket provided by Wilson.

"Other side, sir," the official said. "Your seat is the other side of the tree."

"Which side's the Indian Ambassador?"

"This side, sir."

"Thanks, want a word with him first."

He mounted the platform and sat down in the almost empty row behind the contingent of Indians. A bawling voice rang out on the maidan. "Atten-UN!" Good God, unmistakable Aldershot! He craned forward and saw that a display of massed drill had begun. It was being given by Gurkha infantry troops drawn up in an enormous square with geometrical precision.

"Pres-e-e-e-n . . . UM!" The stocky figure of the Sergeant-Major, the thick neck, were as characteristically British as the barracks-square English of the command, the intonation of the megaphone voice. Even the bawling bulldog face . . . But the complexion after all was brown, the eyes Mongolian—the Aldershot manner, like the medal ribbons, must have been won in British cantonments in India and in the Burma campaign.

"Slo-o-o . . . UM!"

The long files of men, stretching away across the pale dry grass to the eucalyptus trees, responded with uniform movement like threads of a mechanical loom, as a thousand rifles lifted, a thousand bayonets flashed in the sun.

Birkett glanced at the Indians in the row in front of him. He recognized a young man he had met on his first night at the Everest. He leaned forward and said, "Mathai not here to-day?"

"Krishna? Isn't he?" He looked round. "No, that's odd. Still— married man, you know." He gave Birkett a white grin over his shoulder. "I expect he's having a private Tattoo at home with his wife."

"Hope she's not such a hard taskmaster as that fire-eater out there." He looked up as someone came down the empty row towards him. It was the journalist with the sealed eye.

"Major Birkett, I forgot to ask your political views."

"Thought you were just writing an article, young fellow, not a full-scale biography," Birkett said.

"The people of this country have recently been politically awakened, sir. They are interested in the politics of distinguished visitors."

"Sorry, you'll have to skip it—already talked too much."

"Bad policy to offend the Press, old man," a voice said behind them.

Birkett glanced up. "Oh, hello, Potter."

Potter stood grinning down at Birkett, clasping the back of Birkett's chair with his left fist. He kept the right in his pocket. "Decided not to pack it in after all, old man?"

"No, changed my mind."

"Now, that's funny, old man. Just what I told Mrs. Kapoor. 'No, it'll take more than collywobbles to keep Major Birkett away from the Tattoo,' I said. 'I expect he's already changed his mind and sneaked back to the other side of the platform.'" He pulled away the chair next to Birkett to enter the row. "Mind if I join you, old man?"

"Not at all." He noticed that Potter's right hand remained in his pocket as he manipulated the chair with his left. It gripped something bulky with a protuberance that jutted forward into the seam.

"Major Birkett, you will please give me an answer in a nutshell." The journalist turned the sealed-up, sunken eye to one side to take better aim with the other. "You incline towards conservatism or socialism?"

"Difficult to say—could have told you a week ago, but my ideas are in the melting-pot just now."

"That means something's cooking." Potter gave the journalist an exaggerated wink and pulled roguishly at the end of his moustache. "And I can tell you what, only you'll never believe it. Major Birkett's a Communist. He's hatching a plot to assassinate the King. He's hoping to do it this afternoon."

The journalist's eyes twinkled with amusement. "That is a funny joke, sir."

"Major Birkett didn't find it funny. Did you, Birkett?"

"Killing," Birkett said.

"Well said, old man." Potter kept his eyes fixed on Birkett. Birkett continued to watch the Tattoo. The journalist remained silent, aware of some tension between them, some mutual preoccupation that made him suddenly feel shut out and alone. He looked longingly from one to the other. They must have a beautiful friendship, he thought. I would give anything in the world to share such a friendship. But it is impossible because I belong to a different race, which they think inferior, and have an ugly sealed-up eye. And he turned slowly and walked away, and he knew that the two men were too absorbed by their beautiful friendship to notice him go.

Potter said, "Yes, it was really killing, that joke. Only I noticed you didn't laugh, old man."

"Too far-fetched. A joke must have some sense to it. Why should anyone want to assassinate the King?"

"It would create chaos, old man. A very desirable state of affairs for political opportunists. They make capital out of chaos—if one can speak of anti-capitalists 'making capital.'" Birkett glanced at him. Potter still held him with the grin, but it was a grin of something like genuine humour—not the frozen grin of this morning, and set nothing astir in his memory.

He fancied now that he had been letting his imagination run away with him; there was no similarity really between Potter and the man who had been tailing him on the *Maid of Islay*. He felt curiously relieved, though he didn't know why. It made no difference whether or not Potter had tailed him before, because the fact remained that he was tailing him now.

"Well, no sign of any bullets flying yet," he said.

"No, I reckon the chap would wait until a bit later on," Potter said. "Choose some moment when the act could achieve the maximum dramatic effect."

"Sorry, all too subtle for me."

"Naturally, it's not your line. You're an honest straightforward soldier. It takes a professional diplomat like me to appreciate subtleties of that sort."

Potter's tone made it clear that he knew Birkett was no more an honest straightforward soldier than he was a professional diplomat. It was intended to make it clear. What the devil was his game?

Birkett glanced down at Potter's hand thrust into the bulging pocket, the protuberance pressing into the seam. It beats me, he thought. Still, if he wants to lay down his cards I won't stop him. In fact I'll encourage him to lay down a few that I'd like to see—starting with the gun.

He said, "Yes, a diplomat uses subtlety as his weapon as a rule, and leaves the more lethal sort to the soldier. That's why I'm surprised to see you with a firearm."

"Firearm?"

"That's a gun you've got there, isn't it?"

He jerked his head towards Potter's pocket. Potter was momentarily disconcerted. He glanced down and said uneasily, "Gun? That's just—just a few sandwiches I brought along."

228

"Wilson's excelled himself. One of 'em's got a muzzle."

"A chicken-bone . . ."

"Come off it, Potter."

Potter grinned and said, "All right, I suppose old Potter had better come clean—can't compete with those X-ray eyes, old man! The truth is that Potter's secret passion is pigeon-pie. I was hoping to bag a pigeon this afternoon."

"At the Tattoo? Watch out nobody gets hurt."

"Actually I'm quite a crack shot. The only person who'll get hurt is—" He hesitated, fixing his eyes steadily on Birkett from behind the horn-rimmed goggles.

"Well?"

"The pigeon." Potter slowly and mechanically bared his teeth in a grin again—the same frigid, hostile grin of this morning, hoisted like a flag declaring merciless war. And once again, in the dim pool of Birkett's memory, there was an uneasy stirring.

My God, he wondered, was I right after all? Was it really Potter on the *Maid of Islay*?

He looked away, concealing the new access of anxiety that accompanied the memory. He wished he knew for sure. Well, since Potter was being so obliging, perhaps he'd turn up that card too . . .

"I've never cared for shooting pigeons myself," he said.

"Now if you'd said pheasant or grouse—not that I'm a sporty type, but I've had some good days with a gun on the Renfrewshire moors and the Fells of Arran." He added, "By Jove, that's a lovely island, Arran! Know it at all?"

"Yes, spent a week there once, old man. Hideous crossing from Ireland—drunk all the time on potsheen."

"That's the Irish Aran. One 'r'." He fancied that Potter's confusion, carefully underlined by the reference to Ireland, had been deliberate to keep him guessing. "I meant the Scottish Arran."

"Ah, Hebrides—never been to the Hebrides, old man."

"No, it's off Glasgow. You go from the Clyde-steamer called the *Maid of Islay*."

"*Maid of Islay*? That seems to ring a bell . . ." He closed his eyes reflectively. "Yes, I can see myself standing on a quay somewhere—I believe it *is* Arran. Steamer alongside—the *Maid of Islay*! Lot of people going aboard—and a fine upstanding soldierly man something like you—I believe it is you!" He opened his eyes again and gazed at Birkett through the goggles. "I say, what an extraordinary coincidence, old man!"

Birkett shook his head. "Can't have been me. I'd have remembered you anywhere—that moustache and those glasses. Unless of course you were in a different— 'disguise,' shall we say?"

"Yes, as a matter of fact I was," Potter said gravely and confidentially. "I forget just which disguise I was using at the time, but I only adopted this one quite recently." He touched the huge absurd airman's moustache, the horn-rimmed goggles, with a big blunt forefinger.

"Those lenses are plain glass, of course?"

"No, I was going to get plain glass but the oculist chap couldn't get my point about 'disguise,' and put old Potter through his paces. It appeared I was myopic—should have been wearing the wretched things for years." He unhooked the glasses from his ears and held them out to Birkett. "Have a look, old man."

"Take your word for it."

"But of course the moustache is false," Potter said quickly.

"Looks genuine enough to me—let's just say 'designed to give a false impression,'" Birkett said.

"That's it exactly, old man. Damn' clever of you."

He stared at Birkett with mock gravity. Well, there it was. So it really had been Potter. Potter who had tailed him on the *Maid of Islay*, given him the worst few hours of his life . . . He glanced at his wrists, remembering how they had anticipated the bite of steel. Why had he been reprieved? Well, Potter had no secrets, No doubt he would also turn up that card . . .

A huge guffaw suddenly exploded in his left eardrum. He turned, startled, to see Potter throw himself back in his chair and bring his big blunt hand down on his knee with a resounding slap of delight. He rocked back and forward, uttering more joyful guffaws and declaring, "Rich . . . Oh, that was rich! Never enjoyed myself so much in my life—wish I could have kept it up!"

Birkett frowned. "Kept what up?"

"That mad-hatter's conversation—I haven't the faintest idea what it was all about. I've been pulling your leg, old man. I'm afraid I'm not the chappie you seem to think . . . Oh, that was rich about the disguise! Only wish I was in disguise, but I'm afraid I'm just a common-or-garden Foreign Office wallah with myopia and a rather ridiculous moustache—all right, I know it's ridiculous and God knows why I hang on to it, though no doubt the psychiatry boys could explain."

Birkett said drily, "No doubt they could also explain the gun in the pocket."

Potter threw back his head with another delighted guffaw. "But that was the best of all! There isn't a gun in my pocket!"

"Sandwiches, eh?" Birkett said.

"Nothing, old man. The pocket's got a hole in it."

Potter pulled his hand from the pocket, and the lining after it. His forefinger was stuck through a hole in the seam. He flapped the lining to show it was empty.

Birkett found it difficult to conceal his astonishment. He had been certain about the gun. Its existence had been as real to him as the chair on which he was sitting. He wondered if Potter had made it vanish by some conjuring trick. But no, it was plain as a pikestaff—the bulging outline that he had seen in Potter's pocket had been nothing but the fist, the jutting finger. The gun had been a figment of his imagination.

"Yes, couldn't be much emptier than that," he said. He was relieved to find that his tone had sounded casual. He felt profoundly shaken. He had lost faith in himself. If he could let his imagination play such a trick on him, in what other ways 1night he not have been deceiving himself? Suddenly everything that he had taken for granted had lost its certainty, and he stood on shifting sands. Had he imagined everything else that he had supposed about Potter? Had Potter really been pulling his leg? Had it not really been Potter after all tailing him on the *Maid of Islay*?

Was Potter not even tailing him now? Was he nothing but the Foreign Office wallah he maintained?

He suddenly remembered Mathai—he had been forgetting to keep watch for him. I must get a grip, he thought. He cast his eyes inconspicuously over the faces of the crowd round the platform, saying to Potter, "Anyhow, I'm most relieved. I'd have wondered what British diplomacy was coming to—I mean if you really had been carrying a gun."

"But I am, old man."

"Now, no more of your leg pulls, Potter."

"Dead serious this time, old man."

"You just said you hadn't a gun—and I believe you."

"I only said I wasn't carrying a gun in my pocket, old man. Never carry a gun in my pocket. Carry it the same place as you."

"Me? I'm not carrying—"

"No, but when you do, like the night that you and the wife—sorry, didn't mean to bring it up again, old man. Anyhow, she mentioned feeling something in the heat of the fray—well, where you don't usually expect to feel anything, and she couldn't make head or tail of it, poor girl. But naturally I twigged at once because I've always found it the handiest place myself for carrying the old pea-shooter. Here, like to see?"

He unfastened a button of his shirt and slid his hand under his left armpit. He drew something out and held it just inside the opening of the shirt for Birkett to see.

Birkett nodded. It was a gun all right. So now all his conclusions were reversed again and he was back where he had started—and Potter was on his tail and it had been Potter on the *Maid of Islay*. The parlour tricks were presumably Potter's softening-up tactics. Intended to get him rattled. And they had succeeded—though thank God the shell was more or less intact and Potter didn't know it. He said, "But that's not a gun for pigeons."

"It depends on the sort of pigeons one goes for, old man." He slid the gun back into the holster under the armpit and buttoned the shirt. "I only go for the big ones."

"Chaps who carry that sort of gun usually keep quiet about it. So I'm wondering why you make a point of showing yours off?"

"Now, that's a good question, and I'm glad to answer it," Potter said. "The fact is that it occurred to me there might be a pigeon somewhere round here that was thinking of taking a flutter. Well, I don't like to shoot pigeons without fair warning."

Birkett said, "Pigeons aren't used to such consideration. They're usually shot out of hand. Sure it's the pigeon you're thinking about?"

"No, frankly I don't give a hoot for the pigeon. I regard it as vermin. There's only one sort of pigeon I'm glad to see, and that's a dead pigeon in my pie. And that's where this chap's going to end up. Oh yes, don't worry, he's been earmarked a long time for Potter's pie. There's nothing in the world he can do to avoid it. But I'm afraid that if he takes a flutter in this crowd he might cause a disturbance, and somebody might get hurt. Some innocent unsuspecting person who'd never harmed a fly—or even a pigeon— and whose misfortune, if he happened to be in the public eye, might have disastrous and far-reaching effects. Some person like— the King."

Birkett was no longer listening. His attention had been caught by a young man in the crowd. It looked like Mathai, but he kept his head turned away as he pushed through the crowd and Birkett could not be sure. He went out of sight behind the end of the platform.

I believe that was him all right, Birkett thought. I believe he'd spotted me and was making off to avoid me. I'll have to move fast.

He glanced at Potter. Well, no time to invent explanations. Nothing for it but to go like a scalded cat.

He jumped up and started down the row, but he had not taken a step before he was jerked to a standstill. A big hand was clamped over his wrist.

"Steady on, old man," Potter said mildly. He was leaning forward, his arm outstretched towards Birkett's as casually as a doctor's feeling a pulse; but his grip was like a steel handcuff that almost crushed Birkett's bones.

"For God's sake, Potter . . ." Birkett stopped as he caught sight of the young man again, emerging into an open space in the crowd—it was not Mathai after all. He shrugged and moved back to his chair.

"There's a good fellow," Potter said, and unclamped the restraining hand.

Well, this is certainly a fine situation, Birkett thought. Here am I trying to stop Mathai from assassinating the King, and here's Potter—whose object is also to prevent the assassination—stopping me from stopping Mathai. And no harm done that time, but what about next time when it may really be Mathai? What's to be done then?

Well, no use trying to give him the slip again. Nothing to be done except tell him the truth—tell him I've switched horses, and that we're now both on the same side, in the remote hope that he'll believe it.

He glanced at Potter, whose attention was now fixed on the scene of pageantry that had begun to unfold on the maidan—on the jog-trotting squads of infantry, the gunners trundling up artillery in preparation for battle. He said, "Potter, I want to talk to you. This is very important."

"Sounds most intriguing, old man," Potter said indifferently, without turning his eyes from the spectacle. "I'm all ears."

"You think that I'm still at the old game, Potter. But you're wrong. I've chucked it."

"Good for you!" Potter said as if humouring a child.

"I've joined the prevention squad, Potter."

"Really, old man? Well, good show!"

"I'm not here to make mischief, but to prevent it—the same as you." Potter remained apparently absorbed in the pageant and he went on, "You'd better listen to me, Potter, or you'll be responsible for what happens—for the very thing you're trying to prevent."

"Hang on, I'll be with you in a minute old man. I just want to watch those little chappies—I say, you don't think they're actually

234

going to fire those guns? I'm afraid if they do, old man, we'll all get blown to bits."

"There's somebody who is going to fire a gun—unless you let me stop him."

"So long as he doesn't use me for target practice, old man."

Birkett said evenly, "You're a fool, Potter. I'm trying to help you. You've got to believe me and give me some rope."

"Rope, old man? Certainly, all you want."

"Good chap, that's more like it. So if I suddenly scoot off—"

"I thought you were talking about rope, old man. I've been keeping a piece specially for you. Fine quality, take twice your weight—and nice easy—running noose on the end."

Birkett said grimly, "I see, you mean that sort of rope." He was silent as the artillery commander gave the order to fire, and flames leapt from the mouths of half a dozen cannons. A moment later their thunder hit the platform with the solid impact of a wall. Two Indians in the next row held hands like frightened lovers.

The noise rumbled away towards the distant hills, and Birkett went on, "Yes, you've been keeping it a long time for me, haven't you? Remember you dangling it on the *Maid of Islay*. Always surprised me you didn't make more use of it. Matter of interest, what was the idea?"

"Not admitting that it was me, old man. I'd say that if it had been, my only reason for not using it would have been that I hadn't enough to make a decent job. So rather than disappoint you altogether, I'd have dangled it just to let you know it was there."

"Friendly warning to scare rne off, eh? But I don't quite see—I mean, how was I expected to catch on? It was only because I'd been tipped off by a friend who'd found out what you were up to—you must have slipped up somewhere . . ."

"Yes, how careless of me," Potter nodded gravely. "Bad show."

Birkett smiled. "I see it was that sort of slip-up—so you knew I'd get the tip-off and be on the lookout for you. Well, I congratulate you, Potter. It was a good bluff."

"No, waste of time, old man. Dangle a bit of rope for some chaps and that's enough—never want to see the stuff again in their lives. But other chaps are gluttons for rope. Dangle bits in front of their faces as often as you like, but they'll always bob up again somewhere asking for more—never satisfied until they've got a nice long piece of rope all for themselves. So in the end you take pity and oblige. That's why I've brought some along for you, old man."

"This is an independent country, Potter. You're poaching on other people's preserves."

"You're such a grasshopper, old man. Always jumping from one country to another—can't keep passing on the files. But don't worry, I'll invite in the local chaps when the time comes. In fact, I've heard they've got quite an expert here in handling ropes."

Another blast of noise swept the platform. Smoke hung over the maidan like fog.

"I'm afraid your rope's going to be wasted, Potter," Birkett said. "I'm not a killer. I've never killed anybody in my life, and I'm not proposing to start."

"Don't doubt it for a minute, old man. Too smart, a chap like you, to do a job like that yourself—no future in it. Best to get some other chap to do it for you. Always find some nice young chap ready to oblige. Like that young Mathai, for instance." He looked elaborately round the platform. "Hello, not here! Wonder what's happened to him?"

"Couldn't say."

"Well, turn up later no doubt. Meanwhile, I reckon I can't go wrong by sticking to you."

"That's just where you can go wrong. Potter, for the last time—"

"Excuse me, old man, but I'm losing the thread," Potter said, peering curiously at the turmoil of smoke and men on the maidan." Has the battle just got out of hand, or are they celebrating victory?"

An hour later the spectacle drew to its close. The band broke into a stirring tune for the final march-past. The King rose from his golden chair to take the salute.

Birkett once more cast his eyes over the crowd. He held his breath. There had still been no sign of Mathai.

The column of lancers passed before the peepul tree. Next came the infantry and guns. The officer at the head of each section yelled his commands as he drew level with the tree, and the faces of his men jerked mechanically sideways, their hands lifted in salute.

Another troop of lancers brought up the rear. Birkett watched their slow approach across the dry dusty grass, the riders reining back their impatient horses to the walking pace of the infantry.

Another five minutes, he thought. Just keep away for another five minutes, Mathai, then it'll be over. Please don't come now, there's a good chap. I don't want to see you die, laddie. I'm fond of you, and I don't want to see you die any more than the King.

And I want my chance with Lakshmi. So just another five minutes, laddie, that's all . . .

The faces of the lancers, under the blue striped turbans, jerked towards the King, jerked back again. The dust rose round the horses' hoofs, settled again behind the tail of the column. The music stopped and the King carefully lowered his hand to his side. He turned to General Ranju, suddenly grinning with relief as though at the lifting of a burden, like a schoolboy when the bell rings after the last class of the day.

The band struck up a spritely tune. The puce Cadillac glided forward over the grass. The King started down the steps, the diminutive General tottering after him on the little pointed shoes.

Birkett grinned at Potter.

"Well, one look at that gun of yours must have been enough for that pigeon. Not risking a flutter today."

Potter said quietly, "No, good show."

"Sorry, you've been done out of your pigeon-pie."

"That'll wait."

And at that moment it happened—happened so quickly that it was over almost before he knew it had begun. He had been glancing along the platform towards Lakshmi, and just then caught sight of her—caught only a brief glimpse before she was blocked from view again by rising spectators, but long enough to see her frantically signalling and pointing. He sprang forward, too quick for Potter who had relaxed his vigilance, and fought his way through a confusion of Indians and chairs to the edge of the platform—and a violent movement at once drew his attention to Mathai.

He was part of the crowd that had surged forward round the far end of the platform to watch the King's departure, and that was being held back by a line of soldiers. He was fighting his way to the front with a mad frenzy. His eyes shone with fervour. Nobody tried to stop him. A moment later he burst through the line between two of the soldiers. He was a dozen yards from the King, who was about to enter the puce Cadillac. He was waving the gun.

"Mathai!" Birkett cried out. "Mathai!"

But his voice was drowned by the brassy skirmishes of the band. And then he heard the shot and at the same moment saw Mathai stumble over the boot of one of the soldiers and sprawl headlong on his face.

Birkett turned to look at the King, and for a moment thought the bullet had found its mark. He saw the King clutch with one hand at the door of the car, while the other hand jerked to his breast. But a moment later he realized that it had only been his first instinctive reaction to the sound of the shot, and that the bullet must have gone wild, for he immediately recovered and turned towards Mathai. One of the soldiers had thrown himself upon him and was grappling for the gun. Mathai's limbs flew out galvanically in all directions, and performing a violent contortion, he managed to break the soldier's grip, rise to his knees, lift the gun to his temple. But just then two more soldiers hurled themselves on to him from behind, pitching into him with such force that his body, hinged at the knees, came down and struck the ground like a spring trap.

Christ! Birkett thought. Christ!

The soldiers were still struggling to wrest the gun from Mathai's hand. Suddenly the gun went off and a bullet tore into the bodywork of the Cadillac. The shot caused the soldiers momentarily to relax their grip, and Mathai wrenched up his arm. He brought the gun to his head and pulled the trigger. His body jerked, twisted, and then lay still. The next moment it had been swallowed up by the converging crowd. And it was only then that Birkett noticed the little group standing near the car, and the King going towards it, and the group parting to make way for him—and then he saw the little lifeless body stretched on the grass; with the little pointed polished shoes splayed out sideways, the gold epaulettes askew, and the little bald head, from which the over-sized cap had fallen and rolled away on the ground. He had not thought of the General being bald, and somehow the head, was smooth and pink as a baby's, looked almost indecently naked, taking the dignity from his death and making it rather absurd.

So Mathai died with blood on his hands after all, he thought. It must have been that shot that went wild, and killed General Ranju instead of the King.

He watched the soldiers push back the crowd from round Mathai. He could see one of Mathai's thin brown legs with the trouser rucked up to the knee, and one of the thin beautiful hands flung out on the grass. It looked dead and unwanted, like an old abandoned glove.

He felt somebody standing behind him. He knew without looking round that it was Potter.

"Good show, old man," Potter said. Birkett said nothing.

"Quite a nice little flutter, old man."

The brassy music suddenly stopped in mid-note, like the voice of a person who finds himself still talking loudly when silence has fallen upon a room.

"Yes, that pigeon must be feeling very proud of itself," Potter said. "And now I wonder how it's feeling about going into Potter's pie?"

Chapter Eighteen

"I'm sorry, Major Birkett, but I can only tell you that the boy put it in your room with the tickets," Wilson said. "And if it isn't there now, its gone—and 'gone' at the Everest means 'won't come back.'"

"Look, I'm supposed to be off in a few minutes. How d'you expect me to go without my passport?"

Wilson gloomily contemplated the disordered heaps of bar chits on the dining-room table, where he was "catching up with accounts." They looked as if they had been tipped there from a sack. "Frankly, I'm only astonished the tickets didn't go as well. So I suppose that's one thing to be grateful for."

"That's right, only a ruddy passport lost, so that I can't use my ticket anyway—we ought to declare a day of thanksgiving."

"I suppose you can get a new one from the Embassy, though it'll take a filthy time. If you like I'll ask Mr. Potter—"

"Skip it." He turned abruptly and went upstairs to Lakshmi's room. She was just finishing her packing and the room, deprived of the feminine articles that had taken away the barrack-room blight, looked bleak and unfamiliar. "Right, all set? We must get moving."

"Good, you found it?" she said.

"My passport? No, it was left in my room with the tickets but someone must have pinched it. No good worrying." He took one of the air tickets from his pocket and slipped it into her handbag on the bed. "I'll stick this in now, or I may forget it at the airport."

She let the lid of the suitcase fall. "You mean you're not coming?"

"No, I can't come without a passport. I'll follow as soon as I can get another."

She stood up slowly. "I'm not going without you," she said.

"Now don't give me any of that. An hour ago you were saying you couldn't wait to get out of here."

"I meant for us both to get out."

"Sorry, but now you'll have to go on your own. You can wait for me up in Simla—give you a chance to think things over and decide what you really want to do."

"But I've already decided."

"Never mind, you must go."

"No."

He turned in silence and went to the window, and stood looking out at the trees with their purple parasitic blossoming of bougainvillaea, and the big trees in the ground across the road with the huge white ornate facade of a palace beyond—the palace of General Ranju where he might have been lunching today, and where instead the General's young wife was now sitting in her white mourning robes. He remained silent another minute and then he said tersely, without turning, "All right, if you want to stick with me I shan't stop you. It's by your own choice, and I shan't keep thanking you, or telling you you're a fool and I'm not good enough for you. Only first I want to be clear that you know what you're doing." He turned stiffly in the window and faced her. "Here, take a look. That's the lot. It wouldn't add up to much at the best of times, and now I reckon I'll be more a liability than an asset as a hunted man."

"Hunted?" Her fear, which had never been far away, was all at once back in her eyes. "But you said this morning that they'd nothing—no evidence . . ."

"None so far as I knew. But that was before Potter pinched my passport."

She said quickly, "I'm sure that was one of the boys."

"Very likely. Only don't kid yourself, whoever it was he'd been put up to it by Potter. And that means he must think he's got some way he can get me. He's keeping me on hand while he cooks something up." He wondered again about the heaven-helper that he had suspected Potter of taking from his room. It was the only bit of evidence that Potter might have against him that would count for anything in a court of law. Mathai in fact had not used the pills that Birkett had given him—he had evidently decided to rely on the gun for self-destruction, or else had forgotten in the excitement to tuck one into his mouth—but they had found the pastille tin with the pills in his pocket, and Potter could show that the pill he had taken from Birkett's room was in all respects similar. But how could he prove that it had come from Birkett's room? And supposing he could, how could that be regarded as proof of Birkett's complicity? No, he still couldn't see it—nor any other reason for Potter's hopes of getting Birkett into that pie. He went on, "Anyhow, the fact that I'm on the run just makes me a worse risk, and you can take it or leave it. It's the reason for it that you've got to face—what I've done, and what I am," He glanced round, then stepped over to the wastepaper basket beside the dressing-table and snatched out a thin limp newspaper from amongst the litter. "You ought to keep this—take it out now and again to freshen your memory."

The paper, run with Indian backing, had played down the assassination, relegating it to an article of its own so that no shadow should fall on the main feature proclaiming the Tattoo a triumphant success. The headline was in modest lettering.

HIS MAJESTY SPARED IN MAIDAN SOOTING
RANA FALLS VICTIM TO YOUNG MADMAN

Birkett ran his eyes down the column. It was written in rudimentary English with grammar and spelling as unpredictable as the type. The first few inches were devoted to the King's narrow escape, and it was only in the sixth or seventh paragraph that the hapless victim of the "tragic shoooting"—the word seemed to defy every effort of the typesetter—was named. The assassin who had taken his life was described. Only as a "foreigner," until the concluding sentence of the article which gave further details almost as an afterthought: *The gunman has been identified as K. Mathai, 27, Indian in Embassy employment, believed gone off his mind.* Thus the epitaph of a young man with beautiful hands and ideals, who had given his life for martyrdom and a place in world history—and whose only memorial was two lines of dim print in an obscure corner of a newspaper that few people read.

He repeated aloud, "'K. Mathai, Indian, believed gone off his mind . . .' That's right, that was my handiwork—I'd twisted his mind around so that he was no longer responsible for his own actions."

Lakshmi said, "You tried to stop him. You'd seen it was wrong. That's all that matters."

"Listen, just now I'm your blue-eyed boy, because we've been having an affair and rolling in the hay—and when a woman's had a good time rolling in the hay with a man he can carve up his own mother under her nose and toast the pieces over the fire, and she'll still think he's got a soul as white as the virgin snow. But one morning you're going to wake up and find the scales have dropped from your eyes. And you're going to take one look at me lying there beside you, and think, 'I'm in bed with a monster.'"

She closed her eyes and shook her head, and said softly, "I shall never think that."

"You don't think you'll go on being in love with me for the rest of your life?"

"Yes."

A retort was checked on his lips as the simplicity and certitude of her reply took effect on him. He was suddenly profoundly moved.

"It's your last chance. You know what you're doing?"

"Yes."

"Right." He smiled grimly. "All I can say is that Mathai's not the only one who's 'gone off his mind.'" He started for the door.

"Where are you going?"

"Might as well tackle Potter—see if I can get a line on what he's up to."

He went downstairs. He glanced into the bar and the dining-room, where Wilson was still catching up with accounts, and learned from him that Potter had gone off after lunch, and was expected back about tea-time. He went outside and restlessly strolled

243

about the grounds. Half-an-hour later, as he was about to enter the hotel again, there was a crunch of tyres and he saw the Embassy Land-Rover come round the bend of the drive.

It pulled up before the steps and Potter got out, clutching a bulging briefcase.

"Five minutes, old man," he told the driver. He went quickly up the steps, ignoring Birkett.

"Just a minute, Potter. I'd like a word." Potter stopped reluctantly, and half turned.

"I believe you've got my passport," Birkett said. Potter stared at him non-committally.

"I'd like it back, if you don't mind," Birkett said.

Potter regarded him for another moment, then abruptly rested the briefcase on a raised knee, opened the flap, took out Birkett's passport and held it out to Birkett without a word.

Well, I'm blowed, Birkett thought. That's the last thing I expected.

He found it difficult not to betray his astonishment. "Thanks," he said tersely.

Potter put his hand into the briefcase again, and pulled out an envelope.

"You can also have this back."

He handed the envelope to Birkett, then fastened the flap of the briefcase and turned smartly away up the steps.

Birkett examined the envelope. He felt some small hard object in one corner. He opened the loose flap and peered inside. It was the heaven-helper.

He stared at it in fresh astonishment. This gratuitous return of the pill struck him as even odder than the return of the passport.

"By the way, Birkett."

He looked up and saw that Potter had paused at the top of the steps.

"There's something I would like to tell you, in case I don't see you again . . ." Potter hesitated, a trifle awkwardly.

"I'm afraid you will see me again, so far as that goes," Birkett said. "Too late to catch today's plane now. I can't get off until tomorrow."

Potter hesitated another moment, and then repeated, "However, in case I don't see you again . . ."

Birkett frowned. Now, what did that mean? He couldn't make it out at all.

"Well, it's nothing very important," Potter went on. "It's just that—well, you know that time Betty went up to your room? I suppose you think I put her up to it?"

"Didn't you?"

"No, that's one trick I never got up to—using my wife in that way. No, if it's any consolation to you, she went of her own accord."

"And left pretty quick of her own accord, too. Don't worry, Potter. There wasn't any monkey-business."

"No?" He looked at Birkett, and then said quickly, "Well, she told me there wasn't, of course. And anyhow, naturally I'd trust her. I mean whenever she—well, when anything like that happens, I know there's never anything in it . . ."

Good Lord, he doesn't know anything of the kind, Birkett thought. He's wearing a pair of horns. Fancy old Potter wearing a pair of horns!

"Anyhow, I just thought I'd tell you . . ." Potter stiffened and abruptly held out his big hand. Birkett took it in surprise. "Well, goodbye, old man." Potter turned and disappeared into the hotel.

Birkett stood thoughtfully for another minute, and then followed slowly inside and went upstairs to Lakshmi's room.

"Well, I've got my passport back," he said.

"Oh, I'm so glad!" Lakshmi exclaimed. "That means we can go tomorrow!"

"I hope so . . . Only I wish I knew what Potter was playing at." He told her about the pill.

"But I think that's wonderful," she said. "I think it means that he really believes you tried to stop the shooting, and that you've had a change of heart. He's just trying to show you that the past is all forgotten."

"Potter forget the past? Not on your life. At best he's just bowing to the inevitable because he knows he's got nothing on me."

"I'm certain everything will be all right now—I have the feeling."

"The only feeling I've got is that I'll feel a sight easier tomorrow once we've shaken the dust of this place off our heels." He returned to his room, where he had left his suitcases ready packed for his attempted departure earlier in the afternoon. He began to unpack a few articles that he needed for the night, but then hesitated, possessed by an increasing uneasiness, and an odd disinclination to unpack further.

Just then there was a knock at the door and a roomboy came in. He began to strip the bed. It was not even Birkett's own roomboy.

"Here, what are you up to?"

"Changing sheets for Mr. Potter, sir," the boy said.

"Eh?"

"I work Mr. Potter's room, sir. He told me he will sleep here tonight."

At that moment Wilson appeared in the doorway. "Here's your account, Major Birkett. I'm sorry you're leaving, but I don't blame you. On the contrary, it was my advice from the first to go to the Royal."

"What's this all about? Who said I was going to the Royal?"

"Nobody, Major Birkett. I just took it for granted that since you were leaving the Everest—"

"I'm not leaving the Everest—not until tomorrow."

Wilson gave him a curious look. "No? Well, that's funny. Mr. Potter came to me in the dining-room just now on his way out, grinning all over his face—he's had his eye on your room for some time—and said, 'I hear Major Birkett's found his passport and is leaving tonight.' I said it was too late, you'd missed the plane. He said, 'I didn't say he was leaving Kathmandu, I only said he was leaving.' I asked where you were going to spend the night, and he just grinned and said, 'Couldn't say—I expect in his coffin.' I thought the joke was in rather bad taste, and just said, 'Well, anything rather than the Everest,' and then off he went to the Singha Durbar."

"The Singha Durbar? Why should Potter go to the Singha Durbar?" The Singha Durbar was the vast palace, formerly the residency of the hereditary Rana Prime Ministers, that now housed the entire Nepalese government. "Anyhow, it'll be shut on a Sunday, won't it?"

"There's one department that won't—not after that business yesterday," Wilson said significantly.

"What's that?"

"The police department—the local Scotland Yard." He leant confidentially towards Birkett. "There's a buzz going round the town—I heard it from my boys—that Mathai was put up to that job yesterday by a certain foreign person acting on behalf of certain foreign interests, and that there is another foreign person here who knows who that person is, and who is giving the police a line. According to the buzz he spent three hours with the police at the Singha Durbar yesterday after the Tattoo. Well, I can tell you that for three hours yesterday after the Tattoo Mr. Potter was not at the Everest, and remembering that he has gone to the Singha Durbar now, you may draw your own conclusions."

"And you think he's really on to someone?"

"According to the buzz, that certain person behind Mathai is as good as done for—and we're all going to get a big surprise when we find out who it is." He added gloomily, "I'm only praying it won't turn out to be the British Ambassador, because if it is, they'll tear down the Embassy and this hotel brick from brick . . . Well, if you're really staying on, Mr. Potter will have to wait until tomorrow." He left with the roomboy.

Birkett looked round the room. This could be the last room without bars that he ever slept in, he thought. And according to Potter, he'd already slept in it for the last time . . .

He thought of making a bolt for it. But where should he go? India?

No, India would not give him asylum—it would play ball with Kathmandu and join in the man-hunt. Anyhow, you were too conspicuous as a European—you could be picked out in a jiffy.

Then what about Sikkim? No, Sikkim was virtually part of India, and the same objections applied.

Apart from India and Sikkim, the only other country adjoining

Nepal was Tibet. Well, he'd be all right in Tibet. And he could move on from Tibet to China. But Christ, Tibet was a tidy walk.

And supposing it was all a false alarm? He didn't want to live out the rest of his days in China because of a false alarm—because of some buzz started by the hotel boys.

But it wasn't only the buzz. It was Potter repeating insistently, "In case I don't see you again." And that crack about the coffin. After all that, he'd be a fool not to bolt for it . . .

On the other hand, he still didn't see what Potter could pin on him—what evidence he could possibly have. Potter hadn't even got the heaven-helper any more, so why should he get the wind up? No, he was going to sit tight, he wasn't going to get scared off like a frightened rabbit . . .

He paced restlessly about the room. He could not make up his mind whether to go or stay. Sweat broke out on his forehead with the agony of his indecision. There was a knock on the door. He jumped. But it was only the bar boy. "Telephone, sir."

"Who is it?"

"A Nepali man, sir. He wouldn't give name, just said, 'I must speak to Major Birkett—quick!'"

Birkett hurried downstairs. The bar was empty. He picked the receiver off the shelf behind the counter." "Yes?"

"Major Ronald Birkett?" The voice sounded weak with anxiety and came faintly over the crackling line.

"Yes, who's speaking?"

The voice hurried on, talking English with an accent, falling over itself to convey its message. "I cannot tell you my name. I am ringing you at great risk. I have been waiting for an hour for the opportunity to use the instrument to warn you as a . . ." The voice disappeared in a burst of atmospherics.

"Can't hear you," Birkett said. "Speak up, man!"

"I am a comrade, Major Birkett. I am employed in—in certain government clerical duties, and I have reason to know you are in danger, Major Birkett, comrade. Last night . . ." The voice broke off, and Birkett could imagine the nervous backward glances at the door, the sweating palm holding the receiver ready to slam down on the hook.

"Hello," he said impatiently. "Hello, are you there?"

The voice came back. "Last night a fellow countryman of yours, Major Birkett, aroused suspicion against you for conspiracy in the attempt on the life of His Majesty and the murder of General Ranju. There was no proof so I did not warn you. But now proof has been received. It is from India. One of our comrades has betrayed . . ." There were more shattering explosions on the line and Birkett caught only disjointed words of what followed. "Someone . . . or Delhi contact . . . shameful treachery . . ."

Not Gupta? Birkett thought. Not that old revolutionary fighter? He was staggered. He couldn't believe that Gupta had sold him down the river. But who else? There was no one . . . Suddenly he remembered. The resentful eyes, the sandals clopping like a carthorse pulling the brewer's dray, the laboured hunt through the telephone directory to keep him waiting. That jealous old hen of a secretary—what was his name? Desai . . . Yes, Desai—he hated my guts. Still, I never imagined—

The voice returned again, gabbling with renewed fear. ". . . meeting now to discuss formalities and matter of protocol. The military is to make the arrest. They have sent for the officers. It will be soon. You have one hour . . ." The line went dead.

Birkett slowly replaced the receiver. He remained for a minute standing erectly behind the bar. All his anguish and uncertainty had gone. He had always hated uncertainty—sooner a whole armoured division coming slap bang at you in the open field than a handful of hidden snipers in the trees. At least you knew where you stood . . .

And now he knew where he stood—exactly.

He left the bar and went up to Lakshmi's room. The roomboy had just brought her tea on a tray. He jerked his head for the boy to get out, and pulled the door closed behind him. He said, "Now, listen. I've just had word that they're coming to arrest me in one hour. Once they arrest me I'm as good as on the gallows—and it may be what I deserve. But I'm not ready to go yet because thanks to you I'm only just learning how to live. And I want to live properly for a bit before I go. So I'm going to do a bolt for Tibet. It'll be a bit of a hike, but I'll make it all right, and so could you if you don't mind risking a few blisters, and maybe some frost-bite. We'll probably end up in China. And I'll warn you straight—we'll have no friends, no money, and we'll have to start a new life from scratch. And that'll mean hardships that will make crossing the Himalayas seem like a holiday at the seaside."

Lakshmi stared at him in dismay. She said, "You mean we'd never come back to India?"

"Probably not," he said. "No."

She sank weakly on to the bed.

"All right, I'll come back in ten minutes," he said. "You must make up your mind by then. Now, how much money have you got? Cash—not travellers' cheques."

She shook her head and looked round in a daze for her purse. He spotted it on the dressing-table and went over and opened it himself. He took out the wallet and glanced inside—three rupees.

"You're in the same boat as me. I'll have to get Wilson to change my cheques. Must have cash for food in the villages."

He went downstairs but the dining-room was empty. He went through to the bar.

"Where's Mr. Wilson?" he asked the bar-boy.

"Bhautgaon, sir."

Birkett swore. Bhautgaon was several miles away. Wilson sometimes went there to visit a strapping whisky-drinking English nurse, and always stayed away hours. And since he carried the key of the safe in his pocket, that meant no cash. "All right, get me paper and an envelope."

He took out his pen and travellers' cheques while he was waiting and signed all the cheques that remained. They amounted to £130. The boy returned with the paper and he wrote a note for Wilson.

Dear Wilson,

 Fifty quid to garage for jeep—not worth half. Rest for outstanding hotel bill and items I've pinched.

R. Birkett

He sealed the note and the travellers' cheques in the envelope and gave it to the boy. "Now let's have the store-room key."

"Mr. Wilson's got it, sir."

"Come off it. It's on a hook under that bar."

"No, sir."

Birkett dived round the bar to look for himself: the hook was indeed empty. Well, that really dished it. He'd counted on getting the tent, sleeping-bags, and other kit that Wilson kept handy for guests wanting to go off on trek. He couldn't set off for Tibet, over the highest mountains in the world, without any kit—he hadn't an overcoat or even a decent sweater to his name. He'd have to break down the store-room door.

He went along to the store-room at the other end of the building, and heaved at the door with his shoulder. But it was made of heavy wood and there was no give in it at all. He might as well have tried to break into a Bank of England vault. He could have opened the lock with a piece of wire—but that meant several minutes finding the wire, and several minutes fiddling with the mechanism. He couldn't afford the time. No choice but to skip it.

God, this was a bad start. No cash. No kit. The only bit of luck was that he still had the jeep.

He returned briskly down the corridor, pausing in the hall to tear down the map of Nepal that was pinned up beside the letter-rack. It was a fancy pictorial map, dotted with pictures of pagodas and big-game, that showed only the roads in the Kathmandu valley and none of the mountain tracks. Hardly worthy to be called a map at all, but anyhow better than nothing. He stuffed it in his pocket and set off for the kitchen.

The kitchen was deserted except for the cook, in grubby khaki shorts and singlet, asleep on a bench against the wall. Birkett spotted an empty wooden case and took it over to the store-cupboard. Supplies came daily from the bazaar and there was little in stock, but he found two tins of coffee, two packets of tea, a bag of sugar, a small quantity of rice, some biscuits, and a few tins of sardines and corned beef. He piled them into the box and went over to the dresser. He looked quickly through the drawers and took out a tin-opener and a handful of cutlery. He put them in the box with the supplies and dragged the box across the kitchen.

The scraping of the box on the stone floor woke the cook, who opened his eyes in time to see Birkett take a joint of cold mutton out of the ice-box. It was the joint ear-marked for the guests' supper.

He rubbed his eyes and looked again. He saw a pound of butter follow the joint into the box on the floor.

He slowly peeled himself off the bench. He crossed the kitchen and stood watching Birkett, his hands in the pockets of the grubby khaki shorts.

Birkett ignored him and continued to empty the ice-box.

Presently the cook said, "You're taking all the food."

"That's right," Birkett said.

"What are you going to do with all that food?"

"Eat it, of course."

The bar-boy came through the swing door from the dining-room, and stood watching with the cook.

"What's he doing?" he asked the cook after a while.

"He's taking all the food."

The bar-boy had a smooth happy face with laughing Mongolian eyes. He began to giggle. "Why don't you stop him?" The cook shrugged. "I'm not a Gurkha mercenary from the hills. I'm a civilized man from the valley, a specialist in food, and I'm only paid to cook, not to fight. However, you can stop him if you like."

The bar-boy shook with a fresh outburst of merriment. "No, I'm a specialist, too. I specialize in washing dirty glasses and bottles, and am not paid to fight either."

Birkett slammed the door of the ice-box, summed up the two boys with a shrewd glance, decided that the bar-boy looked the most amenable, and told him, "Take this box out to my jeep. Come on, jump to it, if you don't want your bottom kicked!"

The boy, still shaken by giggles, lifted the heavy case on to his shoulder.

"I forgot to mention," he told the cook, "that I am also a specialist in carrying boxes."

He carried the box out through the swing door, and Birkett returned upstairs. Lakshmi's room was empty. He went along to his own room and found her standing over his suitcase, repacking the toilet articles he had taken out for the night before deciding not to unpack further.

"Thanks, very thoughtful of you," he said. She did not look at him. He said, "Well, what is it? Yes or no?"

She closed the lid of the suitcase. She looked dazed, as though she hardly knew what she was doing. She nodded, still without looking at him.

"You mean 'Yes'?" he said.

"Yes," she said in a barely audible whisper.

"You really know what you're doing?"

She said, "I can't just let you go and never see you again."

"Right, then we're off. All we need now is blankets. You can whip them off the beds while I rustle up some boys to help with the baggage."

He found two roomboys in the corridor, and between them they carried everything downstairs. The news of Birkett's raid on the kitchen had spread quickly and half-a-dozen boys had gathered cheerfully on the steps to watch the departure. The only discordant note was struck by the cook who stood sullenly apart with hands sunk in the pockets of the food-stained shorts.

Birkett took out his wallet. He gave his few remaining rupees to the boys who had helped him. They asked where he was going.

"Sikkim," Birkett said. "I need some walking to shake up our livers after all the luxury—living at this place, which is the Sikkim road?"

"Past the maidan, sir."

"Right. 'Bye chaps."

The jeep shot off, Birkett swung left at the gates towards the maidan.

"Not that anybody's going to be fooled by that red herring," he said. "They're bound to hit on Tibet as the most likely place we'd make for. We'll have to avoid the main tracks once we're clear of the valley."

They turned off the Sikkim road beyond the maidan and doubled back to another road leading across the valley. Soon they had left the town behind. The jeep jolted and rattled on the rough stony road between the endless paddy-fields. Twenty or thirty miles ahead the steep green hills rose abruptly from the plain, and stretched back in unbroken succession to the line of snow peaks that barred the horizon from one end to the other. Lakshmi was silent. She had not spoken a word since they had left the hotel. Birkett knew that she was still unable to grasp properly what had happened to her. Only an hour ago she had still taken for granted that she would be back in India soon. And now suddenly she was not going back to India at all, was never going to see it again. It lay behind them—each moment took them farther away. And instead she was going to an unknown world, shut off from all that was familiar to her behind the barrier of ice and snow.

She sat jolting about on the hard seat of the jeep, her mind dazed, her feelings numbed.

Soon the sun began to set. The great snow ranges turned to gold and then were flushed with pink. And her feelings thawed and she felt a responsive flush of warmth.

She thought she had never in her life seen anything so beautiful as that magic world of golden peaks and pink snow. It held her in a spell of utter enchantment. It was like a symbol of her future.

I was right to come, she thought. I'm so thankful I came.

A minute later the glow suddenly faded. The cloak of beauty had been whipped away to reveal the brief illusion. The magic world had vanished, and in its place was a world that was cold, grey, hostile. She felt betrayed.

They rattled and jolted on through the dust. Her heart ached, with dismay. She wanted to cry out to Birkett that she had made

254

a mistake, that she wanted to go back, that she must return to India or she would die. But somehow she could not utter a sound. Darkness dropped over them like a black box. The last chink of daylight was shut away. The box was sealed. She was trapped.

Chapter Nineteen

Birkett woke and heard the twittering of birds and saw daylight through the trees. He jumped up: he had meant to be on the move by dawn. The grass bed that he had made for Lakshmi was empty. She was sitting in the jeep with a blanket over her shoulders.

"Hello, wasn't my mattress comfortable?" he said.

She glanced at him without replying. There were heavy shadows under her eyes. She had not slept all night.

"I'll manage something better for you once we get organized," Birkett said.

She watched him walk off up the track. She felt no emotion at the sight of him. She tried to recall the passion that only yesterday had made separation from him seem an intolerable anguish. But now he might have been a stranger She wondered what madness had possessed her to come with him.

He's a hunted man, she thought. I'm running away with a criminal.

He came back. He said, "There's a nullah just up there with only a footbridge over it, so we couldn't have got any farther last night if we'd tried. Still, we must have come up a good thousand feet—more than I'd expected with the jeep." He began to unload the baggage. "Sorry, you'll have to shift."

She got out and stood shivering miserably with the blanket clutched round her. Her sari trailed in the wet grass, and the earth was damp and cold to her feet in their flimsy sandals.

You mean we've got to walk now?" she said.

"That's right."

"How many miles?"

"Not a clue. Anyhow you can't reckon this sort of trip in miles—at least not horizontal miles. It's the vertical miles, up and down, that count. But at a rough guess I'd say it'll take us a month."

"A month? Walking?"

"That's only to the border—it'll take a sight more to Lhasa. But don't worry, I'll organize something for you to wear, and you'll be surprised how easy it'll go after a bit. The first week's the worst."

She watched him pull another suitcase out of the jeep, whistling to himself. She said, "I've changed my mind. I'm not coming with you."

"Yes you are." He went on whistling.

"You can't make me. I'm going back."

"Not today, you aren't. Not till you've given yourself a chance. You can see how you feel this time tomorrow when we've had time to get organized. Then if you still want to go back I'll find somebody in a village to see you back to the plain. Now I'm going to dump the jeep. It's the first thing they'll be scouting for, and no point in making their job easier than need be."

He drove the jeep forward a few yards to the brink of a ravine, and then got out and released the hand-brake. The jeep moved off slowly down the slope. It gathered speed, then turned over and crashed and somersaulted from rock to rock, shedding a seat cushion, the flat metal bonnet cover, the tubular supports of the hood. A wheel spun in the air like a quoit. It was more than Lakshmi could bear. The jeep was the last tangible connection with the familiar world, and watching it smashing to pieces on the rocks was like seeing her own life destroyed. She hid her eyes, put her fingers to her ears to shut out the sounds as it went on crashing its way down.

At last the ravine was silent again.

"Now you can sit on a suitcase and twiddle your thumbs for a bit," Birkett said. "There's grub in the box if you want it. I'm going to follow the track up to a village and try to get porters."

"How long will you be?"

"Depends how soon I find a village."

He found one after a couple of miles. A crowd of children and curious villagers gathered round as he explained with signs what he wanted. Shortly a young man appeared in the entrance of the village store and asked him in Urdu if he was an officer from the Indian Army.

"I used to be in the Indian Army," Birkett said.

"Then we have a mutual friend, sir," the young man smiled, "Who's that?"

"Please come inside. You shall see him, sir."

Birkett ducked under the low lintel. They entered a room behind the shop. It was dim and full of smoke from the cooking-fire, with only a tiny window and no chimney. The young man's wife squatted at the fire stirring a large copper bowl. There was nobody else in the room. The young man proudly pointed to an old newspaper photograph on the wall and exclaimed, "Our mutual friend!"

Birkett peered through the thick fumes and recognized the face of Field-Marshal Sir William Slim. Alongside was a snapshot of the young man as a Lance Naik in Gurkha uniform.

"Fourteenth Army, eh?" Birkett said. "Good chap."

An hour later he was back with Lakshmi, and three porters, supervised by the young ex-Gurkha, were roping the baggage and hoisting it on to their shoulders. The party started back to the village. Lakshmi struggled along in silence. Soon the skirt of her sari had been ripped by thorns, and the narrow thongs of her sandals were broken. She was obliged to walk barefooted; but she still did not say a word. She knew it was her own fault for not insisting on going back. She had been a coward—afraid to stand up to him. But nothing would stop her going back tomorrow.

They reached the village and entered the smoky little room behind the Gurkha's shop. They sat cross-legged on the matting and the Gurkha's wife placed a bowl in Birkett's hands. She filled it with a milky liquid.

"Chang," the Gurkha said. "Our rice beer."

Birkett drank from the bowl. The woman promptly filled it up again.

"Steady on, you'll have me tight as a coot! I must keep a clear head because we've got a problem on our hands," Birkett said.

"Some friends from Kathmandu invited us along for a trip in their car. It was only supposed to be for a couple of days. But we got so smitten with the countryside that we decided to send them home without us and see a bit more on foot. We reckoned we could buy some kit in a village. But our friends had no sooner disappeared down the road than we realized we'd left all our cash in the car. Now we're absolutely flat. However, we've a good few things in our bags that we don't need, and so I'm wondering if we can do some barter?"

"What articles do you require?" the Gurkha asked.

"Boots and clothes for my wife first of all," Birkett said. "Then we need cooking-pots, some good thick blankets, and a decent piece of canvas—there's a piece I've already got my eye on that's rotting away on empty hen-house as you enter the village. Also some cord, a strong needle and thread, a chopper, and a good sharp knife."

"Several of those articles I have in stock in my shop, and since you are a friend of my friend, Sir Bill Slim, I wish to present them as a gift. The rest you can get by barter."

Many villagers had already gathered outside to peer at the foreign baggage stacked in the open-fronted shop; and when Birkett and the Gurkha squatted on the raised floor and began to open the cases the numbers quickly multiplied. Birkett took out a blue worsted suit. "What do you think this'll fetch?"

The Gurkha looked gloomy. He said, "It is very nice, sir."

"Fifty quid it cost me in London."

The Gurkha told the villagers, "This is the clothing of a superior British gentleman. I have seen such clothing worn in Darjeeling. Who will buy it?" There was silence. "The material is woolly and warm," the Gurkha urged. "If it was cut into small pieces and fluffed, it could be used for padding a coat."

The suit was sold for five rupees. Next a man pointed to a red biscuit-tin with a sailing-ship on the lid that Birkett used for oddments. He offered two rupees. This started some brisk bidding and the tin was finally knocked down to him at nine rupees.

"But that's more than the suit!" Birkett exclaimed. "And he never even asked what's in it!"

"You must remove the contents and sell those separately, sir. He has only bought the tin. A red tin with a pretty decoration and a secure lid is a valuable commodity. The purchaser is a shrewd man. He will resell it at a profit."

"Well, what's he got that's worth nine rupees? Any decent boots?"

"I should take the money, sir, and buy boots from another man."

The dealing lasted two hours. The most lucrative line proved to be Lakshmi's silk saris, and after profitably disposing of several he finished up with all the more important articles he required, and in addition an old rucksack left behind by a Himalayan expedition with the name *W. Brutsch, Zermatt* in faded ink inside the flap, and ninety-seven rupees in cash.

"Now I want some porters who can stay with us a week or two until we get into the Sherpa country," he said.

Three porters, one of them an ex-soldier with a knowledge of Urdu, were found without difficulty and terms arranged. He obtained some information about the track and they set off.

The track climbed for an hour and then dropped steeply, so that soon they had lost all the height they had gained, then abruptly shot up again. It was the same all afternoon. Lakshmi gasped for breath as she struggled along behind Birkett. She wore yak-hide boots and a pair of Birkett's khaki drill slacks, the legs shortened with scissors and a cord holding in the tucks round her waist. She had never walked like this before in her life. She had never walked anywhere if she could help it—"going for walks" was an English madness, like climbing impossible cliffs and mountains, that no Indian could comprehend. Only her dread of losing face before the porters enabled her to keep going, saved her from dropping from exhaustion. And she followed in a daze behind the rucksack on Birkett's back that moved away endlessly along the path. She seemed to have been following it as long as she could remember, all her life.

At last Birkett stopped. "Right, we'll halt early for our first camp. We've a lot to get organized."

She collapsed on the grass and lay with her eyes closed. She heard Birkett briskly instructing the porters, "Cook-house here—tent under that tree-porters' camp over there by those rocks." He detailed one porter to fetch wood, another water. After a while he came over to her. "Easy job for you—potatoes."

"Potatoes?" She stared helplessly. "What am I to do?"

"Peel 'em, of course."

He left her struggling with the potatoes and disappeared with the chopper. He returned with a load of bamboo poles on his shoulder. He dumped them on the ground beside the sheet of canvas for the tent, selected the most slender ones, and chopped them into six-inch lengths.

"Still at those potatoes? Never mind, skip the rest—time for needlework." He knotted some cord to one of the pieces of bamboo. "Better than stitching the cord straight onto the canvas for the guy ropes. They'll take more strain if you stitch on the bamboo like this crosswise . . . No, wait a minute, we can go one better." He turned back the edge of the canvas into a hem and made a hole through the bottom. He threaded the cord through the hole until the bamboo was caught in the fold and held it anchored. "This'll save stitching each one on separately. You can just hem-stitch right along." He started off the stitching for her and then set to work with chopper and knife on the stouter bamboo to make pegs and poles.

"By Jove, I get a real kick out of bamboo—nothing you can't make with it! Know you can even make cups? Well, mugs, more like. You see, look here, the joints are sealed. So if you cut across here just below the joint and then up here where it's hollow . . ."

An hour later the improvised tent was pitched.

"I'll make a proper tent later when I can get some skins. A proper tent with flaps that will keep out the wind . . . My word I'd better start dinner before it gets dark. I could kick myself for forgetting candles down in that village. Memo for the next shopping-list. Meanwhile, I'm afraid you'll have to skip reading in bed." He held up a potato on the point of a knife. "You've left in all the eyes!"

He made mutton stew. She was ravenous and no food in her life had ever seemed more delicious; she felt bound to give him credit for his skill and ingenuity as a cook. She also admitted to herself a sneaking admiration for his other accomplishments during the day. Only this morning, the world fallen about their ears, they had been stranded with nothing. And now he had created this whole little world of his own with the porters to fetch and carry, the two neat beds side by side in the tent, the orderly arrangement of equipment and stores, the magnificent stew.

Few Indians would have been so practical, so resourceful, she thought. He makes my husband seem as soft as a woman.

Her hunger was no sooner satisfied than she was nodding: she went to the tent and was asleep before Birkett came in and stretched himself in the bed beside her. And in the morning she was still sleeping when he rose and went off for a stroll.

He returned to find her washing the supper dishes, using the same water in which she had peeled the potatoes, and holding them at arm's length like a duchess. By Jove, he'd a tidy bit to teach her, he thought. But skip it this morning.

"Well, you've earned your breakfast all right," he said. "What d'you fancy? Fried eggs?"

After breakfast he organized a routine for striking camp and put her in charge of packing up the kitchen. He said nothing about her going back to Kathmandu. She did not mention it either. The porters hoisted their loads on to their backs, pulled down the plaited thongs over their foreheads to take the weight.

"Now we're not going to race," Birkett said. "It's steady and slow that does it. Steady and slow."

He adjusted his rucksack, picked up his walking-stick, and started up the track without looking back, and Lakshmi silently followed.

The track continued like a switchback for the next few days, sometimes dropping down into dense sweltering valleys, sometimes climbing to altitudes where the wind had a bite though they had not yet risen above ten thousand feet and were still a long way from the snows. There was seldom a day when they did not come across a village, and the farther they travelled from Kathmandu the cleaner the villages became: no longer were there mangy dogs, excrement in the streets, babies with sores seething with flies. They obtained all the food they needed by cash or barter, including eggs, chickens, yak's meat and vegetables, besides milk, chang and arak for drinking. They also secured an old paraffin lamp and skins for a tent, iodine and bandages in case of need, and two shepherds' cloaks of yak's wool.

At first Lakshmi's body was nothing but aches and pains. But after a week she began to recover and feel the exhilaration of new strength in herself, and soon they were covering more ground in a day's march than they had covered in two or three days at the outset. Now each ascent took them higher and the villages began to proclaim their increasing proximity to Tibet, they had entered the Sherpa country where the men strode through the streets in embroidered boots and hats and the women wore colourful striped aprons and buttered pigtails; and they often came across red-robed monks and heard monastery bells booming out across the potato fields. Beside the track prayer flags fluttered in the breeze from slender leaning bamboos.

It grew much colder: they traded Birkett's watch and the last superfluous items in their baggage for padded clothes, fur-lined hats and gloves, and embroidered Sherpa boots of felt with yak-hide soles. Their diet also changed with the altitude. Chickens, eggs, meat had disappeared: even yak's meat was for some reason no longer obtainable, but only yak's blood, dried and solidified into hunks that looked rather like liver, and that—their first reluctance overcome—became their staple food, with garlic which grew wild in abundance and provided a free vegetable for their meals.

No trees grew up here except juniper, whose wood they mixed with yak's dung as fuel for cooking. It burnt with a pleasing smell that flavoured food and tea. Dwarf rhododendrons covered the slopes in profusion. And the earth was so thickly carpeted with flowers that they crushed anemones and violets underfoot, and the embroidered patterns on their high felt boots could no longer be seen for buttercup pollen. The great white mountain barrier towered over them. It had become part of their immediate world, nearer each time they looked, until they felt they could reach out and touch it. They met a caravan of yaks bringing Tibetan salt and learnt that it had crossed the pass into Nepal eight days ago.

Birkett said, "And we move faster than yaks, so I reckon five or six days should see us safely over the border."

The next day at the entrance to a valley they were brought to a standstill by the sight that met their eyes. The whole floor of the valley was a brilliant blue.

"By Jove!" Birkett exclaimed. "Oh, by Jove!"

The blue was too bright for cornflowers—they had never seen such blue. They went forward and were soon knee-deep in the azure sea. Birkett picked one of the flowers whose petals opened voluminously like a breakfast cup of the finest china.

"It's a poppy," Birkett said. "I wouldn't have believed it if you'd told me, but that's what it is—a blue poppy."

It was only noon, but they were so enchanted with the valley of blue poppies that they broke off the day's march; and after they had lunched they wandered away from the camp, lay down amongst the blue poppies, and made love. And Lakshmi cried out that it had never been so beautiful and that it must have been an act of creation—she felt convinced of it with her whole being, for it could not have been so beautiful otherwise.

Birkett said, "Well, I don't know how they stand in Lhasa for maternity hospitals."

"Do you think they'll mind that we're not married?"

"We could probably get married in Tibet so far as that goes. The Tibetans are polyandrous. A woman can have all the husbands she wants."

"I wouldn't really mind if we never get to Tibet. I'd like to go on wandering like this forever."

She wanted to stay in the valley another day but Birkett said, "No, we must move on tomorrow. We can't afford an extra day or we'll have nothing to pay for food or porters. I'm worried enough as it is that the money's not going to spin out to the frontier."

But the next day a miracle happened. Half-way through the

morning they met two Frenchmen with porters returning from a preliminary survey for an expedition, and whilst pausing to celebrate the meeting with a bottle of arak, an idea all at once occurred to Birkett. He turned to Lakshmi.

"You've still got those travellers' cheques, haven't you?"

She nodded and he turned back to the Frenchmen. "You can't spare any cash, I suppose? We're nearly cleaned out, but we can give you travellers' cheques that you can cash when you get back to Kathmandu."

Birkett's arak had put the Frenchmen in a convivial mood: they pressed three hundred Nepalese rupees on him despite his protestations that two hundred were quite sufficient.

He laughed. "Well, by Jove, the American Express claim you can cash their cheques pretty well anywhere, but I'll bet they never knew you could do it on the roof of the world."

They were already on the point of parting company when one of the Frenchmen said, "By the way, I suppose you've got your visas?"

"Visas?" Birkett was puzzled, since he had made out that they were only intending to go as far as the Tibetan frontier and then return to Kathmandu. "You mean for Tibet? But as I explained—"

"No, I mean for Nepal."

"Nepal? Good Lord yes, we've got those. We couldn't have got into the country without them."

"The visas for entering the country are only for Kathmandu. Haven't you got district visas?"

"No, what are they?"

The Frenchman took out his passport and flicked over the pages. A large number were occupied by rubber-stamped visas signed by the Nepalese Chief of Protocol.

"You use up your passport quicker in Nepal than any other country in the world," he said. "We've been through six districts and it's a full page for each. You must have come through as many. I can't understand how you haven't been pinched."

"Stuck to the small tracks, I expect that was it," Birkett said.

"Anyhow the worst must be behind us now. Nobody's likely to pinch us between here and the frontier, are they?"

"There'll be a Check Post."

"Check Post? What's that?"

The Frenchman laughed, "I find such innocence charming!" He explained that the Check Posts were situated along all the main tracks, in particular near the frontiers, to check the movements of travellers and goods. They were run by the military.

"Aren't equipped with radio, are they?" Birkett asked.

"Yes, I have reason to know because we got one Post to send back a message for us to Kathmandu. Why do you ask?"

"I was just thinking that—well, if they'd suspected in Kathmandu that we'd gone off without visas, they might have warned the Check Posts to keep their eyes skinned." They'd have warned them all right—it made his heart skip several beats to think how blithely unaware they had been of this danger. "Anyhow, better watch our step. Don't happen to know where the Check Post is on this track to the pass?"

"No, we only joined it yesterday. But your porters are sure to know."

"You're much handier at this language than me. I wish you'd ask them for me."

The Frenchman spoke to the three Sherpas that Birkett had taken on ten days ago after sending the first porters back to their village. Only one had ever been along this track as far as the frontier. It had been some years before but he remembered that the Check Post was on the frontier itself, right up on the pass.

Birkett said, "You might ask him to give me plenty of warning before we reach it."

"You can't miss the pass. We could see it even from over where we were. But I'll certainly ask him for you." He spoke to the Sherpa. "He'll be delighted. Independent fellows, these Sherpas—always glad of a chance to do authority in the eye. Now, any messages we can take back to Kathmandu?"

"Yes, best regards to a chap called Potter at the Everest," Birkett grinned. "And I'm sorry he's been done out of his pigeon pie."

"What does that mean?"

"Ask him. Anyhow it was certainly a spot of luck knocking into you. We'll miss that Check Post now,"

But three days later, despite the Frenchmen's warning, they ran slap into it. They were still a good couple of days from the pass, though they had come within sight of it the day before, when the porter had pointed it out and grinned, "Chickposs." But either his memory was faulty or the Check Post had changed its position since he had last been along the track. They never found out which—once the error had become apparent it was too late for a post-mortem.

It was in the morning. They had set off early from their night's camp at the foot of a ridge and made the steep ascent ahead of the porters. They reached the narrow gap at the top and paused just beyond to wait for them. The pass had broken once more into their full view. It was many thousand feet higher than where they stood, across a steep valley—only one more descent and then they would begin the last long climb to the frontier. Birkett noted with satisfaction that the wide saucer of the pass was covered only partially with snow. And he was running his eye over the dark lanes between the white patches, looking for the best route, when all at once Lakshmi said, "There must be somebody about. I can smell juniper and yak-dung burning."

Birkett sniffed. "More than I can. Probably still tasting your breakfast."

"No, I can smell it. I'm sure."

She took a step farther down the track and stopped dead. Birkett went to her side. The track twisted sharply round to the right from the mouth of the gap and beside it, set back in the shelter of the ridge, was a grey stone building with smoke seeping from the roof. A crude flagstaff was set in the ground before the entrance. It flew the Nepalese flag. A soldier in padded jacket squatted on a rock near the flagstaff. He was cleaning his rifle. His breath steamed in the cold air. He was not thirty yards from them.

Birkett reached out for Lakshmi's arm to pull her away. But just then the soldier looked up and caught sight of them. His hands paused on the rifle. He stared at them curiously.

"I'd better try talking to him," Birkett said. "It'll look too suspicious if we shove off now. I'll ask him if it's the Check Post, and say we're going back to see what's happened to our porters—and then we'll have to go like scalded cats."

But at that moment the door of the building was flung open and half a dozen soldiers with rifles came tumbling out. The soldier jumped up from the rock and joined them as they formed a squad near the flagstaff. An officer appeared in the doorway. He paused, slowly pulling on his gloves and looking curiously at Birkett and Lakshmi. His breath steamed like a simmering kettle. After a minute he pulled the door closed as if he had forgotten about them, went over to the men, and called them to attention.

"We'll just skip off," Birkett said. "But take it easy till we're out of sight."

But they had not taken a step before the officer looked round sharply. He must have had eyes in the back of his head.

He said in English, "Where you go, please?"

"We're just going to check on our porters," Birkett said.

"No. You stay here, please."

He turned back to his men. Birkett and Lakshmi stood waiting unhappily. After a while the officer left the squad and came over. He was tall for a Nepalese with high cheekbones and a small black moustache. His face was smooth with two cleancut holes for the eyes.

"Where you come from, please?" he said.

"Kathmandu," Birkett said. "We've come farther than we meant—we're thinking of heading back."

"No, I mean what country."

"Switzerland—we're Swiss. My wife's from Ceylon but of course she's Swiss now."

The officer studied them carefully. After a minute he called a corporal from the squad. He gave him an order and the corporal ran to the building. He turned back to Birkett.

"You got district visas?"

"Good Lord yes, pages of them," Birkett said. "That's one thing we're all right for."

"Show me, please." The officer held out a hand.

"Sorry, they're with the rest of our stuff with the porters. Shall we slip back and get 'em?"

"No. You stay here please."

He glanced round at the building. They stood waiting in silence with steaming mouths. Presently the door opened and the corporal came out. They could hear a radio receiver peep-peep-peeping inside. It was silenced again as the corporal pulled the door after him. He came over at the double and handed the officer a piece of paper. The officer carefully studied it. He held it averted but the sun behind his shoulders made the writing show through, and Birkett could see two words in large clumsy Roman letters sandwiched between the lines of Nepalese script. He read them back-to-front. They were BISKETT and KAPOOR.

The officer looked up. "What your name, please?"

"Brutsch," Birkett said.

"How you spell?"

"Here, like this." He took off his rucksack and showed the officer the faded ink legend inside the flap: *W. Brutsch, Zerrnatt.*

The officer studied it without expression for a full minute.

"What that second name, please?"

"Zermatt—that's a place in Switzerland."

"That's where you come from?"

"No, we live in Basle but we go to Zermatt to climb. You've probably heard of the Matterhorn—you climb that from Zermatt."

The officer compared the name on the rucksack with the name on the paper. Birkett glanced back along the track. Thank God, still no sign of the porters. They would be lost as soon as the porters arrived with the baggage and passports. Their only hope was to get away first.

The officer said, "Your name not Biskett?"

"No, Brutsch."

"You know that name Biskett?"

"Never heard it in my life."

"You know the name Kapoor?"

"No."

''What this lady's name, please?"

"Brutsch—used to be Sen before she was married."

The officer examined the paper again. He looked puzzled.

"You tell lies, please?"

"No, why should we?" Birkett laughed. "Anyhow you can see yourself from our passports—except that I'm afraid our porters must have missed the track, and if we don't get after them quick we're going to lose 'em."

The officer appeared to consider the idea of letting them go.

"You come straight back?"

"Why not?"

"All right, but please——" He broke off as something behind them caught his attention. "These your porters, please?"

Birkett looked round. He saw the three men coming round the bend in the track, stooping under their humps of baggage.

"Yes, they're the chaps," he said grimly.

The officer ordered the porters to put down their load. He watched them in silence. Presently he noticed some old white lettering on the outside of a valise. He went over and examined it. The letters unmistakably spelt *Maj. R. Birkett.* He looked carefully at the piece of paper and then at the valise again. His face remained expressionless. He did not look at Birkett. After a while he turned his attention to Lakshmi's suitcase. The name Kapoor was still just legible on a torn label. He compared it with the paper again. Presently he looked up.

"Your name Biskett, please?"

"Near enough," Birkett said. "Birkett to be exact."

"This lady's name Kapoor?"

"Yes."

"Why you tell lies, please?"

"Sorry," Birkett said. "Very silly."

The officer nodded as if he accepted the lie as natural and did not hold it against Birkett. "Now you go inside lock-up, please. Excuse me, conditions here very simple. But tomorrow you go back with soldiers to Kathmandu, so for one night you will not mind. You understand, please?"

Chapter Twenty

Birkett squatted on his haunches in the darkness and pried his fingers into the cracks round the big rough stones. He got a purchase with his nails. He pulled and wrenched at the stone but could work no play into it. He rested his hands for a minute and then tried some more stones, but although the wall had been built without cement they were all wedged solid. His nails were broken with trying to loosen them. He gave up.

"A tunnel's the only answer," he said. "But I could never get a tunnel through by tomorrow." There was a low moan from the corner. "Hello, Willy's off again."

He could hear their fellow-prisoners roiling about restlessly. The only light in the lock-up came from a two-inch gap over the door and at first they had thought themselves alone. They had been there an hour before a sudden groan from close at hand in the darkness had made them jump out of their skins. They had spoken to their companion but he had taken no notice. They had thought he must be sick. But when food had been unceremoniously pushed through the door, he had been quick enough to scramble across the lock-up and grab the first bowl; and in the light from the doorway they had seen the red-skinned Sherpa face, with the long greasy black hair and gold earrings and wild eyes of a pirate.

"Well, better face it," Birkett said. "We've no hope of breaking out of this place."

He went over to the door, stooping under the low roof, his eyes smarting in the thick layer of smoke underneath it. He peered through the gap under the lintel. The lock-up was near the main building and he could see the flagstaff and the track, and on the far side of the track the ground dropping steeply away into the valley; and he could see the pass beyond the valley with the white patches of snow and the steep escarpments rising on either side.

"Talk about a kid looking into a sweetshop window," he said. "It's sheer ruddy torture."

He realized that his feet were icy. He began to stamp them and fling his arms about his body.

"My word, it's parky. You want to move about a bit, too." Lakshmi was sitting on the damp floor with her back against the wall. She said, "I can't bear the smoke. I choke if I stand up."

"Yes, they say there's no smoke without fire, but they'd have a job to find the fire in this place." He went down on his knees beside the smouldering pile of yak's dung to try and poke some life into it. But the fuel was too damp. "Hopeless. Let's give you a rub."

He began to chafe Lakshmi's feet and legs. The Sherpa rolled over again and sat up rocking backwards and forwards on crossed legs.

"What's Willy up to now?"

The Sherpa broke into a rapid monotonous chant: "*Om mani padme hum, om mani padme hum.*"

"He's saying his prayers," Lakshmi said.

"If he's praying they'll bring us another meal, I'm all for it. But I fancy the lions only get fed once a day in these parts."

"*Om mani padme hum.*"

"Good old Willy. Here, let's have your hands now."

The bar of light over the door paled as darkness fell. There had been no sign of any more food.

"No hope now," Birkett said. "We'll have to fall back on emergency rations."

He pulled something out of his pocket like an old piece of leather. It was dried yak's blood. He had always kept some handy to chew as they walked. He divided it into two. Just then there were footsteps outside. The key clattered in the lock.

"By Jove, I believe Willy's prayers have been answered!" A crack of fading light appeared as the door creaked open a few inches.

A hand thrust through a bowl of soup. The Sherpa scrambled forward on hands and knees and grabbed it. He bore it off to his corner. The door shut again. The bolt was pushed home and the big padlock clanked back into position,

"Hey, what about us?" Birkett said.

"He's probably gone back for ours like he did this morning."

"Yes, but he didn't lock the door again this morning."

He rose and peered through the gap over the door. This morning a guard with a rifle had accompanied the soldier bringing their food. He had waited outside while the soldier had gone back for the second bowl and then the third—carrying two at once was evidently beyond his capacity. But now there was no guard outside and he was sure he had heard only one person's footsteps. The soldier must have been alone. He listened for the footsteps to return. The only sound was the Sherpa noisily sucking at his soup. Several minutes passed and the soldier did not come back.

"That's too bad," Birkett said.

"Are you starving?"

"Yes, but I was thinking of something a lot more important than that. If the chap was alone I might have made short work of him and we could have skipped off quick. They'd never have caught us in the dark. But I'm afraid we've missed our chance. Here, we're going to need this after all."

He turned back from the door to give her a piece of the old leathery fragment, but stopped tensely as he heard footsteps again. They stopped outside and hands fiddled with the padlock. He stood back against the wall near the door. The door opened and through the crack he saw the stooping form of the soldier as he pushed through another bowl. He looked like a bulky chrysalis in his padded jacket. He was alone.

It looks too easy, Birkett thought. There must be a snag.

The door closed again. It was bolted and locked and then the footsteps retreated.

Well, I'm damned if I can see the snag, Birkett thought.

He stood tense and silent for a minute and then made up his mind. The tension left him. He became cool, brisk, detached.

"Right, we're off—on your feet quick."

Lakshmi said, frightened, "You're not really going—"

"Yes. Just do as I tell you. Quick, over here. Never mind the smoke. That's right—here, flat against the wall. Don't move until I say 'Scoot'—and then go like lightning. Over the track and straight down the hillside. I'll be right behind you . . . watch out you don't trip over my stick and rucksack. I'm leaving them here to grab on the way out after I've tackled the soldier." He heard the footsteps approaching again. "Don't worry, it's going to be as easy as pie."

The lock clattered and the bolt slid back. The door creaked open a few inches and he saw the soldier push through the bowl with one hand, holding the door with the other. The bowl was right at Birkett's feet. He started to close the door again, but before he could do so Birkett thrust his foot into the gap and sent the door flying back with a crash. At the same time he grabbed the soldier's collar and heaved him clear of the doorway.

"Scoot!"

Lakshmi slipped soundlessly past him and disappeared into the shadows. The soldier clutched at his legs. Birkett found a second handhold on his trousers and lifted him clean off the ground: he had forgotten Gurkhas were such featherweights. He gave a heave and released his hold, sending the man sprawling across the floor. He turned to grab the rucksack and stick, glancing through the door at the same time and seeing that the coast was still clear. Too ruddy easy, he thought. They're not even trying. He swung the rucksack on to his shoulder and started forward-and just then a yell pierced his ears and he was struck from behind as though by a charging bull. His first thought was that it must be the soldier who had somehow managed at incredible speed to recover himself. Then, dropping knapsack and stick to defend himself, he saw the red-skinned face with the long black hair and gold earrings and wild pirate's eyes—it was the Sherpa.

The man was attacking him with flailing arms.

"Get off me, you ruddy madman!" Birkett shouted.

He thrust the Sherpa away and turned for the door again. The Sherpa let out another yell and leapt on to his back. Together they

275

rolled on the floor. He struggled violently to break the lock of the man's arms around him. He saw the soldier picking himself up. He broke free but before he had scrambled to his feet the Sherpa had caught his legs and he fell heavily again, and he saw the soldier coming at him and at the same time drawing something from a scabbard at his belt—and then he saw the long shiny sliver of steel.

Christ, it's a bayonet, he thought. He's going to stick me with a bayonet.

He saw the point lunging towards his stomach, and there flashed across his mind an image of Lakshmi waiting for him in the dark not knowing what had become of him, and at last returning and finding him skewered like a chicken with the bayonet through his guts . . . And then, without knowing exactly how it had happened, he had broken free of the Sherpa with a violent contortion, kicked the shiny steel from the soldier's hand and sent him toppling backwards, and regained his feet. And then he was bolting for the door and not bothering this time about stick or rucksack but going like a scalded cat past the flagstaff and across the track, and plunging over the crest of the slope and slithering down into the dark.

Presently he stopped and listened. He could hear nobody following.

He noticed a feeling of dampness round his middle. He felt his clothing. It was quite wet. He could not make it out. Then he realized that it must be the soup. They had probably knocked over the bowls and been rolling in it, what a waste.

He looked round for Lakshmi. He saw a crouching shadow and went to investigate. It was a rock.

Another shadow caught his attention. He went over but it turned out to be a rock again. There were shadows everywhere like squatting figures, and he went from one to the other. He had to be close enough to touch them before he could be sure they were only rocks.

He heard voices. He looked up and saw four or five bulky little figures silhouetted at the top of the slope. One of them carried a lantern.

Well, I wish you luck, laddies, he thought. You'd have a job to find me with a battery of searchlights in this country, never mind an old hurricane lamp.

Soon the figures disappeared. Just then he felt a wet trickle down his leg.

By Jove, I don't believe it's soup at all, he thought. I believe I've wet my trousers, well, that's a lark—fancy wetting my trousers at my age!

He suddenly noticed his hand. It looked black in the dim light as though covered with indian ink. He realized that it was blood and that it had come from his clothes.

That's funny, he thought. I can feel some nice bumps and bruises, but nothing worse,

He touched himself experimentally. There was a spot on his stomach that was a bit sore when he prodded it.

It must have been that bayonet, he thought. It must just have pipped me.

He screwed up his handkerchief and pushed it under his shirt to cover the spot, and then continued the search for Lakshmi. He was beginning to get really worried. He worked his way down slowly, methodically traversing a wide stretch of the slope. His anxiety mounted with each traverse: the farther he went from the Check Post, the greater was the possibility of divergence—the smaller the chance of finding her.

He felt the first flutter of panic. My God, supposing he'd lost her? He decided to risk shouting. He cupped his hands and bellowed, "Hello there!" in one direction and then another. He heard the echoes ringing out from across the valley—and then more faintly another call from somewhere below. It was Lakshmi. He could almost have burst into tears with joy and relief. He hurried down the slope and presently saw her dark shadow moving towards him.

"By Jove, I'm glad to see you," he said. "I was afraid I'd lost you."

"I thought the best place to wait was down at the stream. What happened?"

"Friend Willy went berserk—or maybe he was trying to earn remission. He held me down while the soldier stuck in his bayonet."

"You're not hurt?"

"No, just scratched me. Might just stop and tie it up if we've anything for a bandage."

"We've got bandages and iodine."

"No, we haven't. They were in the rucksack. I had to skip it. And my walking-stick too, which is much worse."

"I'd better look at you."

He stretched himself on a rock. As he leaned back his head there was a warm oozing in his throat. I don't like that, he thought. Still, maybe just a bit of phlegm . . . He put his hand to his mouth and spat on the palm and then looked at it. It was splashed with black.

"Look here, where it went through your jacket," Lakshmi said. "Right through the padding."

He wiped his palm on his collar—no point in alarming her. "Well, thank God for the padding. Saved my kidneys."

"I can't see much in this light."

"Never mind, just tie it up. You can use my shirt-tails." The shirt was so tough that she could not tear it and finally Birkett removed his jacket and sweaters and took off the whole shirt, and she folded it into a pad to cover the wound, leaving the sleeves to tie round his body to keep it secure.

"Aren't you cold?" she asked.

"Ruddy frozen."

"It won't take another minute."

"Then we must move off quick," Birkett said. "And go hell-bent all night."

"You're sure you feel all right?"

"I feel fine. Only I'd feel a sight better if I'd got my stick." They crossed the stream and began the steep ascent. The moon rose at their backs and threw their shadows on the slope. They helped themselves to keep going by imagining that the shadows were trying to give them the slip and that they must at all costs keep pace to prevent them. It was hard work because nothing could daunt shadows. They moved as easily as water, rippling over scree, darting up the side of boulders and sliding away over the top.

The massive peaks over their heads stood out sharply in the moonlight. And the white patches on the pass looked so near that Lakshmi exclaimed, "we'll reach the snow in another hour."

"Another twenty-four hours more like," Birkett said. "We shan't get within miles of it tonight."

He felt another warm oozing in his throat. The bayonet must have punctured him good and proper—he only wondered that he felt no more pain. And he remembered the old sad jut-boned horses in the Aranjuez bullring in Spain and the scented Spaniard with the soft hands and pearl tie-pin who had looked amused when it was gored: "There is no suffering to the horse. The horse suffers absolutely nothing." Perhaps the Spaniard had been right.

But an hour later he felt the pain beginning. Here it comes, he thought. And he knew by the way it was coming that it had weight behind it—that he had seen only the tip of the elephant's trunk round the corner, and the elephant was still to come.

And by Jove, it's going to be some elephant, he thought.

Lakshmi said, "How are you feeling? Oughtn't you to stop for a bit?"

"No, I'm not stopping."

He was afraid to stop in case he could not start again. He must at all costs keep after that shadow. And he kept after it as the moon rose and the shadow shrank and moved round him like the hand of a clock until it was pointing out to the side and he could keep after it no longer.

"All right, the tables are turned now," he said. "We're the leaders with our fat little shadows on our tails. Mustn't let 'em catch us. Never live down the shame of being caught by a fat little shadow."

The cold bit into their faces and fingers but was kept from further inroads by the heat generated by their bodies as they climbed. It was only occasionally, when they were obliged to drop down, that the balance was lost. Then the cold, finding resistance had collapsed, would mercilessly exploit its advantage, launching simultaneous attacks at every weak point and every where winning ground, until they began to climb again and the invasion was stopped.

The moon disappeared. The mountains became great looming black shapes; but the moon had scarcely abandoned the summits to obscurity before they were rescued by the first dawn light which spread quickly down their flanks.

"Stop and let me look at your wound," Lakshmi said. "I'll be able to see now."

"No, I'd rather not stop."

"But you've not stopped all night."

"And I shan't all day, if I can help it. But you stop and rest for a bit—I'll go on slowly."

She did so, and he cut down his steps until he was almost marking time, though moving at the same rhythm as before. He felt that if he kept up the rhythm he could go on forever. He had passed into a kind of stupor that blunted his pain and made him unconscious of passing time. Once, looking to see if the sun had yet risen clear of the ridge from behind which he had seen it begin to emerge in the quivering splendour of liquid gold, he was astonished to find it had vanished. Gone—the sun! Suddenly he spotted it high up in the sky. He realized that hours must have passed in what he had taken for a few minutes.

Towards midday he started abruptly from the stupor and exclaimed, "We must be out of our minds! You know what we're doing?" He pointed to an old dried-up pile of yak's dung. He realized that they had been passing droppings for some time. He had also vaguely noticed the worn stones, the changed texture of the turf, but their meaning had not registered. "Walking slap-bang in the middle of the track!"

They veered off at a sharp angle but kept being driven back to the track by the difficult terrain, and finally found themselves at the bottleneck of a valley—a valley so empty and desolate that it night have been deliberately scoured of all features that offered chance of concealment, the rocks broken into fragments no bigger than a fist. Even the milky waters from a glacier, that lower down became a swollen torrent raging amongst boulders three times the height of a man, here spread themselves so thinly over their wide stream-bed that they seemed to be laying themselves out for inspection, declaring every pebble.

They toiled along the track in the burning sun for six or seven miles. The valley remained empty of life except for themselves. But not twenty minutes after diverging again, they caught a glimpse of the track as it continued a hundred feet below them, and saw two soldiers with rifles coming down from the direction of the pass.

"Do you think they're looking for us?" Lakshmi said.

"No, they wouldn't be looking so sprightly as that if they'd set out after us last night. Probably a regular patrol. But I'm still thankful we didn't meet them coming round the corner."

Later he suddenly felt himself weakening. His feet no longer moved mechanically—they had become like weights of lead and every step required a new purposeful effort that drained his strength further. He looked up at the pass.

Another four hours, he thought. I've got to keep going somehow for another four hours.

The earth began to squelch under their feet like sponge. It was brown and fibrous, the grass rotted from long burial under snow. They passed a soggy patch of snow dripping away in the glare of the sun. They were dripping themselves from the heat and coldness seemed unimaginable—until all at once they entered the icy shadow of a cliff and the draughty air penetrated their clothes and touched their skins like chilly hands. Here the snow was white and hard and crunched under their feet. They found themselves up against a deep drift and were obliged to make a detour.

It meant only a few hundred extra yards. But the setback filled Birkett with dismay. He felt a new draining of his strength. He was like an arrow with force nearly spent that could be brought to grief short of its target by the faintest contrary wind. He remembered his walking-stick. He felt sure that it would have made all the difference—that with stick in hand he would have been striding up here jauntily, immune to fatigue. Its loss was the worst misfortune that had ever befallen him . . . He remembered fishing it out of the Irrawaddy, and trying to throw it away and the stick coming back because it liked him. And all the years since then that it had been his loyal companion. He had lost his dearest and oldest friend. He was overcome with grief.

Lakshmi said, "Look, there are people!"

"People?" He could see nothing for the tears that streamed from his eyes because of the walking-stick. "Where?"

"Right on the pass. There's a whole line of them."

He wiped his eyes with his sleeve. "Those aren't people. You'd never see people from here—those are cairns. Still, we——" He had been going to say, "Still, we must be getting near if we can see the cairns," but a fresh upsurge of emotion caught at his voice. After a long time he realized that the unspoken words were still repeating themselves in his head like a broken gramophone record. It occurred to him that since he had got them ready to speak, and then failed to release them, this was bound to happen, and that they would continue to repeat themselves until spoken aloud.

It's obvious, he thought. If you bring words up from the bottom compartment of your brain into the top compartment, they can't go down through the valve again, so unless you speak them they're stuck. I don't know why I never thought of it before.

Presently he heard himself say, "Still, we must be getting near if we can see the cairns."

Lakshmi said in surprise, "The cairns? But we saw them an hour ago—don't you remember?"

"Sorry, that's right. Going a bit dotty."

"I can see prayer flags now," Lakshmi said.

"Nearly there."

The gradient eased as they came up to the pass. It was about half a mile wide. They avoided the track and kept over to the left-hand escarpment. It faced south and in the shelter of its foot the snow had melted, leaving a corridor of spongy earth and dry flat rock. They had only about fifty feet left to ascend to the highest point of the pass, when the arm of snow on their right took an abrupt inward turn to the escarpment and sealed off the corridor. They were at a dead end—there was no way to avoid the snow without returning to a point several hundred feet lower down and repeating the ascent on the other side. It would have taken an hour.

Birkett's steady trudging steps did not falter. He went straight on towards the snow.

"Going on through," he said. "Not deep."

He entered the snow at the same trudging rhythm as if he hardly noticed it was there. The surface was mushy and offered no resistance, but after a dozen yards he was wading knee-deep. He had to struggle with increasing desperation to maintain his momentum. Suddenly he sank to his waist. He tried to plough forward without interruption but found his right foot was stuck. He tried with all his remaining strength to drag it free. It remained wedged. And finally, nearly twenty hours after breaking out of the Check Post, he came to a standstill.

"Muck this snow," he said. The tears streamed from his eyes. "Muck this ruddy snow."

Weariness overwhelmed him. He was tempted to close his eyes and drop down there, but knew that he must somehow get out before he collapsed. He manoeuvred his foot and it came free. He turned and floundered back towards Lakshmi, ten yards behind him. He felt his knees giving way. He stumbled against her and, somehow supporting each other, they gained the edge of the snow. They covered the few remaining yards to the foot of the escarpment where the ground was bare dry rock. They collapsed together, locked in embrace—and before they had finished falling, Birkett was already unconscious.

Chapter Twenty-One

He awoke the next morning in the first sunlight. He could dimly remember moments of semi-consciousness during the night when he had been aware of the intense cold eating into him, of a brilliant moon high up in the sky, and of Lakshmi lying in his arms as lifeless as marble. He remembered wanting to reassure himself that she was not dead, and finding that the cold had rendered him incapable of movement or speech.

He still ached with cold. But now he felt the sun begin to caress him with comforting tenderness. It was the most beautiful sensation he had ever known.

Lakshmi lay with her eyes closed, her face a pale dead mask.

He tried to speak her name. His jaw was still numbed, and his voice was slurred.

She briefly opened her eyes, and then closed them again. It was another hour before her muscles had thawed out sufficiently for her to stir, and at last drag herself on to her knees. Birkett tried to rise, but without success.

"Well, I'm afraid I'll never move from here under my own steam," he said. He felt completely drained of strength, and now that the cold no longer numbed him, he could feel the ache of his wound—an ache that spread through his blood like a poison, sending out insidious creeping tentacles, like the fungus of dry rot, to every part of his system.

"Let me look at you," Lakshmi said.

It took several minutes to remove her gloves from her purple swollen fingers and undo the buttons of his jacket. She found the pad over his wound was stuck to the flesh as if with glue.

"It'll only start bleeding again if you pull it off," Birkett said. "Skip it and let's have breakfast."

She took the piece of yak's blood from his pocket and they each had a bite.

"Well, it's really been ruddy marvellous, the last month, hasn't it?" Birkett said.

"The best month of my life," Lakshmi said.

"You've certainly become quite a handy little cook."

"I've become a different person," she said. "You've changed me as much as I've changed you."

"That's it, we've both changed each other."

They chewed in silence for a bit.

"Only now we'd better face it," Birkett said "I'm finished."

"I shall go for help."

"Where to? The Check Post? And let 'em restore me to full health, just to string me up? Not on your life! I'd rather die up here in the sun."

"I meant from the other side, won't there be some sort of frontier post over the pass?"

"No, that porter who'd been over this pass said there was nothing for a hundred miles on the Tibetan side."

"He might have been wrong. He was wrong about the Check Post. I shall go and look."

"You can have a quick squint if you like. But you might bring me a bit of snow before you go—I've got a tidy thirst on this morning."

She made a little pile of snow beside him, and helped to pull him up to a half-sitting position against the sloping rock.

"Now, you'll have to drop down again and come up on the other side of the snow," he said. "And you mustn't be more than a couple of hours at the outside. You must be back before midday— so that you can get well on your way back to the Check Post before dark."

"I thought you didn't want me to go to the Check Post."

"Not for help. But if there's nothing doing over the other side, you've got to leave me and go back by yourself." She stared at him. He said, "Look, I'm done for, and I don't care a hoot—especially after this last month we've had. But I'm not taking you with me. You might not get through another night up here, so you've got to leave me today."

She shook her head. "I'm not leaving you."

"You must."

"Perhaps I shall get help."

"All right, that's another matter. But I want you to promise me that if you don't get help, you'll leave me and go back to the Check Post."

"I'll see when I come back."

"I'll have no peace of mind while you've gone, unless you promise first."

She avoided his eyes. "All right, I promise."

"Good girl."

She turned and walked slowly away down the slope between the escarpment and the arm of snow. Twenty minutes later he saw her come up again on the other side of the snow. She waved to him and went on towards the top of the pass.

He lay with the warmth of the sun on the full length of his body. He heard a humming overhead like the singing of taut wires. He looked up. Three or four thousand feet above the opposite escarpment there was a ridge with an overhanging cornice of snow. The snow was streaming from the cornice in a long white plume.

He realized that the humming was the wind. Here in the shelter of the escarpment there was not a breath of wind, but that streamer of snow must have been half a mile long, and the wind up there blowing at gale force.

He lay listening to the wind humming like ten thousand telephone wires, and thought about dying. He knew that Lakshmi would find nothing over the other side, and that he would never leave this rock alive.

He thought about the pill that Potter had so mysteriously returned to him. Once Lakshmi had gone, he could use it to finish himself off. Make a quick clean job of it.

He decided to make sure that he still had it. It took him fifteen or twenty minutes, with his swollen gloved fingers, to unbutton his jacket and extract it from an inner pocket. The envelope was falling to bits but the pill was safe inside.

The effort of taking it out had exhausted him, and he lay back with it in his hand. He had told Lakshmi that he did not care a hoot about dying, but it was not exactly true. He cared a great deal about dying in some ways, because it meant missing all the years in which life might have gone on being as good as it had been in the last month, and it meant missing being married to Lakshmi and making a home with her, and having kids. He cared about that very much.

But in one sense it had been true that he did not care, because now he could die with the knowledge that he had lived. For forty-eight years he had not lived, but had been a prisoner chained in darkness behind locked doors. And then he had met Lakshmi and she had touched some springs in him that had caused the doors to fly open one after another, letting in sunlight and fresh air. And he had begun to live—to experience for the first time the sheer joy of being alive.

He would have bitterly regretted dying before this had happened. But now it had happened, and he could die with a sense of fulfilment. He could accept death with equanimity because he had learnt the value of life.

It was the only thing of importance that he had ever learnt. It was the sum total of his forty-eight years of experience. And if he had gone on living he would have had to work out everything afresh from this new starting point. He would have had to start thinking again from scratch, on the basis of this new belief in the fundamental value of life.

He looked at the pill in his hand.

If I take it, I will be killing myself, he thought. I will be ending my life with an act of destruction, and denying what I have just learned to believe.

No, I won't take it, he thought. No matter how bad the pain, I shall bear it until the end.

He did not have the strength to throw away the pill, and he

screwed it up in the remnants of the envelope and pushed it inside his jacket. He saw from the sun that it must be nearing midday. He looked round for Lakshmi but there was no sign of her.

It was another hour before he saw her again beyond the arm of snow. She went out of sight and presently reappeared, coming up the slope between the snow and the escarpment. Her face was expressionless as she stopped beside him.

"There's a big arch with Tibetan writing over the track on the other side of the pass," she said. "There's nothing else."

"Never mind," he said. "I've just been thinking that I wouldn't have belonged in China. I don't really belong anywhere just at the moment, so I couldn't have chosen a better place to die than right here on the frontier."

"You're not going to die," she said. "I don't believe it."

"You must believe it—and you must leave me."

She shook her head.

"Yes, you must go now," he said. "You promised."

"I didn't mean it," she said. "I didn't look at you when I said it. I'd no intention of leaving you, so please don't try and make me."

"I must make you."

She turned without looking at him and walked slowly away down the slope. After twenty minutes she reappeared, coming slowly up the slope again.

She held a bunch of tiny flowers in her hand, their delicate petals like little bright jewels of red, yellow and blue—the brilliant primitive hues of flowers springing up under the heels of the snow.

"Look, they're all different," she said. "I only picked one of each kind."

She knelt beside him and began to lay them out, counting them in a row on his lap. "Seventeen!"

"They're beautiful." He reached for her hand and held it. He said quietly, "Now, look at me,"

She knew what he was going to say and shook her head, keeping her face averted, refusing to risk herself to the persuasion of his eyes. She tried to withdraw her hand, but he held it.

"You're going to do exactly as I tell you," he said quietly and firmly. "You're not going to ask questions, or think about it at all—you're just going to do it."

She was silent, shaking her head.

"Yes, you're going to get up now. And you're going to turn and walk away down the hill. And you're not going to look back. And you're going to follow the track down to the Check Post and tell them that I'm dead, and that you wish to go back to India. Now, go."

She went on shaking her head, and trying to withdraw her hand, but he still held it. Then he saw her tears coming, and he let it go, and she moved apart from him and squatted with her back to him, crying.

"I'm not leaving you," she said. "You can't make me leave you. I don't want to live if you've gone. I want to stay here and die with you."

He was exhausted with the effort of trying to persuade her; he had no strength left to go on. I've failed, he thought hopelessly, and she's going to die because of me. He laid back his head, looking into the sky where the white cornice trailed its long white pennant of snow, hearing the wind singing overhead, and Lakshmi still crying. Tiredness overwhelmed him, and he closed his eyes and fell into a doze, and dreamed that he lay with Lakshmi in the valley of blue poppies, with the big blue flowers like china breakfast cups gently swaying over their heads and that soon they would be safely in Tibet.

And then he woke up suddenly. And he knew how he could make Lakshmi leave him, so that she would not die.

She had not moved whilst he slept but still sat with her back turned.

He said, "I've just been dreaming of 'our valley,' where we made love."

She was silent.

"You might be going to have a baby," he said.

He saw her stiffen a little.

"I don't know," she said. "Perhaps."

289

"You were certain about it at the time."

"I was carried away—I just had the feeling . . ."

"I've always felt sure you were going to have a baby."

"It makes no difference now."

"It makes all the difference. It means you've another life to think about besides your own."

She said nothing.

"It was you who taught me to create instead of destroy," he said. "If you don't go, you will be destroying what we have created together."

After a while she rose slowly and walked away for a few paces, and stood with hands pressed against her body as if trying to feel if there was life inside her. She stood silently for a long time. At last she said : "All right, I'll go tomorrow."

"I'd rather you went today."

"No, it's too late. But I'll go tomorrow."

"You're not looking at me."

She turned and held his eyes.

"I promise," she said. "If you still want me to go tomorrow, I promise to go."

2

In the morning it was not until two hours after the sun had risen that she stirred and detached herself from him. She dragged herself to her hands and knees.

She saw that he was conscious and that his eyes were open. She tried to pick up the remaining fragments of yak's blood from the rock, but could not grasp it in her swollen fingers.

She used both hands and succeeded in lifting it between them. She held it to Birkett's mouth.

He tried to take a bite but his jaw was too stiff with cold. "Never mind," he said. "I'm not hungry."

She put the fragment down on the rock again and got to her feet. Her legs nearly gave way beneath her. She walked about unsteadily for a bit, bringing the muscles back to life, and then came and stood beside him. Her lips were purple and swollen. Her face was expressionless.

She said, "You still want me to go?"

"Yes."

She avoided his eyes. She went over to the nearest snow and scooped up some between her hands. She came back and put it beside him. She did not look at him. She returned to the snow for another handful. She continued back and forth, building up a pile, and not once looking at him, and he knew that she did not trust herself to do so without losing her resolution.

She pressed down the pile of snow to make it hard, so that it would last longer, and then added more snow until the pile was about two feet high. Then she removed her jacket, took off a jersey, and came and knelt beside him.

She unbuttoned his jacket, still without looking at him, and put the jersey over his body inside the jacket for added warmth.

"You'll need that jersey," he said.

She shook her head. The jersey would not make much difference to him but he did not protest any more. He knew that she wanted to leave him something of her own, and that it would even be a comfort to her to suffer from lack of it, for his sake.

"'Well, by Jove, that's nice of you," he said.

She carefully buttoned up his jacket again.

"Where will you have the kid?" he said. "Will you go to your parents?"

"Yes."

"They'll understand?"

"They will be shocked at first," she said. "But they will take care of me."

"Well, thank heavens they're well off, because although I've quite a bit of money sitting in the bank, I can't think of any way of seeing you get it. Even if I was capable of writing a will, we've no pen or paper."

"I don't need money."

She sat back on her heels, looking at him to see how she could make him more comfortable, but still avoiding his eyes. She noticed that his head was against bare rock. She began to remove a glove. It was already burst at the seams with the swelling of her hands, and she had to rip it more to get it off.

"I'd have thought twice about having an Anglo-Indian kid in the old days," Birkett said. "But people have become more liberal in the last ten years, and by the time our kid has grown up they will have become a lot more so. And apart from social prejudice, I'm all for a bit of mixing of blood."

She lifted his head gently and put the glove behind to cushion the hardness of the rock.

"Now, that's really an unnecessary refinement," he said. "And you'll need that glove for going down."

"No, I don't need it."

"I'd much rather you kept it. Still, I'm bound to say it makes it very comfy."

She looked longingly for some way to make him more comfortable. She said, "What else can I do?"

He tried to think of something to please her.

"You can fish my handkerchief out of my pocket so that I can have it handy," he said. "Just in case it turns chilly up here and I catch a cold."

He also pressed her to take the remaining piece of yak's blood, but she would not do so. She suddenly dropped down beside him and buried her face in his neck. He felt her trembling. She clung to him as if she would never leave go, and the trembling grew worse.

He knew she must go quickly or she would not go at all. He wanted to tell her to go but the words stuck in his throat.

If I haven't the strength, he thought, how can I expect it of her?

Presently she released him. She got up, still without looking at him, and began to walk away.

She stopped after a few yards and turned round. She brought her hands together—the bare purple swollen hand and the gloved hand with splitting seams. She lifted them gently, palm to palm, in the gesture with which she had first greeted him in the Delhi

292

club, and that was a gesture of both greeting and farewell, and as she did so she looked at him for the first time since she had started to go.

He dragged his hands up from his side. They were like weights of lead. He drew them together before his face.

She held his eyes steadily. After a few moments she dosed her eyes, her hands still before her face. Then she dropped her hands and turned without opening her eyes until she would no longer see him, and began to walk away.

She walked slowly down the slope. She did not look back. He watched her go over the curve of the slope, and soon she was gone.

His feelings were numbed and he felt nothing at first, He closed his eyes and fell into a doze.

Later he awoke feeling cold. He opened his eyes and saw that steely grey clouds covered the sun. The pass looked cheerless and bleak.

A sense of loneliness and desolation possessed him. His heart began to ache.

A lonely death was surely the most bitter and terrible fate that a man could be called upon to bear. And he had been left to die alone on the roof of the world.

Shut out on the cold bleak roof while the rest of the world sat below at its fireside. Abandoned even by the woman who had professed to love him.

He knew that Lakshmi had only gone because he had persuaded her. Yet now he could not help reproaching her for allowing herself to be persuaded, for deserting him on his death-bed for an unborn child.

His anguish grew until it became like all the anguish of his life, all the anguish of loneliness and rejection put together.

> *Oh, Mr. Middleton,*
> *I've got such a pain!*
> *Quick! Some Osbaldiston's Syrup*
> *To make me well again . . .*

It's my old bogey back again, he thought. Just when I believed that I'd got rid of it, that I'd really changed.

He tried to feel himself changed, to remember the truths about himself that he had learnt. It occurred to him that his anguish was only self-pity—the self-pity of a child crying for his mother.

And it's time I grew up, he thought. I'm out of my nappies now. It's time I stopped crying for Mummy like a kid.

I'm going to take a strong line with myself, he thought. I'm going to drag out self-pity by the roots. I'm going to beat the bogey if it's the last thing on earth that I do.

It was warmer that night because of the clouds. The next morning the sun reappeared. The air sparkled. He remembered thankfully that by now Lakshmi would be nearing the Check Post. He no longer cared what happened to himself provided she was safe.

He knew that he had beaten the bogey. His victory gave him an exhilarating sense of freedom. He thought that in all his life he had never felt so happy and free.

But by Jove, I feel peckish this morning, he thought. I could eat a yak. Well, I've got a bit of yak's blood, and that's better than nothing.

He picked up the fragment. There were about two bites left. He ought really to spin it out for two meals, but he decided to treat himself to a feast and polish it off in one.

He took a bite and chewed with relish. He was about to put the remainder into his mouth when a bird flew down from the escarpment and lighted a few yards away on a rock.

"Hello, birdie-boy," he said. "What are you doing up here?"

It was the first living creature that he had seen at the pass.

"But I'm afraid if you've come for breakfast you're going to be unlucky," Birkett said. "You're not on the unit strength for rations."

The bird cocked its head and looked at him sideways. It was about the size and colour of a thrush but prettier and more delicate. Birkett noticed a featherless patch on its back, with a small red wound as if a bigger bird had attacked it with vicious beak.

"So you've been in the wars too, have you?" he said. "Well, that's different."

He broke off a tiny morsel of the yak's blood and threw it towards the bird. The bird hopped down from the rock and pecked at it inquisitively. It picked it up, juggled it at the tip of its beak, and then swallowed it and flew off as if it had just remembered an urgent appointment.

That night it snowed. The big soft flakes fell on his face with a gentle tickling caress. It was quite warm in the snow and the next day, his fifth at the pass, he felt as strong and cheerful as ever.

He carefully excavated his body from the snow before it melted on him. The sun came up and he watched the fresh snow round him begin to glisten and drip, and wear thin in patches like trousers going through at the knee. And the first little island of brown earth had just appeared when the bird flew down and alighted beside it, with a quick little run to break its momentum, leaving a trail of delicate little fans in the snow.

"Morning, birdie-boy," Birkett said. "I'm afraid this morning the cupboard's bare."

The bird began to peck at the soggy earth, moving about with fastidious little steps, and sometimes stopping to cock its head appealingly at Birkett, like a dog seeking signs of its master's approval. It stayed all day, and then shortly before sunset flew off abruptly.

The next morning, Birkett's sixth day at the pass, the bird did not come. He anxiously scanned the escarpment and the sky. He was afraid it might have been attacked by some bigger bird again.

"What's happened to you, birdie-boy?" Birkett said. "Where are you, eh?"

His anxiety about the bird preoccupied him all day, and when it had still not appeared by sundown he was in despair, he felt certain he would never see it again.

Darkness brought a wind that flailed him with icy knives.

He knew he could not survive it for more than an hour or two. Drowsiness mercifully overtook him.

Well, I've closed my eyes for the last time, he thought. That's the end of old Birkett. Passed away peacefully in his sleep in his forty-eighth year.

He awoke in breathless sunshine. He had been so certain of not waking again that at first he thought he must be in some Elysian pasture, and that it must be true after all that there was, life after death. The discovery that he was still alive filled him with dismay. Now he must face another long tedious day without even the company of the bird, and then die all over again. Just then the bird alighted on the ground a yard from his face and cocked its head at him. Birkett could have wept for joy.

"Morning, birdie-boy," he said. "What have you been up to, eh?"

He wanted to tell the bird how much he loved him. He wanted to explain that all his life, until recently, he had been incapable of loving; and that now his heart, as though to make up for loss of time, was filled with so much love that it felt as if it would burst; and that the bird had now become the object of all this love because it was the only other living creature at the pass, and its life represented to Birkett the miracle of all life . . .

"That's a nasty place on your back, birdie-boy," he said. "You've got to watch yourself. You're not going to have me around to protect you much longer, you know. I've already been here seven days. Yes, I've clocked up my first week today. Not bad for an old codger, eh, birdie-boy?"

He felt himself weakening all that day, and in the afternoon lacked the strength even to talk to the bird. That night there was a heavy blizzard. He was still conscious in the morning but too weak to brush the snow from his body. The sun came up and it began to drip and soak through his clothes.

The bird flew down and tried to alight in the snow, but floundered, and fluttered in the air again and. settled on a rock. "I'm afraid I'm not so hot today, birdie-boy," Birkett said. "Only just holding on by the skin of my teeth."

His whole body was possessed by a new feeling of sickness and despair. He kept crying and could not control the tears. He felt a stranger to himself. He longed for death.

He thought of the pill again, and in his sickened condition no longer felt any scruples about using it. He would take it and end his life quickly.

He fumbled inside his jacket. He managed to find it at last, and detach it from the soggy remnants of the envelope. The effort had exhausted him. He lay back to recover his strength again, the pill in his hand.

And then all at once an extraordinary realization came to him, and he knew at last why Potter had given him back the pill.

And once he knew this, he knew in a flash much else besides. For it provided the key to everything about Potter that had puzzled him.

And he began to laugh. His whole body shook with laughter.

The fact was that he need not have lain here dying at all. He need not have fled from Kathmandu, but could have gone to India with Lakshmi and had children with her, and lived to a ripe old age. Because the arrest, that he had believed imminent, had all been Potter's bluff.

He saw it all now with perfect clarity. Potter, of course, had not had a single hit of effective evidence against him. But it had taken more than lack of evidence to daunt Potter. He had been determined to get Birkett just the same. So he had carefully contrived to put the wind up him by a variety of means.

The Sunday session of the Security Department at the Singha Durbar, the rumour set afoot amongst the hotel boys, the warning telephone call, had all been part of Potter's carefully calculated kick in the pants, to precipitate Birkett into headlong flight.

And once Birkett had been put to flight, there had only remained for Potter to drop a word in the official ear that Birkett was knocking around Nepal without district visas, and they would soon be on his trail. And if they pinched him, Birkett, thinking they were going to string him up, would try and save them the trouble by finishing himself off first—with the pill.

The pill so thoughtfully provided for the occasion by Potter; And if they didn't pinch him, and he skipped over the border into Tibet, well *tant pis*, it would be a pity to see him escape the fate he so richly deserved, but anyhow, one way or the other, he would be safely and permanently out of Potter's hair.

This was the only explanation that fated all the facts, and the only explanation that accounted for Potter laying all his cards on the table, and of making no secret of the fact that he was on Birkett's tail. And Birkett's failure to hit on it sooner was all the more lamentable since only the previous day, at the Tattoo, Potter had admitted to bluffing him before, on the *Maid of Islay*.

But no doubt he had intended that as a double bluff. Birkett wasn't likely to believe, after Potter had openly admitted to bluffing once, that he was up to precisely the same trick again. And so this time the bluff had worked. And here he lay dying in the snow on a Tibetan pass, a rounded pigeon neatly skewered for Potter's pie. And past even caring. Now all he could do was laugh.

He noticed that he was still holding the pill in his hand.

No, I made up my mind not to destroy myself, he thought. And I won't. I'll live my life right through to its natural end.

He decided that it would be safer, in case he weakened again, to remove the temptation and throw the pill away.

He rested a minute, and then flung the pill from him with all the strength he could muster. He saw it fall a few yards away on the brown soggy earth where the snow had melted. And it was only at that moment that he remembered the bird.

Oh God, he thought. I hope he didn't see it.

He glanced round for the bird. He saw it flutter down from its perch on the rock and alight two feet from the pill with its quick little run.

He watched with dismay as it advanced towards the pill with fastidious little steps.

"No, birdie-boy!" Birkett cried out. "No!"

The bird pecked at the pill inquisitively.

"Birdie-boy! Leave that alone! D'you hear?"

The bird picked up the pill in its beak. It tossed it away playfully, stepped after it, and picked it up again.

"Birdie-boy!"

Birkett, without thinking of what he was doing, without any

thought except that he must reach the bird, began to struggle from the position on the rock in which he had lain without moving for a week.

He succeeded in heaving himself to his hands and knees. His limbs gave way and he sprawled with his face in the brown slushy earth. He struggled to rise.

"Birdie-boy! Birdie-boy"

He crawled another foot or two and then sprawled in the mud again. The bird lifted its beak in the air, juggling the pill at the tip.

"Drop that, birdie-boy! D'you hear? Drop it!"

The bird took no notice. It juggled the pill playfully in its lifted beak. Suddenly it opened its beak, and the pill disappeared down its gullet.

Birkett froze in the midst of his renewed struggles to rise. He stared with held breath. The bird took several quick delicate little steps and began to peck at the earth.

It's all right, Birkett thought. The pill's been affected by the damp. It's not going to work.

Just then the bird was shaken by violent spasms. Its smooth feathers flew out in disorder. Its beak opened unnaturally wide and it uttered a savage, demented squawking,

The commotion lasted for only a few seconds and then subsided as if a clockwork motor inside the bird was running down. The squawking diminished to a faint noise in its throat. It fell over on its side. The beak continued to open and close like scissors, and a moment later it was still.

The dead bird lay tilted with one leg sticking into the air beak half-open, a dull film over its eyes.

"Birdie-boy!" Birkett cried. "Birdie-boy!"

He floundered forward through the mud. He sprawled again just within reach of the bird. He took the tiny soft body into his hands and held it to his cheek.

He felt its warmth already fading. The tears flowed from his eyes and the soft little body grew damp in his hands.

"Birdie-boy. Birdie-boy."

He knew that this was the last terrible punishment for all his years of not loving. He could bear it for himself because it was deserved, and it was not from self-pity that he wept but for the fading warmth that could never be restored. He had come to Nepal to take the life of a king, and now his heart was breaking because he had accidentally taken the life of a bird.

"Birdie-boy. Birdie-boy."

He lay sprawled on the soggy earth with the bird clutched to his cheek. The damp little body grew cold. Towards evening the wind dropped and heavy clouds muffled the pass. Darkness fell. It began to snow.

Lightning Source UK Ltd.
Milton Keynes UK
UKHW010757010721
386450UK00001B/168